T0271520

GHOSTED

Also by Rosie Mullender

The Time of My Life

GHOSTED

Rosie Mullender

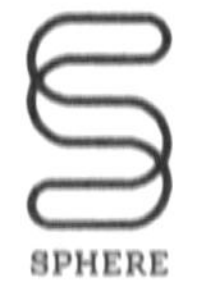

SPHERE

First published in Great Britain in 2023 by Sphere

1 3 5 7 9 10 8 6 4 2

A CIP catalogue record for this book is available from the British Library.

Hardback ISBN 978-0-7515-8525-4
Trade paperback ISBN 978-0-7515-8526-1

Typeset in Caslon by M Rules
Printed and bound in Great Britain by Clays Ltd, Elcograf S.p.A.

Papers used by Sphere are from well-managed forests and other responsible sources.

Sphere
An imprint of
Little, Brown Book Group
Carmelite House
50 Victoria Embankment
London EC4Y 0DZ

An Hachette UK Company
www.hachette.co.uk

www.littlebrown.co.uk

For Chris

Who we miss so much, every day

Chapter 1

Before Andy had tried to contact her from beyond the grave, Emily was panicking about the guacamole going brown. Later, remembering this, she wished she'd realised just how lucky she'd been to be spending her time worrying about avocados, instead of the afterlife.

Zoe poked a finger knuckle-deep into the gloopy green dip, which Emily was dolloping into a row of tiny, jewel-hued mezze bowls.

'Not until the adults get here,' she said, slapping Zoe's hand away from the bowl.

Zoe grinned, sucking dip off her finger with an exaggerated smack. 'Nice guac,' she said, nodding approvingly.

'Why do people keep calling it guac, like they're mates with it? It's guacamole, not your uncle guac,' Emily said, decanting habas fritas, stuffed olives and Percy Pigs (regular and veggie) into more bowls. It was a snack combination that she hoped said, 'I'm well travelled and sophisticated, but fun, too! Plus I am, of course, considerate of our veggie and vegan guests.'

There was a lot of pressure on the nibbles.

'Where did you get these bowls?' Zoe asked, peering into them.

'I got them from the global aisle in TK Maxx,' Emily said. 'But if anyone asks, I found them for sale on an adorable little stall run by a local craftsman during my travels around Mexico.'

'When did you pretendy go to Mexico?' Zoe asked. 'Was that before or after you went fakey interrailing around Europe and phoney backpacking through Thailand? I don't know how you haven't been caught out yet, when the furthest you've travelled is a school trip to the Jorvik Viking Centre.'

Emily snorted, then looked around as if she was worried someone other than Zoe might have overheard her.

'I watch a lot of documentaries,' she said, arranging and rearranging the bowls on a serving tray. 'Plus no one really listens to other people's travel stories because they're too busy waiting to talk about that time *they* helped build an orphanage in Peru, or ate raw llama livers. You just have to say vague stuff like, "Chichén Itzá is just stunning in winter," and people totally believe you've been there.'

Zoe laughed. 'I don't get why you're so worried about this party anyway,' she said, twerking a spiraliser aside with her bum as she hopped onto the kitchen counter. 'It's not like Jada and Simon give a crap about how glamorous you are. They've shared a desk with you for yonks and know all your dark and terrible secrets. Including that you come from Essex, *not* Winchester, and that you didn't know how to pronounce "segue" until you were in your mid-twenties.'

Emily tutted. 'True. But Jess and Mel only know New Emily, not the old, rubbish one. I've got appearances to keep up. Plus, Jess works in magazines, and Mel works in TV.

TeeVee!' she added, gesturing at the telly through the kitchen door to emphasise her point.

Along with Jada and Simon, Emily was a copywriter at a small advertising agency based in Camden. She'd been thoroughly over-excited when Mel, who she'd met through work, had suggested they go for a drink with her best friend, Jess, to celebrate the end of the project they'd been working on together.

Mel was the kind of friend she'd always fantasised as a teenager about her adult self making. Since moving to London, she'd worked hard to make a handful of glamorous-sounding friends – plus Jess and Mel were actually *nice*, too – and now she had them, she was going to do everything in her power to keep hold of them.

She eyed her mezze spread critically, her hands on her hips. 'Do you think the Percys should go on their own tray? Like a dinner-then-dessert kind of vibe?'

'What I *think* is that you've gone completely mental,' Zoe said. 'No one is going to care that much, I promise. Honestly, if I'd known you'd turn into a desperate cliché, I'd have tried to put you off moving to London. I used to have to stop you wanging on about how enormous Martin Baker's willy was, not how best to impress your hipster mates.'

'Ah, Martin,' Emily said fondly, remembering her first proper boyfriend. 'Although I'm *not* a desperate cliché, thank-you-very-much. I'm just trying to fit in.'

'I know,' Zoe said, rubbing Emily's shoulder affectionately. 'But I kind of miss the girl from Greenleaf who'd have vomited if you tried to feed her an avocado. The one whose beauty regime involved a quick squirt of body spray nicked from Superdrug, who thought a night out at Pizza Hut followed by

Hollywood Bowl was the height of sophistication. I wonder what *that* Emily is doing now?'

'She probably died in a tragic accident,' Emily said, squeezing more lemon juice into the guacamole. 'Maybe her polyester shell suit caught on fire, or she choked on a Findus Crispy Pancake.'

'Or Martin Baker's willy ...?' Zoe said, and Emily managed a laugh.

'Don't forget how miserable Old Emily was,' she said, leaning on the kitchen counter next to Zoe. She reached over for her hand and they linked little fingers. 'You always seemed to let the way people treated us wash right over you, but I could never do that. This is my chance to prove they were all wrong about me. And about you, too.'

Even before she'd stepped on the train to London from Essex four years earlier, Emily had never felt quite good enough. At school, all the kids from the Greenleaf estate, where Emily and Zoe had grown up together, were treated like outsiders. Emily had been determined to leave the estate behind her at the first possible opportunity, and Zoe had happily agreed to tag along.

But while Zoe had moved to London with the twin aims of going to gigs without having to miss the last few songs, and of sleeping with as many hotties as humanly possible, Emily had seen it as her chance for a completely fresh start.

She could forget all about her past, work on making herself a new person, and make friends with people who had no idea who she'd once been. She'd done everything she could to leave Old Emily behind her – the one who had about as many prospects as the cartoon miner on a box of Golden Nuggets – and bag herself a future that was completely different from her past. A future where she felt safe and secure, and her kids would never be sent next door to borrow 50p for the electric key so they could watch *Home and Away*.

But despite her best efforts, she still felt like the girl whose dad had walked out on her, who was rejected at school, and whose only friend in the world was Zoe. Everyone in London seemed so *together*. It felt almost impossible to compete.

Most of her wages went on clothes she couldn't afford, and she spent her time at the gym feeling permanently on edge in case she was using the machines wrong (she'd once been flipped off a treadmill like a gangly pancake and had to change gyms out of sheer embarrassment).

She wasn't entirely sure her job at an ad agency, which she'd pursued solely because everyone on *Mad Men* was as glamorous as hell, was right for her. It certainly involved far fewer puppies than was ideal. And she'd ended up moving out of the flatshare she'd lived in for a while with Zoe.

She'd told herself her poky one-bed flat, carefully decorated in shades of stone, grey and cream, was a much better fit for New Emily's life, no matter how much she missed Sunday mornings spent watching hangover telly with her best friend. And it was unfortunately necessary if she was going to cosmically order the life she wanted, which *Bijou* magazine – '*For women who know where they're going!*' – said was all the rage.

Only sometimes, Emily wished she could skip straight to the 'after' photos of her new life – the one complete with a great job, a successful man, and a hot-pink KitchenAid.

Still, hopefully tonight would be a significant stepping-stone towards her transformation: a smart-but-casual dinner party thrown in honour of her two newest (and coolest) friends in her small-but-tastefully-decorated flat. She just had to pray no one moved her neutral-toned throws and rugs and saw how tatty everything was underneath.

'I know you think I'm crazy,' she told Zoe, looking at her earnestly, 'but tonight really means something to me. I really really *really* want it to go well.'

'Oh? You should have said,' Zoe said, raising an eyebrow, and Emily pouted at her. 'Am I even allowed to mention to your hallowed guests that I cut hair at a crappy salon in Hackney for a fiver a pop? Or is that the equivalent of Kate Middleton hanging out with a chimney sweep?'

'You can say what you like about your present, just don't drag up the past,' Emily said firmly.

'And have you briefed Jada and Simon on this too?'

'Don't worry, they know full well that Greenleaf isn't a subject for discussion beyond the one-foot radius around our desks. But it's OK, I've got enough dirt on them for them to keep schtum. Simon would rather die than have it be widely known that he failed the audition for *Tipping Point*.' Zoe snorted.

'My main worry is that Jada and Simon and Jess and Mel haven't met each other before, and there's no guarantee they'll get along, is there?' Emily said, letting go of Zoe's finger and opening the fridge door. 'It's like when your mate tells you you'll definitely get on with so-and-so because they're exactly like you. Then you meet them, and their favourite film is *The Human Centipede*, they don't like baked potatoes, and they have a really annoying laugh. Then you're left feeling mortally offended. I don't want that to happen tonight, do I?'

'They're just people,' Zoe said, arching an eyebrow and popping a Percy Pig into her mouth while Emily's head was in the fridge.

Emily shut the door, clutching a lemon. 'There's no such

thing as *just people*, Zo. People are judgemental and terrifying, no matter what *Bijou* magazine might say. "Blah blah, no one's looking at you in your teeny-weeny bikini; they're too busy worrying about themselves" etc. My arse! They might be worrying about themselves, but only after they've weighed up how cellulitey your bum is compared to theirs. I guarantee it.'

'Do *you* do that?'

'Of course not. I'm too busy worrying about myself. But as we've established, I'm not normal.'

Zoe laughed. 'OK, so let's look at it this way: what would you say if our roles were reversed, and it was *me* having a mini-stroke because some friends were coming round?'

'I'd tell you that they'll love each other, and they'll love you too, no matter what happens. How could they not? You're totally adorable.' Emily leaned over and squeezed both of Zoe's cheeks, making her look like a hamster. She scowled and swatted her hands away.

'Exactly,' Zoe said. 'I've seen your magazines, and I know one of their fave mantras is that you should treat yourself the way you'd treat your own best friend. Yet here you are, convinced that everyone's going to think you're worse than Hitler five minutes after setting foot in your flat.'

Opening the cutlery drawer beneath her knees, Zoe grabbed a spoon and tucked into the tub of melting ice cream sitting on the counter. Emily had pulled it from the freezer in favour of more ice, after *Bijou*'s article on PARTY TRICKS FOR GROWN-UPS had warned that any good hostess should consider running out of ice a fate worse than death.

'Don't dribble that everywhere,' she warned Zoe.

'Sure thing, boss!' Zoe said, leaning over and wiping a smear of ice cream onto Emily's nose with her spoon.

Emily swiped it off and sucked her finger clean. Not for the first time, she wondered why everything that was good for you – eating lettuce, press-ups, doing crosswords to fend off Alzheimer's – was boring and rubbish, while all the fun things in life, like mainlining Chunky Monkey ice cream, were terrible for your health.

'Just ... please try to relax a bit. Otherwise you'll die of a heart attack, then you won't have anyone to impress, will you?' Zoe said, wiping ice cream off her chin with her sleeve. 'This is a small gathering of people in your flat, not the Met Ball. And whether you show them New Emily or the old one, they'll love you and each other. I promise.'

'Thanks, Zo,' Emily said, half-hugging her while arching her chest and overpriced Zara cardigan as far away as possible from the sticky tub clutched in Zoe's hands.

Emily knew Zoe was right: she was attaching far too much significance to a handful of friends popping over for tacos and nibbles. But she'd spent the last few days playing every possible dinner-date-disaster scenario through her head, and was desperate for the evening to go well.

'Fuck!' Emily yelled as the doorbell rang, clutching a hand to her chest.

'Jesus, you have *got* to calm down,' Zoe said, tossing the nearly empty ice-cream tub onto the counter.

'Don't open the door too quickly. We don't want them to think we've been panicking,' Emily said, spinning in a circle as she looked around the kitchen, before hastily scooping the tub into the bin and wiping down the counter.

'*We* haven't been panicking,' Zoe said, leaving the kitchen, walking the few steps across Emily's tiny living room to the front door, and swinging it open.

'Welcome one, welcome all!' she said, loudly. Emily plastered on a bright smile – one that said, *Having cool London friends round to my cool London flat is totally normal and cool* – and drifted calmly out of the kitchen.

'Hey, guys!' she said, spotting Mel and Jess standing on her doormat. 'Welcome to my flat. Make yourselves at home.'

And with that, the lights above them flickered out, plunging everyone into darkness.

Chapter 2

In the next few seconds, Emily felt every drop of blood in her head plummeting towards the floor. She was sure she was going to throw up, or faint. Or throw up *then* faint.

'Is this a surprise party?' Mel asked, peering into the living room as if a cake covered in candles was about to appear.

'Well, it is quite surprising,' Emily said weakly.

'Power cut,' Zoe announced, sticking her head underneath Emily's net curtain. 'The whole street is out.'

'That's amazing news. Fantastic,' Emily said, taking some deep breaths and fighting the urge to have a panic attack.

'Can we come in anyway?' Jess asked, poking her head around Mel's back. 'I'm dying for a wee.'

'Of course, sorry. Come in,' Emily said, ushering them inside. 'Loo's just there.' Plucking her phone from her pocket, she used the torch to shine a beam of light onto her bathroom door. Jess grinned and dashed past her, while Mel raised her eyebrows and handed her an expensive-looking bottle of wine.

'I don't know whether to take your coat or send you home,

where there are things like heating and lighting available,' Emily said, glad that the darkness was hiding the tears she was blinking back. She'd planned the evening so carefully and now it was ruined.

'Power cuts don't often last long. As long as you've got a few candles, it'll be fine,' Mel said. 'Have you? Got candles, I mean.'

'Of course I have. I'm a millennial, I've got billions of them. Although they're all different smells, so I'm not sure how well that's going to work out. It might be like walking past a branch of Lush. Zoe, can you get Mel a glass of wine while I dig them out?'

'Sure thing, boss,' Zoe saluted.

Emily tried to look calm and collected as she headed for her bedroom and rummaged around her chest of drawers, looking for scented candles.

Everything's going to be just fine, she told herself, taking some more deep breaths – in through the nose and out through the mouth, just like her meditation app recommended.

As she placed the candles around the living room and lit them using Zoe's cigarette lighter, along with some tea lights they'd found in the cupboard under the sink, Simon and Jada arrived at the open front door.

'Is this some kind of weird sex thing?' Simon asked. 'Because if it is, I'm totally into it.'

Emily looked up and grinned at him, then shot a nervous look at Mel, who was busy pouring wine into her best glasses. She let out a sigh of relief when Mel barked out a laugh.

'It's a power cut, I'm afraid,' Emily said. 'But please, come in anyway. I'm hoping it won't last too long.'

'Cool, I love a power cut,' said Jada. 'Very eighties.' She handed Emily a bottle of wine that looked significantly cheaper than Mel's, which was fine by her: posh wine just meant worrying about pairing it with the right food (which almost definitely didn't include tacos), or pronouncing the name wrong.

With candles glowing in every corner, their light flickering against the books and ornaments on Emily's shelves, the room actually looked quite cosy.

As her guests grabbed their glasses and settled variously between the sofa and the plump cushions she'd scattered across the floor, Emily handed out the bowls of snacks she'd so carefully prepared, and felt her heart sinking. All that effort, and no one could even tell which Percys were vegetarian. Their ears all looked the same in the dark.

'According to the power company, the lights aren't coming on any time soon,' Zoe said, sitting cross-legged on the fluffy living room rug, her H&M knickers boldly on show and her face lit up by the light from her phone. 'There's been an equipment malfunction, appaz.'

'Oh god, this is a disaster,' Emily groaned, giving up any pretence of feeling OK about the situation. 'I'll leave it up to you guys to decide what you want to do. I can't exactly cook tacos over a Fig and Bergamot candle, can I? You can all go home if you like and I'll reschedule.'

'Don't be silly, it's just a power cut,' Zoe said, squeezing Emily's arm. 'We can order pizza from a place further out. It'll be fun. Like those novelty restaurants that charge you a fortune to eat in the dark.'

'Wine tastes the same whether you can eyeball it or not,' Jada agreed, and everyone nodded. Both Zoe and Jada knew how important tonight was for her, and Emily could have hugged them both with gratitude.

‘Then cheers, everyone. And thanks for coming,’ Emily said, raising her glass.

‘Cheers,’ everyone agreed, clinking their glasses together, and Emily allowed herself to feel a small spark of excitement. Perhaps everything would be OK after all.

By midnight, even though the flat she’d spent so long cleaning and tidying was now scattered with greasy takeaway boxes, Emily was finally starting to enjoy herself. She had to admit that the party had gone better than she’d ever hoped for – perhaps thanks to, rather than in spite of, the power cut.

She’d spent several tortured hours over the last few days imagining a deathly silence descending over dinner, forcing her to start a last-ditch conversation about discontinued snacks. But sitting in near-darkness had turned out to be a brilliant ice-breaker.

Simon and Jada had quickly hit it off with Mel and Jess, happily comparing tattoos, bad dates and – after five or six cocktails – STDs. Once the wine had disappeared, Emily’s carefully curated cocktail cabinet (a FJÄLLBO from Ikea strung with battery-powered fairy lights) had gone down a storm, and by decanting her precious ice from the freezer into a bucket and placing it precariously on the windowsill outside in the November air, it had lasted for most of the evening.

When the battery on Emily’s phone finally died, and her Spotify playlist was forced into silence halfway through Lizzo telling the room why she was one hundred per cent that bitch, she assumed everyone would call it a night. But instead, after rejecting Simon’s tipsy suggestion that they play strip I-spy, they started swapping scary stories.

Passing a candle around, they took it in turns to tell their spooky tales, their faces lit by candlelight, until Jess broke the tension with a story about a haunted Portaloo that was more hilarious than terrifying, and Jada came up with a new idea.

'The only thing better than ghost stories is speaking to real ghosts. Let's make a Ouija board,' she said, grinning mischievously. 'Have you got a big piece of card we can use, Emily?'

Emily glanced around the group to make sure no one was pulling an expression that said, *Didn't you know Ouija boards are, like, totally passé?* before replying, 'I've got a box of organic spelt muesli I can dismantle. Will that do?' Zoe rolled her eyes.

'Bingo,' Jada said, giving a thumbs-up. 'Grab a tumbler, if you've got one. And a Sharpie.'

Everyone looked on curiously as Jada set up a makeshift Ouija board on the coffee table, the stacks of bracelets on her wrists jangling as she wrote the numbers 0-9, 'yes' and 'no,' and the letters of the alphabet across the back of the card in thick black pen. Finally, she placed a glass upside-down in the centre of the board.

'Are you sure about this, Jada?' Emily asked, eyeing the board suspiciously and trying to sound less nervous than she felt. 'Everyone's got that one friend with a story about a girl who heard about this other girl who got possessed by angry spirits after playing with a Ouija board. Then died.'

'It'll be fine, Grandma,' Zoe said, giving her a reassuring hair-ruffle before leaning out of the living room window and lighting a cigarette. Emily hastily smoothed her hair back down and looked enviously at the smoke pluming from Zoe's lips into the night air.

'Sure I'm sure. It'll be a laugh,' Jada promised blithely, shuffling closer to the table, which had been dragged into the centre of the living room rug. 'Besides, a power cut isn't a power cut without a Ouija board, is it?'

'I'll have to take your word on that one,' Emily muttered.

'Come on – down you get,' Jada instructed Mel and Jess, who were curled comfortably on each end of the sofa like bookends, each clutching a cocktail glass. 'No one's chickening out – you have to join in, or else.' Jess slid off the sofa and sat beside Emily.

'I'll have to take my leg off if I'm going to get under that table,' Mel grumbled, easing her way out of the comfy indent she'd made in the corner of Emily's sofa. Simon raised his eyebrows as she deftly released her prosthesis and twisted it off, before sliding up to the table between Jada and Jess.

'Come on, Zo,' Jada said, and she took one last drag on her cigarette before flicking it into the street below.

'Budge up,' she instructed Emily, breathing into her palm and sniffing it. 'Sorry about the smell.'

Emily tutted, while secretly feeling jealous. She and Zoe had smoked their very first furtive cigarettes together in the small playground that sat at the centre of Greenleaf. Sitting huddled underneath the slide, Emily would scrawl EMILY B LOVES MARTIN B, IDST on its side in black eyeliner in between puffs of Mayfair Lights.

Since moving to London, Emily had given up smoking, documenting the process on Instagram Stories with photos of herself perched on her sofa, daintily eating a fat-free probiotic yoghurt with captions like, *Day 12: munchies kicking in!* because it felt like The London Thing To Do. Meanwhile, Zoe didn't give a hoot that, in the kinds of circles Emily wanted to move in, nobody who was anybody smoked.

'Oh, bore off,' Zoe had told Emily cheerfully, after listening to yet another of her interesting facts about how quickly you can go trampolining without wheezing after you quit. 'I've seen those Instagram women you're basing New Emily on. They think eating truffle fries and buying expensive lounge-wear count as vices, because they're *dicks*. If you want to turn into a dick, you go right ahead, but count me out. Besides, you're just jealous,' she added correctly, blowing a perfect smoke ring into Emily's face.

Emily dutifully shuffled her bum across the rug to give Zoe room. Tugging her short black tube dress a centimetre further down her thighs, in a futile attempt not to flash her crotch when she sat down, she plonked herself between her and Jess.

With Emily and all five of her guests now sitting around the table, the others' fingers joined hers on the bottom of the glass at the edge of the board.

'I can't believe you've never done this before, Emily,' Jada said, grinning. 'I spent half my teens making up fake messages to scare my mates and trying to get in touch with Michael Jackson.'

'Dead Michael Jackson showing up in a room full of teen-age girls *would* be pretty scary,' Simon said. Emily tried to nudge him in the ribs without taking her fingers off the glass, and nearly toppled over. 'Even if it does work, the only person I know who's died is my ancient Scottish great-granny. I only met her once, and all I remember is that she gave me a packet of Fisherman's Friends, telling me they were sweets, which means she definitely went straight to hell. If she tries to get in touch, it's hardly going to be a Hallmark moment.'

Emily grinned at him.

'OK. Are we ready?' Jada said, lowering her voice to a

whisper. Everyone around the table nodded. 'Then how about everyone shuts up, then shuts their eyes.'

'Maybe apart from Mel?' Emily said. 'We need someone to read the messages, and out of the six of us, I reckon she's the most honest. That way no one can cheat.'

'Charming,' Zoe said, as Emily smiled shyly across the table at Mel.

'Good plan,' Jada said. 'Close your eyes, and Mel will read out any messages that come through. 'Spirits, are you out there?' she said, lowering her voice and making it sound all mysterious. 'If you can hear me, please give us a sign.'

The room went silent. Then everyone yelped as the glass suddenly lurched towards the letters written on the board, taking their hands with it.

'Everyone, keep your eyes shut,' Mel ordered. Emily could feel her straining to read the board.

'That's an E,' Mel said, as the glass moved slightly to the right. 'And an M.'

Emily gasped as the glass moved again. Although it was a heavy tumbler, it felt like it was on casters, rolling effortlessly around the table rather than being forced by someone's hand. Her skin prickled, and Zoe started breathing heavily beside her.

'It's an I,' Mel said. Suddenly, Emily felt very hot. 'Now an L . . . And a Y.'

'Stop it!' Emily yelped, pulling her hands from underneath the others' and opening her eyes. Her heart was thudding wildly. 'OK, you can stop mucking about now.'

'Yoinks, Shaggy,' Simon said, in his best Scooby Doo voice.

'Who was doing that?' Mel asked. Everyone looked at each other, frowning, before shaking their heads.

'I don't think it was any of us,' Jada said. 'Everyone had their eyes closed and was barely touching the glass. It . . . it felt like it was moving on its own.'

'Then you're making the letters up, right, Mel?' Emily said, uncertainly. 'Which is fine, obviously,' she added hastily.

Her skin was prickling with goosebumps, and she was starting to wish Jess hadn't had the brilliant idea of forcing the last of the Percy Pigs into the remains of the bottle of gin. The resulting 'Pigtails', as Simon had christened them, were delicious, but Emily could feel every last sickly mouthful lurching about in her stomach.

'Mel wouldn't muck about with stuff like this,' Jess said firmly.

Mel's face glowed pale white in the light from the candles. She shook her head. 'It's honestly what it spelled out. Maybe it's a subconscious thing?'

'How about we try it with just you then, Emily?' Jada asked, trying to make her voice sound light as she grabbed her phone and scanned the instructions she'd used to make the board. 'It says here that at least four people are needed to play, but what does wikiHow know?'

'They only say you need four people because they're assuming at least one of them will be willing to wind up their mates,' Mel said, reaching across the table to squeeze Emily's hand. 'But if there's really a ghost in your flat – which there blatantly isn't – it'll still work with one person, right? So let's try it, if only to set your mind at rest.'

'I suppose so,' Emily said, annoyed at herself for feeling rattled. Believing in horoscopes and ghosts, just like her mega-superstitious Auntie Suze, was definitely Old Emily-type behaviour.

It's all in your mind, there's no such thing as ghosts, she told herself as she put her hands back on the bottom of the glass and closed her eyes.

'Right . . . is there anyone there?' Jada asked, ditching the spooky voice.

Emily felt an odd sensation flooding through her hand, like it was being dipped in treacle. Then the glass shot to the left again, and she let out a yelp. She wasn't moving a muscle. The tumbler felt like it had a mind of its own as it moved swiftly around the board.

'E - M - I - L - Y - A - N - D - A - N - D - Y,' Mel read aloud, sounding shaken. 'Emily and Andy.'

With difficulty, Emily ripped her fingers from the bottom of the glass, which felt like it was covered in glue. She was shaking all over.

Suddenly, the lights around the room flickered back to life, and Emily shrieked. Everyone looked up, startled. Zoe shuffled closer to Emily, who was trying hard not to cry, and put an arm around her trembling shoulders.

'God, are you OK?' Jada said, kneeling down beside Emily. 'I'm really sorry, I thought it would stop if it was just you. What happened? And who the hell is Andy?'

Chapter 3

'No one. I don't know anyone called Andy,' Emily said quickly, as Simon grabbed the grey woollen blanket that was draped over the back of her sofa and pulled it gently around her shoulders. 'At least, no one who died, anyway. It must be electromagnetic fields, or ley lines or . . . Alexa or something.'

'The electricity *did* come back on pretty much at the same time,' Simon said, thoughtfully, looking at the ceiling and waving his hand over the Ouija board. 'It's not impossible that it's something to do with static.' Picking up the glass, he started examining it.

'I knew a guy called Andy once,' Jess said. 'He moved to Essex, which is kind of like being dead? Maybe it's a cry for help from beyond the M25.' Zoe opened her mouth to speak, before seeing the look on Emily's face and hastily closing it again.

Emily let out a laugh that sounded fake even to her. She was shaking, but didn't want the night to be memorable solely for the spectacle of her freaking out over a stupid game. 'This is silly. I don't believe in all this stuff, anyway,' she said, trying to convince herself as much as her friends. 'There's bound to be a logical explanation for it.'

'As long as you're really OK?' Jada said, looking sheepish. 'I didn't mean to force you into doing this then scare the bejesus out of you.'

'Of course I'm OK,' Emily smiled, trying to act like someone who wasn't fully intending to leave her bedroom light on that night, and every other night, probably for the rest of time.

'Remember those sleepovers as a kid, where you'd watch a slasher film, then your dad would tap on the living room window and scare the crap out of everyone? Those were the best. And, well, I guess tonight has been a bit like that, hasn't it? A lovely trip down memory lane.'

'Power cuts, Percy Pigs and a séance is a pretty retro combo,' Zoe agreed, giving Emily's arm a reassuring squeeze. Only she knew that Emily had never been to a sleepover in her life. She'd never held one, either, knowing that the girls in her form class would rather eat their strawberry-scented rubbers than set foot on the Greenleaf estate.

Emily had managed to glean what went on at them by eavesdropping on the popular girls, who'd giggle together on Monday mornings over their evenings spent drinking illicit vodka and reading the rude bits out of their mums' Jackie Collins novels. She'd longed, more than anything, to be invited too, but knew she was a million miles from it ever happening.

'Right, it's time for everyone to skedaddle now,' Emily said, faking a yawn. 'My Cat's Miaow presentation is due on Monday, and you're buggering up my exciting Sunday schedule of getting up early and finishing the PowerPoint I've been polishing up for Charles.'

Talking a bit louder than necessary to dispel the uneasy atmosphere that had settled over the flat, everyone started getting ready to leave: rummaging around for their coats and shoes, swearing at Uber apps and checking Citymapper for the night-bus timetable.

Zoe leaned over and gave Emily a quick hug. 'Do you want me to stay over?' she asked in her ear as she slipped on the ancient denim jacket she'd been wearing since high school. It should have gone to a charity shop long ago, but it had been her most treasured possession as a teenager, and she refused to part with it, even though it was falling apart at the seams.

Emily was constantly amazed by the way Zoe could wear something like that and feel completely confident, while she could be clothed head-to-toe in designer clothes – or at least, their copycat equivalent – and still feel rubbish.

'I'll be fine,' Emily said quietly. 'As far as we know, Andy's still alive and well and torturing the lucky lady he dumped me for with his air guitar and stinky socks.'

'As long as you're sure,' Zoe said reluctantly, wiggling her toes into a pair of paper-thin ballet pumps. She was always complaining about her feet being cold, and textured pavement bumps feeling like daggers, but she preferred to spend her money on cigarettes and pints of lager rather than shoes with proper soles.

'I'll text you tomorrow,' Emily promised her, opening the door and kissing each of her five friends on the cheek as they filed out of her flat.

Shutting the door behind them and double-locking it, Emily paused, before pulling the chain across it too. As soon as it snapped into place, a huge wave of adrenaline overwhelmed her. Legs wobbling, she scanned her make-shift cocktail cabinet to see what was left of the haul of cheap alcohol she'd dragged home from Aldi on the bus and decanted into brand-name bottles.

There were only a few dregs left in each, so she poured everything into a glass and added a cocktail cherry to the half-dissolved Percy Pig ears floating in her drink. Reaching behind her, she tugged the zip of her dress down and let it slither to the floor. Sighing with relief, she rubbed her stomach as she breathed out fully for the first time in hours.

Her stomach rumbled, and she suddenly realised it was almost 2 a.m., and she was starving. During the evening, she'd nibbled on a slice of pizza and a handful of habas fritas, claiming to be full. She didn't want to look greedy in front of her guests, or Hulk out in her bodycon dress. But now no one was there to see her eating, she slipped on a pyjama set, headed to the freezer and rummaged in its depths for her tub of emergency ice cream. It had almost completely melted thanks to the power cut, but she wasn't feeling fussy.

Grabbing the spoon Zoe had used earlier from the depths of the sink, she shuffled to the sofa, curled herself onto it and turned on the TV. Deciding that watching *The Greatest Ever Celebrity Wind-Ups* was a foolproof way of warding off evil spirits, she pushed up the volume to just below neighbour-bothering level.

Mary, the ancient-looking woman who lived upstairs, somehow had the aural powers of a child hearing a packet of Maltesers being opened from three rooms away. She was fond of banging on the floor with the heel of one of her marabou mules if Emily made too much noise.

She picked up the soft grey blanket Simon had draped around her shoulders, wrapped it tightly around herself, and picked up her phone. Bringing up Facebook, she decided to put her doubts firmly to bed. She only knew one Andy: Andy

Atkins, who she'd started dating almost exactly a year ago, before he'd suddenly ghosted her.

Her fingers shook a little as she typed his name into Facebook, telling herself that in just a few seconds she'd be laughing at how scared she'd been, and texting Zoe about it. She realised that she was afraid, more than anything, of what – or rather *who* – she might find on his Facebook page.

Andy had been completely different to the other men she'd dated since moving to London. In line with her personal transformation, she'd been looking for someone who was solid, sensible and (preferably) solvent. In short, the opposite of the father who'd disappeared from her life when she was just a child.

Despite the fact that Andy was none of those things, and that she'd only intended their relationship to be a fling, she'd found herself falling for him, and over the five months they'd been dating, her New Emily mask had gradually slipped.

Feeling confident and happy whenever she was around him, she'd started to wonder, just a little, if perhaps she'd been looking for the wrong kind of man – and whether someone like Andy could actually be what she needed. Which had made it even more painful when he'd suddenly ghosted her. Throughout their relationship, she'd wondered whether she should be looking for someone better than Andy. Or at least, someone less chaotic. But as it turned out, it was he who had decided she wasn't good enough for *him*.

After waiting a few days for him to get back in touch, she'd blocked him from her phone and unfriended him on social media. It was a bit extreme, but she couldn't bear the thought of opening Instagram and stumbling across a photo of him with his arms wrapped around another girl's shoulders. A girl who was better than her in every way.

He'd proved to her that she'd been right all along: Old Emily was all too easy to abandon. She needed someone dependable and sturdy in her life, who wouldn't suddenly vanish into thin air – and the way to get him was to focus on making herself the best person she could possibly be, and never allowing herself to slip back into her old habits.

More determined than ever to make herself worth sticking around for, she'd doubled her efforts down the gym, devouring online tutorials on everything from achieving an especially perky ponytail, to how to throw the perfect dinner party.

So now, as she typed Andy's name into her phone for the first time in eight months, she worried she was about to see the woman he'd left her for, and that it would dent her already shaky confidence even more. Maybe she'd been 'the one before The One', and she'd be faced with a series of wedding photos of Andy and someone who possessed all the things she lacked but was so desperate to achieve: a perfectly flat stomach, effortlessly smooth hair, and thighs to match.

She shook her head clear. There was no point speculating. In a moment, she'd know exactly what Andy had been up to since he'd dumped her. As her fingers hit 'search', she felt a wave of nausea at the thought of what she might find.

Then froze when Facebook produced a single suggestion.

She blinked, trying to stop the words swimming in front of her eyes. Instead of Andy's profile page, with its photo of him grinning goofily while clutching five shots of tequila in both hands like he'd won the lottery, she'd found a memorial page.

In sombre black and white, it said:

Remembering Andy Atkins

Chapter 4

One Year Earlier

Emily @EmilyBlotters90
Broke my PB at the gym y'day. 5k in 22 mins 3 secs!

Andy @AndyAtkins88
In reply to @EmilyBlotters90
I love peanut butter too! U should take more care of it tho. Why were u at the gym with it? I hate exercise, blurgh.

Andy @AndyAtkins88
In reply to @EmilyBlotters90
P.S. When are u gonna let me take u out for tacos? Dunno how you've resisted me this long, TBH.

Emily couldn't help smiling at Andy's ridiculous tweets as she lay in bed that Sunday morning. Having smashed her personal best the day before, when her alarm had gone off at

7 a.m., she'd decided that keeping up with social media was a much more important pastime than going to the gym again and pretending to enjoy unholy-hour Zumba.

Since he'd started following her six months earlier, Andy always replied to everything she wrote almost instantly – which presumably meant he didn't have anything better to do all day than flirt ineptly with strangers on Twitter. And for the first time, she wondered if he might actually be just the thing she was looking for: a Winter Boyfriend to see her through to the new year.

Despite daily, careful moisturising, the cold weather meant Emily's legs were the texture of tree trunks. Her bed was more tempting than braving the cold to spend hours in a box full of sweaty men heroically picking stuff up, then putting it down again, which meant she'd skipped the gym a few too many times over the past month.

She'd also found an incredible recipe for hasselback potatoes on TikTok, which she'd *accidentally* discovered tasted even more amazing when you used them to scoop up cheese dip, even though every mouthful made her feel a wave of guilt.

All of which meant she was feeling much less sexy than her best, but also about as horny as a rhino in a rose bush.

After a series of unsuccessful dates – and the absence of any long-term prospects in her life – Emily had started her hunt for a Winter Boyfriend back in September. Since moving to London, it had become a seasonal tradition, like posting a cute bobble hat/fallen leaves/red Starbucks cup photo on Instagram in October, and being annoyed by the wave of Elf on the Shelf Facebook posts in December.

Emily was generally happy to be single and free in spring and summer, when she got to wear flirty dresses, lovely gold sandals that made her ankles look tiny, and huge, flattering hats.

But being single in winter was absolutely crap. Cold-weather meals – hotpots, roast dinners, entire bags of potatoes – were made for sharing, preferably under a blanket on the sofa. Your skin started to dry up and slough off the second you so much as glanced at a pair of tights, and, without summer pedicures, your feet turned into nubbly little trotters, so the very idea of pulling someone new was terrifying. She also needed moral support – and a distraction – to sustain her through another Christmas Day spent in Essex with her mum and Auntie Suze.

Surreptitiously sexting her Winter Boyfriend while pushing dry turkey and burned roasties around her plate was the best part of the season, but with November well under way, she was getting a bit desperate. She'd rinsed Tinder, Bumble and Happn, but no one even remotely suitable had popped up.

She'd once spent a whole day at the National Gallery wearing one of her most intellectual-looking outfits (a pencil skirt left over from her temping days, paired with a frilly blouse that she hoped would look like a purposeful nod to Romanticism), trying to think poetic thoughts as she gazed at paintings of nudey renaissance women who clearly had no trouble embracing their wobbly bits.

She was fairly certain that the men she was interested in – well brought up, ambitious, and reliable enough never to contemplate nipping out for cigarettes one afternoon and never coming back – spent most of their free time hanging about in cultured places like that.

But instead, she'd almost been trampled by rampaging groups of schoolchildren, who tore around the galleries like a herd of wildebeest, pausing only to point at nativity scenes and shout, 'LOOK, IT'S BABY JESUS'S WILLY.' The closest she'd got to some action was when a man with mad-looking hair had sidled up beside her in front of Venus at her Mirror and muttered, 'She should be facing muff-wards, if you ask me. Lovely bum, mind.'

'How do you people get *everywhere*?!' she'd demanded, before stalking off.

She'd left clutching a desk tidy shaped like a pencil sharpener instead of the numbers of several eligible men. But now, looking at Andy's latest cheesy tweet, she started to wonder if what she needed right now was staring her in the face. Clicking on his profile – '*The only thing better than a guitar is TWO guitars!*' – she saw that, unlike most of the other guys who tried to woo her in two hundred and eighty characters or fewer, he only flirted with *her*, rather than with most of the women on his feed.

All his other tweets were about his band, or food, or photographs of his many injuries, usually gained when he did something very stupid.

Andy @AndyAtkins88
Check this out!!! Tried 2 hammer a nail in with my 4head. didn't work. #Ouch #ThugLife.
Via Twitter web app

Emily had never really considered Andy a serious contender before – dating the kind of man who'd once broken his wrist jumping off a bin felt a bit too close to home for her liking, and she was trying to move on from her past, not invite it into her flat for a shag.

Andy was firmly in the 'break-glass-in-case-of-emergency' category of Twitter flirtations. But what was being single in November if not an emergency? Hoping she wasn't making a huge mistake, Emily opened her direct messages folder and tapped out a post.

@EmilyBlotters90

You've absolutely stunned me with the revelation that you don't like going to the gym. How on earth did you get that dad-bod without doing a billion and one crunches?

@AndyAtkins88

I know, right??? It's a miracle. i'm just one of those people who's naturally toned, i guess?

Another question . . . If I agree to go on a date with you – ONE DATE – will you stop sending me terrible jokes?

I don't know what ur on about, cos my jokes are completely on fire at all times, but the answer is yes! When ru free for a night of Andy's Ultimate Romance?

Oh God. How about this Thursday? I finish work at 6 p.m.

Bayou Bar, 6.30, cocktails?

Stalker much? That's a bit too close to my office. Where do you work?

You don't have to be a stalker to know u luuuurve Bayou Bar, you just have to be on Twitter. I'm London Bridge, so I'll find us a nice pub. Not sure the local Spoons is ur scene, even though it's only three quid a pint

Emily almost confessed that she was a big fan of Wetherspoons and its delicious cheap booze, but decided dropping her cocktail-loving online persona in front of a man she hadn't met yet was too risky. Instead, she replied:

Too right. OK, see you Thursday x

Emily threw her phone onto the duvet, smiling at the thought of finally meeting Andy Atkins in the flesh. He seemed funny and sweet, and although he was a million miles from the kind of man she intended to settle down with, they could potentially enjoy a bit of fun together between now and the new year.

On the evening of their date, Emily was surprised to find herself feeling nervous when she turned up at The Hide Bar, a tucked-away place in London Bridge that she'd never been to before. She usually only felt this way when she was due to meet someone who ticked all her boxes, rather than a man who gave every impression that he lived in one.

Half-expecting Andy to have booked something ironic for their date – laser tag followed by dinner at the Cereal Killer Café, for example – she was impressed to see that the bar he'd chosen was the perfect spot for a grown-up first date.

Then, when a cute-looking guy with scruffy blond-brown hair wearing baggy jeans and a clean but faded grey T-shirt approached her, she relaxed a smidgen more. Andy looked a lot cuter than in his profile picture.

'You must be Emily,' he said, grinning, his blue eyes almost disappearing completely into his friendly face. 'I worked it out because you're her, and I know what she looks like. Eat your heart out, Sherlock Holmes.'

Emily surveyed him as she laughed. He had sandy eyebrows and eyelashes, and a swathe of stubble across his chin. He had a nose that you might describe as cute – small and slightly turned up at the end – and he was surprisingly tall and broad-shouldered. He reminded Emily of a big, shaggy bear, and she couldn't help thinking how good he'd look if he had a shave and a haircut and was forced into a suit.

'Andy, I presume?' she said, reaching out a hand. But instead of taking it, he pulled her into a hug.

'Handshake schmandshake. We've been following each other for months on Twitter,' Andy said, before releasing Emily from his arms, grabbing her hand and leading her to the spot in the corner where he'd reserved a table. As soon as they sat down and Emily had ordered a negroni, she realised she already felt completely relaxed.

Andy was quick to laugh – at her jokes, rather than just his own, like most of the men she dated – and constantly ruffled his hair with one hand, as if it might accidentally settle into neatness if he didn't pay it enough attention.

His manners were pretty appalling – as soon as his bottle of Corona arrived at the table, he tossed the wedge of lime poking out of the top onto the table in disgust, drops of beer splashing the front of Emily's dress.

'Fruit is for cocktails, not beer,' he said sternly, shaking his head in disappointment. 'Are they trying to help me ward off scurvy or something? The girls at work recommended this bar, but it's not my usual type of place.'

'You don't say,' Emily said, smiling. Ironically, Andy would look far more at home at the Dog & Duck, the local old-man pub back in Essex that she hoped never to step foot into again, than in a place like this. Meanwhile, she fit in perfectly in her trusty tailored black skater dress.

'Where do you work then?' Emily asked, trying to keep the burning curiosity from her voice. 'I couldn't work it out from Twitter.'

She'd wondered more than once if Andy's bottomless self-confidence and 1990s skater-boi wardrobe could be thanks to the fact that he was secretly stinking rich, like those Californian tech billionaires who dress terribly, but basically run the universe.

'I'm launching a dazzling career in temping,' Andy said, and Emily quietly put aside her fantasy. 'Setting the world alight with my unrivalled photocopying and filing skills, and currently working at an ad agency that's full of the worst people on earth.'

'Hey, I work in advertising! And we're not *that* bad,' Emily said indignantly, slapping his arm. 'Well, not all of us. Ninety per cent, tops.' Andy had somehow managed to manoeuvre his chair around the table to get closer to her without her noticing. Apparently, he had some moves.

'Trust me, none of the ten per cent have landed at Urban Muse, which is where I'm currently stuck.'

'Please tell me you've got some hot gossip about the tossers who work there?' Emily said. 'Or the "legendary creatives and disruptors", as they no doubt call themselves. I promise not to tell anyone, except almost everyone in my office.'

Andy grinned, launching into some wildly indiscreet stories about his employers, before slapping the table with both palms and leaning forward in his seat. 'Your turn to answer some questions now. What is it Hannibal Lecter says? Quid pro quo?'

'You're basing your dating style on a cannibal? That's so smooth I'm surprised you haven't slithered onto the floor.'

'Actually, it was in *Dating for Dummies*, which I read from cover to cover at lunchtime,' Andy said, taking a swig of his third beer. 'It says not to pick your teeth, don't assume you're getting laid, and to ask lots of questions,' he added, counting on his fingers.

'So . . . What about you? What about your life? Let's start at the beginning. Have you got any brothers and sisters? A mum and dad? Pets? Dark and terrible secrets? Actually, not those. Chapter eight says to save the dark secrets for the third date.'

'Oh god, I'm genuinely worried that you actually read this book now,' Emily said.

'Don't worry, I'm just kidding. I only finished the first chapter, even though it was printed in a really big font. I'm a very slow reader.'

Emily laughed so hard she nearly spilled her drink. 'You don't want to know all that boring stuff,' she said. 'The past's the past, right?' Waving Andy's questions away with her hand, she shifted uncomfortably in her seat.

These days, she was New Emily, ambitious copywriter and negroni-lover (at least she *tried* to love them, even though they were confusingly bitter for something that looked so much like Irn-Bru, which was delicious). She didn't want to think about Old Emily – Spotty Blotty, as she'd been known since Year 9, despite having perfectly normal skin for a thirteen-year-old – unless she absolutely had to. Except apparently, Andy had other ideas.

'I really do want to know all that "boring stuff",' he said, adding air quotes with his fingers. 'I'd love to know what makes you tick. Apart from overpriced cocktails that taste like nail polish remover, that is. You always seem a bit like you're putting on a bit of a show on Twitter, if you don't mind me saying so.'

'Why would I possibly mind you calling me a big fat fake?' Emily said, raising an eyebrow.

'I don't mean it like that,' Andy added, hastily. 'And I'd never call someone fat, either, for the record. But it sometimes feels like you put on this . . . front, when you really don't have to. I mean, no one likes pumpkin spiced lattes that much, surely? And although you're always tweeting about work and the gym and stuff, like that's all that matters to you, you're really funny and friendly when you reply to the goofy guys who try to chat you up. Based on your feed, I wouldn't think you'd give them the time of day.'

'Goofy guys? I don't know who you could possibly mean,' Emily said, taking a sip of her drink to hide her blushes. How had Andy seen through her in about three seconds flat? No one else had questioned the online persona that she'd so carefully honed before.

Although, on the inside, she felt a world away from the glossy girls she followed on social media, she'd read enough articles about confidence being a state of mind to know that half the battle was projecting the right image. All her accounts were deliberately curated to show off New Emily in the best light, each photo taken umpteen times before being uploaded, even if it was only a snap of a cup of coffee with some interesting foam art.

But, apparently, Andy hadn't been fooled. She'd assumed he'd been impressed by her glossy smokescreen, and that was why he'd asked her out – but instead, he wanted to see what was underneath.

She examined his face. He seemed genuinely interested in her, in a way she hadn't really experienced before. There was no artifice about him at all – he wasn't pulling out all the stops, trying to impress her to get her attention. At least, she *hoped* this wasn't his idea of pulling out all the stops. And besides, he'd been so indiscreet about his workplace, she had her own ammo to use against him if he decided to tell everyone her deepest, darkest secrets.

So, for the first time since she'd moved away from Essex, Emily told someone the whole truth about her childhood. She told him about her sarcastic, scatty, borderline-alcoholic mum, who lived on the tenth floor of a concrete tower block. She told him about her kind-hearted Auntie Suze, who'd moved in with them after her dad had left abruptly when she was just eight years old.

She explained how her mum had seemed to give up on her, treating her like an inconvenience after her dad had left. And she told him about his classic went-out-for-fags-and-never-came-back exit, which you assume never happens in real life, until it happens to you.

'I mean, come on, Dad. Try to use a bit of imagination,' she said, managing a laugh as she swallowed down the lump that had formed in her throat. Taking a sip of her drink with a shaky hand, Emily felt light-headed, like she'd jumped off a cliff without looking down to see what might be below. She braced herself for Andy to make a stupid joke about her dad living a double life as a spy to hide his discomfort.

But instead, 'That sounds really hard,' he said seriously, as Emily gave him a brave, wobbly smile.

'Do you mind?' he added, leaning over and holding her hand. 'This hand-holding is for me, not for you, by the way. That was ... wow. But Emily, look how well you've done. However she behaves on the outside, your mum must be so proud of you.'

'If that's the case, she's hiding it *really* well,' Emily said, and Andy held onto her hand as she explained how, on her eighteenth birthday, her mum had announced, 'Well, thank fuck that's over. You can look after yourself now,' and stuck pretty much to her word ever since. Andy winced.

'Well, she sounds absolutely great, and I just can't wait to meet her,' Andy said, and squeezed her hand.

Emily had been on plenty of dates where the guy had nodded enthusiastically through every one of her anecdotes, then got her name wrong at the end of the night. It was refreshing to meet someone who seemed to really hear her, instead of pretending to listen while weighing up their chances of getting her into bed.

'Thank you for telling me all that. I feel a bit honoured, actually,' he said, straightening up.

'Enough about my tragic, fatherless past. What about you?' she asked, relieved to be changing the subject. Needing another drink, she smiled at their waitress to get her attention.

'You're not secretly related to the Royal family, are you? Because that would be really great.'

'I hate to disappoint you, but my mum is just your regular, old-fashioned mum,' he said. 'She potters about hoovering under Dad's feet and forces me to FaceTime with her living room ceiling every time I call her. My parents are older than most – in their sixties now – but it means they've always been there for me. I can't imagine what it must have been like growing up without that.'

Emily nodded. 'So what do you do for fun? Apart from injuring yourself for no reason whatever chance you get?'

Grinning, Andy launched into his own life story, talking equally passionately about his beloved cat, Dandy, the 'indie-pop-rock-whatever' band he was the guitarist and backing singer for, and tacos – a subject Emily didn't yet realise she was about to become very familiar with.

'Tacos are more like an art form than food, see?' Andy enthused. 'There are so many different styles – different meats, different sauces, corn and blue shells, soft ones, crispy ones dipped in chilli sauce and fried. And so many toppings. Like there must be a billion combinations. And the best bit? They're perfect for soaking up alcohol.'

Then, pretending it hadn't been part of his plan all along, Andy had suddenly decided to drag Emily out into the cold night air to try her first-ever taco. Andy had been aghast that she'd never tried one (they were one of Zoe's favourite foods, but at about 350 calories a pop, Emily had always declined), and somehow surprised that she'd never eaten food served from a truck painted with Day-Glo skulls before.

As she ate globs of juicy meat, standing in the street next to the group of beery smokers shivering outside a nearby pub, she had flashbacks to her clubbing days, which were never complete without something greasy from Prima Doner, the kebab van stationed outside the Pink Lagoon nightclub back home in Essex.

It certainly wasn't her idea of a glamorous London date. But Andy's enthusiasm had been too endearing to resist, and she couldn't deny it: tacos were as delicious as Zoe had always claimed they were. That was the moment she'd decided Andy was The One. The One to get her through Christmas and the new year up to about March, anyway. The perfect Winter Boyfriend.

The clincher came when Andy greeted the man selling the *Big Issue* outside London Bridge station like an old friend.

'Long time no see, Andy,' the man said, as he handed him a rolled-up magazine.

'Sorry, Frank,' he said, dipping his hand into his front pocket. 'I haven't temped around here for a while. Here you go. Keep the change.'

Andy handed over a £10 note, and Emily felt a burst of warmth in her chest. Having always dreamed of looking after rescue dogs for a living, she often felt guilty that the most useful thing she ever did at work was changing the conversation around what the modern woman expects from her favourite brand of vitamin gummies.

To offset her advertising-wanker footprint, she did some volunteer work for a local homeless shelter, helping the charity by writing their fundraising blurb. She was passionate about their cause, but the last guy she'd dated – who was called Sebastian, which she'd seen as a sign that he might be a bit posh – had looked confused when she'd bought a copy of the *Big Issue.*

'Is it any good, then?' he'd asked, plucking it out of her hands.

'Yeah, it is actually,' she'd explained. 'But the main point is that it helps homeless people to earn a living and get off the streets.'

'You do know most of them are there in the first place because of drugs though, right?' he'd said, handing back the magazine with the tips of his fingers, as if being homeless might be catching. 'That three quid is probably going on Special Brew.'

On her way home, Emily had paused at the mouth of the Underground to unmatch herself from Sebastian on Tinder with a muttered, 'Bye, fuckface.'

So, as Andy chatted comfortably with Frank, asking about his kids and his dog, Emily couldn't help smiling. Andy was clearly cute, funny *and* kind, and he'd made her feel a lot more like her old self than the new one – in a good way. She'd even stopped sucking in her stomach after her third cocktail.

And although she had a strict no-shagging-before-the-third-date rule in place – New Emily's perfect man being far too much of a gentleman to expect sex after just one date – she didn't hesitate to take him home with her.

Later that night, Emily and Andy lay side-by-side, pinned gently together by their sweaty skin as they recovered from a particularly enthusiastic romp on her living-room sofa. That was when Emily had discovered that Andy's take-me-as-I-am, limes-are-for-idiots approach to dating, which she'd found so refreshing, had actually been his best attempt to impress her.

'I brought out all my best lines! No wonder you couldn't resist me.' He grinned, in between nicknaming her boobs

Ant and Dec ('This one is Ant, obviously, because he always stands on the right.')

'Those were your best lines?' Emily laughed, wrapping her naked body, which was glowing with post-sex endorphins, in her grey blanket. 'Jesus Christ, it's a wonder you ever manage to pull.'

Andy shrugged. 'Why do you think I stick to Twitter, where I can woo women with all my amazing jokes?'

'Oh god. Please stop talking before I start regretting all my life choices. Let's see if you're as good in bed as you are on the sofa, shall we?'

Emily let out a scream of laughter as Andy shot her a wicked grin, leaped off the sofa, threw her over his shoulder, and ran with her into the bedroom.

Chapter 5

Sitting on the same sofa where they'd enjoyed that first, fun-filled night together, Emily's heart felt like a hard rock in her chest as she scrolled through Andy's memorial page. It was filled with pictures posted by his friends remembering their time with him.

He was smiling widely in all of them, whether he was drinking in his favourite south-London pub, covered in mud after playing 'Punch the Potato', the painful variation on volleyball he'd invented, or smoking a bong in his front room wearing swimming trunks and goggles.

Each photo was captioned with a heartfelt tribute, the spelling as hit-and-miss as Andy's had been.

Rest in piece, Andy. Miss u every day.

RIP bruv.

There is an extra angle in heaven today.

This sux. Peace out.

Andy was a dickhead, but he was our dickhead. i hope they have tacos in heaven, my friend.

Emily's stomach lurched again as she remembered the message on the Ouija board: EMILY AND ANDY.

Apart from Zoe, no one at her party knew she'd even dated Andy in the first place. She'd avoided discussing him at work, for the same reason she'd avoided introducing him to Zoe, or meeting his friends. Because, much as she'd loved spending time with him, it felt too much like a step towards becoming a proper couple.

She couldn't ignore the nagging voice at the back of her mind reminding her that she was supposed to be looking for the kind of man who could offer her and her future children some security, rather than one who considered temping four days a week to be selling out to The Man.

Like scoffing a six-pack of Cadbury's Creme Eggs then posting an arty shot of a Hotel Chocolat selection box on Instagram, Emily had considered Andy her guilty secret, best enjoyed in private. To shore up her carefully honed image, she needed to be seen as the kind of person who dated confident, successful guys, not temps who sniffed the armpits of their T-shirts in the morning to see if they could stretch to an extra wear.

She'd even asked Andy not to post about their relationship on social media, claiming it was company policy not to date within the industry – and, ever trusting, he'd believed her.

So, since no one knew about Andy, it was almost impossible for her guests to have faked the Ouija board message to scare her, and Zoe would never do such a thing. She was honest to a fault and hated deception of any kind – she even viewed Emily's push-up bra and bum-boosting pants as a form of subterfuge. So did that mean Andy really *had* tried to contact her?

Scrolling back to the very first posts on his memorial page, she froze as she read the tiny captions underneath them: 9 March. Less than a week after Andy had ghosted her and she'd deleted him from her life, one app at a time. Except now, it looked like she'd been wrong all along. Instead of ditching her, Andy had died.

The back of her neck prickled as she scrolled through pages of memories posted by friends of Andy's she'd never even met. He'd regularly asked her to come out with the group of men he fondly referred to as Knob-out, Banjo, The Trevinator and Vaseline Alan, but she'd always made excuses not to. She certainly wasn't keen to find out how they'd achieved their nicknames.

But now, as she read their messages, she felt a pang of regret that she'd turned down their invitations. They were the people Andy had loved more than anyone else in the world, and they had clearly loved him back: everyone had a different favourite memory of him, from the time he'd tried to eat eight hotdog sausages at once, to his dream of eventually living in a converted taco truck.

Although it had been eight months since he'd died, there were still plenty of recent posts. His friends seemed to be using the page as a kind of message board, to check in with each other and make sure he wasn't forgotten.

As she flicked back through their posts and photos, it didn't seem real that someone who had been so alive could possibly be gone. And Emily also realised something strange: no one seemed to know exactly how he had died.

Someone had posted a link to an article titled, BRIXTON MAN DIES IN MYSTERY FALL, so she clicked on it. Facebook disappeared from her phone with an elegant sidestep, and was replaced with a page from the *Brixton Bugle*. She scrolled through it, her eyes widening at every line.

An inquest has returned an open verdict following the death of a local man. Andy Atkins, 31, of Chaucer Road, Brixton, was found dead on Thrift Street, Soho, on the evening of Monday 7 March. He died of head injuries from a suspected fall, the cause of which is unknown.

Atkins, who formerly attended Wren Hill High School, was believed to have been working in the area at the time of his death. Coroner James Ward commented that suicide or misadventure were suspected causes of death, but neither could be confirmed.

A spokesperson for the Metropolitan Police commented that, after an investigation, no other person was under suspicion, and that they were satisfied with the verdict.

What on earth had happened to him? He certainly hadn't seemed suicidal the last time she'd seen him. As she recalled, their last conversation had been about Simon Cowell's hair. Andy didn't seem to let life's weightier issues get to him – although Emily knew better than most that the person you projected to the world didn't necessarily reflect who you really were underneath.

The other possibility was that he'd fallen somehow. Maybe he was looking out of the window at a cat – Andy loved cats – and leaned too far? Or perhaps he was pushed? Although why would anyone want to hurt someone as nice as Andy?

Emily shook her head as it ricocheted between the shock of knowing Andy was dead, confusion over how he had died, and the sudden realisation that he hadn't ghosted her after all. Thinking about any one of them felt like someone had suddenly attacked her chest with a giant ice-cream scoop. But worst of all was *how* she'd found out Andy had died: the message on the Ouija board.

Desperate to stop her brain whirring, she downed her makeshift cocktail, closed her eyes, and tried to think clearly through the fog of booze and exhaustion blanketing her body. When she thought about things logically, she knew the message that had appeared – 'Emily and Andy' – wasn't real.

New Emily didn't believe in ghosts, or horoscopes, or coincidences. She believed that you make your own luck, that love was something you had to work at rather than happening at first sight (and should be achieved using your head as well as your heart), and that people who thought everything happens for a reason were just trying to excuse their own lousy decisions.

But Old Emily had been entranced by all things magical and mystical. When she was small, her dad had taken her to see a magician who was performing in the local pub. He'd called her up onto his makeshift stage and asked her to clutch a broken watch in her tiny, clammy hand.

When, after a couple of minutes, she felt it coming to life, softly ticking inside her fingers, she'd been so astonished she'd almost dropped it. But she'd since learned that the magician's act was simply a trick – the warmth of her hand heating up the rusting parts so they temporarily sprang back to life.

Emily thought hard about what could have happened with the Ouija board. She'd seen enough Derren Brown shows on TV to know how suggestible your mind can be. Perhaps she'd heard about Andy's death somewhere without connecting the dots, and this was her subconscious's way of bringing it to her attention? Or perhaps, in some shady part of her brain, she was aware that it was almost exactly a year since they'd met, and she'd summoned up the message through guilt?

'*That must be it*,' Emily told herself. But as she drifted into an uneasy sleep, she couldn't stop a memory creeping into her mind – of the strange, sticky sensation that had flooded through her fingers, and how the glass had moved beneath them, gliding effortlessly across the board as if an unseen hand was guiding it.

Chapter 6

'Oh, for absolute pity's sake ... Not my Mango throw ...'

The next morning, Emily woke up on the sofa with her limbs tangled in her blanket, which was covered in sticky puddles of melted ice cream. Absorbed by the news of Andy's death, she'd forgotten all about the tub she'd pulled from the freezer the night before.

As she sat up, she winced – she'd slept with her head at a painful angle, and her neck was as stiff as a board. As she turned it gingerly left and right, neither of which she could do properly, the memory of everything that had happened the night before, from the power cut to finding out Andy was dead, hit her all at once, sending her heartbeat haywire.

She took several calming deep breaths before bundling the blanket in her arms and heading for the kitchen. Stuffing it into the washing machine, she switched on the kettle.

Her hand hovered over the jar of instant coffee she'd bought, officially for when Zoe came over, but really for when she had a moment of weakness. But then she reminded herself, 'You are what you eat,' and made a cup of acai berry green tea. It tasted like hot bin juice served out of a jockstrap, but it was her favourite wellness TikToker's breakfast drink of choice – which meant it was hers now, too.

While in the movies, turning into a shiny new version of yourself involved a handful of shopping-mall-and-makeover montages, and the odd, tiny hiccup, like choosing the wrong height of Gucci heel then collapsing into fits of giggles, Emily had found that improving yourself in real life involved lots of small decisions that made your life worse in the short term, but were designed to make you a better person overall.

Tearing features from magazines with titles like, 15 MAKE-UP LOOKS TO WIN HIM OVER IN 15 SECONDS FLAT!, and following swathes of social media accounts that focused on self-improvement, she'd been confused at first. Was she supposed to learn how to love herself, speak her truth, embrace her wobbly bits, and ignore salads, because going on a diet was anti-feminist?

Or was she supposed to squeeze herself into a pair of booty shorts and a crop top, eat nothing but quinoa (preferably after learning how to pronounce it) and, as one influencer had it, 'find out which items in your wardrobe give men the ick'?

Both types of accounts – the ones that told her she was perfect as she was, and those that told her she was a piece of garbage until she learned how to contour her face properly – seemed to be equally sure that they held the secret to achieving confidence and success, which left her completely baffled.

Unsure which route to follow, she'd chosen to channel the spirit of her favourite childhood movies. Anne Hathaway's transformation from geek to chic in *The Princess Diaries* had been a pivotal moment of her youth, so she'd decided to focus on giving herself a whole-life makeover.

It had been a lot less fun than it looked online – not once had she sat on the edge of a cliff at sunrise clutching her knees in a baggy jumper – and despite her best efforts, she still didn't exude the effortless confidence of the girls in her Instagram feeds. Still, she lived in hope.

'Big picture,' she muttered to herself, wincing as she sipped her disgusting tea.

Back on the sofa, her laptop sat accusingly on the cushion next to hers. Although she'd been on an emotional roller-coaster over the previous twenty-four hours, she needed to work on the presentation she was due to present to her boss, Charles, tomorrow. And, if she was lucky, Oliver Beauchamp, the ad agency's new Creative Director, too.

An email from the company's CEO had been sent to the office a month earlier, declaring Oliver to be 'a proper fucking brilliant talent I can't wait to start disrupting with'. Ever since, the gossip thread on the office's instant message service – which Simon had titled Consumer Insights, just in case Charles was hovering – had lit up with chat about the new recruit.

It hadn't taken long for Ellie, the office assistant, to send everyone in the group Oliver's LinkedIn profile, Instagram page, Twitter handle and – though Emily had no idea how – his dating profile.

Oliver was starting tomorrow, and everyone had spent the last fortnight excitedly speculating over his taste in women ('And maybe men too,' Claude had suggested, hopefully), how often he went to the gym, how many children he probably wanted, and what they imagined he smelled like – 'vanilla', 'woodsmoke', and 'just super fucking lush' being the most popular guesses.

Every single woman in the office – minus Jada, who disapproved of inter-department romances because they shored up the patriarchy and were a 'prehistoric throwback to the days when secretaries felt obliged to shag the boss', plus Claude, who had decided to throw his hat into the ring because, 'Who wouldn't wanna tap this?' – had their eye on Oliver.

And although Emily had told Jada and Simon she totally wasn't interested in him either, because she was far too career-driven and self-respecting and yada yada, she was absolutely going to give it her best shot. From what she'd read, he appeared to be the perfect man for New Emily – driven, successful, gorgeous, well dressed, and a million miles away from the guys back on the Greenleaf estate, whose ambitions barely rose above being able to afford a new West Ham shirt each season.

In the back of her brain, Old Emily muttered mutinously that she didn't stand a chance with Oliver, especially when she'd be competing against the ultra-groomed, totally put-together women in the office, who all came from posh backgrounds and seemed to treat having a job like an amusing hobby.

But New Emily had become an expert at disguising her lack of self-confidence. When she put the effort in, she looked every bit as good as Ellie, whose father, unbelievably, gave her a £500 a week allowance just for clothes. She'd become used to laughing and nodding when her privately educated workmates talked about things she didn't have a clue about, just like the girls at school with their Jackie Collins novels.

And as long as she was careful not to take things too far and overstep the mark – like the time she'd tried to pronounce 'hors d'oeuvres', having only ever seen it written down on the company's Christmas party menu – there was no reason Oliver couldn't be convinced that she was every bit as good as them.

Sighing, Emily flipped open her laptop, drumming her manicured fingernails on the touchpad as it loaded up her pitch. The agency she worked for, HoRizons Creatives (on her first day, Simon had told her no one knew why the R was capitalised, but that he reckoned it stood for 'Right Wankers'), was pitching against some of the country's top agencies for the chance to lead Cat's Miaow's new multi-million-pound advertising campaign, to help sell its sachets of organic, paraben-free, all-natural cat food.

Usually, only the company's senior creatives would work on the big idea, spending weeks populating enormous, complicated spreadsheets, writing on the windows with erasable markers to make their ideas seem urgent and interesting, and sighing loudly about having to stay late in the office, despite being paid about a billion pounds an hour.

Spotting an opportunity to show what she could do, Emily had quietly worked after-hours on her own idea for the campaign. After she'd told Charles she'd like the chance to share her idea, he'd promised her twenty minutes of his time to present it to him – and as tomorrow was Oliver's first day, there was a good chance he'd be there too.

If so, she'd have the perfect opportunity to dazzle him right off the bat. She might not be naturally glossy and poised – but she *was* naturally brilliant at her job. Sharing her ideas at work was the one time she never felt like an imposter. And, unlikely as it might be, if they both thought her idea had potential, they might even choose it as HoRizons' official pitch to Cat's Miaow. It was a huge opportunity, so Emily was determined to make her presentation as perfect as possible.

Before she started, she couldn't resist taking another quick peek at Andy's memorial page. There was already a new post since last night, from someone charmingly named Billy the Fist. He'd posted a photo of Andy on stage with his band, Remington 11. Bathed in blue and red light, his eyes partly closed as his fingers worked the strings of his guitar, Emily wished she'd seen them play live. She'd been invited, of course, but had always declined.

Underneath the photo, Billy's message said,

> this gig was awesome, feels like yesterday. hope ur up there jammin with kurt cobain, mate.

Next, clicking on a tab she really must remember to remove from her bookmarks before tomorrow, Oliver Beauchamp's LinkedIn profile filled her screen.

She already knew every inch of his photo, its moody black-and-white filter accentuating his wavy dark-brown hair, swathe of stubble, and deep-blue eyes, which she'd seen in colour on his Hinge profile. She'd even read a couple of the industry articles he'd posted, even though they had incredibly boring titles like, 'Shifting your brand to reboot engagement in a frictionless landscape'.

Emily's brain started whirring unpleasantly again, adding tomorrow's presentation into the mix of things it wouldn't stop prodding her to think about. There was only one person she wanted to talk to about all of this, and as long as they didn't get trapped in one of their conversation spirals about whether Adam Driver was ugly-hot or just hot-hot, Emily would have plenty of time to work on her presentation afterwards.

'Are you OK? Is WhatsApp broken?' Zoe joked when she answered after just a couple of rings. It was a fair question: she and Emily only ever used their phones to text each other and send videos of animals and babies falling over. Both agreed that the phone daring to actually ring was a gross invasion of privacy, and that Gen X's bleak memories of using landlines instead of mobile phones were probably the reason they required so much therapy.

'Your best friend in the whole wide world calls for a chat and that's the first thing you think? Shame on you. Shaaaame,' Emily said, switching the TV on to *Sunday Brunch* and snuggling down into the cushions of her sofa. Upholstered in thinning pink cotton, it was quite a few leagues away from the smart, duck-egg blue sofa of her dreams, but it was also the most comfortable thing she'd ever sat on.

'You're the one who reckons only serial killers, drug dealers and your Auntie Suze use the phone to actually call people,' Zoe said, the grin showing in her voice. 'What do you expect me to think?'

'Fair point,' Emily conceded. Then, taking a deep breath, she said, 'I've got something to tell you, actually. You're not going to believe this . . .'

'You're freaking kidding me?' Zoe shrieked when Emily had finished explaining what had happened to Andy – so loudly, she had to pull the phone away from her ear. 'After all that *Scooby Doo* shit that happened last night? Hang on, I'm putting you on speakerphone so I can look it up.'

Emily heard a rustling on the other end of the phone as Zoe looked up Andy's memorial page.

'Holy shitballs,' she breathed, when she'd found the page. 'So Andy *is* dead. How do you feel about it? Are you OK?'

'I don't know, really,' Emily said, realising she was shaking. 'I mean, it's been ages since I last saw him . . .'

'And I *never* saw him,' Zoe said, pointedly.

'. . . But part of me still expected us to bump into each other again one day, you know? And I had a whole speech prepared to deliver to him when I did. You know . . . "*How could you just throw what we had away*?" etcetera. It's weird to think he's just . . . *gone.* And look at the date under the earliest posts.'

'March? Wasn't that when . . .'

'He ghosted me? Yep. Which means I've spent eight months thinking he'd callously ditched me, when actually he'd been . . . How do the TikTok kids put it? *Unalived.*'

Emily swallowed. Even to her own ears, she sounded glib and cold-hearted. But somehow, she didn't want to admit to Zoe how much the news of Andy's death had upset her. After all, she'd moved on, hadn't she? And besides, she'd made such a show of pretending not to care about him ghosting her at the time, Zoe might think she was putting it on if she told the truth.

'Wow. That's a lot to take in. Do you know what happened to him?'

'It looks like he fell from a building in Soho. He was found on the street below,' Emily said, shivering at the thought and pulling a cushion – whose colour was alleged to be 'hint of vole' – onto her lap.

'Poor Andy,' Zoe breathed.

'The weird thing is that they don't seem to know *how* he fell. Like, whether he tried to kill himself, or if it was an accident.'

'Or he was pushed?'

'Oh god, don't say that,' Emily said, standing up and turning the lights on against the dark storm clouds that were swiftly gathering outside her living room window. 'Who would want to hurt Andy? As far as I can make out, the worst thing he ever did when he was alive was to ghost me. And it turns out he didn't even do that.'

'Speaking of ghosts ... It's weird about the Ouija board, isn't it, now we know Andy is actually dead. I mean, does what happened last night mean that he was actually *there*? That he was trying to contact you?'

'Of course not,' Emily said lightly, trying to conjure up New Emily's attitude to the supernatural, which was that ghosts and the afterlife definitely didn't exist, while Old Emily quite fancied hiding behind the sofa. 'But it is strange, isn't it? Even if I did believe in all that stuff, and Andy's ghost was moving my hand last night, why would he get in touch with me?'

Emily looked up as the lights above her flickered. She frowned, hoping the brewing storm wasn't going to cause another power cut.

'Maybe he wanted you to know he was dead? For all we know, his ghost might have been watching over his funeral all, "*Where the hell is my bloody girlfriend?*"'

Emily laughed. 'I wasn't actually his girlfriend, remember,' she said.

'You were as good as though, right?' Zoe said. 'Even if he hadn't said it using actual words. Have you wondered what might have happened if he'd asked you to be his girlfriend before he died? Maybe you would have realised right away that he didn't just ghost you.'

Emily winced. She hadn't thought of that. But Zoe was

right: if she'd been more confident of Andy's feelings for her, she might have realised something bad had happened to him, and tried harder to get in touch. Instead, she hadn't even gone to his funeral.

'But now you know, right?' Zoe added, her voice filled with hope. 'So that means you *were* good enough for him after all, and you can stop dating men like Hedge Fund Fuckwit and find another Andy to date.'

The line went silent for a moment as Zoe and Emily recalled her dates with Anthony, a hedge fund manager she'd been matched with on Tinder two months ago. On their first date, the waitress at their restaurant had greeted him like a long-lost friend and asked if they both wanted 'the usual', making Emily realise she wasn't quite the special snowflake she'd hoped.

On their second date, at another eye-wateringly pricey restaurant, a waiter had placed a small chair in between her and Anthony's seats. She'd stared at it, panicking – *Bijou* had never mentioned this – until her date had burst into laughter and told her, not particularly kindly, 'It's for your bag.' She'd perched her knock-off Louis Vuitton handbag on it, blushing bright red, wondering what kind of bag might need its very own chair.

'That twinkly-eyed old geezer in *Pretty Woman* was super polite when Julia Roberts didn't know which fork to use,' she'd complained to Zoe, as she'd struggled not to laugh. 'But he was really rude.'

Then – the final straw – she'd declined his offer to go home with him at the end of the night. This was partly because after seven courses of what were essentially blobs of foam on a series of increasingly tiny sliced vegetables, she was bloody starving and needed to grab something proper to eat. And partly because she'd realised that while Anthony might be a good prospect on paper, he was also an absolutely massive twat.

'You're either frigid, or after my money,' Anthony had announced as she'd made her excuses not to get into an Uber with him. 'But either way . . . I'm afraid to say . . . I'm out.'

'He honestly said it like that. Like he was on *Dragon's Den* and didn't like my idea for reusable bog roll,' Emily had told a giggling Zoe on her way home on the bus, sipping a smoothie through a fat plastic straw and staring longingly at the brown paper bag of fries being torn through by the guy sitting on the seat opposite hers.

After The Anthony Incident, Emily had decided to be more careful about who she agreed to go on a second date with.

'I get your point, but I'm not taking a step backwards – not after all my hard work,' Emily said now. 'Dating Andy was an enjoyable blip, but a blip nonetheless. I've eaten far too many salads and done way too many burpees for it to go to waste. I need to stick to the plan. I need to find a man who has a bit of class and ambition, as well as enough cash not to encourage our kids to nick loo rolls from the pub toilets whenever they get the chance.'

'Call Richard Curtis, quick. I think my heart's melting,' Zoe said, and Emily could practically hear her dramatic eye-roll down the phone. 'I know you've worked hard on forging New Emily in the fires of Mount Makeover, but don't you think there are more important things to focus on than a guy's career?'

'Well, of course, but I want someone who matches my ambition,' Emily said. 'And I don't want to end up supporting someone on my own, if I can help it. You can't pretend money isn't important *at all.* I've been poor and – newsflash – it really sucks.'

'Well, I know that, obviously,' Zoe said, trying to hide her exasperation. 'And I do understand why you want someone you can rely on. You've been through a lot. But I also think you're looking in the wrong places. A man can be hilarious, sexy, fun *and* reliable, you know. And surely personality is what counts?

'I don't care if Future Mr Zoe prefers Nando's to Nobu – I just want him to be my perfect puzzle piece; someone who's a bit weird and wiggly, and who fits in with *my* kind of weird and wiggly. I don't want some ordinary guy with three straight edges and a knob, who could happily spend the rest of their life with any girl who has three straight edges and a hole.'

'You'd want *some* kind of knob, presumably?' Emily said, snorting.

'You know what I mean,' Zoe said. 'I don't want the kind of man who would fit with any one of thousands of girls. I want one who is exactly right for *me.* And you should want the same, Em. You're too special to end up with someone who's dull as dishwater, just because they know about pension plans.

'Plus, newsflash: dating is supposed to be fun. Waxing your bits to within an inch of their lives, spending half your life down the gym, and pretending not to like cake every time someone in the office has a birthday sounds rubbish.'

'OK, New Emily's regime isn't that much fun,' Emily conceded, trying not to sound offended. 'But anything worth doing involves some effort, right? It's like revising for your A-levels – you might miss out on a few afternoons down the pub, but you'll reap the rewards later on. I've worked too hard to settle for second best.'

Emily sounded uncertain, and at the other end of the phone, Zoe paused. 'You do know that your dad didn't leave because you weren't good enough either, right?' she said gently. 'He loved you; anyone could see that. He was just young and an idiot. You don't have to be this perfect version of yourself to find a guy who'll take care of you. You just have to find the right one.'

Emily nodded, forgetting Zoe couldn't hear her. In front of her on her laptop were two photos: one of Andy on stage with the band he was sure would eventually bring him fame and fortune, and Oliver looking calm and confident in his LinkedIn profile, his photo perched above a long list of the industry awards he'd won.

She knew now that Andy hadn't abandoned her. But who was to say what the future would have held if they'd stayed together? Emily knew all too well that easy-going charm like Andy's can be irresistible – but that it becomes a lot less fun when youthful exuberance gives way to adult responsibilities, and you're left to deal with them on your own, like her mum had been.

Her eyes flicked from Andy's face to Oliver's and back again. And she knew, no matter what Zoe had to say about wonky puzzle pieces, which kind of man New Emily had to choose.

Chapter 7

'It's so nice to meet you, Oliver.' Emily smiled, widening her eyes and biting her lower lip. 'I love your past campaigns, and really can't wait to work with you. You smell amazing. Is that Hugo Boss? I thought so. Also, your bum is really excellent. Good work. How would you like a lovely new wife?'

Emily batted her eyelids at her reflection, then sighed heavily. 'I've gone insane,' she muttered to herself, twisting round to check her back for bra bulges.

Today was her big day – the day she'd meet Oliver and present her idea for the Cat's Miaow campaign. Riddled with nerves and self-doubt after ending her call with Zoe – which had inevitably gone on for almost two hours – she'd spent her Sunday checking and re-checking every last detail of her presentation, slathering her feet, face and hair in various lotions, and working through some soothing yoga poses.

Whenever her heart had started thudding with anticipation, she'd tried to think calming thoughts about lavender and tinkling bells, but had found her mind being dragged in an endless cycle through thoughts about the Ouija board, the fact that Andy hadn't ghosted her after all, Oliver, and the presentation, which meant she felt more tense afterwards than when she'd started.

Thanks to a million Instagram slogans, she knew finding love was impossible unless you loved yourself first, warts and all. But those slogans were inevitably accompanied by pictures of pert, flicky-haired women who seemed to find it all too easy to love themselves. And as the clock ticked towards 9 a.m., Emily felt even more conscious of her shortcomings than usual.

She knew that across London, all the other straight, single women at HoRizons Creatives (plus Claude) would be spending their mornings grooming themselves to perfection, ready for a fun game of Who Gets to Shag Oliver First, and that their 'perfect' – boosted by great genes and the confident glow of privilege – would look a lot better than hers.

For reasons no one could quite work out, Oliver had been head-hunted from Barter, Bugle and Hegilly, the agency that had shocked the industry by making their name a few letters shy of that of one of the biggest ad agencies in the world. Immediately, a lawsuit had been launched against them for impersonation and copyright infringement, which they'd deftly defeated.

The result was that they became an overnight success. They claimed the lawsuit was their first publicity stunt, purposefully triggered to prove they knew exactly how to grab headlines. It was an audacious move, and now, Oliver was being hailed as some kind of advertising whizz. As well as playing a part in the whole lawsuit hoo-haa, his campaign for a new trainer brand had gone viral worldwide. Showered with awards, he'd become the advertising equivalent of a rock star overnight.

No one had a clue why he'd decided to move from being a big fish in a big pond to being a giant fish at a small agency like HoRizons, but there were plenty of theories flying around the Consumer Insights messenger thread.

Chrissie: He's probably decided to scale down his work commitments so he can spend more time with his beloved grandmother

Ellie: Or volunteering at an animal shelter. He looks like he loves animals

Marni: Maybe he's just freeing up time to find a wife?

Claude: OR HUSBAND.

Jada: Guys, are you aware of how terribly 1950s of you it is to try and shag the boss? It's totally unreconstructed.

Simon: Isn't using the term 'guys' to address both men and women, like, totally problematic?

Jada: Shit.

Competition for Oliver's attention was fierce. So although she would never have admitted it to Jada and Simon in a million years, she was wearing her sexiest underwear, after *Bijou* magazine had claimed it's easier to 'get your flirt on' if you 'rock a seductive look inside and out!' (before going on to insist, in a hastily added side-note, that a woman definitely didn't need a man to be happy).

She'd rewatched her favourite contouring video, and after half an hour's careful work, her cheeks and nose looked marginally slimmer than before.

Then, she'd finished it all off with her black skater dress, carefully styled so it looked different from the last eight times she'd worn it to the office. Her favourite fashion Instagrammer never wore the same outfit twice, while posting earnest Reels about the importance of embracing pre-loved fashion (as buying stuff from charity shops, which Emily had done for half her life, was known these days). After pondering this contradiction, she'd decided accessorising the same old stuff was the best way forward.

Thanks to a nervous 5 a.m. start, by the time Emily had decided she was completely Oliver-ready, there was still almost an hour to go before she had to leave her flat. Although the words 'cat', 'miaow' and 'food' had lost all meaning on the hundredth re-reading of her presentation, she thought there was no harm giving it one last check.

Grabbing her laptop, she smoothed her dress over her knees, and perched it on her lap. Hovering her mouse over the presentation document, she frowned as she spotted a folder hidden among the dozens scattered messily across her desktop, which she'd almost forgotten was there.

Labelled ANDY'S SONG, she hadn't noticed it for the last nine months. But now, with Andy on her mind, she guessed her gaze had been drawn to it. Opening the folder, she hovered her cursor over the single file inside, which was labelled AllYouNeedIsEm.mp3.

She smiled to herself at the memory of Andy presenting her

with the song on Valentine's Day earlier that year. Grinning widely, he'd handed her a USB stick with a heart drawn on its metal case in Tipp-Ex, and a card with a simple but heartfelt question written across the front in huge, neon-pink letters: NETFLIX AND BUM SEX?

The message inside was printed, meaning he'd ordered it off Moonpig.

Emily had laughed when she'd tugged it out of its envelope – it was just such an Andy type of card. But it was also a million miles away from the kind of Valentine she imagined New Emily receiving. Her dream man wouldn't head to the novelty section of an online card shop to find his other half something special for Valentine's Day.

Instead, he'd pick out the perfect card, and write a long personal message about their journey together, in really excellent handwriting. They'd develop a cute tradition where he always insisted on pairing the card with a simple diamond tennis bracelet or pair of earrings, which he'd present over dinner at one of London's hottest restaurants.

Even if that was asking a bit much, Valentine's Day definitely wouldn't involve a request for bum sex in 42-point font.

Now, Emily clicked on the MP3 and smiled despite herself as she heard Andy's South-London twang for the first time in over a year. He'd somehow persuaded his band – which usually leaned towards 1990s grunge – to record a version of The Beatles' 'All You Need Is Love', the word 'Love' clumsily replaced in the lyrics with the word 'Em' instead.

She was surprised to realise it wasn't anywhere as near as bad as she'd remembered. Despite the band itself sounding like a bag of spanners being thrown into a skip, thanks to its insistence on having four lead guitarists, Andy had a lovely voice – and he seemed to really mean what he was singing. She felt her heart thudding painfully, the knowledge that he was gone forever hitting her afresh.

When the song reached the end, she reached for the play button so she could listen to it again. As Andy's voice drifted out of her laptop, Emily's eyes pricked with tears, which she sniffed back in a very unladylike manner to avoid ruining her foundation. Leaning back into the sofa, she closed her eyes, and started singing along to the song. Until she reached the last line of the chorus, and someone else finished it for her.

'Em is all you need . . .'

Opening her eyes, Emily let out a high-pitched scream and scrambled into the corner of the sofa. The someone who had sung the last line of the song was sitting in the armchair in the corner of her front room. A someone who looked horribly, spookily familiar.

A someone, in fact, who looked exactly like Andy.

Chapter 8

Grabbing the TV remote, Emily brandished it in front of her with a shaking hand.

'What the hell? Get out of my house! *Help!*' she screamed.

'Whoa, shit, calm down. You'll wake up Mary,' the someone who looked like Andy said in Andy's voice. Standing up, he held up his palms, then pointed to the remote. 'And what are you doing with that thing? Are you planning to switch me off or something? I'm not sure that'll work, to be honest.'

'How do you know about Mary?' Emily asked, her voice wobbling. Then flung the remote control hard at Andy's chest. Her eyes widened as it sailed straight through his body, hit the back of the armchair, bounced back through his legs, and landed on the rug between them.

They both stared at it in silence, before Emily took a deep breath and screamed again, even louder this time, and jumped behind the sofa, the possibility of creasing her dress forgotten.

'Jesus, stop it! Mary will be down here like a shot. And what are you doing back there? You look like you've seen a ghost.' Andy sniggered to himself.

'What do you mean, what am I doing back here?' Emily shrieked. 'What are you doing ... *anywhere*? You're supposed to be dead. What the hell are you doing in my flat?'

Picking up a cushion from the sofa, Emily flung it at Andy with a shaking hand. It flew through his stomach and landed with a soft flump on the armchair.

'*Aargh!*' Emily yelled, again.

'Will you stop doing that?' Andy asked, stroking his stomach where the cushion had travelled through him. 'It's really rude. At least ... It feels like it's something that would be considered rude ... I'm not too sure yet.'

Andy held up his palms again and backed away, sitting carefully back in the armchair. 'Look, calm down. I won't come near you, I promise.'

Hyperventilating, Emily's legs wobbled beneath her, so she held onto the back of the sofa and tried to take some calming deep breaths, her eyes pinned on the apparition slumped casually in her favourite corner chair.

'Please don't hurt me,' she moaned, tears springing into her eyes. 'I don't want to die.'

'What are you on about?' Andy said. 'I couldn't hurt you even if I wanted to, what with not being solid. I mean, dur. And why on earth would I *want* to hurt you? It's me, Andy, your boyfriend. I've come back! And it seems to be going really well so far. You seem totally stoked to see me.'

Andy laughed to himself, then held his hands up against the light coming from the lamp that sat on the side table next to Emily's armchair. He flexed his fingers, his knuckles cracking loudly, staring with fascination as the light shone dimly through them.

'You weren't my boyfriend, *actually*, because you never

asked me to make it official,' Emily said. 'And how are your knuckles still cracking?' She shook her head, hard. 'What am I saying? This can't really be happening. Andy is dead. This is just a dream. You're overworked, and you've been up since five a.m. This isn't real. It won't last long. Just take some deep breaths.'

Emily squeezed her eyes shut, rubbed her face in her palms, then opened her eyes wide. But Andy was still there. Even though she'd never understood the point of pinching yourself to check if you're dreaming – what's to stop you dreaming that you're pinching yourself? – she rolled up the sleeve of her Zara cardigan and pinched herself, hard.

'Ouch!' she squeaked, rubbing her arm.

'I don't think you're dreaming, Em,' Andy said, looking delighted. 'This is totally sick! I mean, I was dead. And now I'm back!'

He trailed off and started wiggling his hands in front of his face. Although they weren't completely see-through, Emily could still see his nose through them.

Without taking her eyes off him, Emily grabbed her phone, dropping it twice before managing to grip it firmly enough to take a wobbly photograph in his direction. Bringing up the picture, the blurry photo she'd managed to take was of an empty armchair. But here, in her front room, Andy was sitting there as clear as day, just with a slightly faded middle.

Emily made her way slowly around the sofa, sticking to the edge furthest from Andy's chair and keeping her eyes firmly on him. She wedged herself into the corner of the cushions and shook her head.

'There has to be some other explanation,' she muttered to herself. 'There's no such thing as—' she couldn't bring herself to say the word *ghosts* '—whatever that thing is, so there must be another reason he's here. You're pretty tired, you've been stressed at work. There are loads of reasons people hallucinate.'

'That *thing*? Charming.'

'I mean, there was the séance and the whole Facebook Memorial Page thing,' Emily continued, ignoring him. 'Being ghosted then *un*ghosted was pretty huge news. I've been working late on Cat's Miaow for the last few days, and today's Oliver's first day at HoRizons. That's enough to make anyone hallucinate, right? Either way, Andy's *definitely* not here, and he's *definitely* not a . . .'

'Hang on. Who ghosted you?' Andy asked, frowning.

'*You* did,' Emily said, twirling a strand of hair around her finger and trying hard to channel New Emily, who was cool, calm, collected, and knew there was a rational explanation for everything. 'Or so I thought, until yesterday.'

'I'd never have done that to you,' Andy said, looking upset. 'I really like you.'

'See, that's exactly what my subconscious wants to hear. So that proves this is just the result of stress making my mind play tricks on me. And this—' she waved a hand in Andy's direction '—could just be a hallucinatory manifestation. We learned about that in psychology A-level.'

'I don't think I am a hallucinatory manifestation,' Andy said, frowning down at himself.

'. . . Although I'm not sure many people find themselves having conversations with those manifestations,' Emily said. 'Or getting annoyed at them for propping their feet on the arm of their favourite chair, even though they've been told a million times not to,' she added, pointedly.

Andy glanced guiltily at his feet, which he'd slung over the arm of the chair, and hastily swung them back onto the floor.

'How come you can sit in my chair and put your stinky feet over the arm of it when things I chuck at you sail straight through you?'

Andy looked down at himself and shrugged. 'Maybe I'm not actually sitting, but just hovering above stuff, because my brain thinks that's what *should* happen. Like when people have itchy phantom limbs, only with a real phantom.' He swept his hand through the lamp on the table next to the chair. 'See, I'm not solid. Although I do feel pretty real. And I'm definitely not a figment of anyone's imagination.'

'Well, you would say that, wouldn't you?'

'There must be a way of convincing you,' Andy said, looking around the room as if he might find inspiration on her bookshelves. He looked thoughtful for a moment. 'Tell her ditto!' he said suddenly, sitting up.

'Tell her what?'

'That's what Patrick Swayze says to Whoopi Goldberg in *Ghost* to get Demi Moore to believe he's really there, right?'

Emily nodded. A lover of all things 1990s, Andy had persuaded her to watch all of the films of the acting greats of that era, from Patrick Swayze to Arnold Schwarzenegger, early on in their relationship.

'I can't be with someone who hasn't watched *Point Break*. I just can't,' he'd argued. Emily had been more than happy to be educated, especially after discovering that Keanu Reeves had been even hotter back in the day than he was now. In return, she'd made Andy watch *The Princess Diaries* twice.

Their mutual film education meant she was very familiar with *Ghost* – especially the bits where Demi Moore wears a crop top, which Andy always insisted on watching twice – 'for film studies', which he wasn't studying.

'So why don't you ask me something only I could know the answer to? Then you'll know I'm real!' Andy said now.

'What are you on about?' Emily said, clutching a cushion to her chest. 'I can only ask you about things we both know the answer to, which means I could still be hallucinating, numbnuts.'

'Oh, yeah.' Andy looked crestfallen. 'Boo. That's the "oh no" kind of boo, not the haunting kind, by the way.'

'If you *are* a ghost, you're about as scary as a pork chop,' Emily said.

'Pork chops are pretty scary if you're a pig,' Andy said, and Emily laughed. Then clapped her hand over her mouth.

'What am I doing? This isn't happening, and we shouldn't be just . . . *chatting*, like this is somehow normal. I just need to get this presentation over with, that's all,' she said, rubbing her forehead. 'Then when I come home tonight, you'll be gone. Maybe I need to book a weekend at a therapy retreat to give myself some headspace.'

'A therapy retreat? Are you hoping to be bored to death just so you can join me? We used to make fun of stuff like that. It's just a way of getting people to spend a load of money on some peace and quiet, when you could just go for a walk, or sit in a library, and save yourself a few hundred quid.'

'When even my subconscious – which is *you*, by the way – thinks I'm not worth splashing out on, I think that's a good sign that I definitely *do* need therapy,' Emily said, shaking her head. 'And things have changed since you . . . left. I thought you'd run off with someone else, so I redoubled my efforts to improve myself.'

'Project New Emily?' Andy asked, and Emily nodded.

'I wanted to make sure the next guy I dated wouldn't leave.'

'Oh, Em,' Andy said, sadly. 'I'm so sorry. If I'd known you'd turn into the kind of person who'd be into therapy retreats, I'd have put more effort into not dying.'

Emily blinked back tears and shook her head. 'How did you die, anyway? Nobody seems entirely sure.'

'I can't remember,' Andy said, looking thoughtful. 'But to be fair, most dead people can't remember *anything*. You know, because they're dead. I'll have a think while you're at work and see what comes back to me.'

'No, you won't, because you don't exist. So when I get home you'll be gone, right?'

'Don't ask me,' Andy said, with a shrug. 'If I'm a figment of *your* imagination, you should know.'

'OK, well, I think you will be gone. I hope. But even so . . . don't try to follow me to work, OK? If you can walk through doors, that is. Can you? Walk through doors?'

'No idea.' Andy shrugged again. 'I'm brand new. But you look like you're about to have a nervous breakdown, so how about I promise not to try?'

Emily nodded. 'I guess it's better than nothing,' she said, scooping her laptop into her bag with shaking hands and grabbing her coat, all the while keeping her eyes firmly trained on him. 'It's been nice talking to you. I'm sorry you're dead.'

'Me too,' he said softly, as Emily swung out of the front door.

Chapter 9

Although it was a ridiculous expense, Emily ordered an Uber to the office. As well as being late for work, thanks to whatever had just been happening in her front room, she wasn't in the mood to spend the journey pressed against some grubby builder's high-vis vest or sweaty businessman's armpit, especially after she'd put so much work into looking her best.

As her cab wove through the morning rush-hour, causing her to anxiously look at her phone every ten minutes in case she was going to be late for work, she tried her best to push Andy out of her mind.

If stress had caused her brain to manifest him in her front room, worrying even more about it wasn't going to help. She had a big day ahead of her, and she couldn't let anything – not even her brain going temporarily haywire – get in the way of it being a success.

As the cab pulled up outside the office just off Camden High Street where HoRizons Creatives was based, Emily swung out of the passenger door, legs pressed together, and slid her sunglasses onto her face at the same time. In her head, it was an effortlessly slick-looking move, but hit a slight hiccup when her glasses snagged on her ears and fell into the gutter.

'I'll get those,' a voice offered from somewhere above Emily's head. She looked up to see a pair of deep-blue eyes staring into hers.

'Oh, thanks, that's very kind,' Emily said politely, as their owner bent down and scooped up her sunglasses. Her mouth turned drier than the Sahara as she realised the gorgeous eyes belonged to none other than Oliver Beauchamp.

'I'm Oliver. The new recruit at HoRizons.' He grinned, showing a row of beautiful white teeth as he handed her the sunglasses.

Emily managed to look surprised.

'It's great to meet you, Oliver,' she said, hoping her face hadn't turned too pink.

'Am I totally off the mark, or do I recognise you from the company profiles? It's Emmie, right?'

She swallowed. 'Emily, actually. But close enough.' She smiled, hoping she looked sincere rather than slightly crushed. To be fair, most of the other women in the office had cute, two-syllable names that swooped up at the end and sounded like designer shoes – *The Marni is a kitten-heel that comes in three dazzling colourways!* – so really, she couldn't blame Oliver for getting hers wrong.

'After you,' Oliver said, holding open the door to the tower block that held their offices. Emily took her time walking past him, so she could take him in.

Classically tall (apparently he hadn't lied on his dating profile), dark and handsome, his hair was just scruffy enough, and his strong nose just wonky enough to make him look more interesting than your typical tooth-whitened alpha male. He had a sexy pale-and-interesting thing going on rather than the usual corporate-issue tan, coupled with the physique of someone who spent plenty of time down the gym.

He was also beautifully dressed. Most of the company's creatives looked like they'd got dressed by running through a charity shop covered in glue, which Emily didn't understand at all – why, when you had money, would you spend hundreds of pounds on looking like you were poor? But Oliver was wearing a well-cut dark-blue suit with a pop of bright-purple lining inside. His dark-brown leather brogues looked expensive, and it turned out Marni had been right: he did smell like vanilla.

As she passed him, Emily nodded and tried to produce a smile that was sexy but demure, mysterious but open, friendly but cool. Instead, glimpsing herself in the mirror above the front desk, she realised she just looked a bit confused.

'You're the new Creative Director, aren't you?' Emily asked lightly as Oliver passed her, leading the way through the electronic gates in reception before swiping his pass on the touchpad that called down the lifts. 'Are you nervous about your first day?' she added, glancing at her phone. She didn't want Oliver to think she was too invested in this conversation.

Unfortunately, Zoe had just sent her a picture of a piglet wearing red wellington boots with the caption, OMG, HOW MUCH DO YOU LOVE MY NEW SHOES!?

Snorting, Emily tried to disguise her laughter behind a cough and pushed her phone into her pocket. If it had been Jada or Simon beside her, she'd have shown them the text, but Oliver seemed like a proper grown-up, who only laughed at things like *Question Time* or *Private Eye*.

'I'm assuming nobody here bites,' Oliver said, gesturing for

Emily to step into the lift ahead of him. 'And I'm excited to get stuck in. You guys have got some accounts I think I could really make a difference with.'

Emily's heart sank. She'd kind of hoped Oliver would be fun-ambitious rather than boring-ambitious, although in her experience, when it came to men, the prettier the package, the duller the insides tended to be. Her theory was that good-looking people don't need to develop a personality, because everyone's too busy imagining them naked to listen to them properly – the exception being the kind of guy who was an ugly teenager and had time to become interesting before growing into his looks.

'I mean, seven-year-old me is seriously disappointed that I work in advertising, rather than being Spider-Man's best friend,' Oliver added, shoving his hands into his trouser pockets. 'But as far as the pinch-me dream that is any creative's job goes, I'm sure I'll fit right in.'

Emily laughed, and immediately perked up. Maybe Oliver had a human side after all.

'That's weird, because when I was a kid my biggest dream was to write about feminine wipes and to have to use words like "moist" and "intimate areas" several times a day,' Emily said.

Oliver shot her his wolfish grin again, and she felt her insides swoop.

'What accounts do you work on? Apart from Femme & Fab, which I sincerely hope is the one you're referring to,' he asked. Emily noticed he was looking at her, rather than at himself in the mirrored walls, like most people did when they shared a lift.

'Cat's Miaow and Zoo Hotels?' Emily said, making it sound

like a question to hide her pride at working on the agency's two biggest accounts.

'Of course. So you're their star copywriter? The one presenting the Cat's Miaow pitch today,' Oliver asked, raising an eyebrow – a gesture that used just one of his muscles, but turned all of Emily's into mush.

She blushed. It sounded like Charles had already told Oliver about her presentation, which was both a good thing, and a thing that made her want to climb out of the top of the lift, *Die Hard*-style, clamber up the shaft, then run away screaming.

'I mean, I wouldn't say *star*, exactly,' she said, with a modest shrug. 'Maybe wunderkind, at a push. But I think you're going to like what I've done. The pet-owning ABC1 demographic loves dick jokes, right?'

Oliver laughed and raised his eyebrow even further. 'It would definitely make storyboarding the campaign a whole lot more interesting.'

Emily grinned, delighted that Oliver seemed to have a sense of humour, as well as being even better-looking than on his LinkedIn page.

As the doors to the lift slid open, Emily couldn't help noticing the look of annoyance on the faces of the other women in the office (plus Claude) as their eyes swivelled towards the 'ping!' and they realised Emily had got a head-start when it came to flirting with Oliver.

'Good luck on your first day, Andy,' she shot over her shoulder as she stepped into the office, before blushing bright red. 'Oliver, I mean. Obviously,' she stuttered, not daring to turn around to see the expression on his face.

Chapter 10

'Was that Oliver I just saw you sharing a lift with?' Jada asked, craning her neck to watch him walking towards Charles's office as Emily slid into her chair. 'Obviously, I completely disapprove of you trying to date the boss, as it will simply shore up the intrinsic hegemonic masculinity of the office hierarchy, but if you're going to piss Marni off in the process – which her face says you've totally nailed – I guess that balances things out.'

Across the desk, Simon snorted.

'Honestly, Jada, I think I'm in love already,' Emily groaned, deciding there was no point trying to pretend that she wasn't interested in Oliver any more. 'He smells like a bag of mini eggs. I made him smile, like, three times, then I accidentally called him by my ex's name.'

Simon's face abruptly dropped. '*So* smooth,' he intoned.

'Shut up, doofus,' Emily said, picking up a stapler and considering the risk of brain damage before putting it down and lobbing a packet of Post-it notes at his head instead.

'Ohh, Post-its,' Simon said. 'Thanks, Emily!'

'Shit,' she muttered. Thanks to the regular reminders from the office eco-warriors that THIS IS A PAPER-FREE SPACE!!! (via non-ironic paper posters Sellotaped all over the place) Post-it notes were generally frowned upon, and therefore like gold dust. That had been Emily's last, precious packet.

'Mmmm, lovely Post-its,' Simon said, rubbing the wedge of paper over his cheeks, eyes closed in bliss, before writing EMILY N SIMON 4 EVA on a couple and sticking them on the back of his laptop, right in Emily's eyeline.

The three of them watched as Oliver shook hands with the account managers, smiling broadly. Marni, Chrissie and Claude, who were collectively known as the Witches' Coven, on account of being very thin and absolutely awful, were visibly trying to out-simper each other.

'God, he is good-looking, isn't he?' Jada frowned. 'I'm definitely not planning on joining in with the office version of *The Hunger Games*, but I still want to just ... cling to him like a koala bear and lick his face.'

'It's like he's been designed to make us think unfeminist thoughts,' Emily said, switching on her Mac. 'Right now, I've got an inappropriate urge to have his babies then do the washing-up, while wearing really uncomfortable lace undies.'

'For god's sake,' Simon grumbled, looking fed up. 'Why aren't there any normal-looking men in advertising? He makes me feel like a shoe with a face drawn on it. One of Ryan Reynolds' brothers. A meat paste sandwich sitting next to a Pret baguette. Working in this office is terrible for my self-esteem.'

'You can't have scorching-hot good looks *and* a brain the size of a planet, because that's just greedy,' Emily said, typing

'Ryan Reynolds' brothers' into Google and wincing at the result. 'I bet Oliver won't be displaying his *Countdown* winner's teapot on his desk, will he?'

'I guess not,' Simon said glumly, reaching over and carefully rubbing a spot of dust off the spout of his ugliest but most prized possession with his sleeve.

'I meant to ask, how were you after the party?' Jada asked, suddenly. 'I hope you weren't too freaked out.'

Emily's stomach lurched as she remembered the apparition that had appeared in her living room this morning. The more she thought about it, the stranger the whole situation seemed. If she'd woken up in the dead of night and been convinced that her dead ex was floating around in her room, it would have been easy to explain away as a trick of the light thanks to being half-asleep. But Emily had never heard of a ghost turning up at eight in the morning to sit in their favourite chair and have a cheerful chat about the afterlife.

'I've never been to a party where they've raised the dead before,' Simon said. 'Did you work out who Andy was?'

'I don't know anyone called Andy,' Emily said firmly. 'Someone was obviously mucking about. Zoe, probably. No big deal.'

'Yeah, no biggie. You definitely didn't almost wet yourself in terror,' Simon said.

'That was never going to happen. Not within spitting distance of my favourite Mango throw, anyway—' Emily hit 'delete all' on a particularly dull set of Monday emails '—speaking of spooky, Jada, isn't it about time you read our horoscopes?' she added, quickly changing the subject.

Every Monday, Jada brought her nan's weekly copy of *Real Talk!* magazine into the office so she could regale everyone with their fortunes for the week. Jada looked at her thoughtfully. She was incredibly astute, and had a horrible knack of knowing whenever Emily was trying to hide something. She also remembered every single story anyone had ever told her when both they and she were drunk, which Emily found very unfair.

'Right,' Jada said, apparently deciding not to pull at the thread of Emily's discomfort and plucking *Real Talk!* magazine from her bag. She shook it open at the page headlined, 'Fanny Forecasts Your Future,' with a loud snap. 'Here's me:

'Taurus: with the Sun in your third house of communication, this month is all about making spiritual connections. Think about taking up yoga or reaching out to a long-lost friend. Useful. My long-lost friends are lost for good reason, *Fanny*. OK, you next, Emily.

'Sagittarius: Uranus is in your fifth house of romance, so don't be afraid to embrace your fears. Keep your nerve, and you will find life can be full of surprises.'

'I'm not sure Uranus and romance should ever belong in the same house,' Simon said, archly.

'Surprises and romance are a pretty good sign,' Jada said, throwing the magazine on her desk. 'The stars are obviously dead keen for you to have a crack at Oliver. May the odds be ever in your favour.'

'Maybe Oliver isn't the surprise it's talking about,' Emily muttered, rubbing her arms, which were suddenly prickling with cold.

'We just need to find out what star sign he is,' Jada mused. 'If he's a fire sign too, you're golden.'

'It's all bollocks anyway,' Simon said, looking annoyed.

'Horoscopes can't possibly apply to a twelfth of the whole world's population, can they? Unless eight per cent of Namibian Bushmen also landed an unexpected windfall and saw a surprising face from their past popping up last Tuesday. And you never read a horoscope that says, "You're going to have a crap day, and might fall in front of a bus," do you? They're always relentlessly positive because that makes them easier to believe.'

'Ah, how wonderful to see the Rebel Alliance over here beavering away at their work as always,' an amused voice said behind them.

'Oh, hi, Charles,' Emily said, swinging round to face HoRizons' MD. 'We were just, er, talking about whether horoscopes might be woven into the new campaign.'

'You're discussing how to introduce horoscopes into a campaign about cat food, are you? That's a very brave try, Emily, but I'm afraid I'm not quite that gullible. Plus you've already given me the gist of your idea, remember.'

Charles shook his head and tucked his thumbs into the waistband of his trousers. He looked like he worked in a library, or perhaps a potting shed, rather than a cutting-edge advertising agency.

Instead of jeans, designer trainers and an ironic T-shirt paired with mad braces or a terrible hat, Charles was wearing blue corduroy trousers, and a brown and cream checked shirt rolled up at the sleeves, with what looked like an actual vest underneath. His greying, barely there hair wasn't hidden under a baseball cap, and nor did he try to compensate for his balding head by growing an enormous, lumberjack-style beard underneath it.

The younger creatives thought he was past it, but in his

heyday, he'd been responsible for some of the most recognisable advertising campaigns on TV.

'Don't worry, though – I've a funny feeling you spent most of your weekend working on this presentation, young Padawan, so I'm sure ten minutes talking about nonsense won't cause too much harm. Speaking of which, regrettably our meeting has been moved to first thing tomorrow morning,' Charles said, patting Emily on the shoulder.

'Dapper Dentures have pulled their pitch request forward, so we need all hands on deck to prepare for it. Not that I don't find this marvellous opportunity to order my team a stack of pizzas that smell of despair and cost the same as lunch at The Connaught a thrill. Sorry, Emily, I know you've been working hard on it.'

'It's fine.' Emily smiled. *Except I gave up my poxy Sunday night to prepare for it and stressed myself out enough over it to start seeing dead people*, she thought, unhappily.

'I'm sure I'll be suitably impressed when the time comes, seeing as you're my best copywriter,' Charles said. 'And Oliver will sit in too, if that's OK with you?'

'Oh, yes, of course,' Emily said, beaming.

'Are my pithy slogans about vegan milk not good enough for you?' Simon said, standing up. 'It took me ages to come up with the "No Cows, More Wows!" campaign.'

'It was simply wonderful, obviously. Pinteresque, even. But Emily here has her sights firmly set on her next promotion, even when it's less than five minutes since her last one, while you spend half your time with us rehearsing for your next appearance on *Fifteen to One*. Is that not correct?'

'*Pointless*, actually. Filming is in four weeks,' Simon muttered, sitting back down.

Charles nodded. 'Oh, and Jada, I'm sure this has absolutely nothing to do with your earlier conversation, but if you must know? Oliver is a Gemini.' Charles grinned as he wandered off, his hands stuffed in his pockets.

Chapter 11

As Emily slid her key into the front door, she prayed she'd somehow left the TV on when she'd left her flat. Because otherwise, she didn't want to know why what sounded like a scene from *Cobra Kai* was playing out in her front room.

'Wax on, wax off. Haiyyyy-a!' a muffled voice said through the door.

Turning the key and gingerly pushing it open, she peered around it to see Andy's ghost – or her hallucination of him, at least – karate-chopping his hand through her favourite vase on the table next to the armchair, which was shaped like a fish with its mouth open.

'Squish like grape!' he yelled, punching both fists at it and looking frustrated when they sailed straight through.

Emily felt her whole body tingling, the hairs on her arms and neck standing to attention. It was like walking in to see a knife-wielding maniac or a giant spider hanging out in her front room – every fibre of her being was telling her that something was very wrong, and that running away, extremely fast, would be the best path forward.

'Oh, hiya. You can still see me then?' Andy said, leaning his palms on his knees and panting.

'Yes, I can. Just about, anyway,' she said, switching the lights on. He waved at her, which made her knees wobble. She clutched the doorframe.

'Hey, are you OK?' he said, looking worried. He took three steps towards her, and Emily screamed.

'Please, don't come over here,' she said, clutching her chest. 'I'm OK, I just need some water. And a therapist.'

'I'd get you some, but I haven't learned how to touch stuff yet.' Andy looked sadly at his palms. 'Although I'd really like to be able to.'

'So you can scare the bejesus out of people, presumably?'

'I'd just like to feel normal, really. And maybe the scaring-people thing too. But only a tiny bit.'

'Can you go and sit in your chair?' Emily asked. 'Just while I have a think.'

Andy bounded over to the armchair in the corner, and slung his legs over the arm, before grimacing and hastily removing them. Keeping her eyes fixed on Andy, Emily took off her jacket and ducked under the strap of her laptop bag as she pulled it over her head.

Plucking a bottle of water from her handbag, she hung her things up before carefully making her way to the sofa and perching on the edge. Closing her eyes, she took a deep swig of water, then leaned her forehead in her hand.

'So you're really here then?' she said, looking nervously at Andy.

'Yes, sorry.'

'And you're a ghost?'

'I guess so,' Andy said, looking down at himself.

'OK, let me try something again. Sorry if this is rude or uncomfortable or whatever.' Picking up a pillow from the corner of the sofa, Emily took a deep breath and threw it at his chest. Just like it had done that morning, it sailed straight through him, this time landing with a 'flump' in the chair.

'Oh god,' Emily said, shivering. 'That's . . . really disturbing.'

'It's not much fun for me either,' Andy said. 'Although it's not as bad as passing through people, like with the Ouija board. That feels really horrible.'

'So you *were* guiding my hand,' Emily said. 'It felt really weird. Like being dipped in treacle.'

'It feels kind of sludgy for me too,' Andy nodded. 'And tingly. But I do have *some* good news. I think I've found my *ditto* – the proof you need that I'm not a figment of your imagination.'

'Go on . . .'

'Earlier today I heard a commotion outside. Like, loads of yowling and hissing. I was too scared to try and poke my head through the door, but I could hear Mary talking to Fluffy. At least I hope it was Fluffy. She was telling him to stop making such a bloody fuss, and that if he was stupid enough to eat half a packet of rubber bands then he had to suffer the consequences. I think she was taking him to the vet.'

'How does that prove anything?'

'Well, you didn't already know that, did you? You were at work. So if I'm right, and Fluffy really did eat all those rubber bands like a proper silly bastard, then it must mean I'm real. Well, real-ish. Not a hallucination conjured up by your brain, in any case.'

'OK,' Emily said, slowly. 'I guess I could check that out.'

'Can I come?'

'No way. If Mary can see you, she'll want us both to come in for some of her revolting blackberry wine, and the glass will pass straight through you and fall on the floor and we'll have a lot of explaining to do. And if she can't see you, then it doesn't seem fair to bring a ghost up to her flat to spy on her, does it?'

Andy shrugged his agreement.

'You stay put. And can you leave my favourite vase alone, please? I've got plenty of empty San Pellegrino cans in the recycling bin you can practise your karate chops on.'

'Alright, then,' Andy mumbled.

Heading upstairs to Mary's flat, Emily hesitated as she raised her fist above the front door. She wasn't completely sure she wanted to find out that Andy really was a ghost. If it was a choice between suffering from hallucinations and being haunted by her dead ex, she'd choose the nervous breakdown any day. Her GP could deal with stress, but might struggle to prescribe something to help her deal with a terrible case of the undead.

Taking a deep breath, she rapped her knuckle on the door, which swung open within seconds, as if Mary had already been hovering behind it.

'Hello, Emily love. Everything OK?' she asked. She was wearing a pink silk dressing gown tied at the waist and her bunioned feet were crammed into marabou mules, their tufts of pink feathers waving in the draught coming from the hallway. A green headband covered in huge white silk flowers was nestled in her wildly curly grey hair, above a face covered in deep wrinkles. She was holding a cigarette, part of a lifelong, twenty-a-day smoking habit that didn't seem to have given her a moment's ill-health.

'Yes, everything's fine, Mary,' Emily said, suddenly realising that she'd forgotten to make an excuse for her visit. 'I just wondered if you had . . . an egg I could borrow. Please.'

'Of course, love, come in,' Mary said, swinging the door open. 'What is it you're making?'

'I'm making . . . an . . . egg,' Emily said, weakly. 'A boiled one.'

'Fair enough.' Mary frowned, clearly wondering why Emily would choose to have an egg for dinner when she didn't have any.

As she headed into the kitchen, Emily looked around Mary's front room – which was decorated in a riot of clashing floral fabrics and wallpaper – for Fluffy, but he was nowhere to be seen.

'How's Fluffy? Is he OK?' Emily called through to the kitchen, as Mary rummaged in the fridge.

'He's sulking in my bedroom,' Mary yelled back. 'Silly bugger ate a load of elastic bands earlier, and I had to take him to the vet. They were a hair's breadth away from operating on him, but then he started trembling like a nun in a porn shop and crapped the whole lot onto the vet's examination table in a big wobbly ball.' Mary shut the fridge door and wandered back into the living room.

'Lucky it was a fresh packet he'd got his paws on, so I knew how many he'd scoffed. Trust me, love, never get a cat. They're more hassle than they're worth. Here you go,' she said, slightly out of breath from shouting, handing Emily the egg.

She stared at it as if she'd never seen one before. 'Here, are you OK?' Mary said, frowning with concern and touching the top of her arm. 'Do you want some blackberry wine? My latest batch has just finished brewing. It'll put hairs on your chest.'

Suddenly remembering herself, Emily shook her head, and cradled the egg in her hand.

'I'd better not, I've got my water on the boil. For the egg. Thanks though, Mary.' Emily turned towards the hall, leaving her neighbour staring after her with a confused look on her face.

Back downstairs, she paused in front of her door. She could hear Andy *Haiyyyy-a!*-ing again, more quietly this time. What he'd said about Fluffy had turned out to be completely true, which meant she couldn't possibly be imagining him. The only other explanation, no matter how impossible it seemed, was that using the Ouija board had caused Andy to return from the dead.

And now, although she had no idea how, Emily had to find a way to send him back there.

Chapter 12

'I was right, wasn't I?' Andy said, looking up eagerly as Emily pushed open the door to her flat.

'Yes, you were right,' she said wearily, kicking the door shut behind her. Andy backed off and sat in his armchair to stop her freaking out as she slumped onto the sofa. She felt completely exhausted; like she'd just run a marathon then gone jeans shopping. 'I'm not sure what to do with the information though. I mean, you're a ghost, right? And you're haunting my front room. It's a lot to take in.'

'Tell me about it. I'm dead!' Andy said, holding his hand up to the light. 'I still can't get used to being slightly see-through. I feel like a pair of net curtains.'

He ruffled the back of his hair thoughtfully, then stared at his hand and ruffled it again.

'Hey look, I can't touch other stuff, but I *can* move my hair,' he said, plucking at his T-shirt. 'And this. Let me try something . . .' Using the toes of his left foot, Andy wiggled his right trainer off, then tried to kick it across the room. It wobbled in mid-air for a second or two, still attached to his toes by a thin, glowing white line, before being sucked back onto his foot.

Emily felt a shiver rippling through her at the sight.

'Whoa, did you see that?' Andy grinned.

'I did. But can you try not to do stuff like that? If I concentrate very hard, and you stay away from the lights, I can pretend you're just normal Andy, popping over for a drink. Rather than dead Andy, popping over to haunt me. It might help prevent my brain exploding.'

'Roger that,' Andy said, sitting up straighter and putting his hands in his lap.

'Now we've established that you *are* a ghost, we've got to work out what to do with you – the best-case scenario being sending you back to where you came from,' Emily said, clutching a cushion protectively to her chest. 'Which is ... where exactly? Where were you before this? Is it like *The Good Place* out there, with all the fro-yo you can eat?'

'Ugh, fro-yo. No thanks. Honestly, I don't remember anything before this.' Andy frowned. 'The last thing I remember, I was eating Coco Pops for breakfast and wondering when they stopped giving you a free plastic toy in your cereal. Magic FM was on, and my housemate was talking about some party he was going to that night. I've tried really hard to picture what happened next, but there's nothing after that.

'The next thing I remember is hearing a voice asking if anyone was out there. It was like a radio, but one switched on very far away. Then it got louder and louder, until I could suddenly see you and your mates sitting around the coffee table. I didn't really know what was going on, so I put my hand on top of yours, and the glass moved wherever I wanted it to go.

'I sent you that message because I thought you'd think it

was romantic. But instead, you freaked out. It went dark again after that, apart from the odd flicker of light. Like living inside a dodgy lightbulb. Then I heard our song and found myself here, sitting in your armchair.'

Emily looked disappointed. 'So there was no bright light in between? No angels or harps, or Jesus being followed round a technicolour garden by licky lions, like in those leaflets the Jehovah's Witnesses give out?'

'Nope. Sorry. But that doesn't mean there's nothing more out there. Maybe I'm in limbo, thanks to my tragically young passing.'

'So we still don't know how you died,' Emily said. 'You weren't depressed, were you?'

'Not unless something really awful happened at some point during the day, like Remington 11 splitting up.'

'That's good,' Emily said, relieved. 'I didn't like the idea that you might have . . . you know.'

'I hope it wasn't one of those deaths that strangers secretly think are kind of funny,' Andy said, looking worried. 'Like when someone gets squashed by a piano that fell out of a window, or dies on the loo.'

Emily raised an eyebrow. 'How exactly are those things funny? Personally, I can't say I've ever split my sides laughing at anyone's death.'

'What about that big-game hunter who got crushed to death by an elephant after he shot it? You liked that one.'

'That one was pretty funny,' Emily agreed. 'But you don't have to worry, we know what killed you, just not how it happened. I'll show you.'

Pulling her laptop from its bag, she brought up the link to the news article about Andy's death.

'You can come over here and read this if you like. But try not to make any sudden spooky movements, OK?'

Andy nodded, and slowly made his way to the sofa. Emily scrolled through the story as he squinted at the screen. When he'd finished, he looked down and started fiddling with the edge of his T-shirt.

'Are you OK?' Emily said, reaching for his shoulder. Her hand sailed through thin air, and she felt the same weird, treacly sensation as she had done on the night of the Ouija board.

'Ouch,' Andy said.

'Sorry, I forgot. And I didn't think about how weird it must be to read an article about your own death. So I'm sorry about that too.'

'This must be what I was wearing when I died,' Andy said, looking down at his jeans and a stripy blue-and-white T-shirt. In life, they'd been his favourites, but now, both were covered in dust.

'I hadn't noticed this before,' he said, patting the dirt on his chest. 'It's not coming out. Am I going to be dusty forever?'

'I didn't want to mention it yesterday, but you've got a Werther's wrapper stuck in your hair too,' Emily said, pointing.

Andy touched a tentative hand to the back of his head and felt for the gold wrapper, which was stuck in his thick, blondish hair. He tugged at it, but it didn't budge.

Emily stifled a laugh. 'You know, I kind of expected my first ghost to be better dressed,' she said. 'This—' she waved a hand at Andy's general person '—is kind of disappointing. You're not very ethereal-looking, are you?'

'Apart from these,' Andy said, lifting his leg and resting it on the arm of the sofa. He was wearing a pair of pristine chunky white trainers. 'These are cool, but I've never seen them before.'

'They're definitely not yours, they're far too clean,' Emily agreed. 'Plus both shoelaces are done up.'

After they'd been on a few dates, Emily had once asked Andy why his left shoelace was nearly always undone. 'I kind of lose interest after doing one,' Andy had shrugged. 'I guess I don't give it quite as much oomph as the first one.'

Emily couldn't quite decide whether his explanation was kind of adorable, or mind-bendingly infuriating.

'Maybe I was given celestial sneakers instead of a robe?' Andy said. 'Perhaps J-Dog is doing his bit to bring the after-life into the twenty-first century. Shoes do have soles, after all . . .'

'Or perhaps your terrible jokes, along with calling our lord and saviour "J-Dog", explains why he sent you back down here to torture *me* instead of him.'

'Could it be that I'm here to tell you I didn't ghost you?' Andy said. He looked up and held Emily's gaze. 'You know now that I'd never have done that, don't you? I really liked you, Em. Like, really really *really*. And I know how you felt about your dad leaving you. You must have hated me.'

'I didn't hate you,' Emily said, looking at the floor and blinking back tears. 'I just didn't understand what I'd done wrong. Or rather, I thought I knew *exactly* what I'd done wrong: I'd told you all about my past, and allowed myself to relax around you, and you'd decided that you preferred New Emily to the old one.'

'You thought I preferred the Emily who tweets about egg-white omelettes to the one who used to make absolutely banging tacos? Not likely.' Emily looked up and managed a watery smile. 'I'm guessing that if you didn't know I'd died, there weren't fakey spies at my funeral like I wanted?'

'I suppose not. Unless you told Vaseline Alan or Billy the Fist about your brilliant plan, as well as me,' Emily said. 'I'm sorry.'

Shortly before he'd died, Andy had read a magazine article about a man who'd left money in his will especially so his widow could hire three actors to dress like they were spies straight out of *Mission Impossible.*

Complete with long black coats, sunglasses and ear pieces, he'd requested that they lurk menacingly in the background of his funeral, so even his oldest friends would start to wonder if there was a side to him they didn't know about. One very different from his everyday life as a financial analyst from Chafford Hundred.

Andy had been delighted by the idea, and Emily had promised to arrange it for his funeral, should the need ever arise. Obviously, she'd never expected it to. And because she'd been oblivious to the fact that Andy was even gone, he hadn't had the funeral he'd asked for.

'Maybe when we get you home, I can arrange another send-off for you,' Emily said. 'And do it properly this time.'

'Why can't *this* be my home?' Andy frowned.

'Because firstly, I'm not running a ghostly Airbnb. And secondly, we both need to move on. I've got a lot of other stuff going on at the moment, and you can't just stay in limbo for eternity. Don't you want to get to heaven and find out what it's like?'

'I suppose so,' Andy said, although he sounded pretty unconvinced.

'Let's at least look at our options,' Emily said. Opening

Google, she typed in, *How to get rid of ghosts*, and Andy tutted.

Scrolling through the results, they found plenty of click-baity lists – 8 WEIRD WAYS TO TALK TO THE DEAD. U WON'T BELIEVE NUMBER 4! – some fan pages for various horror films, and some cheesy-looking pages advertising psychic services.

'Maybe we need a medium,' Emily said, thoughtfully. 'Or an exorcist. Someone who can help you get back to the other side.'

'Is exorcism the polite thing to do to a valued guest? I'm pretty sure *Bijou* magazine would frown on that kind of behaviour. Plus it might hurt.'

'Lovely as it is to see you again, you're not a valued guest, you're an uninvited one. But don't worry, I'm sure it won't hurt.'

'Then at least pick someone qualified,' Andy said. 'And make sure they're cruelty-free. I don't want to be sent into the afterlife by the psychic equivalent of Rentokil.'

Emily nodded. 'Fair enough. How about this? It says here we need a "supernatural cleansing", and there's a list of mediums who are members of the Spiritualist National Union. They sound legit. Well, as legit as these people can get, anyway. Honestly, I can't believe I'm doing this.'

Emily had always assumed mediums were just making the whole thing up to con the elderly, gullible and bereaved. But then, she'd thought ghosts were a load of rubbish too, and yet here she was having a chat with her dead ex in her front room.

'Can I choose one? It's only fair,' Andy said, leaning over the laptop.

'As long as you pick one who lives in London. I'm not paying for this woman to travel from Ashby-de-la-Zouch,'

Emily said, stabbing at the screen. 'Plus she looks like Alan Titchmarsh. OK. How about this one? He's called Xander Williams.' She clicked on a headshot of a man in his fifties with dyed jet-black hair and serious-looking eyebrows.

'Nah, he looks too much like Ming the Merciless.'

'What about him? He looks like a normal bloke.' She clicked on a link that promised, 'Houses cleansed, spirits laid to rest.' There was a sketch of an old, creepy-looking house with bats flying out of its windows, which looked like it had come straight from the cover of a cheesy 1960s horror book. Next to it was the photo of a friendly looking man in his forties.

'Tony Tyler. Twenty years of unbeatable service. As seen on TV,' Andy read. 'He's been on telly! He must be good.'

'No, it just means he'll be melodramatic and expensive,' Emily said, bringing up Tony Tyler's details and tapping his number into her phone. 'But it's either him or a man who looks like a crap magician, so we don't have much choice, do we?'

Chapter 13

'I take PayPal or cash. No cards,' Tony Tyler said, glancing around Emily's front room without much interest. He was disappointingly ordinary-looking, and at least a decade older than he appeared to be in the photo on his website.

Emily had been half-hoping he'd be wearing a mystical-looking hat, or maybe a cloak, to show off his spiritual credentials. But instead, he was wearing beige polyester slacks, and a blue sleeveless jumper worn over a tatty white shirt, which set off his grey, thinning hair a treat.

Under Tony's watchful eye – 'Can you put it under friends and family rather than business? It's not like you can return an exorcism, is it?' – Emily paid Tony his outrageous £150 fee on her phone, trying not to worry about how she'd pay next month's rent, before heading into the kitchen to make a round of tea.

She came back to find Andy pulling faces, turning his eyelids inside-out and punching his fists through the top of Tony's head as he sat obliviously on the sofa, flicking through his emails.

'Squish like grape! Helloooo? Can you hear me? Anybody in there?' Andy yelled, about an inch from Tony's ear. 'He can't hear me,' he told Emily dejectedly.

'You don't say,' she muttered, before beaming widely at Tony.

'Sorry?' Tony said.

'You didn't say you wanted sugar, did you?'

Tony shook his head, so Emily handed him his tea, before looking meaningfully at Andy and nodding towards the radiator next to her bedroom door. Bending down, she pretended to adjust it.

'Why can't he hear me?' Andy asked.

'I don't know. Maybe he needs to … turn on the force or something,' Emily whispered. 'Let's give him a chance. We know that ghosts actually exist, which means there must be people out there who can see them. Other than lucky old me, that is. And maybe he really does have the gift. He can't be entirely useless if he's charging a hundred and fifty quid.'

Giving Emily a thumbs-up, Andy sat back next to Tony on the sofa, booming, 'Is anybody in there? Switch your Spidey Senses on,' into his right ear.

Emily sat on his other side, clutching her mug of tea in both hands to stay warm. It wasn't a particularly cold November, but her flat felt like an ice box.

'So what's your problem here? I can definitely feel a presence, obviously,' Tony said, with all the energy of someone talking about potting compost, 'but how would *you* describe it?'

Emily knew all too well the tricks magicians, mediums and charlatans of all kinds used to persuade desperate people into believing pretty much anything they wanted to believe. If she was going to find out if Tony was for real, she had to keep her cards close to her chest and not give too much away by accident.

'It's more a feeling than anything else,' she said, cautiously. 'Like a vibe, you know. And I thought I could hear voices coming from the front room when I came home this evening,' she added, looking pointedly at Andy. 'Whatever it is I can sense, I need help getting it to the other side. Or at least out of my front room.'

'And where is this feeling strongest?' Tony asked, resting his tea on Emily's fluffy rug. She stared at it in consternation – the rug was from Habitat, and one of the few genuinely nice things she owned – but she knew it would be rude to say anything.

'Over there, by the armchair,' Emily said, pointing at Andy's chair.

'Yes, yes. I agree,' Tony nodded, steepling his fingers under his chin.

'What a bullshitter!' Andy tutted. Emily glared at him and rubbed her fingers together to indicate that he should shut up, because this bullshitter had rinsed her bank account.

'I mean, look at him,' Andy muttered, as Tony's eyes fluttered dramatically shut, as if he was trying to sense a presence in the room.

'So what now?' Emily said. 'Do you need to tap into your special senses to communicate with the . . . spirit or whatever?'

'I'm not Spider-Man, young lady,' Tony said sternly, standing up. Andy laughed, while Emily surreptitiously plucked his mug from the rug and set it carefully down on the coffee table. 'I can sense spirits all around us, at all times. It's like listening to lots of different radio channels, whispering at me all at once. I just have to put a little effort into hearing what a specific one is saying, that's all.'

Closing his eyes, Tony put his hands out in front of him and gently stroked the air. 'Yes, there is definitely a presence here. I can feel ... I think I can sense an old woman in the room.'

'Charming,' Andy said.

'No, it's definitely not an old woman,' Emily said, shaking her head.

'That's what I can feel, and I'm the psychic,' Tony snapped, opening one eye and frowning at her. 'An old lady ... maybe your grandmother?'

'Both my nans are alive, actually,' Emily lied.

'Oh my god, this guy is such a prick.' Andy laughed, jumping up from the sofa. 'Wooooo! Can you hear me in there?' he shouted in Tony's face.

'Perhaps it was a former tenant?' Tony asked, clearly hoping for some kind of response from Emily. 'These old buildings have a lot of history in their walls, you know,' he added, pressing a palm against her faded and peeling wallpaper and breathing deeply, as if he was absorbing the secrets of the universe from it.

Moving to the armchair, he began carefully examining it, crouching down, rubbing its sides like it was a thoroughbred horse. Then he placed his palms on the seat and closed his eyes, a frown playing across his face. Emily folded her arms and rolled her eyes.

'Yes, yes. I feel a sadness here,' Tony said wistfully. 'Can you say hello to us, spirit? Can you make yourself known?'

'Yes. Hi, Tony. You're an absolute charlatan and a terrible human being,' Andy said.

'Ah, I hear her. Very faintly,' Tony said, frowning.

'Oh, for god's sake,' Emily sighed, rubbing her forehead.

'She says this was her home ... that ... that she died here. I'm sorry to have to tell you this, Emily, but I think she died right here, in this spot, in her favourite armchair.' Tony gave her a woebegone look.

'I bought that in Ikea,' she said.

'Yes, but she placed her chair in this same spot,' Tony said, quickly. 'You must have sensed her, which is why you put your chair here too. She had lived a good, long life, but wasn't ready to say goodbye just yet. SPIRIT! IT'S TIME TO GO! LEAVE THIS PLACE!'

'Jesus!' Andy said, startled. 'No need to shout. But ... hold on—' Andy frowned, and turned around in his seat. He stared at the wall behind the sofa '—I can see a light, Emily.'

'What? Really? Where?' Emily turned around and touched the wall behind her. She felt the hairs on the back of her neck rising. 'It's getting bigger, brighter ...' he said. He was squinting at a spot just behind Emily's right ear, and she shivered. Surely Tony's theatrics weren't real? Surely he hadn't opened up a door to the other side?

'It's calling to me,' Andy said, quietly, getting to his feet.

'Oh my god. Has it actually worked? Tell me everything you can see,' Emily said, staring at Andy's face, which seemed to be glowing with happiness.

'Who are you talking to?' Tony asked, looking around the room.

'It's ... opening up ... I can see people. And faces,' Andy said, his eyes widening. 'People I know. Is that Randy, my childhood dog? I think it is! Hello, boy! It's me!'

'I don't believe it,' Emily whispered, shaking her head and grinning. 'What else can you see?' She didn't care that Tony clearly had no idea what was happening. She felt her skin prickling all over as she stared at the wall, wishing she could see everything Andy could right now.

'What's going on? What is this?' Tony said, staring at the spot where Andy stood. He no longer looked wistful, like he was listening to an old lady telling the tragic tale of her demise. He looked terrified.

Andy took a deep breath and pressed a shaky hand to his chest. Walking slowly around the sofa, he approached the wall, and stretched out his hand. 'I see … An eternal taco truck that never runs out of salsa. And a PlayStation 9. And some really rad trainers that Biggie Smalls designed in heaven. I'm coming, Biggie! Don't leave me behind!' Andy said, his voice cracking. Then he started cackling, and leaped back onto the sofa.

'Oh, for Christ's sake! You bloody bastard!' Emily said. Then she started laughing too, her legs suddenly feeling weak. She was surprised to find she was relieved that Andy wasn't about to head into the afterlife after all. And, more importantly, that a portal to the ever-after hadn't just opened up in her front room.

'What's up with you, mate? You look like you've seen a ghost,' Andy said, grinning at Tony from the sofa. He was deathly white, his whole face sheened with sweat.

'I don't know what this is, but my work is no laughing matter, you know,' he said, his voice rising to a squeak. 'I'll be telling the union about this!'

'Look,' Emily sighed. 'I'm sorry to have lied to you, but the reason you're actually here is because my ex turned up from the dead after we mucked around with a Ouija board, and I hoped you might be able to help him get to where he's meant to be. You know, over to the other side.'

'Hopefully the nice one, not the nasty one,' Andy added.

'But seeing as he's sitting right there on the sofa, taking the piss out of you while you're busy wanging on about some old dear who's supposed to have died in my front room, I can only assume you're a fraud.'

'You're telling me you can see a ghost right here, right now, in this very room?'

'Yes. He's currently flicking double-Vs at you, if you must know.'

'Oh, very funny. Bloody millennials,' Tony said. 'I suppose this is one of your TickityTok pranks, is it? I'm not giving you your money back, so don't ask. House cleansing is a very ancient discipline, and not one to be treated with contempt. I'm going to be reporting this. You won't get another chance. Our community is a very proud one.'

'Emily, he's hurting my feelings by being dreadful,' Andy moaned, covering his face with his forearm. 'Can you get rid of him?'

'Yes, you're right. It's time for you to go, I think, Tony. Andy says you're dreadful, by the way. And I agree. Thanks for your help, though. It's been an eye-opener.'

'And you can bugger off too, if you're even real,' Tony said to the ceiling, as Emily steered him towards the front door.

'Bye, Tony,' she waved, and slammed the door behind him. 'What a waste of money,' she sighed, slumping onto the sofa.

'Is it OK for me to be happy that it didn't work?' Andy said, hopping into his armchair. 'I've only just come back, I'm not ready to leave just yet.'

'I suppose so,' Emily said. 'Although you can't stay here forever. We've got to find a way of getting you back where you belong eventually.'

'I've got a theory about that, actually,' Andy said, leaning forward with a worryingly keen look in his eyes.

'Go on then,' Emily sighed. 'But I'm going to have to close my eyes while you tell me about it, because I'm knackered.' Shuffling deeper into the cushions, she leaned her head on the back of the sofa.

'I think to get to the other side, we need to find out how I died,' Andy said. 'In the movies, ghosts are always wanging on about their unfinished business. Look at Patrick Swayze, chasing down baddies in *Ghost* and making them freak out. And Bruce Willis in *The Sixth Sense* helping that creepy kid. Brackets, spoiler alert. So maybe that's why I'm here. To find out what actually happened.'

'And I suppose you need my help?' Emily said, without opening her eyes.

'Awesome, yes please,' Andy said.

'It's lucky I don't have anything important happening in my life right now, like the biggest presentation of my career, and trying to get a promotion, and . . .' Emily stopped short of mentioning trying to bag a date with Oliver, deciding that she'd already hurt Andy's feelings enough by trying to have him exorcised. 'Never mind.'

'So that's a yes, then?' Andy asked. 'And in the meantime, will you help me learn how to touch stuff? You'd have thought they'd leave ghosts a copy of *Haunting for Dummies*, or at least a number for customer services, but I haven't found anything. It can be like a side-project.'

'Oh, goody,' Emily said, sarcastically. Then, opening one eye to check he wasn't looking, couldn't help smiling at his annoyingly infectious enthusiasm.

Chapter 14

The next morning, Andy followed Emily around the room like a homesick puppy as she tried to get ready for work – and, crucially, for impressing Oliver. She'd been so tired after the antics of the day before, she'd hit the snooze button twice; something she hadn't done since Andy had last been in her life.

It meant she hadn't had time for the long soak in the bath and hot-oil hair mask she'd pencilled in for her pre-presentation prep, back when she'd hoped Andy was a figment of her imagination – which only felt like, ohhh, about a year ago.

But she'd still managed to pull her hair into a messy-but-chic bun using a special technique she'd seen on TikTok, massage cream into her legs in careful, circulation-boosting strokes, and spend an embarrassing amount of time making her eyebrows look totally on fleek.

She was wearing a figure-hugging beige pencil skirt and matching jacket, paired with a pristine cream T-shirt and strappy beige heels, which she hoped struck the right balance between professional and flirtatious. Her wardrobe, like her living room, was a sea of beige, grey, black and white, and comprised what *Bijou* magazine would term 'a clutch of classic separates for chic mix-and-match style.'

She sometimes missed her old, bright wardrobe of clashing colours, slouchy dungarees and floppy jumpers, but fourteen-year-old Emily would have burst with pride if she could have seen New Emily's reflection in the mirror. The teenager she'd once been had always had grubby knees, and her mum regularly forgot to do any washing at the weekend, leaving her uniform already crumpled and dirty on a Monday morning.

Most of her former classmates – the ones who'd teased her equally harshly for having a deadbeat dad and the wrong pencil case – would barely recognise the woman she'd become. Unfortunately, inside she was still the girl who could spill food down herself just by looking at someone else's dinner, so she made a mental note to avoid her usual beetroot and raspberry breakfast smoothie at all costs and pick up some bananas on her way into work instead.

'You look incredible,' Andy wolf-whistled, when she finally emerged from her bedroom and gave him a shy twirl. 'But aren't those shoes going to shatter your ankles within five minutes of leaving the flat?'

'Probably. But it's worth it,' Emily said. 'According to Mary, you don't catch flies with vinegar, or something like that.'

'So you're trying to impress someone, are you?' Andy said, swallowing. He looked worried and Emily's heart sank. She'd done all she could to move on after Andy had disappeared, but for him, their last date felt like it had happened just a few days ago – plus he hadn't had the benefit of a humiliating ghosting to help put their relationship behind him.

'I just need to look smart for the presentation,' she said lightly. 'Think of the flies in this scenario as a lovely fat promotion. What are you planning on doing all day?' she added, swiftly changing the subject. 'Apart from definitely *not* trying to destroy my flat?'

'Could you put the TV on? Until I learn how to walk through walls, I'm kind of stuck here. And maybe you could take the afternoon off? We need to get cracking on working out what happened to me, *and* teaching me how to touch things. Plus I'm brand new, and you shouldn't leave new ghosts on their own for the first few weeks.'

'Isn't that puppies you're thinking of?'

'Woof,' Andy said, seriously.

Emily laughed, despite herself. 'I'll think about it, *if* the presentation goes well,' she said, picking up the TV remote. 'I've worked every evening and weekend for weeks, so a bit of light bunking-off action won't kill me. There you go,' she added, as the telly flashed into life. 'What do you want to watch?'

'Have you got *Paranormal Caught on Camera*? It might have that extra *je ne sais quoi* now I, myself, am all paranormal.'

Frowning with concentration, Emily navigated her way through the maze of her TV's menus until she found the first series. 'There you go. The next one should play automatically. You know, I bet Einstein's ghost isn't using eternity to watch trash TV.'

'Yeah, well,' Andy said, with a shrug, 'not so clever after all then, is he?'

'Why isn't there a law that says you can punch people who suddenly stop walking halfway up an escalator in the back of the head?' Emily said, throwing her bag into her chair and slipping her jacket off. She examined her arm, which was grazed from where she'd fallen over on the steps. The idiot who'd caused her to fall over had wandered off, totally oblivious.

'It's rush hour,' Simon said, seriously. 'That's when all the tourists come out to make commuters want to curl up and die. They never know how Tube barriers work, or to take their backpacks off when the carriages are packed, so how on earth do you expect them to know how to use the escalators?'

'I'm trying to look all amazing for my presentation, and this isn't helping,' Emily said.

'I wondered why you were looking even shinier than usual,' Simon said, gesturing in her direction. 'It's all . . . very . . . *nice*? You look very efficient. I mean . . . Sorry, I'm not so good at the compliments thing.' He blushed, before burying his head in his laptop.

'Thanks, Simon,' Emily said, sincerely, as she tugged her laptop and notebook from her bag. 'In actual fact, I *am* trying to rock a "totally efficient girl-boss" look. There's no way I can compete with Chrissie's legs. Or her tits or her arse, for that matter. Did you see the way she was shoving her cleavage in Oliver's face yesterday? He was at serious risk of suffocation. So I'm going to wow him with my brains and hope against hope that he's less shallow than the majority of the male population.'

'Have you actually seen you?' Jada said, shaking her head. 'It amazes me how you can put so much effort into looking amazing, yet still think you look like a bag of crap. Although you do have a manky tissue attached to your heel.'

'Oh, blast,' Emily muttered, shaking her foot to try and

free it from the piece of paper she'd dragged in from outside. She hoped Oliver hadn't seen it as she'd self-consciously bum-wiggled her way from the lift to her desk. 'This kind of thing never happens to Kate Middleton.'

'Umm, can we please address the fact that you just said, "Oh blast"?' Simon said, looking amused.

'I'm trying to cut down on my swearing,' Emily said, primly. 'Oliver's not going to want to take the kind of girl who might accidentally drop the C-bomb over Sunday lunch to meet his parents, is he? Plus I'm competing with that lot, and you know what they're like,' she added, nodding at the Witches' Coven. 'If Oliver's anything like them, he'd run a mile if he found out I'm from a—' Emily dropped her voice to a whisper '—council estate.'

More than once, Emily had overheard some of her posher co-workers discussing how benefits cheats and dole scroungers were a disgrace to the nation, as casually as if they were discussing their favourite flavour of kombucha.

Emily had been tempted to point out that the average person vastly overestimates how many people commit benefit fraud, and that wealthy tax dodgers account for billions more money lost to the economy – or simply to shout, 'SHUT UP, YOU STUCK-UP TWATS!' – but instead, she'd kept schtum. Just like she'd stayed silent whenever she overheard the girls at school telling tall tales about goings-on on the Greenleaf estate.

'I heard this disabled pensioner was mugged in broad daylight, and instead of helping, everyone just stood around and filmed it on their phones. They even nicked her zimmer frame.'

Emily might have been keen to escape her past, but that didn't mean she was happy to hear people telling clichéd lies about where she came from.

'If you really must try and seduce your boss – which, I reiterate, I wholeheartedly disapprove of – aren't you better off doing it by being yourself?' Jada said now, shaking Emily out of her reverie. 'Surely *Bijou* has something to say on the subject?'

'Sure it does,' Emily said, blowing a stray strand of artfully dishevelled hair off her face. 'It says you should be your authentic self and speak your truth, because life's too short to be fake and any man worth his salt will love you for who you are, warts and all.'

'See?' Jada said.

'It also offers tips on how to achieve the perfect bikini wax, which new foundation gives you flawless-looking skin for only thirty quid, and how to ace the latest wellness trend. Which just happens to involve doing loads of exercise, necking a fistful of very expensive supplements, and getting up at five a.m.'

'Oh,' Jada said.

'Fucking hell,' Simon muttered.

'Erring on the side of caution, I've decided to stick with the latter tactic. Feeling fine about having armpit hair or gnarly toenails doesn't mean the average man is OK with them too, no matter how many TikTok videos they make claiming otherwise.'

'You mean men like Oliver, right?' Simon said.

Emily thought for a moment. 'Yes,' she said, as she scooped up her laptop.

'Honestly, Emily, most men really don't mind that stuff,' Simon said, sounding exasperated. 'You know how we can't find our keys, even when they're right in front of us? That's because our prehistoric brains are designed to see things differently to women. We don't notice things in the same way you do. Which means we don't give a crap about your armpits, or toenails, or . . . hairy bum cracks.'

'Oh my god,' Emily said.

'It happens,' Simon shrugged. 'And the right man won't care.'

Emily swallowed as she was suddenly hit by a memory from her time with Andy. She'd shut the bathroom door when she went to the loo, and he'd been affronted that she felt she had to hide any part of herself from him.

'I can take it, Emily,' he'd said. 'There's no need to hide that stuff from me. We've all got bums, you know.' He'd looked so serious, Emily had burst out laughing, and she'd felt another hole in her glossy smokescreen blowing open.

Since then, though, she'd plugged all the gaps, and built another protective layer around herself, hoping that the more put-together and confident she appeared, the less likely she was to be left nursing a severely bruised – if not quite fully broken – heart.

'I haven't put all this effort in just to terrify him with a hairy vag,' Emily said firmly. 'Now never speak to me about arse cracks again.'

Simon sighed and shook his head as she walked towards The Greenhouse. In keeping with the office's wannabe-Google-headquarters vibe, each of HoRizons' meeting rooms was themed. Summer Meadow had fake grass stuck to its walls and birdsong piped in, The Play Zone's furniture, down to the chairs, was made of Lego, while The Greenhouse was covered from floor to ceiling with plants. It meant that, as she heaved open its glass door, she was hit by a blast of hot, sticky air.

She had five minutes to get ready, and found her hands

shaking as she connected her laptop to the presentation screen. Despite her best efforts, she didn't have the same natural confidence with technology as other people her age. Growing up, she'd never had the latest phone or even satellite TV.

Her school's tech was on its last legs, too, so when she'd arrived at HoRizons, and been handed a brand-new iPhone and MacBook, she'd had to disguise the fact that she didn't have a clue how to set them up. She'd done a fairly good job of muddling through, but still tripped up more often than she'd like – and now was definitely not the time for technology to turn on her like it usually did.

The glass door clanged open, vibrating Emily's teeth and almost knocking over the aspidistra behind it, and Charles swung into the room, followed by Oliver, who quietly shut the door behind him.

Being near him made Emily feel like a walking cliché, because the very sight of him made her knees wobbly. As he pulled out the chair opposite hers, she caught a waft of what smelt like a delicious combination of honey and cinnamon, and she felt herself tingling all over. An image of herself floating across the room towards him, his smell dragging her along by her nose, like Pepé Le Pew sniffing out a sexy lady skunk, popped into her head.

She gave Oliver a small smile that she hoped said, *I'm totally professional, and definitely not imagining us as cartoon skunks in love.*

'Are you ready to dazzle Oliver – I mean, us – with your ideas for the Cat's Miaow account?' Charles said, arching his eyebrow at her. Emily blushed, cleared her throat, and powered up her presentation. This was her big moment.

'OK, so my main idea for the campaign was inspired by one of Oliver's past successes – because it was fresh enough to stand the test of time and frankly, if it isn't broken, why should we spend money fixing it?' she said, raising her voice slightly (one of *Bijou* magazine's SEVEN SIGNS YOU'RE A SASSY, CONFIDENT GODDESS!). 'Without wanting to come across like too much of a kiss-arse, Oliver, your AirLab campaign was a stroke of genius.'

Oliver smiled, and Emily relaxed a little. The arse-kissing line had been put into her notes for being cheeky and assertive – then taken out again for being too rude and presumptive – umpteen times before she'd decided to leave it in.

She clicked onto her first slide, a video of good-looking young people doing backflips and climbing walls, parkour-style, around cities across the world.

'Your award-winning campaign was based on home videos of AirLab fans performing stunts, which meant it cost hardly anything, and came across as really authentic. Using customer content as the basis of an advertising campaign makes sense both creatively and financially, so I've used it as my inspiration for Cat's Miaow as well.

'I thought we could play on the fact that although every cat owner thinks their pet is unique, people who don't have one assume that cats all behave pretty much the same way. The internet is full of memes about cats being evil geniuses and only caring about their owners when they want food, that sort of thing.

'These stereotypes can be annoying for cat-lovers, because when you've got a pet, you know it's special. So, I thought we could turn that whole evil-genius cat trope on its head and show customers that we're on their side. That we understand them, and the way their pet is unique, better than any of our competitors ever could.'

Emily clicked to her next slide. But instead of showing her campaign slogan – the one she'd spent so many sleepless nights coming up with – the screen was blank.

'I'm sorry about this,' Emily said frantically, stabbing at the keys on her laptop. 'That's not the right slide.' Picking up the remote control, she stared at the buttons. They swam in front of her eyes, and she could feel her heart thudding in her chest.

Suddenly, the presentation screen flickered, and went out.

'Hold on,' Emily stuttered, standing up and wiggling at the wires underneath the screen. She felt the hairs standing up on the back of her neck, and whipped her head around to look behind her. Her eyes darted around the room, but there was nothing there, except a sudden blast of cold air.

'Take a deep breath, Emily,' Charles said, and she shot him a tight smile. If Jada had been here, she'd have launched into a diatribe about patriarchal patronisation and the use of calming phrases being used to denote female hysteria in the workplace. But unfortunately (or perhaps fortunately) for Emily, Jada was safely back at her desk.

Trying not to cry as she watched her presentation falling apart before her eyes, Emily thumped the side of the monitor. Suddenly, the screen fizzed back into life, and a giant slogan appeared.

Every cat is unique.
But all cats love Cat's Miaow.

Emily felt her stomach turning watery with relief.

'Here we go. Sorry about that,' she said lightly, trying

not to sound like she'd just watched her life flashing before her eyes.

'So, where were we . . . Instead of playing up the similarities between cats, I thought we could show cats behaving totally out of character. More like dogs, in fact,' Emily explained, her heart hammering. 'We'll ask cat owners to send in content showing their pets' individuality: photos of cats sitting on their owners' heads. Films of cats fetching sticks and stuff. To show that they're not all the same.'

'Do cats even do that?' Oliver said. 'Fetch sticks and, er, sit on their owners' heads?' The corner of his mouth twitched upwards in a smile. 'Mine certainly doesn't. Lazy bugger.'

Emily nodded, trying not to blush. The husky edge to Oliver's voice, which made it sound like he'd just woken up, was making her feel all unnecessary.

'I've found some images that already fit the bill,' she said, getting back into the swing of her presentation as she brought up her next slide. 'Of course, we'd need to get permission to use this stuff – I mean, *content* – but it would get the ball rolling, and it gives you an idea of what's out there.'

A montage of photos played across the screen – cats being cuddled, a cat playing on an iPad in a tiny yurt, even a cat carrying a newspaper in its mouth – ending with a grid of cats all diving for a bowl of food.

'If we ran a Unique Cats competition, like the Parkour one Oliver created for the AirLab campaign, we'd get sent tons of content. People love showing off their pets, but traditionally, cat-food advertisers have shied away from showing real cats, in favour of the polished, fluffy kind. So this would be something really different.

'A condition of entry – small print, of course – would mean

entrants would give us the rights to their content, which we could use as the basis of a TV ad campaign. People won't just be sending in existing films, they'll be making new ones. And, as you can see—' Emily clicked a button, showing a complicated-looking graph showing predicted levels of engagement across different social media platforms '—there's a sixty-three point three per cent chance that we'll go viral.'

Emily counted, *three, two, one* in her head before clicking onto her last slide, which simply said 'THANK YOU', after a feature in an online business magazine had insisted it was 'the ideal closer if you've been granted time by your boss that shouldn't technically be yours'.

'So . . . that's it, really. What do you think?' she said.

The room went silent and Emily held her breath. Then Charles nodded twice, which for him was the equivalent of popping open a bottle of champagne. *Thank goodness*, Emily thought, feeling a flush of triumph. Despite a terrible start, she'd pulled her presentation off. And perhaps keeping her cool in the face of disaster would even go in her favour.

She turned to Oliver, who had an odd look on his face. She scanned it, trying to decipher what he was thinking. She'd worked hard on her idea, and if someone as talented and successful as him liked it, she'd have a real shot at getting even further ahead in her career. Plus, of course, he might fancy her a bit more.

Please, please like it, Emily thought.

'I like this very much,' Charles said, turning to Oliver when he didn't say anything. 'It at least seems like a very suitable jumping-off point for further work, don't you agree?'

Oliver paused. 'I'm pretty sure this is workable, yeah,' he said, sounding uncertain. Emily hoped she hadn't overstepped the mark by leaving in her crap jokes. He tapped his pen on his notepad, looking lost in thought. Then he appeared to pull himself together, looked up, and grinned.

'You're right, Charles, this is a great idea. I'm impressed. And Emily, could you send me some of these videos? My cat does sod all, it would be great if I could teach him to start being useful around the house.'

Emily laughed, her legs wobbling underneath her.

Charles added, 'Of course, we have yet to see our creative teams' *meisterwerks*, so I'm afraid there's no guarantee that your idea will be chosen as the final pitch, Emily, but this is very good work. Their ideas are coming in today, so I'll let you know the verdict shortly.'

'Thank you, Charles,' Emily grinned.

'Well, I'll leave you two to it,' Charles said, standing up. 'As ever, I have people to ignore, emails marked "URGENT!" to delete . . .'

Sitting in the chair opposite Oliver's around the table, Emily let out a little puff of relief at giving her feet a break from her ridiculously high heels, and tried not to wince as her tight skirt cut into her stomach. They were very much a sitting-down kind of shoe, paired with an extremely standing-up kind of skirt.

Emily watched as Charles left the room, her heart beating a bit too hard at the thought of being left alone with Oliver. She had become much better at pretending to match her poised online persona in real life, but it still took some effort. Plus she was always worried she might commit a social faux-pas she wasn't even aware of.

Despite proudly boasting about its commitment to diversity, most of the people who worked at HoRizons – including

Oliver, of course – were from private-school backgrounds. Emily sometimes struggled to work out what on earth they were talking about – what the hell did 'infra dig' mean? – and wondered if they actually taught pupils at private schools this stuff, or if it was just something they'd picked up by osmosis. Emily could tell the difference between Superkings and Marlboro Lights just by the smell, and maybe being able to identify a Savile Row suit at ten paces was just the posh-person version of the same thing.

'So, you've got a cat, have you, Oliver? What's his, her or their name?' she asked lightly, keen to steer the conversation away from 'work chat' and towards 'first conversation of a long, illustrious and sexy union' chat as quickly as possible.

'*His* name is Speedy Tomato. It's from a Stephen King book,' Oliver said, rubbing the palm of his hand with his thumb.

'*The Dead Zone*!' Emily said.

'Wow, I'm impressed,' Oliver said. 'You like his stuff then?'

She nodded eagerly. When she was a kid, one of her mum's boyfriends had been really into horror books. She was too young to borrow them from the library herself, but he'd let her have them once he'd finished with them. When her mum had broken up with him when he was still reading *Carrie*, which Emily had been itching to read, she'd been devastated.

But of course, she couldn't tell Oliver about her mum being a single parent and her consequent string of dead-beat, if occasionally horror-loving, boyfriends. Even if she'd eventually tell him the truth about her past – say, after five or ten years of marriage and popping out a couple of attractive children – now was too soon.

'My mum was really into them when I was a kid,' she said,

blushing at the lie. 'They were her guilty secret when she wasn't busy studying texts for her Open University degree. I wasn't supposed to read them until I was older, but I used to sneak downstairs and take them off the shelf to read in bed. She never even noticed.'

That bit, at least, was partly true. Back then, her mum hadn't seemed to notice – or, at least, to care – that Emily always seemed to have a thick, black- or red-spined book clutched in her small hands, its title dripping with blood or gore, or that she'd started having terrible nightmares.

'I was a total horror geek,' Oliver said, apparently oblivious to Emily's discomfort. 'Although once I read *Pet Sematary*, I kind of went off them a bit. Have you read that one?'

Emily nodded, a chill running down her spine at the memory. 'It was so scary, I had the mad idea of burying it in the garden. But then, of course, I had nightmares about it somehow burrowing its way out of the ground and coming to get me.' Emily laughed. 'How about you?' Oliver added. 'Any cats? Dogs? Kids? Grandkids?'

'No pets, sorry,' Emily said, trying to regain her composure. 'Although I love cats and have always wanted one.' In fact, Emily half-suspected cats were planning to overthrow humanity and become Earth's fluffy overlords, meaning she generally steered well clear of them, but she'd long since learned not to admit it to cat lovers. 'My ex did have one, though. Called Dandy,' she added, feeling a pang of guilt at using Andy to stretch out her conversation with Oliver. 'His dad was called Sandy, and his mum was Mandy, if you can believe it.'

'And the ex? What's he called? Randy?' Oliver laughed.

'No, he was called Andy,' Emily said, glancing at the ceiling and half-expecting the lights to flicker off at the mention of his name. 'But he did have a dog called Randy when he was a kid. I'm not even joking.' She smiled as she remembered him telling her the story of the family tradition that had led to his name.

'It's lucky they never had any more kids, really,' Andy had told her, while she'd tried very hard not to laugh. 'They were going to call another boy Landy, even though it's French and they've never been further than Calais, and a girl Brandy. And if that had happened, there's no *way* she wouldn't have ended up working as a porn star.'

'That's quite something,' Oliver said, shaking his head. Then he glanced at his watch. 'I'd better get going. I've got a meeting with HR to attend. And as you can imagine, I wouldn't want to miss a single exciting second of it.'

'And I'll send you the videos you asked for,' Emily said confidently, standing up. 'Then perhaps you can teach Speedy Tomato Beauchamp a thing or two about fetching sticks.'

'Sorry, who?' Oliver said, looking surprised.

'Your cat. I assume his surname is Beauchamp?' Emily said. 'You know, like when you take a pet to the vet and they're all, "Mr Woofington the Third Smith to room one, please . . ."?'

Emily trailed off as Oliver covered his mouth, trying to hide a grin. 'Sorry, I don't mean to laugh,' he said. 'But it's not pronounced Bow-shamp. It's Beecham. Like . . . the cold and flu remedy. It's from the French, of course,' he added, helpfully.

'Oh, of course,' Emily said, trying to hide her face in her laptop and pile of papers as she blushed scarlet. Seeing as most people in the office had weird surnames, like Brougham, which was mysteriously pronounced 'Broom', she should have checked before opening her mouth. And perhaps changed her surname, which sounded like a stain she couldn't get rid of – *Blott* – in the process.

'What was I thinking?' she stuttered, smiling brightly in the hope that Oliver might think it was a genuine slip of the tongue. 'It's been a long day.' He glanced at the clock that hung on the wall surrounded by shrubbery. She blushed even harder when she realised it was only 9.45 a.m.

'Easy mistake to make,' he said, smiling at her like she was a small child with a crayon stuck in her ear, before heading out of the room.

'Fan-fucking-tastic,' Emily muttered to the yucca by her elbow.

Chapter 15

'So … Are you the future Mrs Beauchamp then, or what?' Jada asked, as Emily slumped into her desk.

'Why couldn't you have said his bloody name out loud *before* the meeting, rather than ten seconds after it?' Emily groaned, resting her head on her desk.

'What do you mean?' Jada said. Then her eyes widened. '*Oh*. Oh dear.'

'Yes. *Oh dear*. What's the point of spending half my life down the gym and half my salary on cute little dresses if opening my big fat gob is going to ruin everything anyway?'

'I'm guessing a reminder that you should be yourself wouldn't be welcome right now?' Simon asked from across the desk.

'No, it would not,' Emily said tartly. 'On the plus side, they seemed to really like my idea, which is the most important thing. Or at least, it should be. My stomach, which feels like it's trying to crawl out of my mouth with embarrassment, doesn't seem to agree.'

Flipping open her laptop again, Emily brought up her

work emails, and sighed. Until she heard from Charles about whether her pitch idea had been successful, she had the immense pleasure of working on the rebrand of Coffee & Co, a hipster café that had recently decided to 'cut through the noise' by serving just one type of coffee (a grande drip-filtered, artisan-roasted, single-bean, speciality-grade, Fairtrade, double-mocha latte).

To demonstrate the business's single-minded dedication to coffee perfection, they planned to stick red crosses over the top of the '& Co' part of their name across all their store signs, and stop selling muffins.

Emily thought it was a stupid idea and secretly preferred McDonald's coffee anyway, but she'd been tasked with taking their branding 'to the next level'. She had a Zoom meeting with someone called Zack, who was a strategic development lead. Emily still didn't know what one of those was, despite having met several.

She tried to look interested as Zack talked her through the rebranding concept.

'We want drinking at Coffee & Co – or "Coffee", rather—' Zack paused to smirk and do air quotes '—to be about moments of reflection, yeah? We want to encourage our customers to take time out to think about what's really important to them in their lives over a cup of really good coffee. A moment of alone-time, just them and their coffee, giving them space to carve out their truth, yeah? We want to create a mood that's irresistible to the discerning, modern, forward-thinking coffee-drinker. Yeah?'

'OK, so it's about taking time to be alone with your coffee and enjoy moments of reflection?' Emily said, resisting the urge to escape by jabbing a pencil through her eye.

'Yeah. But we don't want to be *too* obvious? So we'd like you to steer clear of the words moment, reflection, alone-time, forward-thinking, space, mood, or modern. Oh, and we don't want to use the phrase "discerning coffee drinker", either. Yeah?'

'I get you. Am I allowed to use the word coffee?' Emily asked, through gritted teeth.

Frowning, Zack scanned an iPad he was holding, despite the fact he was already sitting in front of an iPhone and a laptop, and was wearing an Apple Watch.

'Yep, that looks OK,' he nodded. 'That could change, though, yeah? So bear that in mind. We really want to push our boundaries and show people what makes us different from all the rest.'

It was hard for Emily not to let her mind wander between her cringey faux pas in front of Oliver, what Andy might be getting up to in her flat, and the messages popping up on the Rebel Alliance chat group in the corner of her laptop.

Jada: Watching you Cosplay someone who gives a crap about coffee is quite something.

Simon: You'd never guess you prefer your coffee with a Smarties McFlurry on the side. I bet your Princess Leia is amazing.

Jada: Careful, Em. Before you know it, he'll be asking you to staple a couple of bagels to your head and come to work in a bikini . . .

At one point, Emily had to pretend to sneeze to hide an unladylike snort of laughter. Luckily, for some reason, Zack seemed genuinely excited about his own terrible ideas, so for the majority of the meeting, she got away with nodding enthusiastically whenever he paused for breath, which wasn't often.

'This job is abso-blooming-lutely ridiculous,' Emily muttered, after she'd stabbed her finger on her keyboard to ring off the call. 'I don't see the point in trying to sell their signature coffee so hard when it tastes like sweaty balls.' She glanced behind her to check Oliver wasn't within hearing range.

'Don't be so cynical,' Simon tutted. 'Who wants to buy coffee that tastes nice? You want to buy a *concept*, Emily, from people who love the planet and simply don't care who knows it.'

By lunchtime, she'd written just six words: 'It's not coffee. It's a feeling.'

They were six of the most ridiculous words she'd ever put down on paper, but she suspected Zack at Coffee & Co – sorry, Coffee – would love them.

'What feeling's that? The feeling of being completely ripped off by the capitalist machine?' Jada said, when Emily asked what she thought of her latest masterpiece. 'But yes, this is perfect. It's vague and meaningless enough for them to really go for it.'

'I will never understand why you have this job, Jada,' Simon said, shaking his head. 'It's like a turkey getting a job at Bernard Matthews.'

'Money,' Jada said, without looking up from her screen.

Emily glanced at the time in the corner of her laptop. If she was going to sneak out that afternoon, she'd have to start making ominous noises about Women's Troubles soon, as that pretty much guaranteed she'd be ushered out of the office by Charles before she had the chance to go into too much detail.

She stood up, then sat down again when an email from Charles pinged into her inbox.

From: Charles Worthing
To: Emily Blott
Re: Cat's Miaow Pitch

Emily,

I am thrilled to tell you that following a consultation with the creative team, we have collectively decided that your idea is truly exceptional, a conclusion almost certainly not reached because it was also the cheapest to execute by far.

In light of your contribution, I would be delighted if you would work with Oliver to pull together a pitch document for the presentation to Cat's Miaow, which is scheduled for three weeks' time. This is, of course, subject to the charmingly capricious fellows who work there managing to stick to an agreed date for the first time in living memory.

I also think it would be good for you to be one of our presentation leads on the day itself. I believe you're ready for this challenge, don't you?

May I offer you my sincerest congratulations.

Charles W.

Emily stared at the email, a warm feeling spreading from her feet all the way up to her head, which translated into a huge grin.

'What's up?' Jada asked suspiciously. 'You look way too happy for someone who's wearing a skirt that tight.'

'They've only gone and chosen my idea for the Cat's Miaow pitch,' Emily beamed, swivelling her laptop towards her. 'Can you believe it?'

'Lemme see,' Simon said, skimming his way around the desks to read the email. 'Wow, Emily, that really is amazing,' he said sincerely when he'd finished, punching her lightly on the shoulder.

'Thanks, Simon,' Emily said, grinning up at him.

'Very impressive indeed,' said a deep voice behind them. Simon leaped up at the sound of Oliver's voice. Slinking back to his desk, he ostentatiously tweaked the position of his *Countdown* teapot.

'I'm very much looking forward to working on this with you, Emily,' Oliver said, smoothly. 'I think we can come up with some really excellent ideas to push this forward.' Emily sent a silent prayer to her central nervous system not to make her blush, and managed it by thinking about mushrooms, which she hated.

'He's a bit sleazy, don't you think?' Simon said, wrinkling his nose as they watched Oliver enthusiastically greeting the Witches' Coven on his way back to his desk.

'Yes, I think the handsome, nice-smelling, pleasant and flattering man is a total creep,' Emily said, unable to hide her huge smile as she shut her laptop and slid it into her bag.

'So you're still here then? I can't tell you how thrilled I am,' Emily said, as she got home that afternoon and closed the front door, dropping her bag and jacket on the floor and kicking them under the coffee table. Andy had always brought out the worst in her – the bits of Old Emily she tried the hardest to exorcise from her life – and after just a couple of days, she could already feel herself slipping back into her bad habits whenever she was around him.

It was like when she went home to Essex and found the accent she'd tried so hard to drop springing up from nowhere: suddenly, she was full of glottal stops and lapsed consonants. And now, apparently, Andy's disdain for putting things away properly was rubbing off on her, even when he couldn't touch anything.

'Hi, honey. Nice day at work?' Andy grinned from his chair in the corner of the room.

'Discussing cat food isn't particularly thrilling, but one nice thing did happen: my presentation has been chosen for the official Cat's Miaow pitch.'

'Wow, that's huge!' Andy said, sounding genuinely impressed. 'I know from temping at Urban Muse how nuts everyone went when their pitches were chosen. I always knew you were a genius.'

'Thanks,' Emily said. 'And the good news for you is that Charles was happy to let me off early to do some research into cats. I didn't even have to pretend to have period pains. But you'll have to tell me about Dandy, so it sounds like I've actually done something. How about you? What have you been up to?'

'Today's been really boring, actually,' Andy said, frowning. 'Having done extensive research, I can conclude that the ghosts captured on *Paranormal Caught on Camera* are about as genuine as a politician's apology. So I'm glad you're home. I'm ready to do some investigating. And some learning how to karate-chop things. Squish like grape!'

'But you've definitely not been practising on this, right?' Emily said, plucking the fish-shaped vase from the table next to Andy's chair and rubbing some dust off its scales with the sleeve of her jacket.

'Absolutely not,' he said, pulling a serious but completely unconvincing face.

'OK,' Emily said, setting down the vase. 'Where do you want to start?'

Chapter 16

'What exactly are you expecting to find here?' Emily said, picking her way through the tangled undergrowth of the graveyard towards the memorial garden. 'Because if you think your headstone might say, "Here lies Andy, who died after leaning too far out of a window", you're likely to be sorely disappointed.'

Andy coughed and pointed out a passing bee, which was enough to tell Emily that's exactly what he'd been thinking. She looked up at the grey sky, which was starting to let out a fine mist of drizzle, and shivered. She'd half-hoped Andy's idea of investigating his untimely demise might involve taking her laptop to a pub, ordering a nice glass of wine, and doing a light spot of googling. But instead, she'd ended up in a creepy old graveyard looking for Andy's final resting place and praying that she wouldn't be besieged by millions of ghosts now he'd switched on her I-see-dead-people powers.

It hadn't even taken long to find out where Andy's ashes were buried. She'd quite fancied the idea of heading to the town hall, waving a sheaf of papers impatiently at a clerk and demanding to look at the council's burial records, *stat!* But all it took was a quick look on the internet to find out that what was left of Andy's physical self was buried in the small memorial garden at Christ Church on Brixton Road.

'I hate graveyards. They're so spooky,' Andy said, shivering, the lowering sky making it feel much later than 3 p.m.

'Your lack of self-awareness, even now you're dead, really is quite something,' Emily said. 'And anyway, aren't graveyards kind of like Cub Scouts for ghosts? You might bump into some fellow Formers who can help you work out how to touch stuff.'

'I don't want to meet any ghosts!' Andy said, looking alarmed as he followed Emily along a crooked path lined with wobbly paving stones and bordered with knee-high nettles. 'Although I do quite like the name Formers. Sounds like we could turn ourselves into monster trucks if we really wanted to.'

'Not wanting to meet ghosts makes no sense at all, unless you're an introvert, which you're not,' Emily said, stepping delicately from stone to stone to avoid tripping up. 'That's like . . . spiders being scared of spiders.'

'OK, so what if you woke up one day and realised you were suddenly a spider, and were obliged to go and hang out with all your creepy, eight-legged spider mates? Except now they're the same size as you, and expect you to . . . I dunno, make them sandwiches. Are you telling me you'd be totally fine with that?'

'Oh god, no,' Emily said, shivering. She hated spiders. 'I take your point. And what if you came across the ghost of a murderer, and they start chasing you? Can ghost murderers harm other ghosts?'

'This really isn't helping,' Andy said, looking suspiciously at the passing graves, none of which were likely to say, HERE LIES FRED, THE HORRIBLE MURDERING BASTARD, by way of warning.

'Sorry. I'll help you avoid any ghosts if we see one. I'm sure they're nicer now they're dead. That's got to change a person, right? You can't stay grumpy forever. And what would be the point of trying to kill someone who's dead already? Anyway, here we are. Let's find you.'

The memorial garden was a relatively small section of the graveyard, filled with metal plaques and framed by wooden benches that each had their own letterbox brass signs attached to them. Some of the graves featured round urns with flowers poking out of them, and it was easy to see at a glance which were the most recent.

The plaques belonging to the long dead were covered with overgrown grass, their writing worn away. Some of their urns were cracked and half-driven into the mud, as the people who remembered them had gradually moved on or joined their loved ones in the graveyard.

Others had been neglected for just a few years, their vases intact, and still sporting brown stalks sticking up from their tops. Only a couple of plaques looked shiny and new. One took up twice the space of the others, and was topped by an elaborate stone. Shaped like an open book, it was carved with swirly gold writing, surrounded by fresh flowers tied with shiny plastic ribbon, and notes that fluttered gently in the breeze.

Andy walked around one of the benches and got close enough to peer at the inscription. 'Blimey, this one's mine. I know I was always dead popular – excuse the pun – but how did my parents afford that?' Emily wound her way around it to reach Andy's side. She leaned forward and read the writing on the stone aloud.

'Andy Atkins, taken from us far too soon. Survived by a beloved Mum, Dad, and Dandy the cat. We miss you so much.'

Emily felt a hard lump forming in her chest. Through all the drama of the last few days, she hadn't had much time to think about Andy's family, and how devastated they must still be at losing him.

'Poor Mum,' Andy said quietly, crouching down and patting the stone. 'Her only son, snatched from her in the prime of his life, and before he was able to become mega famous thanks to his amazingly rocking band. Hey, what's this?'

Emily crouched down beside him and tugged at a small parcel that had been tucked at the foot of his plaque. It was wrapped in shiny tissue paper that was printed with purple bells.

'Ugh, it looks like food,' Emily grimaced, removing her fingers, which were smeared in grease.

'Amazing! It's Taco Bell!' Andy grinned. 'The king of dirty-but-delicious takeaways. God, what wouldn't I do for a Volcano Burrito right now . . .? Who put it there?'

Gingerly, Emily tugged at a pink Post-it note that had been stuck to the wrapper.

'Stay safe, mate, still miss you,' she read. 'Apparently, this is from Billy the Fist. Dare I ask how he got his nickname or do I really not want to know?'

'It's not as bad as it sounds,' Andy said. 'He's called that because he can't make a proper fist, the silly bastard. Tucks his thumb inside his palm and insists that's how it's done. The first time we saw it, I thought I'd die laughing, but he still couldn't see what he was doing wrong. It was like watching a dog trying to make friends with its reflection.'

Emily smiled. 'That's a *lot* less gross than I was imagining, which is a relief.' She tucked the Taco Bell package back at the bottom of Andy's plaque, and wished he was solid so she could wipe her fingers on his clothes. Instead, she plucked a tissue from her bag, careful not to get any grease on the leather. Unsure of the correct graveyard chic etiquette, she'd changed out of her linen pencil skirt and into black woollen shorts worn with chunky boots, a fine-knit striped jumper and her big coat, her hair falling loosely over its shoulders.

'Hello? Can I help you, love?' a voice said behind them. 'Are you here to see Andy?'

Emily turned, wiping her fingers, and Andy leaped across three graves to reach a woman in her mid-sixties who was carefully navigating the stepping stones towards the memorial garden. She had fluffy light-brown hair, and was wearing a blue padded jacket and matching long blue floral skirt, with a pair of flesh-coloured tights and sturdy-looking sandals poking out underneath.

'It's my mum! Hey, Mum!' Andy said, scampering behind her as she headed towards Emily. 'Maybe you could talk to her for me, tell her I'm here,' he added excitedly, running back over to his memorial stone, like a dog racing between its owners.

'Ah yes, yes I am,' Emily said, as Mandy walked down the path towards her, clutching a bunch of chrysanthemums wrapped in cellophane.

Mandy's skirt caught on a nettle, and as she bent to pluck it free, Emily turned to Andy to mutter, 'I'm not telling your mum you're here. If I suddenly spring "Did you know your son is a ghost and he's come back to haunt my crappy flat" on her, why would she believe me?'

'I've not seen you here before, love,' Mandy said from over Emily's shoulder, making her jump. 'Are you one of Andy's friends?'

'Umm, yes, I am. Or rather I was, obviously,' Emily stuttered. 'My name's Emily.'

Mandy's face lit up. 'Of course you are!' she said. 'You're the girl he was dating, the one he was always talking about. I thought you looked lovely in your photo, but it didn't do you justice. What a pretty girl.'

Emily raised her eyebrows at Andy, but he was too busy beaming happily at his mum to notice.

'That's me,' Emily said, holding her palms up. 'At least, I hope that was me. I'm afraid I was away when he died, so I wasn't able to attend his funeral.'

'Actually,' Andy said, pretending to examine a notebook, 'it says here that you assumed your poor dead boyfriend had ghosted you, so you blocked him on social media and didn't know anything about it.'

'Shush,' Emily whispered.

'I'm sorry?' Mandy said, following Emily's gaze to the spot next to her.

'Nothing, sorry. Just a tic,' Emily said. 'It's a bit nerve-wracking meeting your ex's mum for the first time, especially under the circumstances.'

'Yes. My poor Andy,' Mandy said, kneeling down and gently plucking a speck of moss off his plaque. The cellophane around the flowers crackled as she laid them on the ground on top of the burrito Billy the Fist had left. Emily noticed she'd bothered to peel the price sticker off the side, and had to fight back sudden tears.

'He was a lovely boy. Really kind. And funny, too,' Emily

said, as Mandy made her way to the bench opposite Andy's grave and sat down. 'Do you mind?' she added, gesturing at the seat beside hers.

'Not at all,' Mandy said, patting the chipped varnish slats. 'I actually tried to get in touch with you after it happened, but I didn't know how to. Andy never mentioned your surname.'

Emily glanced at Andy. 'I know how much you hate it,' he said with a shrug, and Emily smiled.

'So it's lovely to meet you now,' Mandy continued. 'I could talk about my boy all day long.'

'I agree, I think you should chat some more about this Andy fella,' Andy said, sitting on the floor in front of the bench by Emily's feet. 'He sounds brilliant.'

'I'm not sure what I can tell you about him that you don't already know, really,' Emily said, plucking at the thick woollen tights she was wearing under her shorts. 'He was obsessed with his band, and with tacos, but you'll know that already. All his friends had stupid nicknames, which made it sound like they weren't close, but I could tell they were really, because Andy would do anything for them.'

'He was a kind boy,' Mandy said, nodding. 'And good-looking, too, when he bothered to brush his hair.'

Emily smiled. 'He once got fired from his temp job because Vaseline Al . . . I mean, because his friend Alan had broken his arm, and Andy's boss wouldn't let him take a day off to look after him. Did you know about that?'

Mandy shook her head, her eyes glinting. She looked at Emily hopefully, as if she was scared that if she said the wrong thing, Emily might stop talking.

'Alan needed someone to help him out while he got used to the cast on his arm, but when Andy called into work, his boss said he had to come in. Andy called him "Rubbish Admin Hitler" and put the phone down on him.' Beside Emily, Mandy chuckled. 'Then he spent the next week at Alan's helping him out. He even took him to the loo. I don't think he was very amused by that, to be honest.'

'He used to time his farts for the exact moment I was helping him off with his pants,' Andy grumbled from the floor. Emily laughed, hoping Mandy would assume she was laughing at her own memories.

'What was he like as a boyfriend? Was he nice to you? I tried to bring him up right, but you never know, do you? Boys can treat their mums like gold dust then run off and be horrible to their girlfriends, can't they?'

'You've got that right,' Emily said, remembering the man she'd dated before Andy. He'd been a total mummy's boy, but abandoned her in A&E with her bottom lip swollen to the size of a lilo after a bee sting, because Arsenal were playing. 'But don't worry, he was an excellent boyfriend. He made me an amazing tape for Valentine's Day – a cover of "All You Need Is Love", but with the lyrics changed.

'And he always remembered the little things. Like he once bought five big bags of Skittles and took out all the purple and red ones, because they were my favourites, and put them in a separate bowl for me. And because I love pizza with garlic dip, he kept spares at his flat in case they got our order wrong.'

Andy looked up at Emily in surprise. Throughout their time together, she'd been worried about getting too close to Andy. Even though their relationship had stretched on for far longer than she'd originally intended – her Winter Boyfriend threatening to become an Easter one by the time Andy had disappeared – she'd never told him how much she appreciated the little things he did for her, in case he got the wrong idea about how she felt about him. Or rather, the right one.

But now, sitting chatting to Mandy in front of Andy's memorial stone, it was easy to remember how thoughtful he'd been. She looked down at him fondly and wished she could ruffle his hair. Or at least pull that ridiculous sweet wrapper out of it.

'I'm so happy he found you,' Mandy said. 'I was worried about Andy, what with him not having a proper job. I knew it might dent his chances of finding a nice girl. Money's important, isn't it? Especially to young girls these days.' Emily nodded, and swallowed down the lump that had formed in her throat. 'If his dad hadn't got ill, and he'd gone to university, things might have been different for him. So I was so pleased when he met you.'

'What do you mean about his dad?' Emily asked.

'Didn't he tell you about that?' Mandy said, pulling a tissue out of her handbag and blowing her nose. 'I suppose he wouldn't. He hated bragging, except about the little things, like his ridiculous stunts. He was more proud of breaking his thumb falling off his skateboard than he was of how kind he was.

'Anyway, what you probably don't know is that Andy had a place at Manchester all lined up, but then his dad got sick with cancer. You know, down there—' Mandy mimed the last two words '—and so he stayed here with us, in London. When his dad was diagnosed, Andy read all these books about it to try and help, and he kept talking about a chapter that said the main carer of someone with cancer needs someone of their own they can lean on. So he gave up his place at university to look after me. I tried to convince him not to, but he wasn't having any of it.'

'No, he never told me about this,' Emily said, looking down at Andy, who was fiddling with his shoelaces. 'And is his dad OK now?'

'Yes, he's fine. He got through it, thank god. But it took three years. By then, Andy had started his band, and enjoyed having a bit of money. He always thought mature students stuck out like a sore thumb, so he decided to skip uni altogether. If I'd known he wasn't long for this earth, I'd have packed him off to Manchester in a flash so he could make the most of his time here.'

Mandy looked across to the main graveyard, where a group of school children wearing little high-vis vests was pressing pieces of paper against the gravestones, and rubbing over them with crayon. Emily wondered if she was remembering Andy's childhood.

'I just wish I knew what happened to him,' she said sadly. 'They said it might be suicide, but I hate to think of Andy being that unhappy before he died.'

'Actually, I wanted to ask you about that,' Emily said, carefully. She looked down at Andy, who nodded. 'I'm absolutely certain Andy didn't kill himself. He seemed fine the last time I saw him, and I think he'd have told me if he was feeling low. I imagine he spent his last morning happily eating Coco Pops and listening to Magic FM as usual.'

Mandy reached over and squeezed Emily's hand, smiling gratefully. A tear slid down her cheek, and Emily squeezed back. 'But it's strange that there are so few details about what *did* happen, so I'm looking into it, to see if I can find out. And I wondered if you knew anything more than what they said in the papers. If you don't mind me asking, that is.'

'Truth be told, love, I'm not sure what I'm allowed to tell you,' Mandy said.

'What do you mean?' Emily and Andy said in unison.

Mandy looked over her shoulder, scanning the graveyard, before lowering her voice. 'Well, he didn't leave a note or anything. Not one that they found, anyway. And like you said, I just can't imagine him doing something like that on purpose. Although it's lovely to hear from someone else who was close to him who thinks that too. But something odd did happen about a week or so after he died. A man came to the house. He said he was from the Criminal Injuries Board, and that because no one knew how Andy had died, me and his dad were owed some money.' Mandy swallowed and smoothed down her skirt.

'I told him outright that I wasn't interested in money. How can money help in a situation like that? But he kept saying we could use it to honour Andy's memory, give it to a charity he supported if we didn't want it, that kind of thing. He was very persuasive, so we both signed some papers, and he gave us ten thousand pounds. Such a lot of money.'

Emily and Andy glanced at each other. 'What did the papers say?' Emily said gently.

'I'm not sure, to be honest. I was such a mess at the time. But he said I wasn't allowed to talk to anybody about what had happened. That they'd come and take the money back if I did, and even remove any memorials I'd bought with it. So I really shouldn't be saying any of this,' Mandy added, casting another nervous look over her shoulder. 'Although I haven't seen hide nor hair of the man who came to see us since I signed those papers.'

'Do you think you still have copies?' Emily asked hopefully.

'Goodness, I don't know. Sandy deals with all that, but he'll have put them away somewhere safe if we do. I used the money to buy Andy his memorial,' Mandy said, gesturing at the elaborate stone. 'And we gave some money to Cats Protection. He always loved Dandy the most. More than his old mum and dad, even.'

Andy shook his head. He looked like he was trying not to cry. Emily squeezed Mandy's hand again. 'I know he loved you very much, Mandy. Even more than Dandy. So don't think like that, OK?'

Mandy gave her a watery smile, then seemed to hesitate. 'This might sound odd, but would you mind if I took your phone number, love? I promise not to bug you or try to befriend you – I'm not that old and daft. But it would be nice to be able to text every now and then, when I miss him the most. His Facebook friends have all got such odd names – Vaseline this and Fistibobs that – I'm not brave enough to ask them if they'd like to talk about him, although I enjoy reading about their memories.'

'Of course,' Emily said, feeling tears pricking the backs of her eyes. 'Here, give me your phone and I'll put my number in.'

Her fingers flew across the keypad of Andy's mum's old iPhone, which had a thick crack across its screen, then she rang the number she'd typed in. She held up her phone as it lit up.

'There you go. Now I've got yours too.'

Chapter 17

'That was so weird,' Andy said, as they walked slowly back to the Tube. 'What do you think all that was about?'

'No idea,' Emily said, pulling her phone out of her bag and pressing it to her ear so she wouldn't look like she was talking to herself. 'But it looks like I was wrong about our trip to the graveyard being pointless, even if we've been left with more questions than answers.'

'Why would the Criminal Injuries Board offer Mum compensation when the coroner recorded an open verdict?'

'That's the thing,' Emily said, pausing at some traffic lights. 'There was nothing to say a crime had been committed. Plus I'm pretty certain that when you *are* the victim of a crime, they don't just rock up at your house with a bundle of paperwork, tell you to keep schtum, and write you a cheque.' A man standing next to her at the lights gave her a suspicious look, and Emily smiled at him.

'There's obviously more to this than meets the eye. Shall we get home and think about what to do next? I'll dig out some cans for you to karate-chop if you like.'

'Can we make a super-quick stop-off first?' Andy said. 'It's on the way home. Kind of. And there's something I really want to try . . .'

'Really?' Emily said, looking up at the darkening sky to the tip of The Shard, which at its highest point was wreathed in clouds.

'Come on, I have to give it a go,' Andy said, jumping on the spot as if he was warming up for a hundred-metre sprint. 'It'll be like base jumping, only without the parachute.'

'Oh, Christ,' Emily said, shaking her head. Even looking up that high made her feel a bit dizzy. 'Can't you start small and work your way up? Like . . . jumping off a post box? Or a small balcony? I'm not sure testing the theory that you can't die twice is the best idea. What if you go splat?'

'Again?' Andy deadpanned.

'Sorry,' Emily said, grimacing. 'I still need to get the hang of Undead Etiquette. I'm pretty sure *Debrett's* doesn't cover this kind of stuff.'

'Don't worry, I'll be fine. I'll jump out of that window,' he said, pointing to the very top of the tower, where the last vestiges of the sunset were reflected and multiplied in the building's hundreds of windows. 'And you stay down here and see what happens.'

'What if what happens is that you're crushed into a disgusting, ghostly pulp?' Emily asked, looking at the glass glinting 300 metres above their heads. 'We've established that you can sit down and rest your legs on the arm of my good chair – so what if your subconscious decides that the natural thing to do, upon leaping out of a very tall building, is to explode into a million pieces?'

'I guess we'll find out,' Andy said, running excitedly towards the glass entrance like it contained free hotdogs, shouting, 'Promise you'll watch me?' over his shoulder.

'Yes, I'm watching,' Emily called after him. Although when it came to it, she chickened out at the last minute. When she spotted Andy's silvery figure plummeting towards the earth, she kept her eyes firmly shut, until she felt a tap on her shoulder.

'It worked!' Andy shouted, pointing into the sky. 'I just walked through one of the windows, and boom! I landed at the bottom!'

'What do you mean, you walked through the window? I thought you were too scared to try walking through things?'

'I know, but none of the windows were open, so I plucked up the courage. Which means I can probably walk through doors, too.'

Emily thought of the protection doors had offered from being followed everywhere by Andy up until now and sighed.

'Watch me do it this time,' Andy said sternly.

'OK,' Emily nodded. Even now he was dead, Andy's infectious enthusiasm was leading her down paths which didn't constitute mature adult behaviour in anyone's book, least of all New Emily's.

This time, after Andy ran into The Shard, Emily carried on watching until she saw him plummeting from the sky like a dart, before landing next to her, his feet hovering an inch from the ground.

'Bloody hell, that is pretty impressive,' she whistled. A man who was talking angrily into his phone about stock portfolios shot her a confused look.

'It's weird – I don't get that rushing feeling in my stomach like I did whenever I jumped off stuff before I died.' Andy laughed. 'It's like, because I haven't got a stomach, it can't go whoosh. But it's still fun.'

Trying to grab Emily in a bear hug, Andy's arms flew through her body. She felt a strange sensation, like she was being dipped in treacle. She caught a faint whiff of Andy's old scent, and her body was instantly covered in goosebumps.

'Eww, that felt weird.' Andy frowned. 'It was like being sucked into quicksand. Brr.'

'I agree. Let's not do that again,' Emily said, rubbing her arms. Even though she was wearing her winter coat, hanging out with Andy was like having her own personal snow flurry following her around.

After that, Andy made Emily wait for him while he rushed to the top of the building over and over, plummeting back down to the ground a different way each time, landing on his back with his arms tucked nonchalantly behind his head, or in a crouch with his fist on the floor in a superhero landing.

Feeling like a parent in the playground waiting for her toddler to get bored of the swings, she began scrolling through her phone. Zoe had texted, asking how the presentation had gone, and Emily was sorely tempted to reply with an uncensored version of how her day was panning out.

Emily: Today has been great, although I'm not sure what my favourite bit has been: landing the Cat's Miaow pitch, bunking off work and meeting my dead ex's mum, or watching Andy's ghost jumping off The Shard, pretending to be Thor . . .

If she sent that, she risked Zoe thinking she'd finally snapped after skipping too many meals. So instead, she tapped out a reply that focused on the thing that, on a normal day, would have been her biggest news by miles.

Today was AMAZING, actually. I landed the Cat's Miaow pitch!

That's incredible! Congratulations!

IK, R? The force is strong in this one . . .

Did you impress Oliver and his gorgeous buns in the process?

Pretty sure I did. Although I also pronounced his name wrong

Hopefully he was too busy looking at your tits to notice. I'm on my way home, but I'll call you when I get there to get ALL the gossip xxx

What, like an actual phone call? Is it the 90s again?

That's how serious I am about the gossip. Nuff said

A few times, as she watched out for Andy in between swiping through TikTok videos, passers-by hovered next to her.

They'd look up at the spot she was squinting at, before they got bored of staring at thin air and wandered off.

At one point, a woman pushing a pram looked from Emily to the building as she watched Andy falling through the sky. The woman seemed baffled as to why she was following empty space with her eyes before letting out a cheer and clapping when Andy landed in a ballet pirouette beside her.

The woman's toddler thought differently, though, and burst into happy giggles when Andy hit the ground.

'He can see me!' Andy laughed, delighted. 'Amazing!'

As he played peek-a-boo with the gurgling baby, Emily couldn't help laughing too, until the baby's mother got freaked out, and hurried the pram away.

'Can we go home now?' Emily pleaded, as Andy plummeted to the ground for the umpteenth time. 'Today has really put me off being a parent. It's boring watching other people having fun.'

'Then can we try to knock stuff over?' he asked.

'I don't know, Andy, I'm knackered,' Emily groaned. 'And I don't want to look totally shagged out in front of Oliver tomorrow.' She grimaced as she realised what she'd said.

'That's the second time you've mentioned this Oliver,' Andy said, frowning. 'Is this someone you're interested in?'

'Well . . . if I'm honest, yes. Yes, he is,' Emily said in a rush. 'He's a new guy at work, and he's clever and successful and smells of Mini Eggs. And . . . and you died, didn't you? So there's nothing wrong with looking for someone new.'

'Then why are you blushing?' Andy said, looking crestfallen.

'Because it's not often you have to justify moving on with someone new to the ex you thought had ghosted you, but turned out to be dead, is it? The fact that you never see the person again after either of those things is kind of the point. But I'm not doing anything wrong, am I?' she added defiantly.

'I guess not,' Andy said, looking at the floor. 'But is he good enough for you? Does he make you laugh? And can he jump from tall buildings in a single bound?'

'Of course he's good enough for me. He's clever, and successful, and . . .'

'Yes, you mentioned those things already. But those are the things New Emily would look for in a bloke. Not the real Emily.'

'Maybe you don't know as much about me as you think,' Emily said hotly. She was fed up with people criticising her attempts to better herself and improve her future, and she could definitely do without it coming from Andy. 'I've moved on. And you need to as well. Which is why we're trying to find out how you died, isn't it? Or am I missing the point?'

'I see,' Andy said sulkily. 'You don't really want to help me. You just want me out of the way so you can woo this Oliver twat.'

'Don't twist things,' Emily snapped. 'He's not a twat, he's really nice. You don't know anything about it, OK?' They both jumped as Emily's phone rang in her hand. 'This is Zoe,' she said. 'I'm going to take this call and have a nice conversation that doesn't involve dead people. Now you've discovered you can walk through walls, why don't you make your own way home and let yourself in?'

'Fine,' Andy said, and turned towards the Tube.

'Good,' Emily shouted towards his retreating back, determined to get the last word in. She watched him carefully avoiding walking through the city workers that crowded the pavement, feeling her heart sinking in her chest. Andy was her ex, and a ghostly one, at that. She shouldn't have to worry about his feelings any more. So why did she feel so bad about upsetting him?

She shook her head in frustration, and perched on the edge of an uncomfortable-looking bench, which seemed to be trying to be a modernist sculpture as well as somewhere to sit.

'Gossip hotline, how may I help you today?' Emily said, grinning as she answered. Then felt her throat tightening with panic as she realised that Zoe was sobbing.

Chapter 18

'Oh god, Zoe, what's happened? Are you OK? Where are you?' Emily stuttered, pressing the phone hard against her ear, as though that might make her answer more quickly.

'I'm fine,' Zoe said, struggling to push her words out between tears. 'I don't want to talk about it on the phone. But can I come to yours and stay the night?'

'Hey, of course you can,' Emily said, feeling sick. 'I'm not home yet, but I'll order you a cab and see you there. Hang tight, you'll be at mine soon. Are you sure you're OK?'

'I'm fine, I promise, I just need to get away from my flat.'

'Stay right there and I'll see you soon.' Emily hung up and called a cab, her fingers trembling as she pressed the buttons, her mind turning over all the reasons Zoe might be so upset. She'd never cried easily, so whatever had happened, it had obviously shaken her up badly.

Running to the Tube and down to the platform that would take her home, she cursed the fact that Andy, being dead, didn't have a mobile phone. She should get back home before

Zoe arrived, but if not, she wouldn't have time to warn him to stay away while they talked.

On the train, she tapped her feet and drummed her fingers on the arm of her seat, urging it to move faster. The doors seemed to be opening and closing more agonisingly slowly than usual, every announcement from the driver asking people to 'move right down inside the carriages' feeling like it took forever, while her mind flicked through the possibilities of what might have upset her best friend.

Had something happened to one of her parents? They were incredibly close, and if one of them got ill – or, god forbid, died – Zoe would be inconsolable. Was *she* the one who was ill? Or had something happened at work? Could a client have hurt her in some way? Emily swallowed hard, trying not to panic.

Out of the Tube, she raced back to her flat, relieved that Zoe wasn't yet sitting perched on her front step, waiting to be let inside. She sent her a quick text.

Home now, ready and waiting x

Traffic is shit. Be there soon

When she opened the front door, she nearly crashed into – or rather through – Andy, who had a look of pure concentration on his face as he stabbed his finger at the light switch.

'Budge up,' she said. Andy stepped aside, and she flicked it on. 'We'll have to leave a light on for you next time,' she added.

Andy silently moved over to his armchair and sat down, swinging his legs over the arms.

'Look, I'm sorry I snapped at you,' she said, as she did a

circuit of the room, turning on the rest of the lights. 'And I know this must be weird, seeing me moving on when the last thing you remember is us being together.' Andy nodded and looked at the floor. 'But this isn't your usual relationship dilemma, so you're going to have to give me time to work out how to do this right. I can't exactly hit Reddit and ask for advice, can I?'

''Spose,' Andy muttered.

'And we don't have time to talk about it now, because Zoe's just called. She's really upset, and she's coming over, so I'm going to need you to scram for the evening.'

Andy frowned and swung his legs off the arm of the chair. 'Is she OK? What happened?'

'I don't know yet,' Emily said, rubbing her face. 'But Zoe never cries, so I need to focus on her, and I don't need any distractions. I'll find some Nirvana videos for you to watch in my room so you've got something to do, if you like.'

'I'd tell you to send her my love, but ... Well, you know,' Andy said, as Emily ushered him into the bedroom and set up her laptop, before firmly shutting the door behind him. While she waited for Zoe to arrive, she poured two glasses of wine, drank half of her own, then topped it back up again, her stomach churning with nerves until the doorbell rang.

'Hey, you,' she said, hugging Zoe tightly as she opened the door. Her face was covered in black rivulets of mascara, and her eyeliner had smudged where she'd rubbed her eyes. Holding one end of Zoe's jacket and letting her spin out of it, Emily hung it on her coat rack, ushered her into the front room and onto the sofa, and thrust a drink into her hand.

'What on earth happened?' she asked gently, holding Zoe's

free hand. It was freezing, and trembled even as she held it tight. 'You can tell me.'

Zoe paused. 'We … we were burgled,' she blurted, fresh tears springing from her eyes, which ran down to the end of her nose.

'Burgled?' Emily said, pressing her hands to her hot cheeks, her body turning to jelly as relief flooded through her. A burglary wasn't half as terrible as the scenarios she'd been imagining. Taking a gulp of wine, she reached over, plucked two tissues from the box on her coffee table, and handed them to Zoe. 'Oh, that's … that's terrible,' she said, trying not to sound too relieved.

'It was really bad,' Zoe said, sniffing hard. 'When I got home from work, the door had been forced open and someone had broken in. They'd rummaged through all my stuff and taken some bits from the others' rooms.

'They nicked the landlord's TV and stereo, too, which I just know he's going to make us pay to replace, even though they're probably worth about a fiver. But worst of all, I don't feel safe in my own home any more.' Zoe shuddered, before sniffing loudly and swiping at her nose with the sleeve of her cardigan.

'Did you lose anything?' Emily asked.

'They didn't take anything of mine, I don't think,' Zoe said, and Emily relaxed even more. A burglary where you didn't lose anything was much less awful than losing a parent. Or a boyfriend. 'I guess I haven't got anything worth taking except my hairdressing kit, which I had on me, thank god. But they nicked Scott's laptop and Mark's DJ deck and gold jewellery. It's lucky I never take this off.' Zoe fingered the thin gold necklace her dad had given her for her twenty-first birthday.

'Well, that's good, then, isn't it?' Emily said, letting go of Zoe's hand and snuggling back into the sofa cushions. 'You're a bit shaken up now, but you'll be fine. And it'll be a great story to tell back home one day.'

Zoe frowned. 'OK, but I'm not fine yet, am I? And I don't think I'll ever see this as a funny story to tell down the pub. It was horrible. And if you still lived in the flat with us you'd be just as upset as I am.'

Emily fingered the edge of one of her cushions. Zoe was right, she *would* be upset – but at the same time, things could be so much worse. Emily half-wished her only problem right now was a burglary.

'And also, can I just get a bit of sympathy for now, please?' Zoe continued. 'My home got broken into. Someone went through my stuff. I'm the one who found out what had happened, and no one else was home. I had to look inside to make sure no one was still there, which was really scary.

'Then I had to call the police on my own, and call the others to break the news. Bethany went nuts in case they'd moved her stuff and ruined the feng shui of her room. And all this after another poxy day spent trying to persuade a load of horrible customers to part with five measly quid for a haircut.' Zoe's lower lip wobbled alarmingly as she tried hard not to cry again.

'You know, you don't *have* to cut hair for a fiver,' Emily said. 'I know someone at Charles Worthington who—' Zoe shot her a murderous look, and Emily shut her mouth.

'Wow, are you competing in the sympathy Olympics or something?' Andy said, from behind the sofa. Emily hadn't noticed him creeping through the bedroom door – literally through it, she supposed, seeing as it was firmly shut – to listen in on their conversation. 'Because you wouldn't even get bronze for that shoddy performance.'

He started slow clapping, and Emily glared back, hoping Zoe wouldn't notice her glowering into thin air.

'Oh, hi,' Zoe said, turning towards Andy with a grateful smile. 'Emily, you should have told me you had company. I'm Zoe, nice to meet you.'

Chapter 19

'She can see me!' Andy said delightedly, grinning at Emily and giving her a double thumbs-up before turning his attention back to Zoe. 'Awesome! Hiya, nice to meet you too.' He took a step forward and raised a hand in greeting.

'Am I not . . . supposed to see you?' Zoe smiled, wiggling her fingers back at Andy.

'It's an in-joke, just ignore him,' Emily said quickly. She felt the back of her neck prickling.

Zoe could see Andy. But how was that even possible? Maybe it was an effect of being inside her flat – or perhaps anyone who had used the Ouija board the night of her party could see him? Which would presumably mean Jada and Simon would be able to see him too. She'd have to remember not to let him follow her to work.

Her heart pounding in her ears, she wondered what she should do next. She usually told Zoe absolutely everything – except when it came to Andy. She hadn't told Zoe how much she'd actually cared for him when he was alive, and had behaved like it was just another piece of gossip when she'd found out he was dead.

And now, something was stopping her from telling the truth about him being a ghost. Andy's secret was something that was just his and hers, and she wanted to keep it that way a little longer.

Plus Zoe's still getting over the burglary, Emily told herself. *I don't want to upset her even more, do I? It's for her own good that she doesn't find out.*

Panicking, her eyes darted around the room as she formulated a plan. She'd always felt a bit guilty for keeping Andy away from Zoe, as she'd been so keen to meet him when he was alive, somehow seeing him as a good influence on Emily. But now, she was glad they'd never met.

If Emily could get Andy back into the bedroom – through the door the normal way, this time – before Zoe realised he was a bit see-through, she might get away with pretending he was someone else. Although it didn't help that he was standing near the corner lamp by her bookshelf, which Emily could see glowing through his left ear.

'Would you mind giving us a few more minutes, please? Girl talk, you know,' she said pointedly, carefully walking around Andy as if he were solid, quickly switching off the lamp, and opening the bedroom door.

Andy grinned a grin that said he wasn't done with having fun yet, and Emily shot him a pleading look.

'You're not going to let me talk to your friend?' Andy asked, looking hurt. 'That's not very nice, is it? Especially after she sounds like she's had a pretty crappy day, Miss Sympathy UK.'

Zoe snorted. 'What's your name then?' she asked, sticking her hand towards Andy over the back of the sofa.

'Oh, he can't shake hands right now, can you … Ben?' Emily said, desperately, leaping from the bedroom door and placing herself between Andy's body and Zoe's outstretched hand. She glared at Andy, mouthing at him to go away.

'He's been a bit under the weather lately. Not himself. Terrible cough. So he's been avoiding unnecessary physical contact, just in case. Haven't you, Ben?'

'I might have a new variant of Covid,' Andy nodded, letting out a fake cough. 'Don't want to be spreading that about, do I?'

'Thanks for the warning. I can't afford to get ill, especially when I don't get sick pay and might have to buy a new telly,' Zoe said, retracting her hand and peering round Emily at Andy. 'So how do you know each other? Is this …' With all the subtlety of a sledgehammer, Zoe stuck her tongue in her cheek and mimed a blow job.

'Oh god, no!' Emily yelped. 'This is …'

'Andy's brother,' Andy said, beaming like his face might burst. He was enjoying this way too much for Emily's liking. 'You remember Andy? The handsome guy Emily was going out with before he tragically died without her even knowing?'

'Oh god, I'm so sorry for your loss, Ben,' Zoe said sincerely, standing up. 'It must have been an awful shock. We've only just found out.'

'Yeah, Emily told me about that,' Andy said, gravely. 'I must say, I was quite surprised that my own brother's girlfriend – who he couldn't stop praising to high heaven – didn't even know he was dead until now. It's a bit shocking, to tell the truth.'

Emily turned pink and gritted her teeth as Zoe started making her way towards Andy. She was a prolific hugger and had such a soft heart that there was a good chance sympathy might get the better of her, virus or no virus. And if her arms went straight through him, Emily worried she might have a stroke on the spot.

'Don't get up,' she said hastily, gently steering Zoe back to the sofa and placing her glass of wine back in her hand – which, thanks to Andy's presence, was cooler now than when it had been poured. 'You've suffered a shock. You need to stay sitting down.'

'Shock?' Zoe said, archly. 'I thought I was supposed to be grateful for the fantastic story having my stuff ransacked would provide me with? Miss Sympathy UK ...' Zoe and Andy exchanged amused glances, which made Emily's heart thud painfully in her chest. Whether it was teenage sleepovers or in-jokes, she hated being excluded from anything. And this felt even more personal.

'Yeah, sorry to hear about your burglary,' Andy said, leaning against the wall opposite the sofa. Emily was relieved to see that against the white paint, he looked entirely solid, and she felt relaxed enough to finally sit down next to Zoe. 'It happened to me once, and it was awful. They took Banksy, my favourite guitar. And it felt really weird knowing someone might have been rummaging around in my pants.'

'No one would have rummaged through your pants, trust me,' Emily said, without thinking. 'They have a special aura all of their own which would put off even the most single-minded burglar.'

Andy laughed, and Zoe shot Emily a confused look, before shaking her head to blink away the tears that threatened to emerge again. 'Maybe I should have expected to be burgled eventually, seeing as I live in a dodgy bit of London. But I just can't seem to get used to it. Although Greenleaf had its fair share of shady characters, no one ever burgled the flats.

'Apart from the fact that we had nothing to steal, there were always too many people milling about at all hours for outsiders to get away with a burglary. And there was an unspoken rule that you didn't target your own. Apparently, word hasn't spread as far as Hackney that robbing your neighbours is arsehole behaviour,' Zoe added, wiping her nose with the palm of her hand. 'Oh, shit, sorry. I'm not supposed to talk about Emily's past,' she said, glancing guiltily at her friend. 'It's one of the Forbidden Subjects, along with losing her virginity to Martin Baker in the janitor's cupboard at school, and the time she had to be cut out of a skirt in Topshop when the zip got stuck and everyone saw her pants.'

Andy burst out laughing, and Zoe sipped her wine. 'Oops,' she said, not sounding very sorry at all, and Emily had to concede she kind of deserved it.

'We might need to discuss those other stories later, because they sound amazing,' he said, raising his eyebrows at Emily. 'But Andy did tell me about Greenleaf, actually – that was the estate where you guys grew up, right?'

Zoe nodded in surprise. 'You told Andy about Greenleaf?' she asked Emily. 'Blimey, he must have been special.'

Emily pulled the cushion she was fiddling with into her lap, and Andy grinned delightedly.

'You do look a lot like him, actually,' Zoe told him. 'Although I've only ever seen him in photos. And his face was usually covered by an enormous taco, or he'd be pulling a face onstage. Emily likes to keep her past and present lives separate, don't you?'

'Apparently not any more,' Emily said, giving up trying to stop Andy from talking and taking a large gulp of wine.

'Well, as far as I'm concerned, it doesn't matter whether you live on an iffy estate or Buckingham Palace, getting burgled still sucks,' Andy said. 'I'm sure losing the family silver is as annoying as the thirty-two-inch TV getting pinched. But you'll be OK, honestly. When we got burgled, we got some money back on our insurance, and used it to throw an absolutely epic party. They never caught the burglars, but three people at the party managed to get arrested. Someone nearly *died.* It was amazing. Every cloud has a silver lining, so try not to let it get you down, OK?'

'Thanks, Ben,' Zoe said, looking up, a smile lighting up her face.

'Isn't it time you headed off, Ben? You've got an early start tomorrow, right?' Emily said, pointedly.

'Umm yeah, sure,' Andy said. 'I didn't bring a jacket, did I?'

'No, you did not,' Emily said, trying to keep her voice calm. Suddenly, she really wanted him out of the flat, even if that meant him going out into the hall and walking through the wall into her bedroom.

'You'll catch your death in that T-shirt,' Zoe said. 'And … why is it so dusty?'

'Goodbye, Ben,' Emily said firmly, opening the front door to let Andy out.

'It was nice to meet you, Zoe,' Andy said, over Emily's shoulder.

'You too, Ben,' she grinned. 'Thanks for the advice.'

'Safe journey home, *Ben*,' Emily said, and firmly shut the door in his face.

'Blimey. You kept him quiet,' Zoe said, waggling her eyebrows, as Emily slumped against the closed front door. 'Is he like a better-looking version of Andy? Because you always said he wasn't really your type, but Ben is cute as a button. As cute as *loads* of buttons, in fact. With bunnies on them.'

'You seem to have perked up,' Emily said, falling onto the sofa next to Zoe. 'He does look quite a bit like him, I suppose,' she added, frowning at the door Andy had just walked through. Because Andy was so ... *Andy*, she'd never really considered that other women might have found him attractive, but Zoe had apparently taken an immediate shine to him. 'So no, he's not really my type. My type is *Oliver*.' She said it firmly, but sounded unsure even to herself.

'In that case, can I have a crack at him?' Zoe said.

'Can you have a crack at my dead ex's brother? No, you can't, you cheeky bugger. Look, I'm sorry I wasn't more sympathetic about the burglary. It must have been horrible. I guess I was thinking it was something *really* awful, that's all.'

'The thing is, I'm not like you – I'm not interested in gathering all these exciting stories about living in London,' Zoe said, carefully sipping her wine. 'I wasn't even that bothered about moving here in the first place, remember? The main draw was us getting to live together ...'

'And maybe bumping into Tom Hardy and persuading him to shag you,' Emily added.

'Yes, and that, obviously. But our flatshare only lasted five minutes before you buggered off to get your own place and cover it in beige cushions. And I'm not ambitious like you, Em. I just want to be happy – whether that means living in a big city, or cutting hair for people at Greenleaf for a pittance. And after the burglary, I just don't feel safe here any more.'

Emily felt goosebumps creeping up her neck, and covered her panic by sipping her wine. She remembered how excited Zoe had been when she'd started her hairdressing course back in Essex. Her parents had been so proud, they hadn't hesitated to open up their flat to a stream of Greenleaf residents, who were happy to be Zoe's guinea pigs.

As the people leaving their hair-strewn kitchen gradually started looking less like they'd had a fight with a lawn mower and more like they'd stepped out of a proper salon, Zoe had begun talking excitedly about the small hairdressing shop she planned to open up. She wanted to stay close to Greenleaf, cutting familiar heads of hair and adjusting her prices depending on how flush her customers were.

Emily had known that was Zoe's dream. But she was also sure that, given the right encouragement, she had the talent to dream bigger. Plus her feet had been itchy enough for the both of them. Desperate to shake off the stain of Greenleaf, she'd painted a picture of their life together in London that Zoe hadn't been able to resist.

Emily's dearest wish was to be the kind of movie heroine who returns to her small, backwater town, and struggles to fit in because she's become so high-powered and glamorous – only without the cheesy ending where she falls in love with a local hick and decides to stay. She couldn't imagine achieving her dream without her best friend by her side. And although Zoe didn't realise it yet, London was the place to be if she wanted to find the happy ending she deserved.

She reached over and linked her little finger with Zoe's. 'You're shaken up now, but you'll feel so much better in a few days' time,' she said, trying to sound enthusiastic. 'There's so much opportunity here. You can get the job of your dreams, a fantastic man. And when you can afford it, I'll help you find your own flat near me. The sky's the limit, honestly.'

'But what if I don't want the sky? What if . . . what if I want to go back to Essex?' Zoe said, in a small voice.

They both looked up at the ceiling as the lights flickered. Emily glanced at her closed bedroom door. Was Andy listening into their conversation? If so, he'd probably side with Zoe – but he didn't know the full story. He tried his hardest to understand her, but he'd always had loads of friends to turn to, and parents who clearly loved him dearly.

How could he imagine what her life had been like, with a missing dad, a mum who made her feel like he'd left because of her, and school friends who treated her like a social pariah? Zoe was the only person who knew what she'd been through, and who knew and loved the real her. So Zoe couldn't go home. Not now, when the future Emily had envisioned for them both was starting to come to fruition at last.

'Don't be daft,' Emily said, forcing a light-hearted laugh. 'Nobody moves from London back to their hometown, until they're married with kids and need Granny to babysit. There's so much more than that ahead of us. And I promise, everything's going to be just fine.'

She pretended not to notice when Zoe uncurled her little finger from hers, and reached for the empty bottle of wine.

Chapter 20

Ravenwood High School, Year Eleven

Zoe was standing just outside the school gates, cheerfully smoking her fifth Mayfair Light of the day about an inch beyond the headmaster's jurisdiction, when Emily practically leaped on top of her with excitement.

'Hey, Zoe. Have you heard? Amanda's having a party on Saturday and Craig's going to be there. Do you reckon that means we'll get an invite?'

Zoe shrugged, blowing wonky smoke rings into the autumn air. Wedging the cigarette in the corner of her mouth and grabbing the top of Emily's strappy satin top, she tugged it upwards to prevent her friend's braless boobs from flopping out.

'I doubt it, Emily, so don't get your hopes up,' she muttered around her cigarette. 'Craig's gone to the Other Side. It doesn't mean everyone from Greenleaf has suddenly become socially acceptable.'

Picking up a tatty purple rucksack from where it rested

between her feet, Zoe shrugged it over the shoulder of her new denim jacket. She'd got it from Topshop instead of the local market, after saving every penny from her Saturday job for months. Her new prized possession, she'd already vowed to wear it until it literally fell apart.

Arm in arm, Emily and Zoe headed towards Greenleaf. As small children, they'd always been happy there, playing together on the monkey bars and swings set that had been cobbled together on a small patch of bouncy tarmac in the middle of the estate. It always felt to Emily like they were being cradled safely in the palm of a giant hand, its long fingers made from concrete and steel.

Back then, they didn't know that thanks to the casual cruelty of schoolchildren, being from Greenleaf was like having a plague cross painted on your forehead, which only other people could see.

It was this invisible stain that had thrown Zoe and Emily together at Cherrywood Primary School. On their first day, the teacher had asked everyone to share where they lived with the class. Then later, when they were told to pair up and find a partner in assembly, Zoe and Emily had found themselves standing alone together, a subtle circle of empty space left around them. Emily hoped, later on, that the teacher had been naive rather than cruel. But either way, from then on, no one wanted to pair up with the girls from Greenleaf.

Even the boy who somehow always had snot running down his upper lip had someone to partner with. Although admittedly, she was gingerly gripping his hand with just two fingers.

At seven years old, Emily and Zoe didn't understand why no one wanted to play with them – it was just the way things were. But, forced together, they developed an unshakeable bond. They giggled through that first assembly and every assembly after it, their wild hair tangling as they pressed their heads against each other's over childish secrets.

But as they got older, they realised that to anyone who lived outside Greenleaf, the estate stood for nothing but trouble. Even the teachers used it as a sort of careless shorthand for inescapable failure.

'I can't get Craig from 10b to behave. He's a total toe-rag. Any tips?'

'Well, he is *from Greenleaf, so . . .'*

When they graduated from primary school to the larger high school, which had more Greenleaf kids in each class, the social division between them and everyone else grew even starker. It was no surprise that most of them behaved exactly as everyone expected, kicking off in classes and not-so-subtly dealing weed in the playground.

But, somehow, Craig Robinson had managed to wipe away the mark that set him apart. Of course, it helped that he was gorgeous. When he'd hit sixteen, he'd blossomed, his burgeoning good looks so apparent that even the female teachers had been spotted looking awkward when he explained, with great sincerity in his newly broken and gravelly voice, why he hadn't done his homework.

It meant that the kids on the Other Side – the ones who had spent the previous nine years of their lives treating him like chewing gum on their shoes that they had to reluctantly put up with – had suddenly welcomed him and his movie-star looks into their gang.

And Emily was desperate to join them. She'd tried everything to try to fit in, to no avail. If she saved her money to buy the same coat as the coolest kid in their year, she'd be laughed at for wearing it the wrong way. When she tried to join clubs in an attempt to find her niche, she found herself shut out of the cliques that naturally formed inside them.

She'd been known as 'Spotty Blotty' since she was eleven, and it had been impossible to see how she could change that while she still lived on Greenleaf. But now, there was a tiny glimmer of hope.

'But if Craig's been let in, maybe he can get us in, too?' Emily said, the excitement making her voice go squeaky. 'You know, like in POW camps when they help each other over the wall.'

'I hate to break it to you, Emily, but he looks like a young Brad Pitt. And you don't look anything like Jennifer Aniston, which you'd have to to get invited to one of Kirstie's parties. And only then if one of the boys fancied you. It's so completely obvious that Kirstie has the hots for him.'

'Come on, don't be so cynical. We must have a bit of a shot? Even just a teeny one? I bet Kirsty's house is amazing. All the places on her road are huge. And I reckon it definitely doesn't smell of fucking mildew.' Emily sniffed the arm of her jumper, which had the musty tang of clothes dried over the back of a chair because her mum couldn't afford the launderette and refused to turn on the heating simply to dry a load of washing.

Zoe sighed. 'I don't know why you want to hang out with those snobby bitches anyway. They've treated us like dirt for years. Why would you even want to be in their gang of twats? When you're born Greenleaf, you're Greenleaf for life.'

Being Greenleaf for life had, once upon a time, been the dream. Blissfully unaware of how precarious life on the estate really was, the kids who lived there felt sorry for anyone who lived outside it. They weren't allowed to play in their local parks alone unless they were being watched like a hawk by their parents, and what kind of fun was that?

Living on Greenleaf meant you had an entire estate to explore. If any kid dared set foot outside that perimeter, a barrage of warning shouts and the odd expletive would spill out from behind the orange glow of a cigarette on one of the balconies. It was the job of every adult on the estate to look out for its kids.

Zoe and Emily felt completely safe there, and never noticed their parents living hand to mouth to feed them, or their anxious eyes scanning the estate's tiny playground for used needles before they were allowed to play.

It was only as they'd got older that they'd started assessing the estate through an adult's eyes – although what Zoe and Emily each saw was very different. Zoe's parents were still together, their cramped but cosy flat reflecting years of happy, messy and complicated, but loving family life.

They were close with dozens of other Greenleaf families, and spent most of their summers sitting outside on fold-out chairs, chatting, drinking and barbecuing. Frozen sausages and burgers bought by everyone chipping in for a big shop would sizzle on a barbecue Zoe's dad would have knocked together from an abandoned shopping trolley, the condiments stored in the baby seat and metal tongs hanging off the handle.

For Zoe, Greenleaf was the place she'd laughed the most in her life, even if much of that laughter had been provided by her friendship with Emily. It was where her family and friends lived, and felt like home – a safe refuge, despite all its flaws.

Emily, meanwhile, had grown to despise it. She wasn't surprised in the slightest that her dad had done a vanishing act. Greenleaf was a place where hope went to die, and nobody who lived there was going to amount to anything. His abandonment of her just proved it. He'd obviously moved on to bigger and better things. Things that were better than *her*.

She didn't blame him for leaving, even if her mum did, loudly and daily. And she didn't blame the kids at school for keeping as far away as possible from the Greenleaf lot. Because if she'd had any choice at all, she'd be far away from them too.

'I don't want to be Greenleaf for life,' Emily said firmly, stealing Zoe's cigarette from her mouth and taking a drag. 'Why can't I have what Kirsty's got? Just because her bloody dad works in bloody London and she's been to bloody Disney World, she's not got unicorns coming out of her arse. If Craig can get us into their gang, then you don't know what might happen. Getting ahead is all about networking and contacts, you know. And that goes for school, as well as afterwards. Probably.'

'You read that in *Bijou*, didn't you?' Zoe muttered, as they reached the edge of the estate and sat on their smoking bench. Throwing her dwindling cigarette into the yellowing grass at their feet and lighting two more cigarettes at once, she handed one to Emily.

'Yeah, I did. They had a copy at the dentist's, so I pinched it. I want that kind of life, Zo, and I don't see why I shouldn't have it,' Emily said, angrily. 'I don't give a shit what Kirsty's lot has done to us in the past. They could be my ticket out of here, and I'll do anything to get it. Even if that means sucking up to her. Even if that means being forced to drink her dad's posh vodka in his nice posh house and eating free pizza. I'm prepared to make that sacrifice.'

Zoe laughed, rolling her eyes before quickly changing the subject. She tried to ignore the nagging worry she felt in the pit of her stomach, knowing that her best friend was about to be sorely disappointed. Beyond Emily's tough exterior, which she'd built around her to protect herself after her dad left, she was a lot softer than she looked, her emotions as easily bruised as a peach.

Craig's admission to the Other Side had been a fluke, a one-off. Zoe saw Emily for who she really was. She saw all her foibles and vulnerabilities, her kindness and humour. She knew about Emily's fierce ambition, her secret obsession with Agony Aunt columns, the way she ate a Twix bottom-first, like a total weirdo.

But she also had the wisdom to see how other people saw her, with her knock-off handbag and see-through, cigarette-burned strappy tops. Zoe could think Emily was wonderful and unique until her head fell off, but from the outside, she knew Emily looked like an identikit Greenleaf kid. She was never going to be accepted.

Sure enough, the next day, Zoe found herself curling an arm around Emily while she rested her head on her increasingly damp shoulder, shaking with sobs.

'I hate those bitches with their stupid shiny hair and stupid shiny shoes,' Emily wept. 'Screw all of them. And I'm sorry about the Doughy Zoe thing, Zo. I really am.'

As casually as possible, Emily had asked Kirsty during break time about her party, hoping to catch her off guard and get an invitation.

'Aww, that's so sweet,' Kirsty had said, her voice full of sugary menace. 'You think because Craig's coming we'll let any old slapper come to our party? Nice try, Spotty, but you've got a long way to go before I'd even let you serve me my McDonald's. Sorry, but you're going to have to spend your Saturday lezzing up with Doughy Zoe as usual.'

She'd shrieked with laughter, high-fiving her mates as they'd sauntered confidently towards their next class. Until that point, Zoe had escaped getting her own charming nickname by keeping her head firmly down and squashing any aspirations she might have harboured to rise up the social ladder at school. But now, they both knew she'd be saddled with the nickname Doughy Zoe for the rest of her schooldays.

'It's OK,' Zoe sighed, stroking Emily's hair with the hand that wasn't smoking. 'They've probably been calling me that behind my back for years. It's just that I don't stick my head above the parapet in the same way you do. I don't care what they think of me.'

'*I* do,' Emily said furiously, sitting up and rubbing her eyes. 'One day I'm going to get the fuck out of here and show them I'm worth way more than they think I am. And I'm not going to let my kids go through the same thing we did. They're going to have nice holidays, and posh clothes, and a dad who sticks around.'

'You're worth ten of those cowbags,' Zoe said, gently. 'And it doesn't matter what you do, to them you'll still be Emily from Greenleaf. So just forget them and try to enjoy your own life. For you, not for them.'

Emily sniffed and lit a cigarette.

'You're right. I know, you're right,' she said, rubbing her

nose with the palm of her hand. But her mind was already made up. As soon as she was old enough, she was going to leave Greenleaf, and everything that attached her to it, as far behind her as possible.

Chapter 21

From: Oliver Beauchamp
To: Emily Blott
Re: Re: Presentation

I'm still trying to figure out the office hierarchy over here, so I wondered if you could help me out? I've spent the afternoon listening to Chrissie, Marni and Claude*, and their jobs seem to involve an awful lot of talking about Ellie's inevitable weight gain (apparently she was caught eating a cinnamon pastry at lunchtime) and something called *Love or Dare*. Is this part of their official roles here?

*If anyone asks, this process is called 'onboarding'.

O.x

From: Emily Blott
To: Oliver Beauchamp
Re: Re: Presentation

It sounds like you're working very hard. I'm worried about you. But yes, I imagine all the things the Witches' Coven* was discussing were very relevant to their work, because they definitely wouldn't ever let their copywriters take up the slack and bask in the glory of success for themselves, because that would be outrageously unprofessional.

I've never seen it, but *Love or Dare* seems to be one of those shows where the women are encouraged to wear no more than 16 grams of clothing, and the men enjoy using random furniture to perform their workouts on. You're welcome.

* This is not their official name, in case Charles asks.

E.x

Love or Dare sounds like it could be extremely important research material to make sure HoRizons has its pulse on the nation's youth trends. Where does one watch such a show?*

*For research.

O.x

I wouldn't have a clue, I'm afraid*, because I'm not some massive pervert who likes watching women frolicking around wearing bikinis you could floss your teeth with.

*ITV, ITV+1, or ITV Hub.

E.x

From: Charles Worthing
To: Emily Blott
Cc: Oliver Beauchamp
Re: Presentation

Hello both, I trust you're well and enjoying the glorious smell that remains in the office a full four hours after someone microwaved haddock for their lunch. Please trust that I'm currently working on getting to the bottom of who the culprit is.

I'm sorry to be the bearer of bad news, but the Cat's Miaow team have, with their usual delightful knack for timing, asked if we can present the campaign ideas somewhat earlier – two weeks from today, in fact. It's going to be a tight squeeze to get a deck ready in time, but Emily's idea was an excellent start, and I'm sure if you put your heads together, you can knock it into suitable shape.

Let me know if you need support, but please be aware that I'm very busy avoiding all my clients' phone calls, and have very little time to spare.

Kindest regards,

Charles W.

From: Oliver Beauchamp
To: Emily Blott
Re: Re: Presentation

Was it just me whose stomach plummeted about 50 floors when Charles's email had the same heading as ours . . .? How fired out of ten would we be if he'd been copied into our emails?

Uses serious voice Regarding this new deadline, I think we need to put in some extra hours tonight seeing as we've spent all day ~~gossiping~~ onboarding.

I'm confident we can nail this – your idea is an excellent one. Personally, I think Speedy Tomato is completely unique among all cats, because he's mine. But he also completely ignores me unless I have food on me.

How about we reduce the agony by heading to Bayou Bar for drinks to talk it over?

O.x

Emily hadn't stopped grinning ever since she'd arrived at work that morning, when she'd found Oliver's first, borderline-flirty email already sitting in her inbox. After pretending for a while that they definitely didn't fancy each other, they'd been messaging back and forth all day, getting very little actual work done.

Now, her smile became even wider as she realised that what Oliver was really proposing, even if not in so many words, was a date. At least, she hoped it was. Old Emily worried that perhaps he was just a bit of an alkie, and didn't like working past 6 p.m. without several drinks inside him.

But she tried to have faith that New Emily deserved this. She'd put enough effort in, after all.

Glancing at the clock in the corner of her screen, Emily noticed it was almost 5 p.m., which meant she could start getting ready – after texting Zoe her news, of course. Not that there was much to do, seeing as she'd spent all day feverishly reading emails and coming up with witty replies instead of doing things that might have dislodged her make-up. Even her lipstick was still intact, after she'd sucked a smoothie through a straw for lunch and turned down all of Simon's offers of a cup of tea to avoid bloating.

Jada followed her into the ladies' to catch up on the gossip, which Emily had refused to divulge in front of Simon, who she had a feeling wouldn't enjoy the conversation. He'd been behaving very oddly lately.

'You've been emailing Oliver all day, haven't you?' Jada demanded, as Emily smoothed her brows into place with a tiny brush that had cost such a stupid amount of money, she'd been forced to forgo her morning coffee for a week.

'*Mayyyybe* . . .' Emily said, pretending to pluck a stray eyelash from her cheek and struggling to hide her grin. 'And maybe we're totally going to Bayou tonight to talk about "work", as well.'

'Wow. This is a difficult time for me,' Jada said, leaning against the sink and watching Emily perfecting her face. 'Firstly, I disapprove of judging a book or man by its cover, but Oliver is so objectively handsome, I'm struggling to hold onto my principles. Secondly, dating your boss is super dodgy, and could backfire horribly.' Emily grimaced at her. 'But thirdly, I know Oliver ticks all of your ridiculously shallow boxes, so I can't help being happy for you. In short, I'm worried, jealous, excited and horny, which is a lot to deal with all at once.'

'Tell me about it,' Emily said, thinking about how Andy would react if he found out Oliver had asked her on a date.

'So what's he like? I've barely said hello to him. Is he just a posh hottie, or is there more to him underneath that expensively cut suit?'

'For starters, he's *really* good at email flirting,' Emily said, adjusting the belt on her black skater dress up a notch. 'And we've developed this thing where we always put an asterisk at the end of our messages instead of a P.S., which is like our first ever in-joke.'

'Oh, cuteness.'

'And he's funny, and not just in that way where he says something a bit self-deprecating, then I feel forced to stroke his ego, then in hindsight it wasn't that funny in the first place.'

'Excellent,' Jada said, sniffing her armpit.

'And he seems really keen to give me the spotlight when it comes to the Cat's Miaow presentation, which obviously never happens, and feels a bit too good to be true. But apparently he used to work with this Mr Miyagi-type character who gave him a leg-up, and he wants to pay it forward.'

'Which could totally be legit.'

'And even if it's just a line, I don't care if it gets me closer to a spot in the Witches' Coven. There. What do you think?'

Emily did a small twirl. But as she turned back to face Jada, she felt a wave of dizziness, her ankle buckling underneath her. She grabbed the edge of the sink and leaned on it, trying to shake her head clear.

'Hey, are you OK?' Jada said, clutching her arm as she clung to the sink. Emily let out a wobbly laugh.

'Yeah, I'm fine. Stupid heels. I think the Greenleaf in me rebels every time I put them on.'

Jada raised an eyebrow at her. 'Is it really the heels, or is it the fact that you spent lunchtime mooning over Oliver instead of eating anything more filling than chewing gum and one of your revolting minus-calorie celery smoothies?'

Emily squeezed her eyes closed, trying to stop her head spinning, then opened them again. Nothing escaped Jada, who was so astute she was practically psychic. It was one of the reasons Emily had decided, when she arrived at HoRizons, to tell her the truth about her past.

At first, she'd tried to present Simon and Jada, her first-ever office deskmates, with the same polished image as the one she pushed on social media. But then one day, when they were working together on slogans for a new range of protein shakes, Emily had breezily mentioned that she hated the gym and could eat whatever she wanted.

She'd expected Jada to be impressed – but instead, she'd laughed in her face.

'Oh, no. You're not one of those flat-arsers, are you?' she'd asked.

'What?' Emily had frowned.

'They're like flat-earthers, except they pedal conspiracy theories about how easy it is to look amazing. Like, they bang on about how little effort it takes to look slim because it's all down to genetics, before going home to do five hundred push-ups and cry over a plate of kale. I know how it works. You've got the same shape as me – you're a total pear – and I know for a fact that you don't eat whatever you want. Unless all you actually want to eat are some sad little lettuce leaves.'

Emily had been so surprised by Jada's honesty, she'd burst out laughing, and hadn't seen much point in maintaining her glossy smokescreen after that. She started revealing the truth about her past to Simon and Jada, piece by piece, until they knew the whole story – and, thankfully, accepted her for who she was in a way she knew the inhabitants of the Witches' Coven never would. They firmly believed that anyone raised on a council estate had to be a workshy layabout who spent all their money on cigarettes and 'flatscreen TVs' (as if there was any other kind these days), and Emily was unlikely to be capable of opening their eyes.

'Maybe I could have eaten a bit more for lunch,' she admitted now. 'But I'll make sure I get some food at Bayou Bar, promise.'

'Do you *promise* promise?'

Emily nodded, and Jada hugged her. 'Then go out there and do your best work, before I start getting conniptions about the patriarchy.'

Chapter 22

As she swung out of the bathroom, Emily paused as she spotted Chrissie hovering around Oliver's desk. She flapped her hand behind her back at Jada, who was following her out, and put her finger to her lips.

Keeping the door open just enough so they could hear what was going on, Emily managed to catch what Chrissie was saying. She was wearing the flirtatious pout she used on everyone new in the office until she'd worked out what they could do for her – which, if the answer was 'nothing', meant the smile was replaced with a bored grimace from then on.

She was also using the simpering voice she used whenever she asked Charles if she could go home early because she had a migraine.

'The printer's broken and I can't work out how to fix it. Can you come and sort it out for me, Oliver? *Pleeease?*' Chrissie stretched the last 'please' out in a nauseating baby voice.

Charles was never taken in by her – 'Much as I have the utmost sympathy for migraine sufferers, Chrissie, I heard you talking to Claude about your plans to go somewhere terrible-sounding this evening. So back to work you go' – and Emily was pleased to note that Oliver looked more amused than aroused too.

'Uh, sorry, I've got somewhere to be. Have you tried calling IT?' he said, hastily pulling his jacket off the back of his chair.

'I think my phone might be broken, too. Please could you help? I'm such an idiot, and so rubbish at techy stuff.'

'Sorry, Chrissie, not my forte, I'm afraid,' Oliver said briskly. 'It's after five, anyway, so why don't you turn it all off and see if it's working in the morning. If not, you're more than welcome to borrow my phone then.'

'Thank you, I'll give that a go,' Chrissie said, through slightly gritted teeth, before turning on the cutesy voice again. 'I didn't think of that, I'm so stupid sometimes. Thank you *sooo* much, you're *such* a sweetheart.'

Oliver shot her a confused smile before heading towards the lift. Emily turned back to Jada, who was grinning. They gave each other a silent high five, and Emily added another positive attribute to Oliver's growing list.

Very nice to look at

Mega successful

Funny, and not just good-looking-person funny, proper funny

Smells like sweets

Loves Stephen King

'That's a good sign, at least,' Emily said in a low whisper. 'It looks like he prefers capable women to the ones who pretend to be crap at stuff just to make men feel good about themselves.'

'Yes, just *imagine* putting on a pretence to win over a man,' Jada said archly. 'What a *terrible* idea.'

'OK, smarty pants,' Emily muttered. 'Lucky for me, not everyone's borderline psychic and can tell how many sit-ups I've done just by looking at me.'

Stepping out of the bathroom, she headed towards Oliver, giving him a small wave, and her stomach flipped. It was one thing hiding behind sexy email banter, which she was thoroughly adept at, but quite another going on an actual date, where there was a much greater chance of New Emily's mask accidentally slipping.

'Right, are we ready to Chat Cat?' Oliver said as she reached him. 'Which we have to promise to do for at least five minutes,' he added sternly.

'I could probably stretch to ten, even though I've been working *super* hard all day,' Emily smiled as they headed into the lift.

Outside the office, Emily and Oliver walked side-by-side until they hit Camden Market's emptying stalls, where Oliver took the lead, confidently weaving his way around the boxes of clothes, jewellery and records being carefully packed away by stallholders. By the time they reached Bayou Bar, Emily's feet were already aching from the sky-high heels she'd been wearing all day. Until now, she'd been trying to sit down as much as humanly possible.

Oliver opened the door for her. Although he didn't actually touch her back as she walked through it, she could feel his hand hovering over it. Her back pulsed with the warmth, as if Oliver's body was filled with static. So when she heard a loud 'Psssst!' behind her, she thought at first that it was an actual crackle of electricity.

Instead, turning around, she saw Andy standing behind Oliver, giving her a thumbs-up above his head.

'Oh, crap,' she said, her Essex accent making an unscheduled appearance, and Oliver's face dropped. 'Sorry,' she blushed. 'I just forgot a call I meant to make. You're a terrible distraction, you know. Do you mind?'

Oliver raised his eyebrows, then nodded. 'Of course, what are you having?' he asked.

Emily ordered a Bellini, then bit her lip as she grabbed her phone from her bag and held it to her ear.

'What are you doing here?' she hissed. 'Aren't you supposed to be at home watching TV and trying to destroy my flat with your magical powers?'

'What are *you* doing here, more like?' Andy said. 'Are you going on a date with that guy?' He stood on tiptoes, trying to catch a glimpse of Oliver inside the bar.

'It's just a work thing,' Emily said, looking nervously at Oliver through the glass doors as he waved his hand to attract the barman's attention.

'Oh, OK,' Andy said, looking relieved. 'I wanted to come and show you my new trick. Still can't touch stuff. But look at this.'

Andy stared at a point above and behind Emily's head, frowning.

'What are you looking at?' she asked, turning around. But

when she turned back, Andy was gone. 'Where are you?' she called, pressing the phone back to her ear when she realised she was shouting into thin air. Then yelped in shock, as Andy pinged back into view in front of her.

'Ta-da!' he said, bowing deeply.

'How the hell did you do that?' Emily said, taking a step backwards. 'You nearly gave me a heart attack. But I must admit, that's pretty impressive.'

'Cool, huh?' Andy said, hopping onto the narrow railing around the entrance to the bar. 'I was sitting on the sofa, staring at the wall and wondering what you were up to, when I suddenly appeared in your office. I got the shock of my life. Well, death.'

'I didn't see you?'

'You wouldn't have. I was in this room full of Lego – I landed right in the middle of the table, which wasn't ideal – with a load of men talking about that cat food you're obsessed with.'

'I'm not obsessed with it. It's my job. I guess that must have been the creatives' meeting,' Emily said, thoughtfully.

'Anyway, I panicked, and wished I was back in the flat, and suddenly I was there again. I did try to teleport myself somewhere else . . .'

'. . . Where, exactly?'

'The Monster Munch factory. I've always wanted to know how they make those tasty little claws.' Emily snorted. 'But it didn't work. I think there's some kind of connection between me, you and the flat, which means I can get to wherever you are and back home again.'

'And can you try that again now? Because I've got a date to get to.'

'So it *is* a date?' Andy said accusingly.

Emily blushed. 'Maybe I'm jumping the gun a bit. It's just a work meeting, really.'

'Work meeting, my arse. He definitely wants to shag you. Can I come? I want to see what this Oliver dude's like and make sure he's good enough for you.'

'Let's assume he is, because there's zero chance of you gate-crashing this meeting,' Emily said. She glanced through the window of the bar to see Oliver holding up her drink and wiggling his eyebrows.

'Go on, I promise not to stay too long,' Andy said, waving at Oliver then marvelling at his lack of reflection in the window. 'It's the least you can do.'

'Because . . .?'

'Because you've only just found out I've died, and it's extremely bad etiquette to go on a date so soon afterwards.'

Emily sighed. 'Is there any way I can stop you?'

'Nope.'

'Come on, then,' Emily said. 'But stay quiet. And you only get five minutes, or else.'

She shook her head in disbelief. Letting Andy gate-crash her date was probably the worst idea she'd ever had. But how on earth were you supposed to argue with a ghost?

She took a second to compose herself before swinging into the bar, smiling at Oliver. He was sitting on a stool at the bar, his jacket draped over the seat beside him. In front of him was an old fashioned, which had been poured over a single huge cube of ice.

'You read my mind,' she grinned, dipping her fingers into the little bowl of habas fritas he'd ordered and throwing a couple into her mouth. As soon as they hit her stomach, it started aching, and she remembered her promise to Jada to order some proper food.

'Ah man, I used to love those crunchy little guys,' Andy said sadly. He perched himself on the stool behind Oliver's, looking frustrated as he tried and failed to grab the edge of the bar to spin himself around.

Emily tried to hop onto her stool as elegantly as possible, even though they were apparently designed to support only a single, tiny bum-cheek at a time. She crossed her legs, hoping it wouldn't cause her to wobble sideways off the seat.

'Should we get the work chat out of the way first?' she said, horribly aware of Andy sitting just a couple of feet away.

'Good idea,' Oliver nodded. 'But first, cheers to you and your brilliant campaign idea. We've got some stiff competition from the other agencies we're pitching against, but I honestly think we – or rather, you – have got something special here.' He raised his glass and touched it to Emily's. She took a sip of her Bellini and hoped that if she chomped her way through enough habas fritas it wouldn't go straight to her head.

'Come on. We both know it's basically a spin-off of the AirLab campaign,' she said. 'Coming up with a Poundland version of an idea that went viral and won a bazillion awards isn't exactly ground-breaking. And certainly not as hard as coming up with it in the first place.'

'How did you do it, Oliver? You're so *amazing*,' Andy said, batting his eyelids. Emily glared at him over Oliver's shoulder.

'Perhaps not, but customers can spot a rip-off a mile away, and I really think this is different enough to fly,' Oliver said, rolling the ice around his drink. 'If we were pitching to another clothing or sports brand, it would be too obvious.

But applying it to cat food makes it feel really fresh. It's not something just anyone would think of trying.'

Emily was pleased with herself for bringing the conversation onto the topic of Oliver's success so swiftly. One of the *Bijou* features she'd torn out from the magazine, which she kept in a tatty folder under her bed along with a bunch of other self-help articles, was titled, HOW TO WOO A MAN IN UNDER 30 MINUTES.

It explained that everyone loves talking about themselves, especially their achievements, so if you steer the conversation that way, then really listen to what your date has to say, they'll recall your meeting positively. They tried to justify it by saying it was something to do with reward centres lighting up the brain, but Emily thought it was pretty obvious that everyone enjoys their ego being stroked.

'So how did you come up with the original idea? If I'm going to break into the Witches' Coven, I'll need to pick your brains, I'm afraid.' Emily went to lean her elbow on the bar, before realising it was too low, and turning the movement into a hair-flick.

'There really wasn't much to it,' Oliver said, his eyes darkening as he scratched his stubble with smoothly manicured fingernails. 'Sometimes these ideas just hit you, you know?'

Emily noticed his chin was a lot darker than it had been this morning. He was literally oozing testosterone through his face. And was he ... *blushing*?

'Oh, come on,' Emily teased. 'Everybody in the industry knows your name, I'm basically fangirling all over you, and your answer is, "there wasn't much to it"? That's terribly disappointing.'

Behind Oliver's back, Andy was frowning.

'I had a moment of inspiration and ran with it, and that

was that, really,' Oliver said, modestly. 'If I could have shared all those accolades with the whole team, I would have, but it was my name on the account so I got all the credit. Pretty unfair, really.'

'Sounds like you were a pretty amazing boss,' Emily said, and Andy snorted. She tried to ignore him, but she could feel her heart pounding harder in her chest as her anger rose. She felt an irresistible urge to prove Andy wrong, and to show him that Oliver was funny and interesting, as well as brilliantly talented and indecently gorgeous.

'So let's get into Cat's Miaow,' she said. 'Tell me more about Speedy Tomato. I don't know much about cats, to be honest, although I've always wanted one. They're so fluffy, and ... soft,' she said, racking her brain for adjectives that were more positive than 'scratchy' and 'Machiavellian'.

'I'm not sure there's a blueprint when it comes to cats, to be honest, which is why your idea is such a great one,' Oliver said, thoughtfully. 'They can be annoying buggers, especially if you've got a shoe collection you don't want to smell of wee. Speedy Tomato acts like he hates me half the time, and I've occasionally been tempted to stuff a few nuggets of Cat's Miaow up my nose just to get a cuddle.'

Emily laughed loudly, and looked pointedly at Andy, who scowled back.

'But then he'll do this thing where he sort of inches towards me for a cuddle, while pretending not to care. I'll be at my laptop, and every time I look up he's sitting licking himself, but he'll be a little bit closer. Until eventually, he's on *top* of my laptop, waiting for his ears to be scratched. I should probably have called him Sneaky Tomato.'

Emily laughed again.

'Oh, come *on*. What's funny about calling a cat Sneaky Tomato?' Andy said crossly, and Emily's cheeks flushed. 'Why are you laughing at this crap?'

'When did you get him?' Emily said, swallowing down her anger to keep her voice steady. 'And why a cat, rather than a . . . bulldog or something?'

'You jest, but I once took a woman back to mine, and she said having a cat was – and I quote – "for sad old single women, not real men". It was the quickest turn-off of all time. I was almost impressed by how awful she was.'

'Oh my god,' Emily said, clapping a hand over her mouth.

'I actually got Speedy because my neighbour died and her daughter didn't want him. She was muttering darkly about driving him to the motorway, dropping him off and hoping for the best, so I thought I'd better step in.'

'And did you make the right decision?' Emily said, taking another sip of her Bellini.

'I think so,' Oliver said. 'Either way, I'm his bitch now, whether I like it or not. Trust me, you'll know if you ever get a cat of your own. But you said you didn't have any pets as a child, right?'

'No, no pets,' Emily said, impressed at how smoothly Oliver had moved the conversation from himself onto the topic of her. Perhaps he was a big fan of *Baron* magazine, which was the male equivalent of *Bijou*. It generally featured lots of photos of shiny cars, expensive suits, and tips on how to charm women into bed.

'Tell me about your family,' Oliver continued, holding her gaze. Emily swallowed. 'Have you got a mum, a dad? A glut of strapping and terrifyingly protective big brothers I need to look out for?'

'No, don't panic. I'm an only child,' Emily said, laughing lightly. She glanced at Andy over the top of her glass. She had a horrible feeling that Oliver was about to push her into a corner she'd have no choice but to lie her way out of, and she had hoped Andy would be gone before that happened.

'What about your dad? Is he going to answer the door holding a rifle if I ever get to meet him? Because I can imagine you were a proper Daddy's Little Princess.'

A memory flashed into Emily's mind: her dad expertly fanning out a handful of playing cards in front of her wide eyes, urging her to pick one. She'd waggled her small hand in front of his face to check he definitely wasn't looking before sliding one out of the deck and peering at it carefully, pressing it to her chest and lifting one small corner to check it, before slipping it back into the pack.

She'd never forget her dad's look of pride when, moments later, he'd asked her to feel in her pocket and she'd pulled out her card: the Queen of Hearts. She'd looked at him with complete awe. At that moment, Emily had thought it was real magic – and that her dad was a real magician, like the ones in Harry Potter. Back then, she *had* felt like a Daddy's Little Princess – until he'd pulled his vanishing act. But she couldn't tell Oliver any of that.

'Am I that transparent? I *was* horribly spoiled, I'm afraid,' Emily said, trying to avoid Andy's gaze. 'I try to hide it, but I guess you can't ever escape your past, right? Although I never did get the pony I asked for every Christmas, which made me feel totally hard done by. I think at one point I even threatened to call Childline.' Oliver let out his low laugh.

'Bullshit!' Andy said, shaking his head. 'Why are you lying to him, Emily?'

'Will you just shut up!' Emily snapped.

'Sorry?' Oliver said, frowning.

'Oh my god, Oliver, not you,' Emily stammered, putting one hand on his knee and covering her mouth with the other. 'I can hear someone talking really loudly in the corner over there. Can't you hear them?'

Oliver peered behind him to see a couple quietly chatting, so engrossed in conversation their heads nearly touched across the table. He looked back at Emily, who shrugged.

'I've got really good hearing,' she stuttered. 'I'm like one of those super-recognisers. You know, those people who have amazing facial recognition that the police use to catch criminals. But with . . . ears.'

'That's . . . weird.' Oliver said, looking confused, and Emily half-slid, half-hopped off her stool. 'I've got to go to the bathroom, anyway. Would you mind asking for a menu? They do a really good quinoa Buddha bowl here, and I'm famished.'

Emily had no idea whether quinoa was on the menu or not, but she wanted Oliver to know she did know how to pronounce *some* weirdly spelled words.

'Sure,' he said. Raising his hand, he clicked his fingers at the barman to get his attention, and stabbed a finger on the bar. Emily looked at him in shock. Wasn't that awfully rude? But then she shook her head. She didn't have time to worry about that now.

Giving Andy a look that clearly said, '*If you don't follow me, I'm going to kill you*,' she hurried into the ladies', ushering Andy into a cubicle and locking herself in before rounding on him.

'Are you kidding me?' she said, her cheeks flushing. 'What's with the running commentary out there?'

'OK, OK, I'm sorry,' Andy said, jumping onto the toilet

to get further away from Emily's angry face and holding up his hands.

'I asked for five minutes of good behaviour, and you couldn't even manage that. Why are you being such a pain in the arse?'

'I could have handled it better, admittedly . . .'

'No shit, Sherlock.'

'. . . But honestly? There's something about this Oliver guy I don't like.'

Emily folded her arms. 'Like what? His piercing blue eyes? His successful, full-time job? Hair that doesn't have a Werther's Original wrapper permanently stuck in it?'

'Hey, there's no need to get personal,' Andy said, gingerly touching his hair. 'All I'm saying is, he makes me feel uneasy. I just can't put my finger on why. Maybe it's because you're not being honest with him. What was all that rubbish back there about being spoiled as a child?'

'Everyone tells a few white lies on a first date,' Emily said, looking at the floor. 'You can't just say stuff like, "Oh, by the way, Mum wants us to get married down the Dog & Duck, cos Bob offers a ten per cent discount if the happy couple isn't knocked up," to a man like Oliver.'

'So it *is* a date,' Andy said, hopping off the loo seat and sitting on it. Even as a ghost, Emily thought, he really was very fond of sitting down. 'And as I recall, you said that kind of stuff to me when we first met, didn't you?'

'Yes, but Oliver's not like you,' Emily said. 'I'm trying to better myself. And that means presenting my best side.'

'This isn't your best side, though, is it? It isn't really you at all. And what's with all this?' Andy said, clicking his fingers in the air.

'Maybe it's OK to do that these days,' Emily said, weakly. 'Oliver went to Cambridge University; he must know what he's doing.'

'Going to a posh university doesn't make you *not* a total wanker,' Andy pointed out. 'Just . . . be careful, OK?'

'Let me guess. If you can't have me, nobody can, right?'

'It's not like that,' Andy said. 'I get that you need to move on, even if it feels like only yesterday that we were together – like, literally, for me. And OK, I'm not doing cartwheels about it. But *him*? Really? You can do better than that.'

'What do you know about it?' Emily said, feeling her eyes pricking with tears. 'Sure, he's not like you. But you disappeared, just like my dad did. And even if I know why *now*, it changed things for me. I've had eight months of thinking you just decided I wasn't good enough.' A tear dripped down Emily's cheek and onto the floor, and she swiped it away. 'Can you go now, please? I feel like I'm getting it in the neck from all sides at the moment, from you, from Jada, from Zoe. And I could really do without it.'

Andy hesitated. He looked pained, and took a step towards Emily, like he wanted to wrap her in a hug. But of course, he couldn't. Instead, he nodded, mutely. Then he stared at the door behind her, blinked, and promptly vanished.

Emily sank down onto the toilet seat and held her head in her hands. She'd been so excited about the prospect of meeting Oliver, who was turning out to be exactly the kind of man she'd been looking for. But she hadn't bargained on Andy coming clattering back into her life, turning what she thought she'd known on its head and throwing a very unwelcome, ghost-shaped spanner in the works.

In a perfect world, she'd put her love life on hold while she helped Andy to work out what had happened to him, and hopefully get him over to the other side. But she'd waited too long for a man like Oliver to come along, and it was too risky to wait, what with the likes of Chrissie, for whom the phrase 'legs for days' might as well have been written, angling for a date. So what was she supposed to do?

Suddenly, her pocket vibrated. 'What now . . .?' she muttered, pulling out her phone and seeing a text from Zoe.

> I just got out of work and I can't BELIEVE you got a date with Little Lord Fauntleroy already. Maybe we should call YOU Speedy Tomato. I hope it's all going well! But not that well, cos I'm hoping to stay at yours tonight. I'm still a bit wigged out about the burglary, and the front door is currently a sheet of plastic.

She'd added a gif of Puss in Boots from *Shrek* looking wide-eyed and sad. Emily rubbed her face, then swore as she realised her make-up might have smudged. Andy would be in the flat, and she could barely trust him to behave himself. But on the other hand, she could hardly say no to Zoe, especially after she'd been less than sympathetic about the burglary in the first place.

Her only option was to give Zoe some warning and hope Andy was sharp enough to come up with a good excuse for his being there. Preferably one that didn't involve them being embroiled in a torrid love affair.

> Sure, of course! Just a heads-up, but Ben might be there. We are NOT bonking, so stop thinking that immediately

OMG, you are totally going to be the meat in a delicious Oliver and Ben sandwich! I'm well jel. I can let myself in with your spare key. Mwah! xxx

Three wobbly dots appeared on Emily's phone, followed swiftly by the Distracted Boyfriend meme, his girlfriend labelled 'Bread', the girl he was looking back at labelled 'More Bread', and the distracted boyfriend labelled 'Tasty Emily filling'.

Sighing, she shoved her phone back in her pocket, swung out of the cubicle – ignoring the odd looks she was given by a group of girls reapplying their make-up in the mirror – and headed back to the bar.

Chapter 23

Before opening her front door, Emily paused, listening. All she could make out was the murmur of Zoe and Andy chatting, so there was no way of telling whether the game was up, and Zoe had found out the truth about Andy. But when she walked inside, and saw Andy propped in his armchair and Zoe curled on the sofa, looking very much like she *hadn't* seen a ghost, Emily allowed herself to breathe.

An almost-empty bottle of wine and single glass were on the coffee table, leaving a wet ring of condensation. Zoe's eyes looked a bit red, and Emily wondered if they'd been talking about the break-in.

'Oh, hi guys,' she said, as she placed her bag carefully on the table and hung her jacket on a coat hook, before whipping off the belt she was wearing, which was so ridiculously tight, it was starting to feel like it was cutting off the circulation to the top and bottom halves of her body simultaneously.

'You're still here then, *Ben*?'

'Uh yeah, I think I sorted your electrical issue out,' Andy

said, shooting her a look. 'It was pretty simple in the end. It was a problem with the . . . transmogrifier.'

'Ahh, of course. The transmogrifier. I suspected as much,' Emily said, hoping Zoe knew as much about circuits as Andy apparently didn't. 'Thanks for doing that. Hang on, I'm just going to get changed.'

Heading into the bedroom, she stripped off her dress, peeled off her fake eyelashes, and picked up the grey satin pyjama set she usually wore as loungewear. When she bought it, she'd reasoned it was the equivalent of dressing for the job you want, rather than the one you have, and would help her cosmically order the kind of man she'd want to peel it off her.

But on the other hand, both Andy and Zoe had seen her looking her worst umpteen times, and with her first date with Oliver a success, she realised it might be a long time before she got to slob out in her own space again. Or fart, for that matter.

Folding her silky pyjamas back up, she dug around in the back of her chest of drawers and pulled on the comfy T-shirt bra and slouchy loungewear set she'd started wearing when she was dating Andy. Then she leaned under the bed and pulled out her guilty secret: a pair of huge, cheap and distinctly unstylish Ugg-style slippers, which were hideous, but made her feet feel as warm and cosy as a bagful of kittens.

Feeling more comfortable than she had done in months, she shuffled into the living room.

'OK, so what was he like?' Zoe said as Emily emerged from her bedroom. Zoe was holding a freshly poured glass of wine above her head for Emily to collect on her way to the sofa.

'Thanks, Zo. But I'm sure Ben doesn't want to hear our girlie chat,' Emily said, catching Andy's eye as she wriggled her bum into the corner of the soft cushions of her sofa. 'I can tell you another time.'

'Don't mind me,' Andy said. 'I'm curious to hear what he's like.'

'Won't it be a bit weird, as the last person I dated was your brother?' Emily asked, pointedly.

'It's fine, honestly,' Andy said, and Emily flushed.

'Don't be a spoilsport,' Zoe said, taking a large sip of wine. 'Spill.'

'Fine,' Emily said, forcing a smile. 'It went really well, actually. He's, like, really *really* nice. Just my type. It was the best date I've had in ages.'

Zoe shot her a suspicious look. Emily knew she could tell she was lying. And although she would never admit it in front of Andy, the date *had* gone a bit weird by the end. There hadn't been any awkward silences, or anything like that. But Oliver had carried on clicking his fingers at the barman, which had made her feel a bit uncomfortable, and he'd occasionally name-dropped people he'd met at his members' club, which Emily was pretty sure was bad form – though she'd have to look it up online.

By the end of the night, she was surprised to realise she didn't have any urge to kiss him – yet she'd still felt a bit disappointed when he'd walked her to the Tube and said goodbye with a quick peck on the cheek.

'And did you tell him about your past? Greenleaf and all that?' Andy asked. Zoe looked at him and frowned.

'I didn't, no,' Emily said. 'But then you have to hold a bit of yourself back, don't you? You can't just go ahead and spill your guts to a new guy straight away.'

Zoe and Andy exchanged looks.

'What? What have I missed?' Emily said.

'Nothing,' Zoe said, quickly. 'But do you think it's a good idea to hide your past from Oliver like that? Surely if he's the right person for you, he shouldn't care where you come from.'

'I will tell him about all that eventually,' Emily said, wondering, even as she said it, whether it was the truth. 'But everyone holds something back on a first date, don't they?'

'I don't,' Zoe said, glancing at Andy again. 'And neither did Old Emily. But then I guess New Emily is a different kettle of fish. Just be careful, OK? I don't want you getting hurt. Neither of us do.'

'I will, I promise,' Emily said, feeling a prick of annoyance. They'd obviously been talking about her behind her back, which was bad enough. But there was an odd vibe in the room, which she couldn't quite decipher. Like something had happened between Zoe and Andy that they weren't telling her about. She'd have to ask Zoe about it – but that wouldn't be possible while Andy was sitting in his armchair, looking annoyingly pleased with himself.

'Don't let us keep you, Ben,' she said, faking a yawn. 'I'm having an early night, and I'm sure you need to get home. Thanks so much for coming and fixing the transmogrifier.'

Andy raised his eyebrows. 'You're welcome,' he said, standing up.

'Thanks for the chat,' Zoe said. 'It's helped me see things a lot more clearly.'

'You're welcome too,' Andy grinned, and Emily frowned.

Andy followed her to the front door, and waved goodbye to Zoe. Swinging it open, Emily's stomach swooped as she realised Andy was standing just behind her, and the door had nearly sailed straight through him. Luckily, he'd managed to bend himself out of the way just in time. Except now, he looked like he was going to fall backwards.

'Careful!' Zoe shouted, jumping from the sofa and reaching for Andy as he waved his arms in the air, trying to keep his balance.

Although technically, gravity only existed for Andy in his mind, he couldn't stop himself from falling. Emily watched in what felt like slow motion as he fell through Zoe's outstretched hands, passing silently through the living room table and onto the rug below.

There was a long pause, during which Zoe stared at the table wide-eyed, her chest heaving. It stretched out like a rubber band until Emily thought she might snap. But then suddenly, Zoe let out a piercing scream, before scrambling over the back of the sofa and onto the floor behind it.

'Oh, shit,' Andy said from underneath Emily's coffee table, staring at its underside.

'Nice one,' Emily muttered.

'Emily! Please tell me what just happened?' Zoe moaned from behind the sofa. 'I thought I just saw Ben falling through the table. But I can't have. So tell me I'm on acid, or I drank too much, or . . . something.'

Emily knelt on the sofa and peered over its back. Zoe looked up at her, her bottom lip trembling.

'It's OK, Zoe. Don't worry,' she said, soothingly. 'I can explain.'

'So what I think just happened really happened? No, no, no, no, no no no *NO* . . .' Zoe started shaking her head from side to side, and clutched her knees to her chest.

'You bloody idiot. You've broken my best mate,' Emily

hissed at Andy. 'Get out from under there and help me. It's OK, Zo, it's not what you think,' she added to Zoe. Then paused. 'Well, maybe it is what you think. What do you think it is?'

'He just FELL THROUGH A FUCKING TABLE!' Zoe shouted, pulling her hands away from her knees. 'What is he? The Invisible Man? A ghost? Or did all the atoms in that table just happen to align at the exact same moment and allow him to magically fall through it?'

'The Invisible Man can't fall through things,' Andy said helpfully, and Emily sighed. 'Sorry,' he said. 'Although I guess I don't have to pretend to go home now, right?' he added, pulling himself up through the table and settling back into his armchair.

Emily scrambled over the sofa to sit next to Zoe and held out her little finger. Zoe stared at it for a moment, before linking her own through it. 'Listen to me. Please don't freak out,' Emily said gently. 'But the truth is, Ben is a ghost. Actually, it's not Ben . . . it's Andy. We told you he was Andy's brother because we panicked. We didn't expect you to be able to see him last night. But . . . well, he kind of came back the night we did the Ouija board.' Emily paused. She'd become almost used to living with a ghost, but could still clearly remember exactly how freaked out she'd been a few days earlier when Andy had appeared.

'So you're telling me ghosts are real?' Zoe whispered, her eyes like saucers. 'And that there's one behind us right now?'

'Sorry for scaring you,' Andy said, poking his head over the back of the sofa. Zoe let out another blood-curdling shriek, and started desperately pedalling herself along the carpet to get away from him.

Andy grimaced. 'Sorry again.'

'Andy, bugger off, OK? Let me deal with this,' Emily snapped, and Andy ducked his head back behind the sofa. 'Zoe, I know this is weird, and I totally don't blame you for freaking out. But Andy's a *friendly* ghost, OK? Like Caspar. Or . . . or . . .'

'Bruce Willis in *The Sixth Sense*,' Andy offered, poking his head above the sofa again.

'Spoiler alert,' Emily tutted.

Zoe had reached Emily's bedroom, and was leaning against the door, panting. 'So you're honestly telling me I've spent all evening talking to a corpse?'

'We prefer to be called Formers,' Andy said. 'At least I do. But yes, technically, you were talking to a dead guy. We had a good time, though, right? You said I was like an agony aunt, only cuter.'

Emily swallowed. So Zoe *did* fancy Andy, and apparently hadn't felt any need to hide it from him. Which wasn't the best friend-etiquette in the world – although, Emily conceded, now might not be the best time to bring that up.

A sudden thudding at the front door caused Zoe to scream again. She clutched at her chest, and Emily worried she might actually have a heart attack.

'What's going on in there? Are you alright, Emily?' a voice called through the door in a broad cockney accent. 'It sounds like Piccadilly bloody Circus in there.'

'It's Mary,' Emily whispered, pointing at Andy. 'Go into the kitchen, and don't come out until she's gone, just in case.' She wasn't in the mood to discover that anyone who was in her block of flats on the night of the séance could see Andy's ghost.

'Zoe, are you alright?' Emily asked, crouching down to talk to Zoe as Andy sloped into the kitchen. Her friend's face was wavering between sickly green and white with shock, and she looked like she was going to throw up. Zoe just stared at her, taking hiccupy deep breaths.

'Clearly you're *not* alright, but I'd better get this,' Emily said, patting her on the back.

'I can hear you in there, and I'm not pissing off until you open up,' Mary said from behind the door. 'If there's a rapist in there, tell him I'm going to cut his balls off.'

Swinging the door open, Emily smiled unconvincingly at Mary, who was wearing her usual evening uniform of pink silk dressing-gown and marabou mules.

'Sorry about the noise, Mary,' Emily said. 'This is Zoe.' Emily opened the door wider so Mary could wave at Zoe, who tried to wave back from her spot on the floor, her hand shaking so hard it went in mad loops instead.

'And I'm Andy,' Andy said, slipping into the front room from the kitchen. Emily sighed. At least he had the decency to give Zoe, who looked like she might start screaming again, a wide berth.

Mary ignored him. 'Are you OK, love?' Mary asked Zoe, frowning as she pulled a packet of Superkings from her dressing gown pocket and lit a cigarette. 'You look a bit shaken.'

Zoe nodded, her eyes widening as Andy walked over to Mary and waved a hand in front of her face. He turned to Zoe and shrugged. 'Can't see me. Or hear me,' he said. 'Aren't you the lucky one, Zoe?' She stared as he made his way to his armchair, leaped into it, and slung his legs over the arm.

'Zoe opened my window to let in some air and a bloody

pigeon flew in, can you believe it?' Emily said quickly. 'It was the size of a bus, and gave her the shock of her life. Didn't it, Zo?'

Zoe nodded slowly, peeling her eyes away from Andy for long enough to turn to Mary. 'Huge,' she croaked, stretching her arms out to indicate that a pigeon roughly the size of a Newfoundland had flown into Emily's front room.

'It, er, flew straight out again, but gave her a bit of a shock. Thanks for checking on us, though, Mary,' Emily added. 'Much appreciated.'

'Ah, I see. I hate bloody pigeons. Like pieces of shit on wings.'

'Don't you mean rats, Mary?'

'Nope. Pieces of shit. Hate 'em. Luckily Fluffy chases them off my balcony, otherwise I'd have to use my gun.' Emily raised her eyebrows. 'Well, as long as you're OK. Do you need a fag, love? You're white as a sheet,' she added to Zoe.

Emily watched Zoe consider for a second, then realise that under the circumstances, there was no way Emily could get angry at her for smoking in her flat.

'Ta, Mary,' she said, slowly getting up on wobbly-looking legs. 'Sorry about the racket.'

'Don't worry, pet,' Mary grinned, flashing a set of pristine false teeth before lighting Zoe's cigarette for her between her puckered, pink-glossed lips. 'I've got a gentleman friend upstairs, so a bit of noise to cover up the sound of our mischief won't go amiss, if you know what I mean?' She cackled.

'I think I just about catch your drift,' Zoe said, sucking on her cigarette like it might save her life.

'You need a glass of blackberry wine, love. That'll see you right. Don't wait up!' Mary winked, waving her dressing gown with a theatrical flourish as she turned to go back upstairs.

Closing the door, Emily breathed a sigh of relief.

'I wonder what pensioner sex looks like?' Andy said thoughtfully, from his chair. 'Balls are saggy enough as it is. Pensioners' balls must be like huge floppy pendulums.'

'Don't even *think* about trying to find out,' Emily said firmly, waving Zoe's cigarette smoke away from her face with an agitated hand.

'Are we going to talk about this?' Zoe said, depositing a trail of blue smoke in the air and a sprinkling of ash on the floorboards as she gestured dramatically towards Andy. 'Is this really happening? Or did the burglary totally unhinge my brain?'

'I'm afraid it's really happening,' Emily said, gently plucking the cigarette from between her fingers and taking a drag. She sighed with relief. 'When Andy first appeared, I thought it was the result of stress too. But he's been here a few days now, and our survey says he really has returned from the dead. I think the Ouija board did it. I knew I shouldn't have trusted Jada.'

'She loves having me here really,' Andy said to Zoe.

'I'm sorry I didn't tell you about him before,' Emily said, 'but I really didn't want to stress you out even more.'

'Same here. I'm sorry I lied to you,' Andy said. 'But I was under strict instructions from Herr Blott here not to tell you. Although if I had, and your heart *had* exploded, I'd have gained a cool spooky dead mate. And maybe you'd know how ghosts can touch stuff.' Andy glared at Emily's fish vase like it was his sworn enemy.

'This is a lot to take in,' Zoe said. 'More wine, please. And this time, make it the good stuff.'

Emily nodded and headed into the kitchen. Grabbing one

of the posh bottles from her fridge, she headed back into the living room. Zoe was staring at Andy from behind the sofa, shaking her head.

'So you're Emily's ex, right?' she asked, her voice still a few octaves higher than usual. Andy nodded. 'And you're dead?' Andy nodded again.

Emily handed Zoe her glass where she was standing, and topped it up almost to the brim. Emily usually refused to pour what Zoe called 'Zoe's Special Measures', on the grounds that her favourite etiquette websites said wine should only be poured up to the widest part of the glass, but now wasn't the time to split hairs.

'Can I try something?' Zoe said.

'Go ahead,' Andy said. Without taking her eyes off him, she plucked a book from Emily's bookcase and threw it at Andy. It flew through his chest, and she shuddered.

'Weird, isn't it?' Andy said.

'It's very weird. And gross, sorry. So I might just stay over here for a bit, if that's OK? At least until I'm drunk.' Holding her wine aloft to avoid spilling it, Zoe slid her back down the kitchen wall and landed on the floor with a bump. Emily handed her a cushion from the sofa, and she leaned to one side to slip it under her bum, wiggling into it to get comfortable. 'So how did you die? Emily showed me the article they wrote about it in the paper, but they didn't seem to know much.'

'I don't actually remember myself,' Andy said. 'Although Emily's promised to help me find out.'

'We have made a bit of a start on the whole detective thing, actually,' Emily said. 'And we uncovered something really weird.' She explained to Zoe what Andy's mum had told them in the graveyard.

'Wow. That *is* weird,' Zoe said, shaking her head. Emily was relieved to see she looked a lot less like she was about to pass out. 'Can I help? I quite fancy playing detective.'

'Sure,' Andy said. 'The more the merrier. Friends?'

'Friends, I guess,' Zoe agreed, and Andy beamed like a rescue dog greeting its new owner. 'Maybe as well as joining the investigation into how you died, I could help you learn how to touch stuff,' Zoe said. 'Although you'd think there'd be a handbook or something, wouldn't you?'

'Like *Haunting for Dummies*? That's what I said,' Andy said, looking pleased with himself.

'As wonderful as Day Three in the House of the Dead has been, I really need to get to bed,' Emily said, with a yawn – this time, a genuine one. 'I'm knackered, and you must be too, Zo, after the day you've had. We can sleep top-to-tail in my bed if you like.'

'I'm too hyper to sleep right now,' Zoe said. 'But I reckon I'm happy on the sofa if I can get a sleeping bag?'

'OK. Andy doesn't sleep, so he can watch videos in my room as long as he has the sound turned down low.'

'I don't mind him staying in his chair if he behaves himself,' Zoe said. 'This is just so incredibly weird. Part of me can't really get my head round the idea that Andy's a ghost. We've spent all evening chatting like he's real.'

'Still real,' Andy interjected. 'Just dead.'

'Sorry,' Zoe said. 'But it's hard to believe he's not just … *normal*, you know? He's not exactly scary, is he? He's got a Werther's wrapper in his hair.'

'How have you got used to this situation so quickly?' Emily tutted. 'This is like when Covid started. Everyone else was busy going nuts, but within five minutes of lockdown you were merrily making home-made masks out of old socks and getting a crush on Joe Wicks. It's not normal.'

'I guess I'm very ... *flexible*,' Zoe said, raising her eyebrows at Andy, who sniggered.

Emily shook her head as she headed to her wardrobe to fetch a sleeping bag and pillow. As she bundled them into her arms, she felt her stomach twisting. She was glad Zoe wasn't too freaked out by the revelation that Andy was a ghost. But at the same time, she wasn't exactly thrilled by the thought of them having a sleepover in her front room.

'Plus you said yourself, he's a friendly ghost,' Zoe called through the doorway.

'I see dead people,' Andy said, in a tiny, shaking voice, before both of them burst out laughing. 'Maybe it's that thing you told me about, Emily?' he added. 'Where if a miserable bastard wins the lottery, within a year they're a miserable bastard again.'

'Hedonic adaptation? Maybe.' Emily nodded, handing Zoe the bedclothes and a pair of flower-sprigged pyjamas.

Emily was surprised Andy had listened to her waffling on about her A-level psychology back when they were together.

'Thanks for letting me stay.' Zoe smiled at Emily. 'And for letting me meet Andy at last, even by accident,' she added, pulling the sleeping bag over her legs from her spot on the carpet and reaching for the bottle of wine Emily had placed next to her.

'Night then,' Emily said, slipping back into her bedroom. Shutting the door, she felt her stomach swooping as she heard Andy asking Zoe what her favourite food was. *Tacos*, she thought.

Although she'd known Zoe would have to find out about

Andy sooner or later, she'd enjoyed having a secret that was just her own, and didn't involve bending over backwards to hide her past. But now, her two worlds had collided, and she wasn't sure how she felt about it.

Settling into bed without taking her make-up off for the first time in years, Emily drifted off to sleep, trying to block out the sound of Zoe and Andy's laughter seeping through the walls.

Chapter 24

The next morning, Emily woke up before her alarm went off and realised she could hear the low murmur of conversation coming from the front room. It wasn't quite 7 a.m., and Andy and Zoe were already awake and chatting – unless Zoe hadn't even gone to sleep. Emily pushed the thought away. It bugged her, even though she knew it shouldn't – after all, she had Oliver in her sights, so what did it matter if Zoe and Andy were getting on so well? But knowing she was being illogical just bugged her even more.

Flinging her covers off, she padded to the mirror. The very thought of having to dress to impress Oliver today was exhausting, especially after the drama of the day before, but she had to keep up the progress she'd made. It was still early days, and she had a long way to go.

Emily sighed as she contemplated the weeks of Kardashian-level grooming ahead of her. Already, after just a couple of stressful days and no trips to the gym, she felt knackered, her skin looked dull, and her hair badly needed a conditioning wrap. Running her fingers through it to get rid of the worst of the tangles, she pulled on her silk dressing gown to help put her in the right mindset for the day, and pushed open her bedroom door.

'Morning, chumps,' she said, stifling a yawn.

'Hey, Em,' Zoe grinned, turning round to face Emily from the spot on the sofa where she was tucked cosily into a sleeping bag, her head propped up on a pillow. Andy was sitting in his armchair, looking frustrated. 'We've been trying to teach him how to move things, but no luck so far. We didn't wake you up, did you?'

Emily shook her head. 'No, and I've got to get ready for work, anyway. Do you want first or second shower?'

'I, er, thought I might hang out here for a bit today if that's OK?' Zoe said, meekly. 'I nearly took someone's ear off yesterday because I was all shaky after the burglary. My boss told me to take some time off if I needed it, and since discovering ghosts exist, I'm hardly likely to be more steady-handed today, am I? Plus Andy asked me very nicely if I'd spend today helping him learn to touch stuff.'

'I thought you wanted me to help you do that?' Emily said, feeling a pang of jealousy.

'I'm happy to let you off so you can concentrate on your presentation,' Andy said. 'And Zoe's really keen to help.'

'OK,' Emily said, trying to sound unconcerned. 'Just stay away from my fish vase. And Zoe, you know where the fridge is, so help yourself.'

'Ohh, yum. Yakult, turkey slices and blueberries for lunch,' Andy said, pulling a face. 'You can order KFC and I can sniff it, yeah?' Zoe grinned and nodded.

'Have you been shoving your big fat dead head through my fridge door?' Emily grumbled. 'That's gross.'

'I like looking at food, even if I can't eat it,' he protested. 'But cold turkey is more of a punishment than a food, except on Boxing Day.'

Emily remembered the one time Andy had gone on a diet when they were dating. He'd lasted three days, complaining the whole time that he was '*literally* starving to death'. He'd also kept a pile of takeaway menus by his bed to read before he went to sleep, like they were porn magazines.

'Do you reckon they call it going cold turkey because people get so sick of turkey curry they can't wait for the Christmas leftovers to be finished with?' Zoe asked.

'Turkey is healthy, and a lean source of protein,' Emily said, wondering since when she'd started sounding like an infomercial for the most boring diet in the world.

'While KFC is delicious, and an excellent source of eleven secret herbs and spices,' Zoe parroted.

Shaking her head, Emily headed for the bathroom and pointedly shut the door on Zoe and Andy's laughter, her eyes stinging.

Brainstorming for one. #Amwriting

Emily tapped the caption into Instagram and held her phone aloft in selfie mode. Perching on one of the bar stools at New HoRizons – the in-office coffee-shop-slash-bar no self-respecting advertising agency in London would be without – she pressed an empty coffee cup to her lips, struck a thoughtful pose, her eyes fixed on a spot somewhere behind the camera, and snapped a photo.

When she'd moved to London, Emily had no idea what kind

of career she was interested in, beyond something that involved writing, which she loved, or puppies, which everyone loved. After watching some of her favourite geeky-girl-to-goddess transformation movies, and a handful of box-sets, she'd toyed with becoming a lawyer, enjoying the idea of writing impassioned closing arguments, before settling on advertising, which seemed to have all of the glamour, but with none of the stress of accidentally getting innocent people sent to jail.

Plus, because most people got their idea of what a copywriter does from watching *Mad Men*, it suited Emily's ambition of forging herself a glamorous-looking life down to a T – even if the reality involved coming up with clever ways to sell super mops and pore strips rather than having lots of sex in pencil skirts and enormous boardrooms.

Most importantly, thanks to HoRizons' need to hire some staff who knew what Pot Noodles tasted like and hadn't gone to university at Oxford or Cambridge to fulfil their diversity quotas, Emily had been a shoo-in for their trainee scheme.

As she applied a flattering but not-too-obvious filter and hit 'send' on her photo, her Auntie Suze's name popped up on her phone.

'Changing the world one photo at a time?' a voice said behind her. She inwardly cursed at being caught posing, before swivelling round on her stool and smiling at Oliver.

'Can't let my fans down,' she said. 'What if they didn't know what I had for breakfast? They might die of curiosity, and that wouldn't be very nice of me, would it? I'm doing them a massive favour, if anything.'

Oliver laughed, holding up his palms. 'Fair enough. I didn't realise you were busy saving lives out here. Don't let me stop you. Although I do have a quick question.' Emily raised an eyebrow.

'There's a new vegetarian restaurant opening this weekend in Shoreditch. It'll be packed full of the kind of people who'll gobble up Coffee & Co's ridiculous new branding, but it looks like fun, and I know someone who knows someone, so we'll get VIP treatment. Fancy checking it out?'

Emily smiled gratefully. The restaurant sounded terrible, but at least she'd be eating fancy vegetables on a date with Oliver. Her mind flashed back to her first meal out with Andy, standing next to a taco truck in the freezing cold. Weirdly, it had been one of the most delicious meals she'd ever eaten, which was when she'd first realised the effect context can have on your tastebuds

'That sounds amazing,' she said. 'There's just not enough good vegetarian food in London, don't you think? Name the time,' she added, glancing at the text from Auntie Suze before opening her calendar.

> **Auntie Suze:** Hey love! It's Auntie Suze here! Don't forget it's ur mum's birthday this weekend. I know she's a pain in the arse, but she's still ur mum. See you Saturday lunchtime? Xx

'Oh, sh ... darn. Sorry, Oliver,' she said. 'I've just had a text from my friend Mel, reminding me that I'm going to the prosthesis clinic with her this weekend. We're going for drinks afterwards and I can't let her down.'

Emily swallowed. Was it OK to tell a lie about your mate's leg amputation as an excuse to get out of talking about your mum, or was she going to hell forever?

'I can't stand between a girl and her noble do-gooding, can I?' Oliver said. 'We'll have to go another time. Shall I catch up with you next week?'

'That would be great,' Emily said, trying to keep the disappointment from her voice as Oliver walked back to his desk, his hands stuffed in his expensive suit pockets.

Old Emily might have been content enough spending her weekend downing cans of beer in the Dog & Duck and possibly catching an STD off one of the bar stools. But New Emily would much rather have spent it drinking posh cocktails and shagging Oliver.

Trying not to feel too bitter about things, she tapped out a reply to Auntie Suze.

Emily: Sure thing. Where we meeting? Dog & Duck or the flat?

Auntie Suze: The flat, I think. Your mum's got something she wants to talk to you about.

Inexplicably, she added a gif of a Minion eating a banana.

'Great,' Emily muttered. She didn't have the energy to wonder what her mum wanted to talk to her about, but she was pretty sure it wasn't anything like an apology for being entirely self-centred from the moment her dad left, or news of a long-lost relative leaving them buckets of cash.

It was more likely that her mum had found a new, terrible boyfriend she wanted Emily to bond with – and whenever she met another one of her mum's long line of men, it inevitably tarnished her memories of her dad. Emily remembered him as someone who was kind and quick to laugh, would make her squeal by scooping her up for hugs, and dazzle her with magic tricks. A man who loved watching old 80s movies from his own childhood – *The Goonies*, *The Princess Bride* – listening to Britpop and fixing cars. Sometimes for free, if their owners couldn't afford the repair fee.

She'd always thought her dad was the best, most fun dad ever. Her favourite photo of him had been taken a few days before he'd left. In it, he was wearing his usual dark blue overalls, over a checked shirt rolled up at the sleeves. He looked tired, his face swathed in stubble, but his blue eyes were crunched into a smile.

Emily had a too-big top hat perched on her head, which was balanced on her ears and almost covered her eyes. She was grinning delightedly at her dad, who was holding out a spread of playing cards, urging her to tap one with the wooden wand, made from an old piece of dowel painted black and white, she was holding in her hand.

She kept the photo in her bedside table drawer. She'd loved to have kept it pinned to her fridge, or even framed in her living room, but that was too risky. People might start asking questions, then wonder how she'd managed to be such a terrible daughter that she could drive her dad away from his family.

All her memories of him were good ones. But when every one of her dad's successors was such a waste of space, she wondered if she was looking at the past through rose-tinted glasses. Maybe, like Darren had done, he also drank milk straight from the carton, standing in front of the fridge door with his top off and his huge, hairy belly wobbling about.

Or perhaps he picked his toenails in front of the TV like her mum's ex Steve did, flicking the bits he found towards the screen and sending them pinging back onto the carpet. Maybe she'd just forgotten those bits about her own father. For him to have left his family without a second thought, he can't have been the man she remembered.

And this weekend, instead of revelling in her blossoming romance with Oliver, she was going to have to endure a very unwelcome trip down memory lane, her dad replaced in those memories by whichever loser her mum was currently dating – plus, of course, Andy would be hanging out with Zoe while she was in Essex, which meant she'd spend the whole time wondering what they were getting up to.

As she reached her front door that evening, Emily heard laughing drifting through it, which stopped abruptly when she slipped her key into the lock.

Swinging the door open, she gaped at the scene in front of her. It looked like her flat had been ransacked. A cold pizza sat in an open box on the coffee table, next to a plate with a half-eaten slice on it. The floor was covered with empty drinks cans, and half the books had been removed from her shelves and were scattered around the flat.

For some reason, there was one of her bed sheets draped over the back of the sofa and – to top it all off – her fish vase was smashed into pieces on the floor next to Andy's chair. Sitting on it, looking guilty as hell, was Andy.

'What the actual fuck is going on here?' Emily said, slamming the door behind her.

'Hi, Emily,' Zoe said, weakly, from the sofa. 'We thought you'd be working late on the presentation.'

'Well, I'm not. I came here so I could work in peace. But . . . have *I* been burgled?'

'No, it's nothing like that,' Andy said quickly. 'I've got some brilliant news.'

'Go on,' Emily said faintly, rubbing her face as she spotted the state of her bedroom through its open door. It looked like it had been tossed through a hurricane.

'I can touch things!' Andy said proudly.

'He wanted to practise, and I kind of forgot to tidy up,' Zoe said from the sofa, where she was hugging her knees and wearing an expression that reminded Emily of the naughty dogs on TikTok who were being shamed for wrecking their owner's homes, or eating a whole cooked chicken.

'Watch this,' Andy ordered, like a toddler about to do a rubbish dance. Kneeling on the floor, he took a deep breath and closed his eyes. Then he opened them and stared at one of the empty cans, before shoving it with his hand. It went flying across the room.

'See?' Andy said, proudly.

'Well done,' Emily said, numbly. She tried to feel pleased for Andy, but it was hard when she took in the state of her room. 'But why is there so much . . . *stuff* everywhere?'

'We were trying out different things,' Zoe said, nervously. 'It turns out he can't pick up anything heavier than a book. But if he tries really hard, he can push them over.'

'Squish like grape?' Emily said, faintly, looking at the shards of pottery scattered next to the armchair.

'Exactly,' Andy said. 'But also, sorry. I got a bit carried away.'

'And this? What was this for?' Emily plucked the sheet from the back of the sofa. It had two holes cut out of it. 'Oh, you're kidding me? Please tell me you're joking.'

'We couldn't resist,' Zoe said, perking up. 'Look at this. It's *so* funny.'

Andy stood up from his chair, and Zoe grabbed the sheet from Emily's hands. She threw it over Andy's head and arranged it over his face so he could see out of the eyeholes.

'Boo,' he said. And Zoe burst out laughing.

'I'm sorry,' she said, wheezing. 'I don't know why I find this so funny, but I just do. It's not even like he looks like a ghost to us! You can still see his feet.'

'Jangle jangle, scary chains. Spooky noises,' Andy said, in a deadpan voice that sent Zoe spinning off into a fresh fit of laughter.

As she fell back on the sofa, wiping tears of laughter from her eyes, Emily felt the corners of her mouth twitching upwards. In any other situation, she'd be joining in with the fun. But jealousy bit into her, stopping her in her tracks.

She'd spent all day walking around in ludicrous heels, trying to impress Oliver and doing some dull-as-dishwater marketing research for the Cat's Miaow pitch, only taking the occasional break to write ridiculous slogans for the world's most pretentious coffee brand – which, Emily figured, was quite an impressive feat when there was so much competition.

In the back of her mind, she'd been worrying about her upcoming trip back to Greenleaf – what did her mum need to talk to her about? And while she'd been carrying around all that stress, Andy and Zoe had been having the time of their lives and wrecking her front room in the process.

Emily had been forgotten – and, she realised, she'd actually been looking forward to spending time with Andy and teaching him how to touch things, and now she'd missed it.

Shaking her head, she knelt next to his chair and carefully picked up the pieces of her broken vase, fighting back tears. She didn't want to spoil anyone's fun. And she didn't understand why she was reacting like a mum who'd missed her child's first steps. But she couldn't help feeling dejected.

'Oh, shit, Emily, I'm really sorry,' Zoe said, alarmed, as a tear slid down Emily's nose. 'We really were going to tidy up.'

'And I'll buy you a new vase,' Andy said, tugging the sheet off his head.

'Where from? Oliver Boo-nas?' Emily said, managing a wobbly smile.

'See? She made a joke. Well done!'

'Let me do that,' Zoe said, gently nudging her away and gingerly picking up shards of pottery from the floor, before wrapping them in paper. 'Pour yourself a glass of wine – that's not yours by the way,' she added, gesturing at the half-empty bottle on the table. 'I topped up your wine collection, and even bought you a nice one.'

'Thanks, I suppose,' Emily said, slumping onto the sofa. Grabbing the bottle, she filled up the empty glass beside it, pouring herself a Zoe's Special Measure. 'Hang on, what have you wrapped that in?' Emily said, squinting at the bundle in Zoe's hands. 'Are those my notes for the Cat's Miaow pitch?'

'Umm ... maybe ...' Zoe said sheepishly. 'They were on the table.'

'Oh, for Christ's sake,' Emily said, putting her head in her hands.

'Oops,' Zoe said, grimacing at Andy and carefully unwrapping the vase. Smoothing out the crumpled pieces of paper, she handed them to Emily, who stared at them numbly.

'Look, we know we fucked up,' Zoe said, crouching down in front of Emily. 'But you've had a really stressy week, so why don't you come out with us and let us cheer you up?'

'Out? Where are you going?'

'Zoe found out that Remington 11 are playing in Brixton tonight,' Andy said excitedly. 'I want to see how they're managing without me. Pretty badly, I assume. And I haven't been to a gig for ages. Wanna come? You always said you'd see the band one day, but you never did.'

Emily looked at her laptop bag, which she'd dropped on the floor when she came home. She'd had a quiet evening of polishing her presentation planned, and perhaps some restorative meditation. But frankly, the gig sounded like a lot more fun. And even if she stayed at home, she knew she'd end up tidying instead of getting any work done.

Surveying the wreckage of her flat, it felt like a metaphor for her attempts to pull away from her past. With Andy back, she was quickly running out of the energy she needed to fight it. With a deep sigh, she pulled herself off the sofa.

'I guess we're going to a gig, then.'

Chapter 25

'Oh my god, this is *amazing*!' Zoe yelled, shrieking right into Emily's ear.

'Are you sure about that?' Emily yelled back, as the fifth pogo-ing gig-goer of the night bumped into her, sloshing his pint onto her shoes. Luckily, when she was getting ready, she'd ignored the pull of her faithful skater dress, and dug her Old Emily uniform of jeans, strappy top and chunky trainers out of the back of the wardrobe. She'd almost forgotten how comfortable clothes that didn't dig into her body could feel.

She hadn't been surprised when they'd arrived at the venue in Brixton where Remington 11 were performing – a small, dingy room above a pub – to find that there were plenty of tickets left. But it was clear that, although the band's fans were few, they made up for it with raw enthusiasm.

Onstage, the band was bathed in red, then green, then blue light, thanks to two old-fashioned projector wheels fixed to each side of the stage. The three guitarists were ear-splittingly loud, apparently competing for who could cause the most nosebleeds among their audience.

Emily was finding it hard to make out the lyrics above the din, although the crowd seemed to know every word of the latest song. As far as she could make out, the lead singer was putting on a faux-American drawl to sing about satnavs.

'Can't get away from satnavs
Wanna protect you from satnavs
Why is the world so full of satnavs?
You are my satnav.'

It was very weird – was the world really *that* full of satnavs? – but then Andy's band had always been anything but ordinary. He'd once written a song about tacos, called 'Taco, My Belle', which included the line, 'Your tasty curves make me say, "Holy Moly!"/with your tender meat and your guacamole'.

'Hey, look!' Zoe squealed, pointing at the stage. Andy had clambered onto it and was dancing wildly behind the guitarists, waving his arms in the air. Every now and then, he broke off to sing into the microphone, even though only Zoe and Emily could hear him.

As the song came to its deafening climax, Andy let out a whoop and dived off the stage, sailing through several of the people below and landing on the floor. They looked around, some rubbing their arms, and Emily remembered the strange sensation she felt whenever a part of Andy passed through her.

'Oh my god, that was amazing,' Andy said breathlessly, pushing through – literally, in some cases – the crowd. 'It's been so long since I played with the band. I don't think much of their replacement guitarist though, do you?'

'No, he was rubbish,' Emily agreed, honestly.

'Your band is amazing,' Zoe grinned.

'Thanks!' Andy said. 'Did you like the last song, "Sadness"? I used to love singing that one. It made me feel like Kurt Cobain.'

'Ahh, *Sadness.* That makes much more sense,' Emily nodded.

'They're taking a break now, but they'll be back on later. I've seen their set list, and they're playing "Buttmunch" in the second half. That's one of the ones I wrote!'

'I guess we're staying then,' Emily said, taking a gulp of warm wine out of the plastic cup she was clutching. 'In for a penny, in for a pound.'

'Can't wait,' Zoe said, her eyes shining as she looked at Andy. Emily hadn't seen her this happy in ages, and as she looked at them smiling at each other, she felt her stomach plunging. OK, so Emily had moved on since she'd thought Andy ghosted her, and things were going pretty well with Oliver – they'd spent most of the afternoon email-flirting again.

She'd also made it very clear to Zoe that she was looking for someone who didn't have to fight the urge to climb up every lamp post he passed, and she hadn't ever told her exactly how much she'd liked Andy when he was alive. But Emily couldn't help feeling a bit disgruntled by how keen she was to hang out with him. What happened to the girl code that said you didn't touch a girl's exes? Did it mean *nothing*, just because the ex in question was no longer alive?

Although, according to her book of mantras, she knew she should be busy 'Embracing the festival of life', rather than feeling hard done by, it didn't sit comfortably with her.

'Hey, there's Vaseline Alan,' Andy said, as a sweaty-looking man with shoulder-length hair plastered to his face made his way towards them through the crowd, heading for the bar at the back of the room. 'We should talk to him. Maybe he knows something.'

Emily nodded. 'Excuse me. Are you Vase ... I mean, are you Alan?' she yelled above the noise of the grungy DJ music being pumped through the speakers. If anything, it was louder than the band had been.

'Yeah. Who are you?' he asked, his eyes flicking over her shoulder and towards the bar.

'I'm an old friend of Andy's. Andy Atkins. Can I buy you a drink?'

At the mention of booze, Alan's eyes lit up. 'Cheers, I'll have a pint, thanks. It makes me play better.'

'I'm sure it does,' Emily muttered. 'This is Zoe, and I'm Emily,' she shouted, before turning towards the bar.

'Are you that bird he was dating before he died?' Alan asked, following.

'Well, I don't have feathers, thanks. But yeah, I was.'

'Although she didn't even know I'd died,' Andy added, shouting pointlessly into Alan's other ear as she ordered a round of drinks. 'Can you believe that?'

'Is there somewhere a bit quieter we can go?' Emily asked, her eyes scanning the room.

'D'you wanna come backstage?' Alan asked. 'I can introduce you to the rest of the boys.'

Emily, Zoe and Andy all nodded, before following Alan through a flimsy black curtain pinned to the frame of a door to the left of the stage. Pushing open a door optimistically marked 'Talent' with his foot, a small roar greeted Alan as he stepped into the room, as if he hadn't last seen his bandmates just three minutes ago.

They were scattered around the room, on a seating

arrangement comprising a small, tatty sofa, some metal beer kegs, and a bar stool. Amid this glamorous setting, a couple of the band were tuning guitars that were slung across their laps.

'Ladies, these are our guitarists, Knob-Out and Twisted Paul, and our lead singer, Banjo String. That there is our drummer, Billy the Adult. And that's our back-up singer, Clam.'

The men all nodded and waved. 'That nickname was my idea,' Andy said. 'It's short for Chlamydia – his real name's Vince Dunn. VD, see? Venereal disease, Chlamydia, Clam.'

'Very creative,' Emily said.

'Thanks.' Alan grinned. 'Guys, this is Zoe and Emily.'

'As in Andy's bird?' Clam said.

'Yes. His *bird*,' Zoe said, clearly enjoying herself.

'I don't remember seeing you at his funeral?' Knob-Out frowned. 'We all thought we might get to meet you there at last. We tried to find you online after he died, but Andy never posted about you.'

'Company policy.' Emily coughed, trying to ignore Zoe's look of surprise. 'And I was out of the country for his funeral. But of course, I would have come otherwise.'

'Poor old Andy, eh?' Alan said, scratching his chest with a hairy hand. 'We was really tight. It's been eight months now, ain't it? He was a top lad, he really was. Here, do you fancy going for a drink after the gig? We could, er, swap stories about him.'

'You cheeky bell end!' Andy protested.

'I'd better not, thanks. I'm still quite raw about Andy,' Emily said, watching as Zoe perched herself on the arm of the sofa, tugged her top down an extra inch, and pretended to be very interested in learning how to tune a guitar.

'Yeah, I was gutted when we heard,' Alan said, suddenly

looking crestfallen. 'He was a nutter, you know, but he was our nutter. The band's not been quite the same without him. His enthusiasm was a big part of what kept us going. He was so sure we'd be world-famous one day. Even though we're actually a bit shit, you know?'

'Speak for yourself, mate,' Knob-Out said, mashing his hand against the strings of his guitar and letting out a strangled yell.

'I guess there's nothing wrong with a bit of self-belief, is there?' Emily said, wincing.

'I wonder what happened to him?' Alan said. 'We never did find out. They said it might be suicide, but that doesn't sound like Andy. He loved jumping off stuff, so I wouldn't be surprised if he just forgot he wasn't Iron Man for a moment and chucked himself off a building.'

Emily smiled at the memory of Andy jumping off the top of the Shard and landing, superhero-style, on the ground beside her. 'That's what I told him.'

'Told who?' Alan frowned.

'Never mind,' Emily said, shaking her head.

'One thing I'm sure of, he didn't top himself,' Alan said firmly. 'He was so excited about that video he was making, so I'm sure he wouldn't have done anything silly. But it's all a bit of a mystery, innit?'

'What video?' Emily asked. She frowned at Andy, who shrugged.

'Didn't you know about it? We thought you would, which is why we tried to find you. He texted me the day it happened. Here, I've still got his message. It's the last one he sent me, so I took a screengrab after he died. You know, just in case.'

Pulling his mobile out of the pocket of his tatty jeans, Alan brought up his photos, scrolled through them, then held the phone out to Emily. She took it from him then read the texts out loud.

Alright mate? U still up for band practice l8r?

Yeah, cool. might be a bit late, cos i'm making a film at work. this bloke reckons it could make me famous, which means Emily will definitely want to be my girlf, right?

What video, mate? Sounds sweet, whatever it is.

'He never texted me back after that.'

Emily's heart thudded. 'So Andy was going to ask me to be his girlfriend?' She glanced at Andy, who was pretending to be engrossed by the beer keg beside him.

'Shit, yeah. Sorry. That's probably not the best way to find out, is it? He'd mentioned he wanted to ask you, but he was worried you'd say no. Said he thought he might not be good enough. He said you was gorgeous, and he wasn't wrong.'

'He needn't have worried, because he *was* good enough,' Emily said, realising as she said it that it was completely true. Andy turned and grinned at her.

'Do you have any idea what the video thing was about?' Alan asked.

'Nope, no idea,' Andy said, shaking his head.

'None, sorry,' Emily said, handing the phone back to him. 'But this conversation happened at six in the evening, right? And my last text to Andy must have been sent at about half past, when I left work. I always texted him when I was finished. But he never replied, which means maybe he died between six and half past – or around then, at least. He was usually pretty quick at getting back to me.'

'Before deciding I'd ghosted her and deleting me from her phone forever,' Andy added, helpfully.

'You could be right,' Alan said thoughtfully. 'I hoped you might know what the film was about, seeing as he mentioned you – you know, that he might have dropped it into conversation to butter you up before asking you to be his missus. But it sounds like he never got the chance.'

Emily felt sick. It had never crossed her mind that she might have had anything to do with Andy's death. Why would it? But judging by the timings of their texts, and Andy's complete inability to leave messages sitting on his phone unanswered, it seemed like a distinct possibility that this video was somehow involved. And if he'd thought whatever he was filming might help persuade Emily to be his girlfriend, then she might be partly to blame. Keeping him at arm's length had seemed harmless at the time – but what if it had somehow led to his death?

'Did the police come and see you too?' Alan asked suddenly.

'No.' Emily frowned. 'Did they visit you?'

'Yeah,' Alan said. 'This geezer came and asked me some questions, then took my phone in for evidence – he wore gloves and put it in a plastic bag and everything, like you see on TV. But I never heard nothing back after that. They posted me my phone back, but the messages about the video were gone. Luckily, they didn't delete the screengrab I'd taken. Not just a pretty face, see?' he finished, tapping his forehead with one finger.

'That's so weird. You'd think if my text arrived on Andy's phone after yours, the police would have visited me, too. Can you remember the name of the man who came to see you?'

'I do, as it happens. I'm shit with names, but it was DS Arnott. Like the fella in *Line of Duty*. I thought he was joking at first and he looked well annoyed.'

'I wonder why they didn't contact me?' Emily said. 'My last text to Andy was pretty bog-standard, but you'd have thought they'd have asked me if I knew anything all the same.'

'Maybe they only got in touch with me because he texted me about his last movements,' Alan shrugged. 'Although it does seem weird that you didn't hear anything.'

'Which makes this our latest clue,' Andy said.

Emily stood up. 'I guess we'd better get going and leave you to your beer, Alan. Zoe, you look like you want to stay back here, am I right?' Zoe gave her a thumbs-up. 'Thanks for your help. And good luck for the rest of the gig. You sound . . . great?'

'No problem,' Alan said, grinning. 'And if you change your mind about that drink, you know where to find me.'

Chapter 26

'You do know we're not about to embark on a trek to the summit of Mount Everest, don't you?' Emily asked, peering into the carrier bag Zoe was clutching, which was filled with crisps, sandwiches and magazines. 'It's thirty-five minutes on the C2C to Essex.'

'I really love train journeys,' Zoe said, by way of explanation, pulling open a bag of sweets and offering Emily a fizzy jelly worm. 'Don't be a party pooper.'

Reluctant to leave Zoe and Andy together over the weekend, Emily had persuaded Zoe to come to Essex with her on Saturday. Now Andy could touch things as well as walk through walls, he was much happier about being left to his own devices for a couple of days, although he was under strict instructions not to destroy anything (else) valuable.

This morning, after Emily had reminded him of his promise – and warned him that Jada knew how to exorcise people's exes using a process she'd read about in *Real Talk!* magazine, involving burnt sage leaves and feng shui, should he decide to misbehave – she met Zoe at Fenchurch Street station so they could make the journey together.

'How do you feel about seeing Baz?' Zoe asked, the train tossing them gently from side to side as it rumbled towards Essex.

'OK, I guess,' Emily said. 'I've known him my whole life, so at least this isn't another new man to get used to.'

Before leaving her flat this morning, Emily's Auntie Suze had texted to warn her that her mum had started dating Baz, her dad's old best friend. They'd run the garage together, and Emily couldn't help feeling a sting of betrayal on his behalf. What kind of person leaps into bed with their other half's best mate, even if said other half had left years ago? Although she was also aware she might be projecting the whole Zoe/Andy situation, however weird that was, onto her mum's.

Even though this revelation was shocking enough, apparently that wasn't the news her mum wanted to talk to her about. She was too scared to let her mind probe too deeply at what that might be.

When they reached Greenleaf, a short bus ride from the station then a few minutes' walk, Zoe headed for her parents' flat, agreeing to meet Emily down the pub once she'd had her fill of batting away her mum's sarcasm and hearing updates about the neighbours' various ailments.

'Good luck, soldier,' Zoe beamed, unable to disguise her happiness at being back.

Emily sighed and looked up at the tower block she'd called home for almost twenty-four years of her life. The local council tended to leave estates like Greenleaf to their own devices, so while the smart estates at the other end of town were kept clean and tidy, it had barely changed since she was a small child.

The yellow paint on the bars of the swings was largely chipped away, just a few patches still clinging heroically to the metal. A bench whose missing seat slats meant you had to perch right on the edge stood next to a bin that was leaning to one side, its base a melted puddle, where someone had set fire to it. Even the loose paving slab next to the playpark was still there – the one she and Zoe had used to try and launch Skittles into each other's open mouths almost two decades ago.

Yet despite the general disrepair, there were signs that Greenleaf's residents had done their best to make the most of their surroundings. The grass around the park was pin-neat, the older residents of the estate banding together to keep the verges trimmed. Despite the melted bin, there wasn't a scrap of litter anywhere, and there was a poster stuck over the NO BALL GAMES sign advertising a jumble sale being held at the Dog & Duck to raise money for the local food bank.

Climbing the concrete stairs to the flat, wincing at their musty smell, and rapping on the frosted glass of the front door – her mum having removed the knocker years ago so she could use it to prop open the kitchen window – her Auntie Suze opened the door, giving her the kind of wildly enthusiastic greeting a Labrador might do.

She was a good half-foot shorter than Emily, and spent the first ten minutes after her arrival stretching up and squeezing her tight, letting her go to examine her face, her palms pressed into her cheeks, then hugging her all over again. Emily's mum stood in the doorway of the living room, picking at her fingernails.

'Bloody hell, you're even more fancy-looking than last time,' she said by way of a greeting, once Auntie Suze had finally let her go. 'Baz is gonna think you was swapped at birth.'

Emily forced a smile as her mum pecked her on the cheek. She'd purposefully dressed down for the occasion, in plain trousers and her third-nicest top, but apparently that was still too OTT.

'Hi, Mum,' she said, handing her a white envelope. 'Happy birthday and all that.'

'Another year older,' her mum said. 'What a treat.'

'You're looking thin, love,' Suze said anxiously. 'What are they feeding you over there? I've heard they're all vegans in London. I don't know how they expect to get anything done without a few sausage sandwiches to keep them going.'

Emily smiled, putting her arm around her aunt's shoulders and squeezing. While her mum was tall and angular, Suze was short and round, and six years older than her younger sister.

They looked nothing alike and had completely different temperaments, but their identical, high cheekbones and pointed chins, which they'd clearly got from Emily's grandad, proved they were definitely sisters, for better or worse.

'I still eat meat, I promise,' Emily said, kissing the top of her aunt's head – although she didn't have the heart to tell her that 'meat' meant the odd slice of turkey, or that she hadn't eaten bread for almost eight months.

'Glad to hear it,' Suze said. 'You look bloody gorgeous, anyway. Hard to believe she comes from the same crop as us, isn't it, Abi?'

'That'll be her dad's genes,' Emily's mum said drily. 'He buggered off the first chance he got, too.'

Emily frowned at her. 'Come on, let's say hello to Baz. I haven't seen him in ages.'

'Try not to act like you're too good for him,' her mum warned as they headed towards the living room.

'What do you mean?' Emily demanded.

'You know what I mean, madam,' her mum said, shoving the door open with one hand so Emily could greet Baz. Seeing him lying on the sofa in his blue overalls brought a memory swooping back to her – of her favourite game when she was little. Her dad would carry her around the garage on his back, looking underneath cars and inside tall storage cabinets while she clung to the back of his overalls.

'Have you seen Emily, Barry?' he'd ask, sounding worried. 'I'm sure it was her shift today, but I can't find her anywhere.'

Emily would giggle her head off as he searched for her high and low, before standing in front of the mirror above the grubby garage sink and pretending to spot her at last, sweeping her off his back for a hug.

'Say hi to Emily,' her mum said, picking up the remote and turning the TV down a couple of notches.

'Alright, Emily, nice to see you,' Baz said, flicking his eyes briefly from the screen to Emily's face and flashing a smile.

'Alright, Baz,' Emily said.

'For God's sake, Baz, can't you look as if you mean it? At least sit up,' Emily's mum said, slapping his legs off the sofa and sitting down in the space they left behind. 'You don't have to stop watching the game.'

'Em don't mind, do you? It's West Ham against Aston Villa. I've got a tenner riding on this,' he said. 'Here, swap over, will you?'

'Men,' Emily's mum said affectionately, swapping seats so Barry could see the telly properly.

'Bloody Fabianski,' Barry muttered now, grabbing the

remote and putting the volume back up. 'He couldn't catch herpes in a brothel, the useless bastard.'

'Charming,' Emily said, plonking herself into the armchair next to the telly. She felt herself falling into a sullen mood, which always happened within minutes of coming back home. It was like the flat had its own electromagnetic force field, which erased all the maturity Emily had developed in the years since she'd left home, sending her back to the years when her mum had called her 'The Incredible Sulk'. Apparently, losing your father at a tender age wasn't enough to elicit any sympathy.

Her mum slid her thumb under the flap of the envelope and tore it open. 'Still got your sense of humour, then?' she snorted, as she read the front.

Emily had chosen a card that was covered in flowers, and said, TO A LOVING MUM ON HER BIRTHDAY on the front. Underneath was a poem written in swirly italics, which began,

I hope your day is as special as you, and as warm as the love in your heart
We have so much fun when we're together, and feel sadness when we are apart.

'Oh, that's lovely,' Suze said, as she took the card from her and read the front. Emily decided it was best not to tell her that it was entirely tongue in cheek. 'I'll get some tea,' she added, squeezing past Emily's mum to the kitchen.

Emily looked around her mum's tiny front room. Not much had changed here either, to the extent that she suspected the dead spider plant on the bookcase was the same one that had been on its last legs in January.

There was far too much stuff crowding the room, and everything in it was mismatched. Although not in a *Grand Designs*, 'I inherited this from my grandmother, who was Churchill's former secretary, while we got this gorgeous mid-century piece from a local flea market' kind of way.

Emily's mum accumulated random furniture almost by accident, but it never seemed to flow the other way. She'd once taken a chair home from a gathering at a neighbour's flat, thinking she'd brought it with her, before realising the next morning that it wasn't hers.

'They can nick one from the next night,' she'd said with a shrug, admiring her new chair.

In this way, the flat was crammed with stuff from other people's lives that didn't quite match. Emily's childhood bedroom had been equally haphazard, splashed with piles of colourful knick-knacks donated by, or bartered with, neighbours. She wondered if perhaps she'd gone too far by sticking to grey and cream in her own flat. It looked sophisticated, but was also deathly dull.

'What's this meant to be, then?' Emily asked, plucking a ceramic elephant from the small table next to the armchair. Its snout curved upwards and was hollow with a hole in the top, while its tail curled around to form a handle at the back. Whoever made it had forgotten to paint pupils in its eyes, so it stared blankly ahead. It was absolutely hideous.

'Teapot,' her mum said, patting Barry's leg.

'What's it doing in the living room?'

'No room in the kitchen, is there?' her mum said, as if that was the most obvious answer in the world. 'Plus it's decorative.'

'If you want to stretch the word decorative to its absolute limits, then yes, it's very decorative,' Emily said.

'Load of piss,' Barry suddenly snapped, making Emily jump. Grabbing the remote, he switched the TV off, took a gulp of beer from a can sitting on the floor next to the sofa, then slapped his knees. 'So how've you been doing, Em? I ain't seen you for donkey's years.'

'I'm fine, ta,' Emily said, her Essex accent already making itself known. 'Been keeping busy. I've got a job in the city now, in advertising. And my own flat. Rented – you know.'

'You look well for it,' Barry nodded. 'Your dad would be proud of you.'

'He's not dead, he walked out, Baz,' Emily's mum said. 'He could tell her he was proud of her to her face if he wanted to, couldn't he? If he could be bothered, the bloody toe-rag.'

'OK, Mum, don't start,' Emily sighed. Auntie Suze patted her hand as she placed a steaming mug of tea on the little table next to her chair.

She smiled. 'Plenty of milk, two sugars.'

'Lovely, thank you,' Emily said, taking a sip and wincing at the sweetness. She hadn't had sugar in her tea in years. 'Auntie Suze said you had something to tell me, Mum. You'd better not be up the duff or there'll be hell to pay, young lady.'

She snorted and took another sip of tea. Then noticed her mum was beaming at Barry and clutching her stomach.

'Actually . . .' she said, and Barry reached over and squeezed her hand, a delighted look lighting up his face.

'You've got to be kidding me . . .' Emily said, her mouth falling open. 'Auntie Suze, is this a wind-up?'

'I'm afraid not, love,' Auntie Suze said. 'Silly buggers.'

'But you're ancient!' Emily blurted at her mum.

'I'm not *that* old,' she said indignantly. 'I had you when I was yay high, didn't I, so all my bits still work.'

'They reckon it's called a geriatric pregnancy at her age,' Barry added. 'You can imagine how much your mum liked that one.' He beamed, and placed his hand on top of her mum's, which was still resting on her stomach.

'And anyway, it was an accident,' her mum sniffed.

'A happy one,' Barry added quickly. 'I've always wanted to be a dad. And here's my chance at last.'

'I can't believe you've been so irresponsible,' Emily said, standing up. 'I'm twenty-eight, old enough to be a mum myself. And now you're telling me I'm going to have a brother or sister? Don't you people know how to use condoms?'

'Don't be so bloody rude,' her mum said. 'I seem to remember taking you to Superdrug for the morning-after pill more than once, so don't get all holier-than-thou with me. And you're having a sister, actually. We're calling her Chanel. That's what you would have been called if your dad hadn't loved bloody *Bagpuss* so much when he was a kid.'

Emily's cheeks flushed as she remembered the way her dad had put her to bed every night, right up until the day he'd left.

'I'm just an old, saggy cloth cat,' he'd tell her, tucking her duvet all the way around her legs and arms. 'Baggy, and a bit loose at the seams.'

'But Emily loved him,' she'd reply sleepily, as he'd kiss her goodnight, before drifting off feeling completely cosy and safe.

She glanced at Barry. He seemed smitten with the idea of being a dad now, but she knew that didn't mean anything. Her dad had been like that too, once. She pictured her as-yet-unborn sister growing up without a dad, just like she'd done – being looked after by Auntie Suze and watching her mum sinking deeper and deeper into drink to cope. And all the while, her mum would hint heavily that it was Chanel's fault her dad had done a runner, leaving her with the same rock-bottom self-esteem Emily had always struggled with.

Despite her determination to move on, Emily couldn't leave her own sister to deal with something like that alone, so she'd have to go back to Greenleaf to take care of her – or at least visit regularly, to check she was OK. It seemed to Emily that every time she took a step away from this place, something happened to drag her back. And now this had happened, she couldn't see how she'd ever fully escape her past.

'Sorry, but I need some air,' Emily said, tears welling up in her eyes. Grabbing her coat from the back of the chair, she ran outside, ignoring her Auntie Suze calling for her to come back, the perfect future she'd worked so hard to deserve dissolving before her eyes.

Chapter 27

'What's going on? Are you OK?' Zoe asked when she met Emily outside the doors to the Dog & Duck.

'I'll tell you everything once we've got drinks,' Emily said, stamping her feet against the cold. 'You're probably going to need one, and I definitely do.'

'Why didn't you meet me inside? It's freezing,' Zoe shivered.

'I haven't been here for ages, and you know what they're like.'

'Fair point.'

The Dog & Duck was the unofficial Greenleaf pub, and anyone from outside the area who accidentally stumbled upon it was decidedly unwelcome.

As a teenager, Emily had been drinking in there when a group of girls dressed up for a wedding had walked in, apparently hoping for a quick drink before the ceremony. Everyone had reduced their chatting to a whisper as soon as they'd entered, as if they'd stepped into a saloon in the Wild West. It took the girls a while to realise everyone was throwing suspicious glances at them, and the hush that had settled over the pub didn't lift until they'd hurriedly finished their drinks and tottered off on their crystal-clad heels.

But now, it was Emily who was the outsider. Although Zoe came home regularly to see her parents, Emily had reduced her visits down to three times a year, at Christmas and on her mum's and Auntie Suze's birthdays, and the Dog & Duck's regulars weren't backwards in coming forwards to show her they thought her rejection of their home turf was bang out of order.

Emily felt a rush of nerves as Zoe pushed open the pub door, letting out a blast of warm air and conversation.

'Alright, Zo?' Bob, the pub's landlord, called over, raising a hand from behind the bar as Emily followed her through the pub and towards the back of the room around crowds of mismatched furniture. The pub had previously been a British Legion hall, and it was cavernously large, its walls still filled with plaques honouring members both dead and alive.

Against one wall, a row of dusty glass cabinets was filled with medals and trophies earned for long-forgotten triumphs, and photographs of legion members proudly wearing their uniforms. Most of the drinkers here could find a member of their family among the names carved into wood or punched into metal, because most Greenleaf families had lived here for generations, moving into the tower blocks from the surrounding housing estates back when they were shiny and new.

Following closely behind Zoe, Emily marvelled at how little the place changed from year to year. Even the pub's regulars – those who were still alive, at least – were sitting in the exact same spots they'd occupied for decades. Their faces were more lined, and the tables were more chipped, but otherwise, it was like Emily had stepped back into 2010.

'Who's this you've brought with you?' Bob squinted, shifting along the bar to peer behind Zoe. 'Is that Pete's girl? Fucking hell, look at Zsa Zsa Gabor over here. Someone get a bin bag to put on the seats, she'll get a grubby arse!'

The landlord's joke triggered a smattering of laughter from the regulars.

'Who the hell's Zsa Zsa Gabor?' Zoe muttered.

Even dressing down couldn't disguise the fact that Emily had toned up and lost weight since her last visit, but she knew if she put up with the digs with good grace, and gave as good as she got, everyone would soon get bored.

'Yeah, quite right too, Bob,' she said. 'Last time I saw something that mucky, I was dating your Mike.'

The regulars who were within earshot guffawed at this one, and Emily started to relax. Zoe leaned over to hug Bob, then shot a contented grin at Emily. She'd never understand why, but this was Zoe's happy place – somewhere, as the song had it, everybody knew her name.

'Nice to see you too, Glamourpuss,' Bob said, leaning over the bar to give Emily a peck on the cheek. His breath smelled of the watered-down glass of rum he always kept behind the bar, which whisked Emily straight back to being a little girl, when her dad would park her in a corner with a packet of prawn cocktail crisps and a copy of *Tots TV* magazine to keep her occupied.

Back then, Bob had been the landlord's son, and would sneak Emily a handful of mini sausage rolls or half a scotch egg from behind the bar to nibble on when she'd run out of crisps.

'Two large white wines, please,' Zoe asked, leaning comfortably on the bar. Emily opened her mouth to ask for

Sauvignon blanc, before remembering that the wine at the Dog & Duck came in two types: red and white, served in miniature plastic bottles.

She glanced at one of the floral-upholstered barstools before thinking better of sitting down. Bob had been joking about the bin bag, but she had no way of knowing how many germs were lurking among the decades of dirt ground into the stool's fabric seat, and she was suddenly regretting choosing to wear her pale-grey trousers, rather than stain-hiding black.

'I'll grab us a table,' Emily nodded, choosing one with wooden chairs that stood a better chance of being clean. Grabbing a tissue from her bag, she gave the table a surreptitious wipe, before depositing her bag on the floor. Knowing how the Dog & Duck was largely held together with old beer stains and cigarette smoke, she'd dug an old one out from the bottom of her wardrobe that she'd kept in case of noughties fancy-dress party emergencies.

As she sat down, the door slammed open, and three generations of Robinsons clattered into the pub. Emily recognised them all: Pat and Paul, their son Craig, his wife Clare, and their twins, who were about five years old.

After his star had briefly risen at Ravenwood High School, thanks to his good looks, Craig had started dating Kirsty, but it wasn't long before she'd got fed up that he couldn't afford to take her out anywhere more glamorous than Pizza Express when it had a two-for-one deal on.

Giving up on his aspirations and returning to his more comfortable life as a social reject, he'd started dating Clare, the pick of the Greenleaf girls, instead. The whole incident had been the talk of the Dog & Duck at the time, and Bob had insisted on calling Craig 'Shit Calum Best' for weeks after he'd broken up with Kirsty.

These days, both Clare and Craig looked a bit worn around the edges, wrinkles creeping onto their faces and strands of grey hair appearing at their partings, even though they were still only in their late twenties, like Emily. The glow that had set them apart from their peers on the estate had been rubbed away, making them look much the same as everyone else.

As Clare tried desperately to herd her boisterous twins into two chairs, Emily could see why.

'I WANNA SIT IN A CHAIR LIKE KYLE'S!' one of the boys yelled, kicking his sibling in the shin as he sat down.

'There's never two bloody chairs the same in here, is there?' Clare muttered, scanning the room. 'Sodding cheapskate.'

In big cities, mismatched furniture was a sign that a place was totally trendy, rather than falling apart at the seams. Emily had no doubt Coffee & Co was filled with tables and chairs exactly like those in the Dog & Duck, except they'd call them 'reclaimed' rather than 'second-hand', and would have paid well over the odds for them. Bob thought paying over a tenner for a barstool on Gumtree was daylight robbery.

'Here you go, you can have my chair,' Emily said, standing up. Her chair matched the one Clare's son Kyle was currently sitting in, clutching his leg and yelling 'OW!' at louder and louder volumes until Paul made a big show of rubbing it better.

'Thanks, Emily,' Clare said, blowing the hair out of her face and quickly looking Emily up and down. 'Nice to see you, by the way.'

Emily wondered what she saw. Someone who'd managed to better themselves since leaving Greenleaf and had made a good decision in not settling down and having kids too young, she hoped. Sitting side-by-side, the twins started swinging their legs and kicking the underside of the table in unison.

'Alright, love?' Pat asked, kissing Emily's cheek as she scanned the room for another chair. 'How's your mum?'

'Don't bloody ask,' she sighed.

'So she's told you then?' Pat cackled.

'Told you what?' Zoe asked, setting two glasses down on the table.

'Mum's pregnant, *obviously*,' Emily said, grabbing a seat from a neighbouring table. 'Because why would a forty-four-year-old woman who's got thirty years of shagging under her belt know how to use the bloody pill properly?'

'Oh, Em!' Zoe said, and clamped a hand over her mouth to stop herself from laughing.

'It's not funny!' Emily protested, unable to stop the corner of her mouth twitching upwards into a smile too. Plonking herself in her seat like a grumpy teenager, she took a large swig of wine.

'I guess it's not,' Zoe said, trying and failing to force her face into a frown. 'A baby, though. Everyone likes babies. Does she know what she's having?'

'A girl. Called Chanel. I can only assume she's doing a bit of cosmic ordering and is hoping she ends up with a career in fashion.'

'You did always want a brother or sister . . .'

'That was years ago, not *now*,' Emily said, picking up a beer mat and worrying at its corners. 'You know what this means, don't you? I was doing everything I could to escape this place, but now I'm going to have a permanent attachment to it, for at least eighteen years. And what am I supposed to tell Oliver? It's embarrassing enough to have a mum still popping out kids at her age. But I told him my parents live in New Zealand and don't know how to use FaceTime. I can't keep popping to Essex to see a baby. I don't know what to do, Zo.'

'Maybe you could find a man who'll stay with you even if you tell him the truth about your tragic past living on a council estate and going to a school you didn't have to pay for?' Zoe said. 'You've barely met the guy, but you're already so worried about what Oliver thinks. Which makes me worry about *you*.'

Zoe leaned over and squeezed Emily's hand. She squeezed back before extracting it, then reaching down to pluck her phone from her bag.

'The only thing you need to worry about is if I find myself dragged back here. You know how hard I've tried to escape, and nothing, not even a sister, is going to stop me making something of myself. In fact . . .'

Before she could change her mind, Emily tapped out a text to Oliver, her thumbs flying over the keys.

I'm sorry we couldn't hang out today, but how about you come over to mine tomorrow evening and we can work on the presentation? I could make us something to eat

Immediately, three dots appeared, making her stomach swoop with excitement.

Sounds good. As you might have guessed, I was planning to work on Sunday anyway, and it would be good to have some company

Emily grinned. 'There,' she said, hitting send and showing her phone to Zoe. 'Can't take that back now. If the past is going to drag me backwards, then I'm going to have to outrun it, aren't I?'

'By shagging Oliver?'

'Maybe,' Emily said. 'But only after we've done some really excellent work trying to sell cat food, obviously.'

On the table beside theirs, Clare and Craig's twins had given up trying to destroy the furniture, and started smashing their identical plastic cars together, giggling uncontrollably every time something snapped off one of them and flew across the room.

Pat and Clare were talking animatedly about someone who, according to Pat, had a 'heart of gold', even though, from what Emily could gather, he'd just been sent to prison. Meanwhile, Craig and his dad were trying to stop the twins destroying their toys but having little luck because they were laughing too hard themselves.

Zoe smiled at them fondly, crossing her eyes at the twins and blowing a raspberry at them before turning back to Emily.

'I know it's a cliché, but blood is thicker than water, Em,' she said, gesturing to the next-door table. 'You're going to have a sister. You can't just run away from that.'

'My dad managed to do it without so much as a backward glance,' Emily said, tears springing to her eyes again. 'The whole point of trying to get a man like Oliver is to make sure my own kids are secure and happy – and not just until their dad gets fed up and fucks off. I wanted my future to be different. But now Chanel's probably going to grow up without a dad, just like I did, and I'll be dragged right back to square one.'

'You don't know that, though, do you? You have to stop judging everyone around here by what your dad did,' Zoe said, spinning her glass by its stem. Behind her, Bob knocked over a tray of empty glasses and she joined the rest of the pub in letting out a hearty cheer. 'You're like the girls at school, making assumptions just because of our background.

'I mean, look at my parents. They've been together for about a million years, they get by just fine, and they're still in love. And Craig,' she added, lowering her voice, 'you were so jealous when he got into Kirsty's gang, but he's right back here in Greenleaf. And he looks pretty happy to me.'

'And knackered.'

'And knackered, yes. But that's kids for you. If you think Oliver is going to change more nappies than the average guy just because he goes to a posh gym, you're in for a bit of a shock. Why don't you give Barry the benefit of the doubt?'

'Should my ears be burning?' said a voice behind their table. 'Your Auntie Suze sent me to come and check on you.'

Emily turned around to see Barry standing behind her, his hands stuffed in his pockets and a cheerful grin on his face.

'You weren't sent here by Mum, then?' Emily asked.

'Nah. I think her exact words were, "If she wants to sulk because I'm creating the miracle of life, then bloody let her." But I agreed with your Auntie Suze. We didn't exactly break the news to you gently, did we? Alright, Zo?'

'Alright, Baz,' Zoe nodded.

'Do you mind if I pull up a pew?'

Emily nodded, sipping her wine, and Barry turned a chair around and straddled it, his arms resting on the back. The sleeves of his stained blue overalls were rolled up to the elbow, and he smelled of grease and Swarfega. It was the exact same way her dad had always sat down when he was about to tell her something important, and Emily felt her heart squeeze.

'Look, Em, I know this is a bit of a shock to you,' Barry said, gently. 'And it's a bit of a shock to us, too. But it's a good kind of shock, now it's sunk in. I promise I'll do right by your mum, and little Chanel. The business is going great, so they won't want for anything. It won't be like when you were growing up.'

A memory flashed into Emily's mind, of the girls at school laughing at her cheap shoes. Nothing she wore was ever quite right. Would Chanel have to go through the same thing?

'No offence, Baz, but everyone thought Dad was in it for the long haul as well, didn't they? And that we'd be fine. And we weren't. Far from it.'

'I get why you feel that way, Em. Of course I do. Your dad left me and the garage up to our ears in debt, and it took me years to set things straight, so his disappearing act affected me, too.' Barry rubbed his face with a large, calloused hand. 'I could have swung for him, if I'm honest with you. But I can promise you now, I won't do anything like that. I did plenty of gallivanting and sodding about when I was young. I'm far too old to be playing silly buggers now. Not every man is like your dad.'

'I'm going to hold you to that,' Emily said. 'I've got my own life now, and Auntie Suze can't go running around looking after a kid while Mum sticks her nose in a bottle, like she did with me.'

'Suze is barely in her fifties, Em.'

'Exactly! Look at her! You know I love her more than anything, but she looks about seventy.' Emily glanced at the table next to hers, where Clare was busy trying to stop one of the twins drawing on his own face in permanent marker, and thought, *and so does everyone else around here.* 'And trust me, I spend far too much on moisturiser and hyaluronic acid peels to want my face to go the same way.'

Zoe snorted.

'I understand that you're protective,' Barry said, 'but all I can give you is my word. How about you come down to the garage after your drink, and I'll show you how it's going. There's something I want to give you, too.'

As soon as she stepped through the open door of Barry's Repairs – formerly Pete and Barry's Auto Shop – Emily was hit by a wave of memories that felt like a fist to her stomach. The smell of the place, a combination of old oil, Swarfega, sawdust and the metallic tang of dismantled car parts, instantly took her back twenty years.

The garage was only small, with room for one car inside and a couple outside on a cramped forecourt, so she walked around its edges slowly, absorbing the stingingly familiar sights and smells, and letting memories overtake her. She vividly remembered all the hours she'd spent here, spinning on the office chair, exploring the metal shelves that stretched from floor to ceiling, and begging her dad for piggybacks while his legs poked out from underneath a car.

Although he was long gone, the shelves were still crammed with plastic buckets filled with screws, nuts and bolts, precariously stacked wheel rims, files of paperwork covered in oily fingerprints, and random tools and rags. One wall was hung with a shadow pegboard, its ghostly outlines of hammers, spanners and wrenches bare.

Emily remembered her dad hanging it proudly on the wall, announcing that the shop would be much tidier from now on, before he and Barry had immediately abandoned the new system for their usual one of leaving anything they were using on the floor once they'd finished with it. She'd loved going around the garage, picking up lost tools, and hanging them up properly.

'You was a right pain.' Barry laughed softly behind her. 'Me and your dad knew where everything was, even if it didn't look like it. Then you'd come along, little madam that you were, and tidy up after us. We'd put a screwdriver down for two seconds, and whoosh! It was gone.'

Emily turned to look at him. He had a friendly face the texture of old leather, with bright-blue eyes and scruffy, mousy-brown hair, which was permanently slicked with oil from where he'd absent-mindedly run his hands through it at work.

'Why do you think he left, Baz?' she asked. 'I'm pretty sure, now I'm older, that it wasn't anything I did, whatever Mum had to say about it. But I want to understand.'

'I can't speak for your dad, Em, but whatever his reasons for leaving, he really did love you,' Barry said, wiping his hands down his front, even though they weren't greasy. 'I've got no idea what was running through that thick skull of his. But he was young. Younger than you are now. He had a young child, a business with a stack of unpaid bills, a stressed-out wife. Maybe the pressure got too much for him.'

Emily frowned. Standing here in the garage where her dad had worked brought it home to her how young he really was when he'd left. She'd been eight years old, which meant he'd been just twenty-six when he'd vanished. Right now – apart from having to find out what had happened to her dead ex-boyfriend and land a promotion at a job that didn't do any real good in the world – Emily had no responsibilities. She'd never really thought about what her dad had had to deal with at her age, even without the added burden of having to live with her mum, who'd mellowed with age, no matter how unbelievable that seemed.

'Thanks, Baz. I know you're probably right. It's just hard to feel it, you know?' Barry patted her gently on the arm. 'What was it you wanted to give me?'

'Here,' Barry said, turning towards a set of metal drawers that were heroically clinging to the last vestiges of their formerly pristine green paint. Yanking open a drawer, which squealed in protest, he pulled out a small blue plastic vase with a domed, ridged lid, and pressed it into Emily's hand with a shrug.

'I dunno where the ball's gone from inside. It must have disappeared yonks ago. But I know it was your favourite, and that your dad would want you to have it. It's only a small thing. I hope you weren't expecting diamonds.'

Emily's face battled the urge to laugh and burst into tears all at once. She chose instead to hug him. 'This might sound weird, but it's better than diamonds, Barry,' she said. 'Much, *much* better.'

Chapter 28

Essex, February 2004

The reflection in the mirror showed a look of pure concentration on Emily's face as she tried to hide the red ball in the palm of her small hand. She was sitting cross-legged in front of the tall mirror propped against her mum and dad's bedroom wall. A cheap magic trick was placed in front of her on the tatty green carpet.

'I place the ball in the palm of my hand like this,' Emily said quietly. 'I say the magic words – abracadabra! – and, ta-da! It disappears. But look. I lift the lid of the cup and see? It's reappeared!'

She looked up and grinned at herself in the mirror. She'd been practising for two hours and had finally mastered tipping the red ball from the cup into her hand, pretending to place it in the palm of the other, then carefully dropping it into her lap as she said the magic word to make the ball disappear.

She sometimes forgot how to open the cup a certain way to show that the ball had magically reappeared – when actually, it was a fake lid painted to look like a red ball – but that was the easy bit. The tricky bit was making the ball look like it had disappeared into thin air, without anyone spotting the trickery behind it.

Another half an hour, and she was pretty sure she'd be ready to show her dad what she'd learned.

'What are you doing in here? How many times have I told you not to come into our room?' a voice demanded from above her head. Looking up, she saw her mum frowning down at her, her arms folded.

'I only came in a little way,' Emily said in a small voice. 'I wanted to practise, and I needed a mirror. There isn't one in my room.' She held up the plastic cup. 'See? I've been learning the ball and vase trick. I'm almost there. I just need a bit longer.'

'And where did you get that?' her mum asked, bending down and snatching the cup from Emily's hand. 'Have you been going through Dad's things?'

'Not going through them … I …' Emily blushed. 'He showed me the trick last week, and I saw where he kept it in the garage. It was just on a shelf. I didn't go through his stuff, I promise. I just wanted to surprise him.'

'He'll have been looking everywhere for that. He'll be so upset and disappointed. You know you're not supposed to touch our things.'

'I'm sorry. I didn't think he'd mind,' Emily said, tears prickling behind her eyes. She'd been so keen to impress her dad, she hadn't considered that he might be missing the trick she'd borrowed. It was meant to be a nice thing; a surprise. But now, she had a horrible twisting feeling in her stomach. The last thing she'd wanted to do was let him down or make him worry.

'Come on. Out,' her mum demanded. 'You can spend the rest of the day in your room. I'll call you for dinner, but I'll be taking this.' She held up the vase, and a tear slid down Emily's face. As she stood up, her hand touched the red plastic ball she'd dropped in her lap, and she clutched it in the centre of her palm.

The hours spent practising sleight of hand meant her mum didn't see her sliding the ball into the back pocket of her jeans before she walked down the small hallway and into her room, and quietly shut the door.

That evening, dinner was spent in silence, her mum checking and rechecking the clock on the wall of the kitchen.

'I'm going to kill your dad when he comes home,' she growled. 'I'd leave him a note telling him the dinner's in the dog, if we could afford a bloody dog.'

'Maybe he's with Baz?' Emily asked, timidly.

'You don't say. Baz and the rest of them down the Dog & Duck, having a laugh while I'm here, stuck on my own with our kid, slaving over dinner. You could use this mash to grout the bathroom by now. I'm telling you, Emily, when you get older, keep your legs together,' she said, lighting a cigarette. Emily looked down at her grubby knees and frowned. 'You'll understand later on,' her mum added. 'And if you can't do that, at least find a man with a bit of class. One who can make some proper money, who won't spend it all down the pub.' She rubbed her eyes and sighed.

That evening, after Emily had gone to bed, her mum poked her head into her room before slipping away. Emily heard her pulling her coat from one of the hooks in the hallway and heading quietly out of the front door.

Emily knew she'd gone out to look for her dad, and

that tomorrow would be awful. Her mum would be barely speaking to him, and he'd trail her around the flat, half-apologising, half-arguing that he needed some down-time after a day at work.

'And it's not like I don't pull my weight with Emily, is it? She comes to the garage so I can keep an eye on her, so you get some time to yourself, don't you?'

These arguments always made Emily terrified – and this time, it would be even worse. It was the first time her dad had been out so late, and not come home or even rung her mum from the pub to tell her where he was. In fact, they hadn't seen him since he'd popped out to buy her mum some more cigarettes that afternoon.

Emily knew he did his best, even if sometimes his best wasn't good enough for her mum.

'But Emily loved him,' Emily whispered to herself in the dark, pulling the covers over her head.

Chapter 29

When Emily had invited Oliver over on Sunday evening, there was one thing she'd completely failed to consider, but which really should have been at the forefront of her mind.

'But *why* do I have to go out?' Andy sulked, as she worried her way around her small front room, making sure the sofa was precisely the right distance from the coffee table, plumping cushions and karate-chopping them in the middle, and artfully draping her grey throw across one corner of the sofa using a 'flip and flop' method she'd found on YouTube.

He hadn't reacted well to the news that she expected him to make himself scarce that evening, especially after he'd been alone for most of the weekend. Zoe had graciously agreed to ghost-sit, but Andy was still less than thrilled to be turfed out of his favourite armchair.

'Because – and call me old-fashioned if you like – there are few bigger passion-killers than your dead ex loitering around while you're trying to boink someone else.'

Andy blushed and looked at the floor. Emily grimaced.

'Sorry, that was uncalled for. I know your situation isn't ideal . . .'

'What? Being dead? That's a bit of an understatement.'

'. . . But I need to get on with my life while you get on with your death. Demi Moore didn't have to put up with this crap in *Ghost*, did she?'

'Please can I stay? Please please please?'

'Not a hope in hell,' Emily said. 'Remember what happened at Bayou Bar? It's not happening.'

'Don't forget to make the end of the toilet paper all pointy, will you?' Andy said sulkily, as Emily karate-chopped another cushion. 'What *will* Oliver think otherwise?'

Emily folded her arms and glared at him. She didn't want to admit that she had actually considered folding the loo roll into pointy corners, before worrying that it would give away the fact that she'd spent the summer when she was twenty-one working as a hotel chambermaid. Oliver and his friends probably spent their summers skiing, horse riding and being patronising to staff like her, rather than picking other people's pubes off tiny bars of soap.

She picked up the cushion and threw it through Andy's head. 'Rude. I've spent all weekend on my own, and I've been really bored without you here,' Andy moped.

'How is it even possible to be bored in your situation? You can walk through walls and touch stuff and are invisible, which means you can go anywhere and do anything. When you were alive you always chose invisibility over flying as your superpower, and now you've got it, but with knobs on, you don't know what to do with it.'

Emily recalled a video she'd seen on TikTok, of a man who'd filled his kitchen with brightly coloured plastic balls and left the house, secretly filming his dogs in his absence. He'd assumed they'd spend the whole time playing, but instead, they'd sat by the door waiting for him, with woebegone looks on their faces. Andy had always reminded her of a slightly dishevelled but well-meaning puppy, and this proved it.

'OK, maybe I was lonely, then. I can go anywhere and do anything, but I can't talk to anyone unless you or Zoe are around, and that's no fun. You kind of owe me.' Emily shook her head. 'How about we make that call to the police before Oliver arrives, then? Surely you have time for *that.* I'm sure some of your cushions can stand to go un-floofed.'

'Alright, then,' Emily muttered, grabbing her phone from the coffee table.

After their conversation with Alan at the Remington 11 gig, Andy and Emily had decided their next step would be to call the police and find out why they hadn't approached Emily to talk to her, seeing as her text to Andy was possibly the last one he'd ever received.

'They might want to talk to you,' Andy said. 'And maybe you know something about what happened without even knowing it, if you see what I mean.'

'Like a clue hiding in plain sight?' Emily said, and Andy nodded.

Emily hadn't had time to call the police since they'd agreed on this plan of action, but now she reckoned she did owe Andy that, at least. Standing up and walking around the room, because she'd read somewhere that it makes the caller sound more authoritative, she dialled the number for the Metropolitan Police and put the call on speakerphone, her heart thudding.

She wasn't sure why she felt so nervous, but had a strange

feeling this was yet another conversation that was going to result in more questions than answers.

'Hoax calls to the Metropolitan Police are a criminal offence,' a bored voice told her when she asked for DS Arnott. 'You could receive a fine of up to five thousand pounds or six months in jail.'

'It's not a hoax,' she said, quickly. 'That really was his name. Or at least, that's the name he gave to my friend. I've got information about a death that happened back in March, in Soho.'

Emily heard a keyboard tapping at the other end of the phone. The officer who'd taken her call sighed deeply, in a way that seemed to say, *We just love people calling us about closed cases out of the blue, because we have hardly anything else to do.*

'I'll put you through,' he said, and the next voice was much more brusque.

'DS Clarke here.'

Emily swallowed. 'My name's Emily Blott, and I'm looking for a DS Arnott. I might have some information about Andy Atkins' death.'

'I dealt with the Atkins case in Soho. And closed it,' DS Clarke said, pointedly. 'You can talk to me. What information do you have?'

'Andy was my boyfriend,' Emily said. Andy beamed at her, and she realised it was the first time she'd ever referred to him that way. 'And apparently someone from the Met spoke to my friend, Vaseli . . . I mean, Alan . . .'

'Thomas,' Andy said.

'Thomas. Alan Thomas. About Andy's death.' Emily could hear a keyboard tapping down the line. The detective was taking notes, at least, which had to be a good sign. 'DS Arnott came to see him, we think because Alan was one of the last people Andy contacted that night,' Emily said, a bit more confidently. 'But I texted him too – we texted all the time – and no one from the force got in touch with me. And . . . well, I wondered if maybe I'd slipped through the cracks. I knew him better than anyone, and I'd love to help if I can. I know the verdict was left open, but it would be great if Andy – his family, I mean – could get some proper closure.'

The tapping stopped, and there was a short silence. 'We never recovered a phone from Mr Atkins' body,' DS Clarke said. 'We conducted enquiries, but nothing turned up. We assumed perhaps it had been stolen from the scene before the police arrived, but the area wasn't covered by CCTV. Which means nobody working on that case spoke to your friend – Mr Thomas, was it?'

Emily widened her eyes at Andy and nodded, before stuttering, 'Yes.'

'But you say Mr Atkins texted Mr Thomas before he died? And that someone visited him in person?'

'Yes. Alan texted Andy about the video he was making, which we assumed was why you paid him a visit. To look into it, you know?'

'A video, you say? And you're sure Mr Thomas actually received these texts? I'm sorry to ask, but we have to be careful. I'm sorry to say people do have a tendency to exaggerate their closeness to a case when something of this nature happens.'

'I'm sure,' Emily said, firmly. 'We turned up at his gig unannounced and he showed us some screengrabs of the messages. It seemed pretty legit to us. I mean, legitimate, officer. Sergeant.' Emily grimaced at Andy.

'If you're correct, then this does change things,' DS Clarke said. 'We'll have to look into this further. I'm sure we'll need to speak to you in due course. But in the meantime, do you have Mr Thomas's details?'

'I don't,' Emily said. 'But his band, Remington 11, is on Facebook. He's known on there as Vaseline Alan.'

'Of course he is,' DS Clarke said, crisply. 'We'll be in touch, Ms . . .'

'Blott,' Emily said. 'Emily Blott.'

Once the detective had taken down her details, she hung up and slumped onto the sofa.

'Great. That made everything about as clear as mud,' she said, puffing her hair out of her face. 'So now we've got a weird bloke offering your mum loads of cash, a fake police officer visiting Alan, and a video nobody seems to know anything about floating around somewhere. The press are normally shit-hot on that kind of stuff – "in the hours before his death, the deceased made a video of himself dancing to Kate Bush. See it on our YouTube channel," yadda yadda. But there was no mention of it in that article. And the police had no idea either. All they mentioned was that you'd been at work. Where were you booked to be that day?'

'I have no idea,' Andy said. 'I do remember that I didn't have any shifts booked for that week. The agency must have called me with a job at the last minute, but it could have been anywhere.'

Emily nodded thoughtfully. Andy's temp job took him all over London, to all sorts of businesses, so the only way of knowing where he'd been would be to ask the police if they would be willing to tell her when they interviewed her.

Andy looked troubled. 'Why would anyone do all this stuff, unless they'd actually had something to do with my death?

I don't understand. I'd never hurt anyone. But did someone hurt *me*?'

'I don't know,' Emily said. 'But I think you were right, Andy. I think you were sent back here to find out how you died. And we're going to find out what happened.'

Chapter 30

'Oh god, there's nothing I hate more than working out budgets,' Emily groaned, rubbing her forehead as she stared at her laptop. 'If I don't look directly at the spreadsheet, do you think it will work itself out? I've heard they can do amazing things with algorithms these days.'

'I'm not sure that's how they work, but you can give it a try,' Oliver said, popping a nori roll in his mouth and chewing thoughtfully.

Oliver had been in her flat for exactly two hours and ten minutes now, and Emily was starting to wonder if he was ever going to kiss her.

Andy had made a last-ditch attempt to persuade Emily to let him stay – 'I don't trust this Oliver guy,' he'd said. 'I just want to make sure you're OK. And if things get hot and heavy, I'll leave. And not just by sitting in the kitchen.'

'The fact that you think I'd even consider that request for five seconds is mind-boggling to me,' Emily had said, before bundling him off to Zoe's place so she could wax her legs and give her hair a hot-oil treatment. Although she was a bit jealous of how close the pair was becoming, she had to admit it was handy having someone available to ghost-sit when she needed it.

Before Oliver's arrival, she'd 'hidied' her flat to within an inch of its life, throwing the animal-ears onesie that had been brought back into circulation since Andy's return into the back of her wardrobe, and displaying the posh bottle of wine Mel had bought round on the kitchen counter, as if buying £30 bottles of wine was an everyday occurrence for her.

She'd spent hours fretting over what to wear, having been thoroughly confused by the advice she'd found online, which told her to opt for something 'functional and comfortable, but still flattering, and a little bit sexy', which made it sound like the ideal date outfit was a push-up bra under a boiler suit.

Eventually, she'd settled on a tightly belted black maxi skirt, a matching cropped blouse, and the heating turned way up so she could show off a small strip of flat-ish stomach without getting too chilly.

When Oliver had arrived, she'd felt wobbly with desire, mainly due to the fact that he smelt like a box of Quality Street – did he somehow have access to a range of confectionery-based aftershaves designed to make hungry women melt? – and was looking ridiculously good in a dark-blue shirt, blue chinos and loafers. She was relieved to see she'd guessed the tone correctly, and her outfit was a suitable match for his.

After some breezy small talk, they'd settled onto her living room rug, their backs pressed against the sofa and laptops propped on the coffee table. Oliver had quizzed Emily about the ins and outs of her idea for the Cat's Miaow campaign, so he could get the full picture of how she envisaged it playing out on various social media channels.

Eventually, they'd ordered sushi, and their chopsticks had clashed as they reached for the same piece of maki. Emily replayed the moment in her head and decided if they were in a romcom, their first kiss would be just around the corner. But instead, after finishing dinner, Oliver had dived into an earnest look at the campaign budget.

'I always find that, after a creative session, working on the numbers serves as a kind of palate cleanser for the mind,' Oliver said – a bit pretentiously, Emily thought. She didn't point out that he hadn't really contributed much to the creative bit, apart from taking notes, but working on a boring spreadsheet had still put a bit of a damper on the mood. Emily was also fairly sure that the Date Night playlist she'd put together was about to start from the beginning again, and Ed Sheeran singing about his love of shapes wasn't going to help.

'We're called creatives, not . . . matherators,' Emily said now, leaning back against the sofa and rubbing her forehead.

'I'm not sure matherators is a real word,' Oliver said, the corner of his mouth twitching upwards.

'Well, it should be. And why are we called creatives, anyway? There are plenty of ways people can be creative, and I don't see why people in advertising get to appropriate it for themselves. I'm sure making a lovely vase or writing a screenplay is more creative than coming up with a new and interesting way to sell toilet paper. So why do we get the honour?'

'It's to make us feel better about the fact that we're using our talents to shore up capitalism,' Oliver said, stretching his arms above his head. Emily looked at him hopefully, in case he turned it into an excuse to put his arm around her, but instead he just put his hands back on his thighs. 'Besides, it's better than calling ourselves "magic makers", which I swear is what the CEO has printed on his business cards.'

'You're making it up!' Emily laughed, looking up at Oliver from behind her hair, which she'd allowed to partly fall over her face, with the express intention of peering seductively up from underneath it.

'I swear I'm not,' Oliver said, leaning over and gently shutting her laptop. For some reason, Emily found the action terribly erotic, and not just because it meant her spreadsheet had disappeared. But then, she realised, Oliver would probably look sexy flossing his teeth. He'd rolled up his sleeves – after literally saying, 'Shall we roll up our sleeves and get to it, then?' – and had very toned forearms.

'We've done pretty well for a Sunday evening. Shall we call it a day and put a bit more effort into vanishing this wine?' Oliver said. 'We deserve some time off for good behaviour.'

I was hoping to get some time off for bad *behaviour*, Emily thought, managing to keep it to herself by taking a large sip of wine.

'Here, did you know you're covered in cat hair?' she said, leaning over and plucking a ginger hair from Oliver's trouser leg. It wasn't her smoothest move, but it was an excuse to shuffle slightly closer to him along the rug.

'It comes with the job of owning a cat, unfortunately,' Oliver said ruefully, batting at his legs with his palms. 'Cats are not kind to clothes and soft furnishings. I would definitely recommend you enjoy some quality time with your favourite outfits before getting one.'

'Actually, I'm getting one soon. A cat, I mean,' Emily said. Then wondered where on earth that had come from.

Oliver broke into a grin. 'Oh, really? That's brilliant. When?'

Emily flushed. She absolutely hadn't been planning on getting a cat, and she wasn't even sure she was allowed one in her rented flat.

But instead of laughing, 'Only joking!' and digging herself out of the hole she'd just created for herself, she found herself saying, 'I'm going to the . . . pound. On Monday. After work,' before turning even redder.

'You mean the cat shelter?' Oliver said, frowning

'Yep. That's the one. I'm getting a rescue, obviously. It's the right thing to do.'

Inching closer to Oliver, she plucked another cat hair from his chest. Looking up at him and widening her eyes slightly, she hoped he'd take the hint.

Then, at long last, he leaned down and kissed her. Emily had expected this moment to be like fireworks going off through her whole body, but instead, she found herself worrying what her breath smelled like after all that sushi.

As they broke away from the kiss and stared at each other, smiling, she glanced at the sofa. Unbidden, the memory of her first night with Andy shoved its way into her head. She angrily pushed it aside, reminding herself firmly, *You're Emily Blott, and you've landed a man like Oliver. Look at the future, not the past. Look at how far you've come.*

She grinned to herself as he slid his hand around the back of her neck and pulled her in for another kiss, but she couldn't help another unwelcome thought intruding: *How the hell am I going to afford a cat?*

Chapter 31

'ChapSticks,' Charles said, his hands buried deep in his pockets. 'What do we know about them?'

'They're sexist?' Jada ventured from her spot sitting cross-legged on a Lego chair at the edge of the Play Zone meeting room.

'They're called ChapSticks because they're for chapped lips, not because they're for chaps, numbnuts,' Simon said, shaking his head.

'Objection,' Claude said, from the back of the room. He claimed to have learned English partly by watching *Clueless* on repeat, which he knew word-for-word in French, and he enjoyed employing random words from the movie in his everyday life. 'Numbnuts is also sexist, yes?'

'At least it makes a change from using parts of women's bodies as insults,' Jada said, glaring at Simon. 'Men's body parts are used for comedic effect, while women's are used entirely differently. It's just another way of preserving negative gender norms, if you ask me.'

Across the room, Oliver was leaning against one of the

Lego-clad walls of the office, his arms folded. Emily tried to catch his eye so she could offer him a slightly treacherous eye-roll, but his gaze was trained firmly on Jada.

'This is a wonderfully enlightening window into the world of Generation whichever-letter-we're-on, but unless you can tell me how dismantling the patriarchy can help us land the ChapStick account, I'm not sure now's the time,' Charles said, pinching the bridge of his nose.

He'd called an emergency meeting to come up with a pitch for the rebrand ChapStick were planning on launching, to capture the 'lip-balm avoidant summer market'.

The word CHAPSTICK was written in bold black pen on the whiteboard behind him, and everyone would be expected to come up with some quick ideas in the meeting that the creative team could use as a jumping-off point – aka steal and pretend were their own.

'Pair up, and let's regroup in ten,' Charles said. 'Meanwhile, I will refresh my tired brain with a delicious cup of tea.'

As Charles left the room, Emily began side-stepping her way around the primary-coloured plastic table towards Oliver, her stomach and cheeks sucked in, and her tongue pinned to the roof of her mouth (which apparently made your chin look sleeker). Then she stopped in her tracks as he turned to Chrissie with a smile. She watched as they agreed to pair up, and blushed bright red.

'Don't worry, you can pair up with me,' Simon said from the seat next to the one Emily had paused at, tapping his pen on the table and sounding amused. 'I'm afraid I haven't got stretchy abs or awesome glutes or whatever, though. Sorry.'

Sitting down with a bump, Emily stared in dismay at where Oliver and Chrissie were bent over a notebook together.

Chrissie burst into laughter at something he'd said, placing a hand lightly on his leg, and Emily briefly wondered how it would feel to headbutt her.

'Try to ignore them,' Simon said gently. 'We've got some very important ChapStick-related work to do.'

'Why didn't he want to pair up with me?' Emily said, unhappily.

'He probably wasn't keen on cracking his shins on twelve pieces of incredibly knobbly furniture to get all the way over here, that's all,' Simon said, putting a hand on Emily's arm.

'I'm getting terrible PE flashbacks right now,' Emily said, remembering how she and Zoe were always the last of the girls to be picked for netball, permanently lumbered with Wing Defence simply because they were from Greenleaf.

'How's it going with Oliver, anyway?' Simon asked. 'Does he have buns of steel and blow his nose on twenty quid notes, just like you always dreamed of?'

Emily laughed. 'It's going OK,' she said, deciding to keep last night's extra-curricular activities to herself. She had a feeling Simon wouldn't be too thrilled to hear her latest piece of Oliver-related gossip. 'At least, I thought it was. I'm trying so hard to be good enough for him, but I seem to be taking two steps forward and three steps back.'

Simon flushed. 'I wish you could see what we see, Emily,' he said, staring at his hand on her arm. 'It's ridiculous that you feel like you have something to live up to. Not like, *you're* ridiculous,' he added, hastily, 'but that you don't feel good enough as you are. Who cares where you came from? You're Emily Blott, the girl who organises every single office birthday collection, helps out at a homeless shelter, and can write the best goddamn cat-food slogans in town.' Emily managed a laugh.

'Plus look at you. You're bending over backwards trying to impress Oliver, drinking those disgusting smoothies and turning down birthday cake left, right and centre, but you've always been gorgeous.'

'Oh, really?' Emily said, raising an eyebrow.

'Yes, really. I'd tell you not to get big-headed, but there's no chance of that, is there?' Simon said, rubbing his nose. 'I just want you to be happy.'

'Well, that's lovely. Thank you,' Emily blushed.

'And since Oliver arrived here, you've seemed really anxious. Why are you so worried about being this perfect version of yourself for him? I thought these days the narrative was all about being yourself, and embracing you for you, etcetera?'

'Oh, Simon, my sweet summer child,' Emily said, reaching over and pinching his cheek. 'Have you been on the internet lately? It's full of women telling their billion followers to be authentic. But that's pretty easy to do when you're borderline perfect as it is. I mean, look at this.'

Emily pulled out her phone and brought up one of the videos she'd saved on TikTok. It showed a slender woman with a perfectly flat stomach, beautiful face and a pneumatic behind, twirling and pouting at the camera. The caption said, WHAT MY FANS SEE.

Then the video changed. The new caption said, THE TRUTH! and the same woman was now rubbing her stomach – which she was pushing outwards, so it protruded very slightly – and grabbing her behind. If you squinted, you could see it had a few small dimples of cellulite. BE YOURSELF, GIRLS! the final caption screamed.

'Oh,' Simon said, handing the phone back to Emily. 'That's . . . weird.'

'Exactly. We're fed this narrative about being yourself, but "yourself" is only acceptable if you look incredible first thing in the morning with no make-up on. Meanwhile, men get fed articles about how dad bods are totally hot because Leo DiCaprio's got one. It's completely unfair.' Emily glanced at her watch. 'Anyway, we've only got three minutes left, and we're supposed to be selling ChapSticks.'

'By the sounds of it, if their slogan was, "Hey, girrrrl! You look like shit, but we can help with that. Buy a ChapStick!" they'd sell out.'

'How about we use, "Sun's Out, Fun's Out!", partner up with Walls, and bring out a range of retro ice-cream flavoured ChapSticks in SPF fifty?' Emily said. 'Job done.'

Simon and Emily agreed she should present their idea to the group, so she could catch Oliver's eye as she stood at the whiteboard. But his attention kept flicking back to the ideas written on the notebook on Chrissie's lap. At least she hoped it was her ideas he was interested in, rather than her long legs. Her stomach sank with disappointment when he didn't even wait for her outside the office to flirt some more.

'Oh my god. You totally got off with Oliver,' Jada said, as soon as she and Emily reached their desk and slumped into their chairs.

'How the hell do you know that?' Emily whispered, alarmed.

'I'm very intuitive.' Jada frowned, folding her arms. 'I could tell by the way he was looking at you.'

'I'm amazed. He barely glanced at me during that meeting.'

'Who's got off with who now?' Simon said, arriving back from the loo at the worst possible moment.

'Emily. Oliver. Last night.'

'In the study with the candlestick?' Simon said, raising his eyebrows.

'In the bedroom with a condom, I hope,' Jada said sternly, turning to Emily. 'Even though he's *her boss*, so she shouldn't be going there at all.'

'Keep your voice down, Foghorn Leghorn,' Emily hissed. 'We didn't go that far, don't worry. New Emily is a *lady*, remember? But thank you for your extremely sexy TED talk about gloving up.'

'Ahh. Now I see why you were so annoyed at him pairing up with Chrissie,' Simon said.

'What was he like?' Jada asked. 'Although I still very much disapprove of this coupling, I want every last sordid detail.'

Emily grinned. 'I'll tell you all about it over lunch, OK? During which I will definitely eat more than just a smoothie,' she added to Simon. 'I need to catch up on my Cat's Miaow work, because we didn't get much done last night, if you know what I mean . . .'

'If only we didn't,' Simon sighed.

Opening up her laptop, Emily wondered what she'd tell her friends over lunch. She liked to be honest with them, especially when they were two of the handful of people in London she could be herself around. But when she thought about how last night had panned out, she felt a knot of anxiety twisting in her stomach.

Not that it had been bad, in any specific way. But there was definitely something missing, which she couldn't quite put her finger on. She and Oliver had spent an hour on the sofa, indulging in some fairly innocent making out. A few times, his hand had snaked towards the hem of her skirt, but she'd placed it firmly back on her thigh. If he was going to be a long-term prospect, she wasn't going to give up the good stuff so quickly.

But she kept finding her mind drifting towards Andy, wondering what he and Zoe were getting up to. Then she began worrying about how her stomach felt to Oliver's wandering hands – could he feel her rolls? She tried to pull her mind back to the moment by telling herself sternly, *You're snogging Oliver Beauchamp! Concentrate!*

But it all felt a little bit paint-by-numbers – as if they were kissing because it was a natural way for the evening to end, rather than because they couldn't keep their hands off each other. Emily's mind also kept skipping, treacherously, to her first night on this same sofa with Andy, which had been so much more fun. She hadn't spent more than half a second worrying about what she looked like back then, because she'd been too busy enjoying herself.

There was no denying, though, that Oliver was the sexiest person she'd ever kissed. Which perhaps meant *she* was the one who was at fault? Perhaps, by deciding before he'd even arrived that they definitely wouldn't be having sex, she'd given off the wrong vibes. Maybe he'd sensed her mind wandering, which prevented him from relaxing into the moment?

Her stomach dipped painfully at the thought that Oliver was probably thinking the same things as her, and was disappointed at how the night had ended. That would explain why he was so keen on pairing up with Chrissie that morning. Perhaps in his mind, he was already detaching himself from Emily and looking elsewhere.

She remembered his parting words, just before he'd left the flat. 'I'd better go, but thank you for a great evening. I'll leave you to get your beauty sleep.' Emily wondered now if the comment had been intended as a dig. Maybe he'd even kissed her because he felt sorry for her – because he'd seen through her and knew that, deep down, she didn't deserve a man like him.

She looked down at her stomach, patting it thoughtfully. Lunch with Jada and Simon would have to be salad – and when she got the chance to be alone with Oliver again, she'd put more effort in. But for now, she had two choices: either torture herself by going over every moment of last night and worrying about what she'd done wrong, or take matters into her own hands, even if she risked rejection.

From: Emily Blott
To: Oliver Beauchamp
Subject: Saturday night

Hiya,

I hope you're not feeling too exhausted after last night's very hard work?*

I'm throwing a bit of a dinner party on Saturday night, and wondered if you fancied joining us? It won't be a big thing – a TV producer friend is coming over, along with a couple of other people, and I think you'll enjoy their company. But most importantly, you can meet my NFBF **

*If Charles sees this email he will NEVER crack my secret code.

** New Furry Best Friend.

E.x

Then, she picked up her phone and tapped out a text.

Emily: Hey Zo. Fancy an exciting evening out at
the cat shelter?

Chapter 32

Having never been involved with the law before, Emily wasn't sure exactly what she'd been expecting to find at Charing Cross Police Station. But after gaping at the imposing columns that stood at its entrance and trotting up the stone steps towards the wooden door, it probably wasn't a bleak waiting room featuring pairs of blue-painted metal mesh chairs, which were welded to the floor against the walls.

Not long after their phone call, Emily had been called into the station to meet DS Clarke and talk about her last conversations with Andy. But of course, the only time she could fit Emily in was the Saturday morning of her dinner party, which she'd set aside for preparing both herself and dinner. Andy had looked so woebegone when Emily had suggested rescheduling that she'd agreed to the meeting, no matter how inconvenient it was.

To compensate, she'd booked herself a blow-dry, and bunged her lamb shank main course, which was apparently both elegant and foolproof, into the oven on a super-low setting before leaving for the station. That way, it could slow-cook all day and she wouldn't have to spend her meeting with DS Clarke distracted by clock-watching.

After checking in at the front desk, she'd been unsurprised to find the chairs in the waiting area had definitely not been designed with sitting in mind. The large room was bleak, decorated with a single poster warning people to get their bicycles security marked. She hadn't realised that waiting to be questioned by the police would be so much like waiting for a dentist's appointment, and she'd forgotten to bring a book. She was glad she had Andy to distract her from her nerves.

Emily's leg jiggled nervously as she waited to be called into the interview room, while Andy pulled faces at a huge Rottweiler sitting next to its even larger owner. He was covered in tattoos, one of which said NO RAGRATS, which Emily decided to assume was intentional. Andy was delighted when the Rottweiler woofed and started happily wriggling on the spot. 'Look, he can see me!' he said. 'And he's just a puppy, really. He doesn't know he's scary.'

'A bit like you, then,' Emily said, realising too late that she'd forgotten to pretend she was on the phone. Still, the Rottweiler's owner barely glanced at her.

'You're a good boy, aren't you? A *good* boy,' Andy told the dog, who immediately rolled over onto his back. Andy went over and tickled its tummy, and he woofed happily.

'What are you playing at, Kevin, you daft sod?' his owner said, reaching down and scratching Kevin's stomach. His hand overlapped with Andy's for a second, and he shivered, frowning at his palm before quickly wiping it on his leg.

'Do you think they've already interviewed Alan?' Andy asked, turning around to look at Emily. She tugged her phone out of her pocket.

'No idea,' she said, holding her phone near her face but not putting much effort into pretending she was having a real conversation. 'But I guess we'll find out soon enough.'

'Ms Blott?' a uniformed woman carrying a clipboard called to the room. Emily raised her hand, and the woman tipped her head towards a door off the waiting room. Her heart thudded as a bored-looking officer behind the main desk buzzed them through to a narrow corridor. The officer led her to a small, grey-painted door, knocked once, and swung it open.

'Ms Blott for you, DS Clarke,' she announced, and left Emily and Andy to make their way into the room. It looked pretty much like every interrogation room Emily had ever seen on police dramas on TV, a plain wooden table filling most of the room, with two chairs either side of it. The only difference was that this room had plain bare walls, instead of a two-way mirror for her to thump her fist against, shouting, 'I KNOW YOU'RE BACK THERE!'

The room also enjoyed the luxury of a tatty stained carpet, and padded chairs upholstered in material that was the exact same shade of grey, and equally stained, as the carpet. Even without Andy's help, the room was freezing cold.

'Would you like to sit, Ms Blott?' DS Clarke said, gesturing towards one of the chairs. She took the one furthest from the door, so Andy could sit down too.

'You can call me Emily,' Emily said. 'If that's allowed?'

'It certainly is,' DS Clarke said, smiling. 'Now, I understand you were the last person to text Mr Atkins . . .'

Emily went through everything she knew about Andy's last movements, looking down at her hands when she admitted that she hadn't known he was dead until a few days ago. At the end, DS Clarke asked, 'And do you have any questions of your own?'

Emily glanced at Andy, who nodded. 'We did have one,' she said.

'We?' DS Clarke asked.

'Me, I mean. I wondered if you could tell me where Andy was working before he died? It would help me paint a picture of his last day in my mind, you know?'

DS Clarke frowned at her notes. 'I'm afraid that's not something I can divulge,' she said. 'The case has been reopened since your phone call, and that's privileged information, for now. But I'm sure I'll be able to tell you in due course.'

'Fair enough,' Emily nodded, then suddenly had a thought. 'Might it be possible to see what clothes Andy was wearing when he died?'

DS Clarke paused. 'I don't suppose there's any harm in showing you the photographs,' she said, and Emily looked alarmed. 'Don't worry, they were taken after the clothes were removed from the body.'

Opening the beige cardboard folder in front of her, she took out a pile of photographs, and sifted through them. Plucking a few of the photos out of the pile, she pushed them along the table towards Emily.

'There you go. Everything's bagged, but hopefully you can see what's inside clearly enough.'

'Thank you,' Emily said. Andy leaned over her shoulder as she spread them out across the table.

'So we were right,' Andy said, plucking at his T-shirt. 'This is what I was wearing when . . . *it* happened.'

'Including these,' Emily said, stabbing her finger onto one of the pictures.

'Yes, Andy was wearing them when we found him,' DS Clarke said.

The photo was of a clear plastic bag, tied up with a cardboard tag around the top. The tag said #05, which Emily assumed was an evidence number. Inside the bag was a pair of pristine white trainers.

'So these weren't some kind of eternal present from J-Dog then?' Andy frowned, lifting his foot onto his thigh. 'But I've never seen them before.'

'No ... but I think I have,' Emily said, now noticing the bottom of his shoe.

'I'm sorry, what?' DS Clarke said.

Andy peered round to see the logo that was hidden on the sole of every pair of the hottest trainer brand of the moment.

'AirLab,' he said. 'Where have I heard that name before?'

Chapter 33

'How do you switch it off?' Emily asked, her hands on her hips as she watched Fluffy – aka Churchill – the cat flinging himself around her living room.

'It says here that cats can get the zoomies if they've had a long sleep. Has he had a long sleep?' Zoe said, frowning at her phone.

'Nope, he's spent all afternoon trying to destroy my sofa,' Emily sighed. 'He should be worn out by now.'

'I like him,' Andy said, grinning as Churchill took a running jump, dug his claws into Emily's curtains, and started climbing his way up them, a kamikaze look of determination on his face.

When Emily had googled 'how get free cat fast?' it turned out cat shelters didn't just hand out moggies to anyone who popped by. Apparently, you had to fill in forms and have a home visit and prove that your landlord agreed that getting a cat was A-OK, when Emily was pretty sure that in her case, it was A-bsolutely not.

She'd panicked for a while – her plan of using a cat to lure

Oliver to her dinner party was fairly reliant on said cat actually existing. Then she'd remembered Mary's cat Fluffy, and had generously offered to catsit for a few nights over the weekend.

Instead of being reluctant to part with her adorable pet, Mary had been worryingly enthusiastic about the idea, dropping Fluffy in his pet carrier at Emily's door as soon as she'd returned from the police station. Alongside him were some sachets of cat food that were half the price of Cat's Miaow but looked and smelt exactly the same, and a cat bed with half its stuffing falling out through several deep claw-scratches.

'Do you want to say goodbye?' Emily had asked, peering nervously through the bars at Fluffy, who looked extremely pissed off.

'Nah, he's a right pain in the arse. It'll be a nice break, if I'm honest. Good luck,' Mary had said, waving over her shoulder without a backward glance. She'd headed back upstairs with the demeanour of someone who would be happily skipping if it wouldn't have given the game away.

Andy had been pleased when it became clear that Churchill – who had been named after a cat in a Stephen King book, for extra 'Oliver Bonuses', as Zoe put it – could see him. Although Emily's temporary feline pal had nearly had a heart attack when he'd tried to jump onto Andy's lap, only to fall straight through it. Terrified, he'd leaped a couple of feet into the air, yowling, before hissing at him from the top of a bookcase.

'Sorry, Churchie. Didn't mean to use up one of your lives,' Andy said, luring him down with some kitty kibble. Within ten minutes, he'd settled next to Andy's feet, purring loudly and occasionally shooting Emily evil looks.

'Are there any more tips, Zo?' Emily wailed now. 'If he doesn't chill out soon, he's going to ruin my dinner party.'

Zoe shrugged. 'It just says he'll wear himself out eventually.'

Emily glanced at her watch. In the two hours she had left before Oliver, Mel and Jess were due to arrive, she still had to get ready, prep her starter, and try not to implode with nerves. Zoe had agreed to come over to help her set up, but there wasn't much she could do about a demented cat.

'I don't know what I was thinking,' she groaned. 'Andy ruined my last party, and now I've done this—' she gestured at Churchill, who was perched on top of her curtain rail, hissing. 'Why am I such a glutton for punishment? Why?'

'I didn't ruin your last party!' Andy protested, holding up his palms.

'There was a power cut,' Emily said. 'That must have been your fault. We know you have a weird effect on electricity.'

Everyone looked at the ceiling as the lights flickered.

'Sorry,' Andy grimaced. 'But remember, you told me you summoned me after the power cut happened. And it affected the whole street, so you can't blame me for that one.'

'Right, I'm going to get ready,' Emily said. 'Zoe, will you get the scallops out of the fridge? I'm pretty sure the fishy dishy bloke on the internet said something something room temperature something.'

'That's quite a memory you have there, Em.'

'What should I do?' Andy asked.

'You sit there, and you do not move a single muscle. I can't control this dickhead—' she waved in Churchill's direction '—but you can promise to behave.'

Andy saluted, and sat carefully in his chair, even though

he couldn't disturb Emily's karate-chopped cushions unless he really tried.

'I promise I'll behave myself, Scout's honour,' he said. 'Don't forget to ask Oliver about my trainers, though. They weren't even released yet when I died, but if he worked on the ad campaign, maybe he'll know where I might have got them from.'

'Of course,' Emily said, nodding as she hurried into her bedroom. Spending all morning with Andy had brought Old Emily to the fore again, so she needed to get herself into a dinner party mindset before her guests arrived. She brought up some of her favourite etiquette websites to get into the zone – a warm-up for her brain, so she wouldn't forget her manners in front of Oliver.

Make sure you have enough room at the table

Handle surprise guests courteously and with good grace

Seat the guest of honour on the host's right, and serve them first

When she was fairly sure she had remembered all the essentials, she was about to throw her phone on the bed and start getting ready when she noticed her mum had texted.

Hey luv, I've got a scan next week, and I wondered if you fancied coming? Baz is busy, and it would be nice if you could get to know Chanel before she arrives.

Her mum was still online and would see that Emily had read her text and was online too. She stared at the message, wondering what to do.

She knew she should play the dutiful daughter and agree to go with her. It would also make her Auntie Suze happy, because she'd tried hard to rebuild bridges between Emily and her mum ever since she'd moved to London.

But she already had enough on her plate without dealing with her mum's geriatric pregnancy and the realities of gaining a baby sister at the grand old age of twenty-eight as well. It was too much. Perhaps after the Cat's Miaow pitch, she'd have more time to decide what to do about her mum. But not right now.

Her fingers hovering over the keypad, Emily realised she was too stressed to even come up with a convincing excuse. Deciding she was harnessing the power of no and setting healthy boundaries (as *Bijou* would probably put it) she quietly swiped WhatsApp closed, threw her phone on the bed, and grabbed her make-up bag.

'So . . . what's everyone's favourite discontinued snack?' Emily asked. Zoe caught her eye from her spot on Andy's armchair and grimaced.

Emily's guests had arrived less than an hour earlier, and she'd assumed that they'd quickly settle into the same easy chat of the party she'd thrown the night Andy had appeared. She'd been too worried about Churchill destroying her front room, pulling off a three-course meal, and the correct way to set the table to consider whether, with Oliver replacing Simon and Jada, the conversation would still flow as easily.

She'd imagined a small, cosy gathering of creative types,

filled with intelligent conversation. But following a short burst of nice-to-meet you chatter, the atmosphere had plummeted. After a couple of awkward silences that had gone on far too long for her liking, Emily had resorted to the conversational topic of the truly desperate.

'I really miss coconut Boosts,' Jess ventured, sipping her wine.

'Although they did leave your mouth drier than the Sahara,' Zoe added, in the silence that followed. Emily shot her a grateful smile for trying, her whole body vibrating with nerves, which caused her to leap out of her seat when someone knocked at the front door. She looked around the room and frowned. All her guests were already here.

Her heart sank when she swung open the door to see Mary standing there in her pink dressing gown and marabou mules.

'I, um, just wanted to see if the chairs I lent you are OK?' Mary said nosily, peering around the door. 'Sorry a couple of them were only stools, but that's all I had. Alright?' she nodded, spotting Oliver, Mel and Jess on the sofa. They were crammed together more tightly than necessary, thanks to Oliver spreading his legs a touch too wide.

'Hey,' Mel waved.

'So it's a dinner party, is it? I love a good knees-up,' Mary said, glancing at her small fold-out dining room table, which Emily had carefully covered with a tablecloth and set with mismatched plates that she hoped said 'bohemian cool' rather than 'skinty no-mates'.

'Would you like to come in for a drink?' Emily said, holding back a sigh, reminding herself to *Handle surprise guests courteously and with good grace.*

'Don't mind if I do.' Mary grinned as she barrelled past Emily and into the living room.

Jess stood up to give Mary her space on the sofa, and Emily swung one of the chairs out from underneath the table so she could sit down. Zoe got up and grabbed Mary a glass, and Emily poured her some wine. She crossed her fingers and hoped Mary wouldn't mention that she was Fluffy's real owner.

'You're a handsome fella, aren't you?' Mary said, shifting herself around in her seat so she could get a better view of Oliver. 'If I was forty years younger . . .' she cackled.

'I'd better go and finish off the scallops,' Emily said, heading for the kitchen, already feeling exhausted.

'How's it going?' Andy asked, as she shut the door behind her and turned on the radio to cover up their conversation.

'It's very sweet that you want it to go well, considering how much you dislike Oliver,' Emily said. 'But you'll be pleased to know it's already going badly. No one's talking, Oliver's manspreading his way across half the sofa, and Mary's turned up. Plus she seems to fancy him too.'

'Ah,' Andy said.

'Yes. Ah.' Emily drizzled some oil into a pan ready to sear her scallops.

'I'm hoping she'll bugger off before I have to serve up the starters.'

'Do you want me to chuck a book at her head to scare her off?' Andy said, looking hungrily at the seafood. 'I could probably manage to pick up a small one.'

'Nope. I want you to stay in here, not making a single peep,' Emily said.

Ten minutes later, Emily ushered everyone to the table,

and tried to angle Mary towards the front door, still clutching her wine glass.

'So, scallops, is it?' Mary said, looking in the direction of the kitchen and sniffing the air. 'My Bill used to love them. I don't think I've had them since he passed . . .' She dabbed her eyes with the sleeve of her dressing gown. Mary had only mentioned Bill once before to Emily, telling her, 'He was even more of a bloody waste of space than his bloody exercise bike,' but she had to admire Mary's chutzpah.

'Would you like to stay, Mary?' Emily asked, through slightly gritted teeth.

'Ohh, lovely. Don't mind if I do,' she said, suddenly cheering up.

'I'll just have to rearrange a few things,' Emily said, managing to sound a lot more positive than she felt as she realised everyone would have to make do with two and a half scallops each so Mary could have a share. 'Would you like to go upstairs and change?' she added, gesturing at Mary's pink dressing gown and slippers.

'Nah, you're alright,' Mary said, and plonked herself at the table.

'I'm not sure about the rest of this crap,' Mary said, shoving her black pudding aside with her fork and spearing a scallop with it. 'But these things are fucking delicious.'

'Glad to hear it,' Emily said, forcing a smile and taking a large gulp of wine. She'd spent a fortune practising her starter to perfection, and although scallops on black pudding with pea purée felt a little bit *Masterchef* 2012, her guests had *ohhh*ed appreciatively when she'd brought the plates out.

She hoped the sawn-in-half scallops weren't taking the

shine off the meal – or the fact that Emily's head was about a foot lower than everyone else's around the table. Her extra, unexpected guest meant she'd been forced to squeeze Andy's armchair between Mel's seat and Oliver's spot at the head of the table.

'So Oliver, Emily tells me you're responsible for that AirLab advert that's all over my telly,' Mel said, nibbling delicately on her slice of black pudding. 'That's pretty impressive.'

'Get some AIR!' Zoe shouted, and Emily briefly wished she'd sat Jess on his other side instead. Oliver gave Zoe a watery smile, and Emily realised he must get sick of colleagues shouting the campaign slogan at him.

'It wasn't that big a deal,' Oliver shrugged. 'Sometimes you just get lucky with an idea and run with it.'

'Look at Mr Modest over here,' Jess said. 'It must be pretty amazing coming up with a campaign that everyone in the world knows about.'

'I had a question for you about that actually, Oliver,' Emily said, glancing at Zoe. 'How would someone get hold of a pair of AirLab shoes before they were launched? I know someone who had a pair back in March, before they were even released. But I don't know how on earth he could have got access to them.'

'They usually keep these things pretty hush-hush,' Oliver said, frowning. 'I'd guess he must have worked for the brand in some capacity – something like design or marketing. Or they were sold illegally. Trainers sell for insane amounts these days, especially the really rare ones, and some of the people who signed an NDA might have thought it was worth the risk.'

'NDA?' Zoe asked.

'Non-disclosure agreement. I had to sign one when I was

sent some pairs of trainers for the campaign, and I would have been in big trouble if anyone else had got hold of them.'

'Interesting,' Zoe said, and raised her eyebrows at Emily. 'Can I ask how you ended up at HoRizons? No offence to Emily, but it's not quite as well known as Binkle, Bonkle and Turnip, or whatever your last place was called.'

'It's Barter, Bugle and Hegilly, actually,' Oliver said, evenly. 'And I chose HoRizons for that exact reason. I could see it had great potential, thanks to rising stars like Emily, and I love a challenge – taking places that aren't quite hitting the mark and helping them to reach it. After my success with the AirLab campaign, I felt like I wanted to give something back.'

Emily reached up and squeezed Oliver's arm. She found it unlikely that he'd really had any idea of her potential before he'd arrived at HoRizons, but it was sweet of him to pretend.

'It sounds like you two have plenty in common,' Zoe said, raising her glass in their direction. 'Emily works for free for homeless people, and you've lent your genius to a middle-weight advertising company.'

'It's the least I could do,' Oliver said, apparently missing the sarcasm in Zoe's voice.

Emily turned pink and raised her eyebrows at Zoe. 'You just wait until you see the Cat's Miaow campaign,' she said. 'It's all totally hush-hush at the moment, but I'm really hoping we win the pitch. Seeing an idea I came up with on telly would be a total dream come true.'

'Speaking of cats, where's . . .' Mary began.

'Are we finished?' Emily interrupted, standing up so abruptly her thighs dragged the tablecloth half a foot towards her chair. Zoe downed the last of her wine and tipped the glass in Emily's direction, waggling her eyebrows. By Emily's calculation, that glass had been her second, which was around the time Zoe tended to start worrying a lot less about Emily's rules on what should and shouldn't be discussed in polite company and a lot more about when her next drink was arriving.

'Would you like some water, Zoe? I've got still and sparkling,' Emily said.

'Nope,' Zoe said cheerfully.

'Great,' Emily said, pushing her way into the kitchen to get another bottle of wine. She jumped at the sight of Andy sitting on the kitchen counter looking bored, swinging his feet through the cupboards below him.

'I thought you'd be hanging out with Churchill in my bedroom by now,' Emily whispered, checking her guests were safely in their seats before gently closing the door behind her.

'I'm bored,' Andy said. 'I wanted to talk to you, and I knew you wouldn't be going into your bedroom any time soon. Not without *Oliver* in tow, anyway.'

'Less of the sarcasm, please,' she said, as she rummaged in the fridge for more Sauvignon blanc.

'Can I help?' Zoe said, poking her head around the door.

'Do you mean, "Where's my wine?"' Emily said.

'Yes.'

'If I give it to you, can you please stop with the little digs at Oliver?' Emily said, turning around. 'Not everyone has the time to do volunteer work, even if they want to, and you know his last company wasn't called Binkle, Bonkle and Turnip.'

Andy snorted. 'I'm only teasing,' Zoe said.

'Well, you're about as subtle as Donald Trump's tan,' Emily said. 'Come on, Zo, you know how nervous I am already, and you're not exactly helping me to impress Oliver.'

'The thing is ... *why* do you want to impress Oliver?' Zoe groaned. 'He is gorgeous, there's no denying that. And he smells weirdly of Toffifee, which is no bad thing. But he's a total conversation vacuum and has barely cracked a smile since he got there. He's a bit up himself, isn't he?'

'He's not *that* bad,' Emily said, uncertainly. 'And I reckon that's allowed when you've got plenty to be up yourself about. He's really funny when you get to know him, especially when it's just the two of us hanging out together. He's probably just a bit nervous.' Zoe gave a grunt of disbelief.

'Look, whatever you think of Oliver, now isn't the time,' Emily said, shoving a bottle of wine into Zoe's hands. 'We can talk about how rubbish you think he is later on, if you like. But for now, just keep the obvious digs to yourself, OK? Make yourself useful by giving everyone a top-up – and no, you can't give yourself one of Zoe's Special Measures – then bringing out the rest of the plates. I've got to finish off my posh mash.'

Zoe nodded, and ducked back into the living room, looking slightly sheepish.

Emily peered into the bubbling pan on the stove and poked a knife into the potatoes. 'Andy, can you stick your head in the oven?'

'Charming.'

'To see how the lamb shanks are doing,' she said, rolling her eyes. 'I'm not quite that sick of you yet.'

Andy looked delighted by what he took as a firm compliment as he hopped off the kitchen counter and poked his head through the oven door. Then looked decidedly less pleased as he withdrew it.

'Were they supposed to be resting?' he said, uncertainly. 'Because the oven isn't on.'

'The oven's not . . . *what*?' Emily said, slamming the knife she was holding onto the kitchen counter and yanking open the oven door. Instead of a whoosh of hot air, she was greeted by stone-cold silence, and the smell of congealing grease.

'Oh my god. When did this happen?' Emily said, turning pale.

'I don't know,' Andy said quickly. 'I didn't do it, I promise.'

Pulling the casserole dish out of the oven, Emily stared at her half-cooked lamb shanks, which were poking out of a lumpy, congealed mess of gravy, and surrounded by a grim-looking ring of hardened fat. She'd meant to check on them earlier, but had been distracted by Churchill terrorising her sofa. 'These are supposed to be slow-cooked,' Emily said, fighting back tears. 'They've been in the oven for *hours*. Andy, did you touch the oven?'

'I might have run through it and into your room when we got back from the police station,' he said, looking nervous. 'I was playing hide and seek with Churchill. But I didn't realise I'd done anything, I promise.'

'You can't play hide and seek with a bloody cat,' Emily wailed. 'And your stupid, interfering, electricity-zapping aura has ruined dinner. What on earth am I going to do now?'

'Mission accomplished,' Zoe said, triumphantly, reversing through the kitchen door, holding aloft a pile of empty plates and the empty wine bottle. Then, 'Oh, shit, is that dinner?' she added, staring at the dish Emily was holding. 'Because it looks really bad.'

'Yes, it is dinner. Of *course* it is,' Emily said, plonking the casserole onto the kitchen counter. 'Because why would tonight go smoothly? It's only one of the most important nights in one of the most important weeks of my life, that's all.'

'Maybe we can rescue it?' Zoe said, dubiously, poking at a soggy lamb shank with her finger. 'Or order pizza?'

'Oh, great idea,' Emily said. 'Because nothing screams "hostess with the mostess" louder than ordering in a bloody Domino's, does it?'

'She's only trying to help,' Andy said, cautiously.

'You just . . . shush,' Emily snapped. 'This is all your fault.'

'Is everything OK?' Jess said, poking her head around the door. 'Do you need any help? Oh, hi,' she added, spotting Andy and looking between him and Emily. 'Sorry, I didn't realise there was someone else in here.'

'Ha!' Andy beamed. 'Today is brilliant. I'm Andy, nice to meet you.'

Emily sighed. 'Andy, this is my friend Jess,' she said, manoeuvring herself so she was standing between them. 'She works in magazines.'

'Nice to meet you, Andy,' Jess waved.

Emily could feel her stomach rolling with nerves. At least, she hoped it was nerves, and not the scallops. She was fairly sure she was supposed to let them reach room temperature before cooking them. But perhaps that was the lamb . . .

'Aren't you joining us for dinner?' Jess asked Andy.

'He's my friend, and he's staying the night. But, well . . . I didn't want to give Oliver the wrong impression, so Andy's keeping out of the way, just for this evening.'

'In . . . the kitchen?' Jess said.

'Yes. He loves it in here. Food, you know,' Emily said. 'You won't say anything, will you?'

'Of course not,' Jess said, although she looked a bit confused. 'My lips are sealed.'

'Right, everyone else out of the kitchen,' Emily announced.

'I'm prepping dinner. Zoe, could you make sure everyone's got what they need?' *And that they don't come into the kitchen*, she added, telepathically.

'How come Jess can see me?' Andy said, when Emily had shut the door on them.

'I can't believe I didn't realise this would happen earlier,' Emily said, rubbing her face with her hands. 'She was there the night we did the Ouija board, the same as Zoe. Which means Mel can probably see you too, as well as babies, dogs and bloody cats. So for the sake of my blood pressure and mental health, can you please just go into the bedroom, keep Churchill quiet, and stay put? I know you didn't do the oven thing on purpose, but I don't want you to … I don't know, accidentally send death rays shooting out of the TV.'

'I'm really sorry about the oven,' Andy said, giving Emily a small wave as he walked through the kitchen wall and into her bedroom. As Andy passed through it, the oven whirred into life, and Emily tried hard not to burst into tears.

Chapter 34

Fifteen minutes later, Emily had found an app that specialised in delivering haute cuisine from high-end restaurants, and paid roughly the same price as a small second-hand car for some stuffed poussin and grilled fish to be delivered in super-fast time.

Taking a deep breath, she swept back into the living room. 'Right, everyone, slight change of plan,' she told her guests brightly, hoping her grin conveyed, 'joyful hostess' rather than 'minor mental breakdown'. 'We've had a slight cock-up with the lamb shanks, I'm afraid. But our main courses will be arriving soon, so just hold tight. Meanwhile – ta-da!'

From behind her back, Emily produced her two TK Maxx mezze bowls filled with half a jar of leftover olives and some Percy Pigs, and a glass crammed with some slightly out-of-date breadsticks. She'd learned from her dad's magic shows that managing to suspend your audience's disbelief relies on the strength of your performance, so she hoped her plastered-on enthusiasm was enough to distract her guests from how seriously crap the nibbles were.

'This is haute cuisine, is it?' Mary said, squinting at the breadsticks as Emily plonked them in the middle of the table.

'Yes, Mary,' Emily said, trying to look elegant as she folded herself into the armchair and took a large swig of the wine Zoe had poured for her. She knew the evening was hanging by a thread, but as long as nothing else went wrong, there was still a chance things could tip in her favour. Perhaps, like the power cut at her last party, this disaster would bring the group closer together.

She was quickly proved wrong when another uncomfortable silence settled across the table.

'So, Oliver,' she said, her voice a few octaves more high-pitched than usual, 'tell us a bit more about how you got into advertising? Mel works in telly, you know. And Jess is the features editor at a magazine.'

'I think you mentioned that already, just a couple of times,' Oliver said, the corner of his mouth twitching upwards. Two hours ago, she'd have thought he was being sympathetic, and found the twitchy-mouth thing unbearably sexy.

But now, especially in light of what Zoe had said in the kitchen, she could see he was actually being a bit patronising. She swallowed down the lump in her throat. Instead of cool, sexy and collected, she was clearly coming across as needy and desperate. She felt a spark of anger – but whether it was aimed at Oliver or at herself, she wasn't sure.

Beside her, Oliver jumped as a loud crash came from her bedroom.

'What's that?' Mel said, looking worried.

'That'll be Churchill,' Emily said, as a spirited yowling and the sound of things being thoroughly broken emerged from behind her bedroom door. 'He's my new cat. Named after the cat from Stephen King's *Pet Sematary*,' she added in Oliver's direction, sounding like a shopping channel hostess. But he was too busy staring in alarm at the bedroom door to notice.

'Is that Fluffy?' Mary asked. 'Bloody toe-rag.'

'No, it's Churchill,' Emily said firmly.

'Hadn't you better see what's going on?' Jess asked, wincing at the sound of breaking glass.

'I'm sure it's fine,' Emily said, swallowing hard to stop herself from crying. 'Percy Pig?'

Suddenly, the bedroom door flew open. Churchill leaped through it and onto the back of the sofa, before launching himself into the middle of the dinner table. He sent the bowl of olives flying, almost hitting Mel in the face. Emily jumped to her feet.

'Oh my god, I'm so sorry,' Andy said, running out of the bedroom. 'I tried not to get him all worked up, but he wanted to play hide and seek again.'

'That's let the cat out of the bag . . .' Zoe said, taking a large gulp of wine.

'Hi, Andy,' Jess said, from the end of the table. 'This is my friend Mel.'

'Hi, Andy,' Mel waved.

'Who's Andy?' Oliver asked, frowning.

'Another name for the cat,' Emily said, desperately, as Churchill stalked his way across the dining table, casually knocking over the breadsticks.

'I agree, Fluffy,' Mary nodded. 'Horrible things.'

'That's Andy,' Jess said, pointing at Andy, who was standing behind the sofa. 'He's just a friend of Emily's.' Jess glanced at Emily and grinned conspiratorially.

'What on earth are you talking about? There's no one there,' Oliver said, looking pale.

Emily thought she was going to throw up. Then she realised that if Oliver and Mary were the only people in the room who couldn't see Andy – and if Mary, who had her back to him, had been telling the truth when she'd claimed she hadn't been able to turn her neck properly since 1998 – there was a small chance she could style this horrifying situation out.

'My friend Andy is here. Can't you see him?' she said, looking concerned.

Churchill curled up in the centre of the table and started hissing at Oliver. Then he swished his tail, knocking Oliver's wine into his lap in the process. Mary honked with laughter.

'Shit, let me get that,' Andy said, grabbing a serviette.

'What's going on?' Oliver shrieked, as Andy – or, from Oliver's point of view, a floating napkin – approached him.

'Argh, sorry,' Andy said, dropping it on the floor and backing away from the table.

'Will you please, *please* just go back into the bedroom?' Emily begged.

'Who are you all talking to?' Oliver asked, standing up. He looked pale. 'Is this some kind of wind-up?'

Jess and Mel looked at each other in confusion.

'What's going on?' Mary asked.

'Don't you worry, Mary,' Zoe said, patting her hand. 'Just enjoy your drink.'

'I think maybe Oliver's had a bit too much wine,' Emily said, soothingly. 'Sit down, and I'll get you some water.'

'Nope. No. I'm going to go now,' Oliver said, almost falling over his chair as he made for the door. His face was covered in a thin sheen of sweat, and he was shaking.

'Please stay,' Emily said, desperately. If Oliver left now, the night would be an official disaster. 'Dinner will be here any minute. You're just a bit drunk and hungry and … *not* seeing things. That must be a thing, right? Like a reverse hallucination?'

'Sorry, but I really need to get going. I don't feel so great,' Oliver said.

'He looks really … spooked,' Zoe agreed, and Emily blinked back fresh tears. Why was she trying to make things worse?

'Shall I get his coat?' Andy said, from the bedroom door.

'Sure. You get his coat and we'll finish him off for good,' Emily said, imagining Oliver's face when it came floating through the air towards him.

'I'll get it,' Mel said. 'Perhaps we should go too.'

'Fine,' Emily said, slumping into her chair. Too much had gone wrong for her to have a hope of rescuing the evening now.

Mel came back holding three coats and a couple of handbags. Oliver grabbed his jacket, muttered, 'See you on Monday,' and headed swiftly out of the door, slamming it behind him. Another awkward silence descended as Mel and Jess shrugged on their jackets and slid their bags over their heads.

'Is the party over, then?' Mary asked, draining her wine glass and looking at the empty chairs around the table.

''Fraid so, Mary,' Zoe said, helping her out of her chair and to the front door.

'These things happen, Emily,' Mel said kindly, squeezing her shoulder. 'Although to be honest, I'm not sure exactly *what* just happened …'

'You'll laugh about it one day,' Jess added. 'Maybe not for a decade or so. But one day. And when you do, *Real Talk!* pays a hundred pounds for readers' dating disaster stories, so it's not all bad.'

'Thanks, both,' Emily said, managing a rueful smile and giving them each a defeated hug. 'I promise not all my social events are complete and utter cock-ups.'

'Well, that was awkward,' Andy said, after she'd shut the front door behind her guests.

There was a silence as Emily felt anger building up inside her.

'That wasn't *awkward*, Andy,' she said, turning red. '*Awkward*, in dinner party terms, is when someone comes back from the loo with their skirt tucked into their knickers. *Awkward* is not when your best friend spends all night making digs at the guy you're dating, your stupid borrowed cat is a psychopath, and your ex-boyfriend comes back from the dead and ruins the bloody lamb shanks. This is what's known as a *disaster*.'

'Neither of us did anything on purpose,' Zoe said, looking hurt. 'And come on, it was quite funny,' she added.

'Funny?' Emily said, feeling a bit hysterical. 'Ha! You think tonight was funny? I mean, obviously you did, otherwise you wouldn't have made all those comments, would you? *That's let the cat out of the bag, haha.* I'm bending over backwards to build myself a new life, and you two think it's all a huge joke. But honestly? I don't think it's very funny.'

'Old Emily would have thought it was funny,' Zoe said, hotly. 'And if Oliver goes off you after tonight, well ... our suspicions were true, weren't they?'

'You don't get it, do you?' Emily said. 'I don't want to be the kind of person who throws hilariously crap dinner parties.

I don't want to be the goofy sidekick in my own life. Tonight was my chance to prove that I've changed, and that it is actually possible to leave a shitty past behind and make something of yourself.'

'Well, thanks. I'm part of that "shitty past" so that's just lovely to hear,' Zoe said angrily. 'Do you know how frustrating it is to watch you chasing this fantasy perfect life? Because that's what it is – a fantasy. For some reason, you seem to think all this nonsense – fancy dinner parties and boring grey throws and drinking smoothies – makes you a better person. But newsflash: it doesn't. It just makes you annoyingly self-centred. And now you're after a guy like Oliver – who, by the way, is fucking dreadful – to complete this picture of bliss you seem to have conjured up, when he's clearly totally wrong for you. It's ridiculous.'

Emily fought back tears. 'You've already made it obvious that you think Oliver is boring,' she said. 'But have you considered that you just don't understand him? He's better than us, Zo. And even if you think it's self-centred for me to try and improve myself, he represents everything I want in my life. And when I have kids, in their lives, too.'

Zoe barked out a laugh. '*Better* than us? No, he isn't, he's a twat. And if your self-esteem is so low you want to fling yourself in front of him, begging him to accept you – just so long as you look the right way and behave yourself, of course – then fine. But don't assume he's any better than me or Andy, because he's not.' Zoe shook her head in disbelief.

'None of this is going to protect you from being hurt again, you know. And I don't think you understand how hurtful your behaviour is to other people. As well as slagging off Greenleaf any chance you get – which, may I remind you, is *my* home, too – you had this amazing guy in your life who was totally into you, but who you kept at arm's length because he didn't fit your picture of the perfect guy,' Zoe said, gesturing at Andy.

'I . . . I didn't,' Emily said.

'Really? Then why wouldn't you meet any of his mates, or introduce him to me? And why did you tell Andy it was company policy not to tweet about dating you, which is clearly bollocks? That doesn't exactly suggest you were proud of him and your relationship, does it?'

'Is that why you kept us all apart?' Andy said. 'Because you were waiting for someone better to come along?'

Emily shook her head, and stared at him in dismay. Too proud to admit she'd made a mistake, she'd missed her chance to tell Zoe how much she'd really cared about Andy when he was alive – and how devastated she'd been when she thought he'd ghosted her. And now, Zoe thought that she hadn't cared about him at all.

'It wasn't like that . . .' she began. But Zoe wasn't finished.

'You tell me off for "misbehaving" in front of your new mates, like I'm an embarrassment. And you ran off to your own flat five minutes after we arrived in London. Do you have any idea how that felt? We were supposed to be doing this together. And I get that you're desperate to move on from your old life. Honestly, I do. But guess what? *I'm* part of your old life. And so is your new sister, who you already seem determined to ignore.'

Zoe's breath hitched in her chest, and Emily swallowed. Deep down, she knew everything her best friend was saying was true. No matter how much she'd cared for Andy when he was alive, she'd never shown him off in the way she should have. She'd treated Zoe like an accessory to her new life, and was already punishing her sister for reminding her of the past, before she'd even been born.

But that didn't mean she was prepared to listen to what Zoe was saying. Not in her own home, and especially not right now.

'If I'm such a terrible bore, why do you bother hanging around me, then?' Emily said, as tears started dripping down her nose. 'I'm trying my hardest to please everyone. But if you don't like me any more, then maybe you should just leave,' she said, pointing at the door.

'It's funny you should say that,' Zoe said, plucking her jacket from the hook beside the front door, 'because I was planning on leaving London altogether, and going back to Essex. You might be happy to turn your back on your family, but I miss mine, and I want to go home.'

Emily stared.

'I'm sick of London,' Zoe said, 'and I'm sick of what it's done to you. I was trying to work out how to tell you, because I didn't want to upset you. I had to talk it all through with Andy instead, because he actually listens to me the way you used to. But tonight has made telling you pretty easy, to be honest.'

Andy looked troubled. 'I was so excited to be back, and to be able to see you again. But you never really liked me the same way I liked you, did you?' he said, shaking his head. 'You wanted a man like *him*. And when I see the way you treat Zoe, it makes me wonder if the person I was in love with was even real.'

'Love?' Emily said. 'You were in love with me?'

Andy nodded, miserably. 'I was. I couldn't help it. You were so kind and lively and fun. But this person you're turning into? I honestly don't recognise her.'

Emily stared at him, her chest aching. Then she looked at the floor, unable to say anything in return.

'Come on, Andy,' Zoe said quietly. 'I think we'd better go.'

Chapter 35

Mum Mobile: 3 missed calls

Emily picked up the corner of the sofa cushion, threw her phone underneath it, and dropped it back down with a soft 'flump'.

'Out of sight, out of mind,' Emily muttered, taking a swig from the bottle of beer on the floor beside the sofa, then pushing her spoon around the soft edges of the tub of Häagen-Dazs resting in her lap.

It had been almost twenty-four hours since Zoe had stormed out of her flat, taking Andy with her, but Emily still felt her stomach swooping with adrenaline every time she thought about the events of the night before. There was no corner for her brain to hide, as it kept leaping from disaster to disaster, trying to decide which moment had been the most excruciating.

Perhaps it was Mary inviting herself for dinner, Andy accidentally turning the oven off, Churchill nearly smashing Mel in the face with an olive bowl, or Oliver's terror when everyone started talking to someone he couldn't see and Andy attacked him with a napkin?

Or maybe it was Zoe tearfully telling her she was moving back to Essex because New Emily sucked so hard, Andy confessing that he'd been in love with her – the crucial word being 'had' – or a courier turning up moments after everyone had fled, carrying a hundred quid's worth of posh dinner-party food? After presenting it with a small flourish, his smile had quickly dropped from his face when he'd surveyed the empty room behind Emily's tear-stained face, which Churchill was still busy destroying.

Whichever moment her brain landed on, pretty much every one of them made Emily want to cry, scream, or cringe herself inside-out.

She'd blown everything, and didn't even have the energy to fix things. Usually, whatever problem New Emily was faced with, she would come up with a meticulous plan of action to try and fix it. Facing social rejection? Move cities and reinvent yourself. Doomed to repeat your mum's mistakes? Make yourself a better life. New guy not feeling it? Throw an amazing dinner party and hope it doesn't fall apart faster than a pair of Primark shoes.

Her life since leaving Essex had been like a chess game, every move carefully considered to bring her closer to her goal. But now everything had imploded, she was at a total loss for what to do. Which was why she was busy burying her feelings underneath an avalanche of beer and ice cream.

She'd tried to call Zoe umpteen times, but she'd hung up on her mid-ring, before switching her phone off. Andy was nowhere to be seen – presumably, he was hanging out at

Zoe's place, making her laugh and reflecting on how much he wished he'd been with her in his last few days on earth instead of Emily.

She couldn't tell him that since his blurted confession she'd realised that when he was alive, despite her efforts to ignore it, she'd been falling for him, too. Her attempts to keep him at arm's length hadn't worked in the slightest, and all she'd achieved was to deny herself the chance to grieve when Andy had disappeared.

To top it all off, even though Zoe's words about her new sister were still ringing in her ears, she couldn't face speaking to her mum, who kept trying to ring her. Every time she gave up, Emily felt guilt sweeping through her, but a conversation about mucus plugs was the absolute last thing she needed right now. Underneath the cushion, as if on cue, her phone let out another muffled ring.

'Nope. Nope, nope, nope,' Emily told it. Then sighed as she realised that while she was desperately hoping to hear from Zoe, curiosity would inevitably get the better of her.

Shoving her hand under the cushion, she grabbed the phone. Her Auntie Suze was calling. Probably just to tell her to answer her mum's calls, but when she pictured her aunt's anxious face at the other end, she couldn't bring herself to ignore her. She hit the green button and put it on speaker-phone, resting it on the arm of the sofa next to her right ear. She didn't have the energy to lift her head up from the fat cushion it was propped up on.

'Hey, Auntie Suze,' Emily said, trying to sound upbeat. 'What's up?'

'Oh, hey, love,' her aunt said, nervously. 'We've been trying to get hold of you all day. Is your phone broken?'

'Probably. Sorry.'

'We've got something we need to tell you. And, well … It isn't good news, love. Is Zoe there with you by any chance?'

'No,' Emily said, shuffling straighter up the sofa and picking up the phone. 'But she's away at the moment. Work thing. You can tell me, though, I'll be OK.'

'It's your dad,' Suze said.

'Is he back?' Emily said, jolting upright. It felt like a bolt of electricity had shot through her entire body.

'No, love. The opposite, in fact. I'm so sorry to have to tell you this, but … your dad's body's been found.'

'His body? I don't understand,' Emily said in a small voice, the backs of her eyes prickling.

'They're building a new bypass up the road. Down by the old offie. They were digging up all the bushes and trees around there, clearing space, I suppose, when they found some bones. They stopped digging right away, of course, and the police were called. They did some tests, and well … It turns out it was your dad. They reckon it was a hit and run, years ago. He ended up in the ditch, and whoever did it decided it was best just to leave him there.'

'When was this?' Emily croaked, swallowing hard. 'After he left us?'

'They can't say exactly when he died,' Auntie Suze said gently, 'but they think it was at least twenty years ago.'

'Which is when he disappeared …' Emily said, tears spilling down her cheeks.

'That's right. And there's another thing. I don't even know how to tell you this bit, love. They found a plastic bag. It was still right there, in his hand. It was from Playbox, do you remember?'

Emily nodded at the phone, swiping the tears off her cheek with her shoulder. She remembered walking around the local toy shop, touching the glittery hair bobbles, the plastic dolls and ponies, the skipping ropes and roller skates, wishing her parents could afford to buy her nice things all year round, rather than just at Christmas and on her birthday.

It had seemed impossible to her that some children could go into a shop like that, choose whatever they liked, and their parents would buy it for them. She knew they existed, but they seemed a million miles away from her life.

'Most of what was inside the bag had rotted away,' Auntie Suze said. 'But you know what they say about plastic, don't you? It takes years and years to decompose. And they found some things inside, Emily. A plastic wand, and a cup and ball.'

Emily froze. Her mind turned to the small red cup Barry had given her when she'd visited her dad's garage – the one her mum had told her off for stealing, and which she'd worried for years was the reason her dad had left. The one she'd reunited with its shiny red ball, and was tucked safely in her bedside table, the only thing of her dad's she had of her own.

'Your dad didn't leave you and your mum all those years ago,' Auntie Suze said, gently. 'He was out buying you a magic set.'

Chapter 36

Jada: I can't believe you've had the audacity to call in sick the Monday after the big dinner party without telling us what happened! Oliver looks knackered. I really hope it's something to do with what you got up to on Saturday . . .

Simon: Can we not pollute the group chat with innuendo? Gross

Jada: OK. DID YOU HAVE SEXY SEX WITH OLIVER? There. That's not innuendo, right?

Simon: This is a violation of my human rights

Reading through her friends' texts, Emily managed a small smile, before rolling over and pulling the duvet over her head. Even if she hadn't hosted the world's most catastrophic dinner party over the weekend and fallen out with both her best friend and her dead ex-boyfriend, the revelations of the day before meant she couldn't face going into the office on Monday.

The Cat's Miaow presentation wasn't until Wednesday, and she couldn't possibly do any more work on it than she already had done, despite the distractions Andy's reappearance and Oliver's bum had provided her with.

Behaving like everything was normal when her whole world had imploded felt impossible, so she'd called in sick, wrapped herself in her animal onesie, and tried to process everything that had happened.

The last shreds of confidence she'd had in her plan to re-invent herself had been obliterated by her aunt's phone call. She was reeling with fresh grief, knowing that her beloved dad was never coming back. But she also understood now that all the hard work she'd put in trying to escape her past, and feel worthy of being loved, had been based on lies.

Andy hadn't ghosted her because she wasn't good enough: he'd died. And now, she knew the same fate had befallen her dad. If she'd known all that time that her dad *had* loved her, that he hadn't been able to just walk away from her without a backward glance, she would have found it a lot easier to love herself the way she was – and cared a lot less about what everyone else thought of her, too, just like Zoe did. What would it have mattered?

After meeting Andy, for a few brief months she'd felt good enough to be liked – perhaps even loved – by someone other than Zoe and Auntie Suze, even when she showed him her real self. And perhaps if she'd known the truth about his death, she would have saved herself from even more pain.

But because of the things she'd wrongly believed to be true, she'd ruined her relationship with Zoe, the best friend who had stuck with her through thick and thin, and hurt a man she loved to chase a fantasy she wasn't even sure she wanted to come true.

She would never see her dad again, and that broke her heart. But there was still time to make amends with Andy and Zoe – if only she could find them, and they would listen to her.

From her duvet cocoon, Emily heard her phone buzzing into life. Slinging the covers off her head, she saw Churchill glaring at her from his spot curled up on her dressing table. Unlike Emily, who had twisted herself, pretzel-like, to fit an idealised idea of herself, he was exactly who he was – essentially, a grumpy, mad ball of fur – and didn't care what anyone thought of him.

'You've got worse table manners than Zoe and Andy put together, but you don't care, do you?' Emily sniffed. 'And you might be a pain in the arse, but Mary still loves you, doesn't she? Kind of.'

Churchill hissed at her, then leaped lightly from the dressing table and onto the bed, curling himself on top of her phone.

'You love pushing those boundaries, don't you, boy? Or is it only dogs people call boy? I have no idea,' Emily said, pushing her hand under Churchill's warm fluffy body and pulling out her phone. She had a new text from Jada on the group chat.

> **Jada:** Umm, have you checked your email, Em? If what I'm hearing on the office grapevine is right, I think Oliver might secretly be a prize prick . . .

Reluctantly, Emily opened the email app on her phone. She really could do without any more disasters right now, but there it was, at the top of her inbox: a very unwelcome email from Oliver.

From: Oliver Beauchamp
To: Emily Blott
Re: Cat's Miaow pitch

Hi Emily,

I hope you're not feeling too unwell. I have been discussing the Cat's Miaow pitch with Charles, and explained that you seem to be struggling under the pressure of being elevated to a key player.

We are both worried about pushing you too far, too soon, so Charles has agreed that it would be best for me to take on the burden of presenting the pitch alone this time, although of course this doesn't preclude you from being front and centre in future. I hope this is the good news we intend it to be, and that we'll see you tomorrow.

Kind regards,
Oliver

'What?' Emily whispered, her chin wobbling. She re-read the email, her heart thudding. Oliver knew how much the Cat's Miaow presentation meant to her. So why on earth would he take it away from her? He must know that she'd never welcome this decision, no matter how stressful the project had been.

OK, so the dinner party had been an unmitigated disaster.

But surely that wasn't enough for him to decide she couldn't handle the presentation? Her competence at work had nothing whatsoever to do with whether she could cook some bloody lamb shanks properly.

Unless . . . Unless this had been his plan right from the start? Andy had taken an instant dislike to him, which Emily had put down to plain jealousy. But he was usually a good judge of character. And Zoe – well, she was a born cheerleader. She would never tread on Emily's dreams unless she had good reason to – or serious doubts about Oliver's character.

So could it be that Oliver had decided to pick Emily's brain for ideas and steal her thunder at the last minute? She thought back to their meetings about the pitch. Oliver was supposed to be a super-talented advertising god, while she was just a lowly copywriter, but every time, he'd ask for her thoughts, then tell her they were a 'good jumping-off point', or 'something to work on'.

Then afterwards, he didn't actually seem to evolve her ideas, or bring anything new to the table, did he? She'd done all the work – and now, she was off the pitch. So perhaps Andy and Zoe had been right all along. Perhaps Oliver *was* the bad guy.

Emily re-read the email – this time, from the perspective of someone who thought that rather than being a gorgeous-smelling, talented sex-god, Oliver was actually a horrible weaselly git. And suddenly, the truth hit her like an unwelcome wave.

'Kind regards? You absolute bloody *tosser*,' she yelled, when she reached the end, flinging her phone to the end of her bed. Tears flowed down her cheeks, and she wiped her nose on the arm of her onesie.

It seemed so obvious to her now. Oliver was going to take her idea and make it his own. He'd shown his true colours by betraying her at her lowest ebb, and was probably rubbing his hands with glee that he'd managed to edge her out of the pitch. Emily wondered, briefly, if the campaign that had made him famous had even been his idea in the first place.

'Maybe I need to take a leaf out of your book,' she told Churchill, who scowled as she picked him up and hugged him to her chest, his fur growing damp from her tears. 'You're not perfect, are you? In fact, you're a noisy, annoying, chaotic twat. But you don't give a damn, do you? As long as someone loves you – OK, feeds you – it doesn't matter. I think it might be time for me to Be More Cat, don't you?'

Churchill yowled grumpily, and batted Emily's nose with his paw.

'I'll take that as a yes.'

Churchill scowled at Emily, then at her phone, as it started vibrating again. Hoping that perhaps the cosmos had heard her and it would be Zoe calling, Emily stretched towards the end of the bed and tried to reach it. When that didn't work, she held Churchill's paws and gently threw his backside towards it, before dragging it across the bed under his bum.

'See, you do have your uses after all,' Emily said, wiping her nose on the arm of her onesie and chucking him behind the ear. She frowned as she saw ANDY MUM was calling. Her timing couldn't be worse. She probably wanted to share a memory of Andy, at the exact moment Emily had driven him away with her behaviour. But she could hardly ignore a call from a grieving mother.

'Hello, Mrs Atkins,' Emily said, answering using her best phone voice. 'How are you doing?'

'Hello, love, thank you for picking up. And call me Mandy, won't you?'

'Of course, Mandy. It's lovely to hear from you. Did you want to chat?' Emily braced herself for Andy's mum to start thanking her for appreciating Andy so much before he died, or sharing memories that she wasn't sure she could cope with right now.

'Actually, I didn't call about that,' Mandy said. 'I've found something, and thought it might help you work out what happened to Andy.'

Emily sat up, the back of her neck prickling. 'Go on.'

'After I met you at Andy's grave, you got me thinking about those papers we were asked to sign. At the time, we didn't really think twice about it. You wouldn't, would you? Not so soon after what happened. But looking back, it seems so odd. Why would they give us that money? I looked it up on the internet, and there was nothing about compensation for open verdicts on there. Anyway, I asked Sandy to look for those papers we signed. He couldn't find them anywhere, but he did find the details of the man who came to the house. He told us we should call him directly if we had any questions, rather than ringing the department, and not to share his number with anyone, because scammers were everywhere. Gave us this whole spiel about confidentiality. But you're not a scammer, are you? And if it'll help us find out what happened to Andy ...'

'So you have his name and number?' Emily asked. 'Hang on, let me get a pen.' Leaning over, she reached into the drawer of her bedside table and pulled out the pen and notepad she used to write out to-do lists when her brain wouldn't shut up at night.

'Go on,' Emily urged.

At the end of the phone, Mandy hesitated. 'Some things are more important than getting into trouble, aren't they?' she asked.

'Yes. Yes, they are,' Emily said gently.

'Then here you go, love. The man's name was Oliver. Oliver Beauchamp.'

Chapter 37

'Oliver Beauchamp? You're sure?' Emily asked, struggling to get the words out. Her heart was hammering wildly, and her ears were ringing. 'What was the number he gave you?'

Mandy read out the number, and Emily checked it against the one she already had saved in her phone as a contact: Oliver Work.

That meant Oliver – *her* Oliver – had been to Mandy's house. In fact, he'd paid her thousands of pounds not to talk to anyone about Andy's death, or to question the open verdict the coroner had given.

It didn't make any sense. How on earth was Oliver connected to Andy? As far as Emily could tell, they hadn't even met. In life, at least. Andy had moaned that Oliver gave him a bad vibe, but that was understandable. And while he *was* wearing AirLab trainers when he died, it was quite a leap from there to think Oliver was involved in Andy's death.

'Hello? Are you still there, love?' Mandy said.

'Oh, sorry. I got cut off for a sec,' Emily stuttered, swiping away a tear from her cheek. 'That's really helpful, thank you, Mandy. I'll have a look into this – but I'll be careful, I promise. No one's taking Andy's memorial headstone away from you.'

'Thank you,' Mandy said, her voice cracking. 'I just want to know what happened to him.'

'You and me both,' Emily said, before saying her goodbyes and hanging up.

She lay back on her pillow, staring at the ceiling, trying to deal with the tsunami of feelings crashing through her. She quickly realised it was hopeless trying to untangle how she felt about everything that had happened over the past few weeks.

Since moving to London and embarking on her new career, she'd learned that the best way to handle disaster was to take action to deal with the parts she could change, leaving the rest to deal with itself – and that, at least, was something she still believed in.

Auntie Suze had taped the Serenity Prayer to the back of the loo door in their flat in Greenleaf. Reading it every time she went to the bathroom, Emily had learned it by heart: *God grant me the serenity to accept the things I can't change, the courage to change the things I can, and the wisdom to know the difference.*

She didn't believe in God – but she *did* believe in herself. She knew that taking back as much control as she could would make her feel steadier and more stable. But this time, it wouldn't involve starving herself so she took up less space, or trying to achieve perfection in myriad other ways. This time, she was going to find out how Oliver was connected to Andy and solve the mystery of his death once and for all – even if she had to do it alone. She owed him that, at least.

Clambering out from under her duvet, she grabbed her laptop from the living room, then took it back to bed with her.

'Right. Let's find out what you were doing the day Andy died, Oliver Beauchamp,' she said, opening her laptop onto Google, then typing out his name, plus the month Andy had died.

The first results that came up were articles in advertising industry magazines, talking about Oliver's previous agency landing the AirLab trainer campaign. Emily clicked on the top entry.

Barter, Bugle and Hegilly triumph again with pitch for AirLab campaign

The industry's most controversial player has added another feather to its cap after winning the coveted pitch for the new AirLab trainers campaign.

Creative Director Oliver Beauchamp – the branding genius credited with dreaming up the risky strategy that saw the agency threatened with a lawsuit before its launch – has been credited with the idea for the new campaign.

Launching next month, it will use video footage sent in by fans of AirLab trainers, performing parkour-style stunts wearing the newly launched styles.

'It's a risky strategy, because you have to rely on members of the public to provide footage of high enough quality to be used on multiple platforms,' Beauchamp told *Pitch Perfect.*

'Luckily, mobile phone quality these days is such that we already had some great examples to show the AirLab team when we made our pitch, proving that we could do it. I'm confident the campaign will be a great success.'

'What a fucking *womble*,' Emily muttered.

Next, she clicked onto an article about Oliver's move to HoRizons.

Rising star Oliver Beauchamp makes shock move to midweight rival

London's advertising scene is still reeling following last night's shock announcement that Creative Director Oliver Beauchamp, of industry leader Barter, Bugle and Hegilly, is leaving for mid-level rival HoRizons.

The agency has remained tight-lipped over the reason for their star member's sudden departure. A spokesperson told *Pitch Perfect*: 'Oliver has been a huge asset to the team, and we wish him all the best in his future endeavours.'

Meanwhile, an insider, who asked to remain anonymous, told our reporter, 'There are rumours going around that there's more to this move than meets the eye. For a creative like Oliver to leave a huge agency like BB&H for a much smaller team, when he's at the peak of his career, is frankly madness.'

When *Pitch Perfect* reached out to him, Beauchamp was unavailable for comment.

Unsurprisingly, there was no mention of Oliver realising what amazing potential HoRizons had, and his desire to build up the potential of fresh young copywriters like her. Emily tapped her fingers on her keyboard, thinking. Something was niggling at her – something at the back of her brain, like a whisper that she couldn't quite make out. She brought up the website of Oliver's old agency, wondering if there might be something there to help her join up the dots.

Perhaps she should head down to their offices, and ask questions herself. Clicking on the map, she squinted as she zoomed in on the red pin dropped on the map. Then jumped as Churchill leaped onto her keyboard, staring at her as if he sincerely wished looks could kill. 'If you're angling for a starring role in the Cat's Miaow presentation, it's too late,' Emily said, poking at him with a forefinger in the hope that he might take the hint. 'Oliver's in charge of that now, so you've got no chance.' Gently tipping her laptop to one side, Churchill yowled and stalked his way to the end of her bed. Emily watched him, frowning, as the whisper at the back of her brain got louder. She looked back down at the map on her screen and froze, as she realised what she was seeing – and the whisper erupted into a roar.

When Zoe swung open her front door after what felt like an age of waiting, Emily watched as a range of emotions washed across her face. Anger, hurt, disappointment and . . . did she detect a hint of relief? She hoped so.

'Before you slam the door in my face, which I completely deserve, please can you hear me out?' Emily asked, from the bottom of the set of stone steps leading to Zoe's front door. 'I've come to do some world-class grovelling, because you won't answer your phone and I'm your best friend and I'm really really sorry.'

'I'm a bit disappointed you're not holding a stereo above your head playing our song, to be honest,' Zoe said, leaning against the doorframe and folding her arms.

'I don't have one,' Emily said. 'And even if I did, I haven't been to the gym for, like, forty-eight hours, so my floppy arms would probably be too weak. I could put it on Spotify if you like?' she added, waggling her phone in Zoe's direction.

'Our song being . . .?' Zoe said, raising her eyebrows.

'Don't make me say it,' Emily groaned.

Zoe made a show of examining her fingernails.

'OK, OK. Our song's "Amarillo". I can't believe you made me do that,' Emily said, faking annoyance, but feeling a swell of relief in her chest. She could see Zoe struggling not to smile, and knew she was remembering the junior school party.

Held before Emily's dad had disappeared and she'd started wanting to fit in, they'd nagged the DJ to play their favourite song over and over, despite the cool kids throwing empty drinks cups at them and complaining that they wanted to listen to Eminem. It had felt like a tiny act of rebellion, and had brought them closer together than ever.

'So can I come in? Please?' Emily said. 'Joking aside, I'm not taking this lightly, I promise. I have a proper apology to make. And I have some news about Andy.'

At the mention of Andy's name, Zoe's expression changed. Emily tried not to feel hurt all over again.

'In that case, come on in,' Zoe said, indicating to Emily to follow her inside. 'Scott has got a girl over, and they're currently getting off with each other in front of *Home and Away*, so we'll have to go to my room. On which note, why are you here so early, and not at work following Oliver around with your tongue hanging out?'

'We'll get to that a bit later,' Emily said, as Zoe led the way to her bedroom. It was large and airy for a house-share, and painted bright yellow. Zoe plonked herself down on the bed and gave Emily a look that told her she wasn't quite ready for her company on it. Emily pulled the chair out from underneath Zoe's desk and sat on that instead.

'Go on then. I'm ready for my grovelling apology,' Zoe said.

'Right, well,' Emily said, suddenly feeling shy. Her entire life had changed in the last forty-eight hours, but now she had to focus on the bit where Zoe had accused her of looking down on her, at least partly correctly, and it made her heart thud painfully. 'Obviously I was an absolute prick on Saturday night.'

'Obviously.'

'But also, it wasn't just Saturday, was it? I realise I've been treating you badly for years now, just because hanging around with you means risking people finding out about my past. When, really, I should have been shouting from the rooftops about what an amazing best mate I've got instead.'

'So true,' Zoe said, the corner of her mouth flickering up.

'In short, I've been behaving just like all those horrible arseholes at school, treating you as *less than* just because of where you came from. Even though it's where I came from, too.'

'Where's this language come from? I thought swearing was too common for New Emily?'

'Yeah, well, New Emily was, as a wise woman once put it, a dick. I've decided to let Old Emily out for a bit. She's been itching to wear a onesie all this time and I never let her.' Zoe laughed, and Emily smiled with relief. 'I was so focused on improving myself, I never thought about how it might be affecting you.'

'Me and my horrifically common background?'

'The one I also share, yes. And which I was wrong to try and run away from.' Zoe raised her eyebrows. 'Can I come and sit there now?'

Zoe nodded, and Emily swung off her chair and sat next to her on the bed. 'I've known deep down for months that you wanted to move back to Essex, and that London wasn't what you hoped it would be, but I just ignored it. Because it was the right thing for you, but the wrong thing for me.

'But of course you shouldn't stay if you don't want to. And I'm one hundred per cent supportive of that. I should never have let it get to the stage where you had to lean on a ghost you'd only just met for moral support. I totally understand if you want to go home, and I'll visit all the time. I'll even help you pack.'

'No, thanks. I doubt New Emily isn't so dead you wouldn't be a nightmare. I have visions of colour-coded spreadsheets . . .'

'My spreadsheets are *gold*. But OK. Whatever you need. And I promise never to act like I'm not incredibly proud to have you in my life ever again. Is that grovel-tastic enough?' Emily turned and held her arms out, and Zoe fell into them for a hug. She squeezed Zoe tight, feeling a mixture of relief that she was forgiven, and sadness that, soon, her best friend in London, as well as the world, would be leaving.

'That's not just top-drawer grovelling, that's . . . a bit weird,' Zoe said. 'What's happened to bring all this on?'

'A few things, actually. Starting with my dad . . .'

Chapter 38

Zoe listened in shock as Emily told her about the accident that had stopped her dad coming home over twenty years ago.

'Oh god, Emily. I'm just so sorry,' Zoe said, covering her mouth with her hands. 'All that wishing and waiting . . . I can't imagine how you must feel.'

'It feels so weird to have spent all these years feeling like I was easy to abandon, even by my dad, only to find that he didn't disappear on purpose after all. New Emily was all about feeling good enough, which of course I never could. Not while I blamed myself for Dad leaving. But this turns everything upside down. After speaking to you, I'm going to call Mum and tell her I'll be at her scan – at every scan, if she wants me to be there for her.'

Zoe reached over and linked Emily's little finger with hers. She had tears in her eyes.

'I'm sorry I wasn't with you when you heard about your dad. But I'm glad you're here now,' she said.

'I haven't even told you about Andy yet, and I'm already knackered,' Emily said, laughing ruefully, swiping at her eyes with her sleeve. 'But I think I've worked out what happened to him.'

Emily explained about Mandy's call, and how it had made her wonder what Oliver's connection to Andy could be.

'That absolute bastard,' Zoe growled.

Pulling her laptop out of her bag and opening it up, Emily clicked on the map she'd seen earlier. A red pin was pointing at a building labelled Campaign House.

'Otherwise known as the home of Barter, Bugle and Hegilly,' Emily said. 'And this—' she stabbed her finger at a small side street running along the edge of the building '—is Thrift Street.'

Zoe shook her head, then added, softly, 'The road where Andy's body was found.'

'Andy can't remember anything past breakfast on the day he died, right? But he was a temp at the time and had done some stuff for ad agencies around the city. So I called up the agency he was with and pretended to be with the police.'

'Blimey,' Zoe whistled. 'Isn't impersonating a police officer a crime and stuff?'

'Totally, but honestly, they didn't give a crap. I had a whole spiel worked out, banging on about the Official Secrets Act and which division I was from, but in the end I just said I was calling from the Met and needed to know where Andy Atkins had been sent on 7 March, and the girl on the phone told me immediately. I could have been anyone.'

'Good old idiots,' Zoe said.

'And, surprise surprise, the day he died, Andy was sent to Barter, Bugle and Hegilly. It meant I'd found a definite connection between Andy and Oliver, but it took me ages to work out how that could be related to how he died. It all pieced together when Churchill jumped onto my laptop and just sat there, glowering at me. I was half-wondering if I should video him for my Cat's Miaow presentation, when it came to me.

'The pitch I've been working on includes loads of example videos to show to the client, see? I've had to include them to help demonstrate what the finished campaign might look like. And I suddenly realised that Oliver must have done the same when he worked up his pitch for the AirLab campaign – pulling together his own footage to use in the initial presentation.'

'You mean ... by making videos? Like the one Andy told Alan about?'

'Exactly. I'm using footage I've found off the internet, because it's just an example. But perhaps Oliver thought his pitch would look even more impressive if he made his own video featuring the actual trainers that would be seen in the finished advert. So I searched through the agency's website, and found a showreel of clips from their successful pitches. And ... well, take a look at this.'

Clicking on another tab, a video appeared onscreen. Emily clicked ahead to the right part of the film, swivelled the screen towards Zoe, and hit play.

The video was captioned 'AirLab Campaign Pitch' and showed clips of young men doing parkour-style stunts on city streets, leaping up walls and onto roofs, and jumping between narrow bollards. Most of the footage was grainy, and none of them were wearing the same pristine, bright-white trainers as Andy – until a familiar figure appeared onscreen.

'Look, see! There,' Emily said, pointing. Andy was wearing his striped T-shirt, jeans, and AirLab trainers. He was standing on the edge of an air vent, and suddenly turned his back to the camera and did a perfect backflip, before grinning at the person behind the camera and giving them a thumbs-up.

'Jesus,' Zoe said. 'So you think this is related to how he died? And that Oliver ...'

'... was behind the camera, yes. Because look at this.'

Clicking back onto Google Maps, Emily selected the satellite view. Zooming in on Campaign House, its pixelated roof gradually grew sharper, until you could clearly see the bright-red air vent Andy had jumped off.

'So Oliver got Andy to help him make his campaign video ...' Zoe said.

Emily nodded. 'And I think he died in the process.' She swallowed. Just a few days ago, she'd thought Oliver was her ticket to the future she'd always dreamed of. Realising that instead, he was a fraud who'd had a hand in Andy's death – and apparently tried to cover it up – had felt like a punch to the stomach. How could she have been so wrong about something she'd wanted so badly? New Emily had a lot to answer for.

'All we need is proof that Oliver was behind the camera, and that he lied about Andy's death, then we've got him bang to rights,' Emily said. 'But I need Andy's help. As well as owing him a humongous apology. Where is he?'

Emily looked around the room, as if she might not have noticed him loitering next to the wardrobe.

'I thought he was at your flat?' Zoe frowned. 'After the dinner party, he came back here for a bit, then he said he needed some time by himself to do some thinking. I assumed he'd transported himself to wherever you were. He was pretty upset, though, Em. I shouldn't have blurted everything out like that, especially not the bits about you and Andy. That was none of my business.'

Emily paused. She'd considered telling Zoe how much she had actually cared about Andy, and admitting that she'd covered up her real feelings simply to save face. But she knew she'd only be confessing to make herself feel better, perhaps making Zoe feel bad for getting close to Andy in the process. Plus Emily had kept Andy at arm's length, no matter what her real feelings were. 'None of it was untrue, was it?' she said, picking up the threadbare floppy bunny toy Zoe had owned since she was born and flapping its ears distractedly. 'Hearing it all laid out like that made me realise how wrong I was, keeping my distance because he didn't match some stupid perfect-man template. And I need to tell him how sorry I am.'

'Maybe he'll remember more about his last day when he sees the video, too,' Zoe said.

'It feels like we're so close to finding out exactly how he died,' Emily said. 'But we haven't got long – the Cat's Miaow pitch is on Wednesday afternoon, and Oliver's planning on taking all the glory.'

'I'm sorry you've been through all this on your own,' Zoe said. 'I didn't like Oliver, sure, but sheesh! This is a *lot*.'

'I'm certainly not going to assume someone's right for me just because they're a bit posh and smell of marshmallows again,' Emily said ruefully. 'You might argue that the cosmos was a tad too enthusiastic about teaching me a lesson, but still. So how on earth do we get hold of Andy? I've never had to get in touch with him before, he's always just . . . been there, being his usual irritating, adorable self.'

'Do you reckon he's got lost, like in *Poltergeist*? Maybe he's trapped in the telly.'

Emily and Zoe looked dubiously at Zoe's tiny flatscreen, then at each other.

'So far Andy being dead has been nothing like the movies, unless the director's cut of *Ghost* features Patrick Swayze plotting to hang around the Playboy mansion, so I think we can rule that one out,' Emily said.

'How about we try this?' Zoe said, picking up the glass on her bedside table and waggling it.

'How is drinking going to help? Any excuse,' Emily tutted.

'No, idiot,' Zoe said, shoving her. 'I mean we could set up another Ouija board.'

This time around, Emily was more terrified that no one would appear when they summoned the undead than of seeing a ghost.

'OK, fingers on the glass and close your eyes,' Emily instructed, her heart thumping. 'And it goes without saying that we don't want either of us mucking about.'

Zoe nodded and placed her fingers on top of Emily's on the upturned glass she'd set in the middle of her DIY Ouija board. Zoe had scrawled the letters of the alphabet, the numbers zero to nine, and 'yes' and 'no' onto the back of a dismantled shoebox in felt tip, and lit a couple of candles to make the room's atmosphere as close to that of the night of Emily's party as possible. It wasn't midnight, but they didn't want to have to wait that long.

'Now we know this thing works, let's just hope we don't bring back someone who isn't Andy back from the dead, shall we?' Emily said, from her spot sitting cross-legged on Zoe's bedroom carpet. 'I can't be doing with two ghosts wandering around asking me to help solve the mystery of how they died.'

When both their fingers were spread across the bottom of the glass, Emily cleared her throat.

'Is anyone out there? We're looking for Andy,' she said, adding, 'Andy Atkins,' just in case. Emily's ears rang in the silence that followed. 'Andy. Andy Atkins. Are you out there?'

'Try telling him you want to apologise,' Zoe whispered.

'I'm looking for Andy to say how sorry I am,' Emily said. 'And to tell him that we've found out how he died. Kind of. Can someone . . . go and get him?'

The glass remained resolutely still in the middle of the board. 'Let me try,' Zoe said, closing her eyes and placing her fingers on the bottom of the glass. 'Andy, we really want to see you. If you're out there, please make your presence known.'

Zoe opened one eye, then closed it again. 'Andy? Can you hear us?' But the glass didn't move an inch.

'Bugger,' Zoe said, leaning back against her bed. 'What do we do now?'

'I guess I'm going to have to go and look for him,' Emily said. 'But where do I even start?'

Chapter 39

Outside the window of the pub, the sky was turning dark with rain clouds. It was time for Emily to move on. She licked prawn-cocktail flavoured salt off her fingers and downed the last of her drink, before reluctantly hopping off her bar stool.

She'd spent the whole morning travelling from place to place, searching Andy's favourite haunts for signs of him. She'd been to The Shard, a handful of street-food markets, and to several grungy pubs around Brixton where Remington 11 played – but there was no sign of him. Pausing for a Coke and a packet of crisps in a pub with sticky carpets and flickering neon signs in the windows, she'd texted Zoe with an update.

What if I never find him? What if that's it, and he's gone for good?

He hasn't got closure yet, has he? So he has to be around somewhere. He might even be back at your flat already, playing hide and seek with Churchill

That would be a very Andy thing to do. I've just got one last place I might as well try while I'm here. Wish me luck

Zoe responded with the 'this is fine' meme – a cartoon dog, sitting in the middle of a burning room, smiling.

Reassuring. Cheers.

The sun was already dipping behind the houses by the time Emily wove her way through the backstreets of Brixton towards Andy's mum's house. She felt her stomach rolling with nerves as she approached the terraced street where he'd grown up, and where his parents (and Dandy the cat) still lived.

If Andy wasn't here, she was out of ideas. And she wasn't sure how she'd feel looking Mandy in the eye, knowing she could have made Andy's last days on earth so much happier, if she'd only believed in herself – and Andy – a bit more. As she reached the house, which had a tiny, neat front garden and a pebble-dashed front, she took a deep breath and pushed her finger on the doorbell, which buzzed shrilly inside. She heard someone shuffling down the hallway towards her, and nervously tapped her foot until the door opened a crack – then swung open when Mandy saw who was standing on her front step.

'Oh, hello, Emily,' Mandy said, breaking into a wide grin. 'How lovely to see you. Do you want to come in?'

'Yes please, if you don't mind,' she said, carefully wiping her feet on the doormat as she stepped into the hall.

'The living room's just down there on the right,' Mandy said. 'Make yourself at home.'

Emily shut the door behind her, looking around the hallway for clues that Andy might be there. A beautiful cat, completely white apart from a black front paw, watched her through the bannisters. It miaowed, then slinked its way down the stairs and wove its way around her legs.

'That's Dandy. He's been ever so wary of strangers since Andy died, but he's been behaving a bit oddly over the last couple of days,' Mandy said, and Emily grinned. She bent down to stroke him, and Dandy arched his back into her hand, purring loudly.

Emily made her way to the small but immaculately tidy living room. Along one wall was a dresser, which was crammed with photos of Andy, tealight candles in brightly coloured glass holders, and little pots filled with flowers. She ran her finger along its edge and felt a pang as she realised that although it hadn't been long since she'd last seen him, she missed Andy. No one in her life had made a joke about underpants for almost two whole days.

Among the pictures, she saw a photo of him with his arm slung around his dad's shoulders. In the picture, Sandy looked painfully thin and pale, and had a tube snaking into his nose. Emily realised it must have been taken when he had cancer, and Andy had decided to abandon his place at uni to support his mum.

Next, nestled among the mismatched frames, Emily spotted a photo of herself. In it, Andy was grinning from ear to ear, and she had her face only half to the camera, her head thrown back in laughter at something he'd said.

She picked up the frame. 'Do you mind?' Emily asked Mandy, holding up the photo as she came into the room carrying a plate of biscuits.

'Of course.' Mandy smiled. 'I love that photo. Andy was so happy when he met you. I really wanted to meet you, but Andy said you had that important job, and didn't have the time. But this photo reassured me that you were the right girl for him. It means a lot to me that he had you looking out for him.'

Emily blushed. 'Can I sit down?' she said, gesturing at the sofa, and Mandy nodded.

'I wanted to talk to you about that – about mine and Andy's relationship,' Emily said, her heart pounding.

'Oh, really?' Mandy frowned. Smoothing her skirt, she sat on the armchair opposite the sofa.

Emily paused. Ever since she'd found out she might have had something to do with Andy's death – that he'd been hoping the video he made with Oliver might persuade her to be his girlfriend – she'd felt eaten up with guilt. She'd made her apologies to Zoe, and planned to make one to Andy, too, when she found him.

But didn't Mandy deserve to know the truth as well? That Emily hadn't been the girlfriend Andy's parents thought she'd been? She didn't deserve to be praised for making him happy.

'I wasn't entirely honest with you at the cemetery, Mandy. And I've got a bit of a confession to make.'

'Oh, really?' Mandy said, frowning. She looked almost scared, like Emily might say something that might add to the burden of pain she was already carrying. And Emily suddenly realised that while telling the truth might make *her* feel better, she would be making Mandy's life a whole lot worse. Emily touched Andy's face in the photo. Until now, she hadn't noticed how much she'd changed since he'd disappeared.

She'd always focused on what was right for her, not really noticing how her behaviour affected other people.

But since he'd come back, she'd felt so much more like her old self again. Like the real her – not the one who hid behind a mask, scared of rejection. And suddenly, she realised something else, too.

'The truth is, Mandy, I never told Andy how I felt about him,' she said. 'You see, I was in love with him. But I never managed to say it out loud. I don't know why not. I think I was scared of falling for someone and risking getting hurt. Only I never told him that. And I really wish I had.'

'I'm sure he knew, love,' Mandy said, reaching over and squeezing Emily's hand. She was smiling, and Emily was relieved that she hadn't chosen to unburden her guilt onto her.

'Ha! I knew I was too awesome for you not to fall in love with me,' a voice said from the doorway.

'Andy!' Emily said, leaping up from the sofa.

'You can't take that back now,' Andy said, grinning. 'I heard everything. I just wish I had a pen so I could take notes.'

'I don't want to take it back. I'm so happy to see you,' Emily said, her eyes shining with tears.

'Who are you talking to?' Mandy said uncertainly, staring at the doorway.

'Well, well, well,' Andy said, folding his arms. 'After all the times I asked you to come and talk to my mum on my behalf, and you said no. You're going to have to now, aren't you?'

Emily grinned back. 'I suppose I am.'

Mandy stood up. 'Please can you tell me what's going on?' she said, her voice cracking.

'I'm so sorry, Mandy,' Emily said, turning towards her. 'I'm not sure how to explain this, and it's going to sound crazy, but … two weeks ago, my friend set up a Ouija board at a party I was throwing. We were just mucking about, but Andy's ghost appeared. And he's been hanging around my flat ever since.'

Mandy took a step backwards.

'I know how this sounds,' Emily said, quickly, 'but he came back to find out what had happened to him, and to stop me from making one of the biggest mistakes of my life. And at this very moment, he's standing right there, in your doorway. He's wearing his stripy T-shirt, blue jeans, and white trainers. And he's got a sweet wrapper stuck in his hair.'

'Werther's Originals?' Mandy croaked, shaking her head. 'I wanted to take that stupid sweet wrapper out of his hair when the police asked me and Sandy to identify him. But they said it could be evidence, so I wasn't allowed.'

'I'm honestly not making this up, Mandy,' Emily said. 'Me and Andy had an argument on Saturday, and I guess he decided to come and see you. He's been asking for me to talk to you ever since he appeared. Perhaps that's why Dandy's been behaving oddly lately – because animals and babies seem to be able to see him. Show her, Andy.'

Andy bent down and called into the hall, 'Here, Dandy, here, kitty.' Dandy stalked into the room, looking aloof, before weaving in and out of Andy's legs. To Mandy, it looked like he was dodging around thin air. Andy chucked Dandy behind the ear before standing up.

'I'm right here, and I'm OK, Mum,' he said, heading for the armchair in the corner of the room. He really did enjoy sitting down an awful lot. 'I don't want you to worry about me.'

'He says he's OK, and you're not to worry about him.'

Mandy shook her head. 'I don't know how you've pulled

off this trick with the cat, but it isn't right, what you're doing,' she said stiffly. 'Why would Andy appear to you, and not to me? That doesn't make sense.'

'Everyone who was there the night of the séance can see him, but only them. And I guess he came back because he had unfinished business. You were right – Oliver Beauchamp had something to do with Andy's death. And I think he's here to make sure he doesn't get away with it.'

'*Oliver* had something to do with what happened?' Andy said. 'What have I missed?'

'So much, your head might explode,' Emily said.

'You seem to know an awful lot about this Oliver,' Mandy said, glancing nervously at the armchair. 'Have you been sent to check I'm not blabbing about the money? Because I don't give a sod about your stupid cheque. You can have it all back, every penny.'

'I do know Oliver. I work with him, but I promise I'm not part of this. And I'm not making it up when I tell you that Andy is here, now. In fact, he's sitting in your armchair, driving me nuts by slinging his legs over the arm.'

'I told him not to do that a million times, but he'd never listen,' Mandy said.

'You and me both,' Emily said. 'It was like training an unruly dog.'

Mandy laughed, despite herself.

'Tell her ditto,' Andy said, suddenly.

'Once again, Andy, that doesn't work outside the film *Ghost*,' Emily said, pinching the bridge of her nose.

'So you reckon you're talking to Andy right now?' Mandy said, looking between Emily and the armchair.

'He wants to convince you that he's really here,' Emily said.

'At least give him the chance. Please? Is there something only you and he would know, that I can ask him?'

'What was the song I used to sing to him when he was a boy, whenever he had a nightmare?'

'Oh, Mum, that's so embarrassing,' Andy said, dropping his head in his hands.

'It's not like you can die of embarrassment, is it, because you're already dead,' Emily said. 'So spit it out, before your mum kicks me out of her house for being a big fat fraud.'

'It was the *Teenage Mutant Hero Turtles* theme tune,' Andy muttered.

'Oh my god. That's amazing,' Emily said, grinning. 'You're right, that's really embarrassing. He says it was the *Teenage Mutant Hero Turtles* theme tune,' she added, turning to Mandy.

'Andy?' she said, looking nervously at the armchair. 'Is it really you there?'

'You can ask something else. Anything you like,' Emily said. 'He really misses you and wants you to know he's OK.'

'Ask him what our special password was – the one I said I'd use if I sent a stranger to pick him up from school, so he'd know if a pervert was trying to kidnap him.'

'He's not the Messiah, he's a very naughty boy,' Andy said, grinning as Emily relayed his words to Mandy. 'Dad loves Monty Python.'

'And what was his favourite Friday tea?'

'Andy's Beige Bonanza,' Emily repeated. 'What on earth was that?'

'Potato waffles, Findus Crispy Pancakes, baked beans and turkey dinosaurs,' Mandy and Andy said in unison. 'Dinner of kings,' Andy added.

Mandy looked pale, and sat down on the sofa with a thud.

'Well, I think you've convinced your mum, anyway,' Emily said, sitting next to Mandy and gently taking hold of her hand. 'What do you want to say to her?'

Andy took a deep breath. 'I love you, Mum. And everything's going to be alright. Although I can't tell you anything about the afterlife, because I haven't seen it yet, Emily's helping me get over to the other side. The fact that I'm here at all means there has to be something after this, right? And that means we'll see each other again. So there's no need to be sad.'

As tears started falling down Mandy's face, Emily delved into her pocket and handed her a tissue.

'Oh, Andy,' Mandy said, blowing her nose. 'We miss you so much. Every day.' She shook her head. 'His dad's never going to believe this. He's down the pub. How will I ever convince him?'

'Tell him he's left his reading glasses in the potting shed,' Andy grinned. 'I was hanging out with him yesterday when he lost them. He's been looking for them everywhere.'

'Why didn't you just move them inside for him?' Emily said, after relaying the news to Mandy.

'He's left them under an upturned plant pot. It was too heavy for me to lift it. But . . . hang on. Tell Mum to come over to the mirror. And would you mind breathing on it for me?'

Mandy frowned as Emily beckoned her over to the mirror then breathed on it hard, her nose touching the glass. The cold air Andy's presence created caused it to bloom with mist. Mandy stared, her chin wobbling, as Andy wrote with his finger in the condensation: I ♥ MUM.

'I love you too, Andy,' she said, bursting into fresh tears as

Emily guided her back to the sofa. 'But what happened to you? What did this Oliver person do?'

Emily and Andy glanced at each other. 'I think I've worked out what happened, Mandy. I can't tell you just yet, because we still need to check a few things. But don't worry. I'm going to make sure he doesn't get away with it. And that Andy can finally rest in peace.'

Chapter 40

'Play it again,' Andy asked, for the third time in a row. Emily pressed replay on the video of Andy on the roof of Barter, Bugle and Hegilly's offices, ignoring the odd looks she was getting from some of the other customers in the sticky-floored pub.

'Are you OK?' she asked gently, as Andy watched what they assumed were some of his last minutes on earth, over and over again.

'So you think something happened to me after this, and I died wearing these?' Andy said, pulling his foot onto his lap and tapping his trainer.

'It's just a theory, but it seems likely,' Emily said. 'Do you remember anything?'

Andy shook his head. 'Still nothing after Coco Pops, sorry,' he said. 'I must have been sent by the agency to work with Oliver. I'd never done a shift at Binkle, Bonkle and Turnip before, which is why I didn't recognise him. Although I knew he was a douchebag from the word go, obviously. But this is definitely me. And that's definitely what I'm wearing now.

Including those shoes, which it turns out might actually be, like, murder weapons.'

'I think Oliver was the one behind the camera, and that's why he visited your mum and paid her that money.'

'Poor Mum. I told you he was a twat,' Andy said. 'My subconscious probably recognised him from when he did me in.'

'You did tell me. I'm sorry for not believing you. And for . . . all the other stuff.'

'Care to elaborate?' Andy said.

Emily sighed. 'For not giving you enough of a chance. For keeping half an eye over your shoulder, looking for someone better. And for never admitting the truth to you, or even to myself.'

'Which was . . .?'

'You heard me telling your mum everything. Don't make me say it all again, you wanker.' Emily tried to nudge Andy, forgetting he wasn't solid, and nearly toppled off her stool. 'I was in love with you too, OK? I was just too idiotic to realise it.'

The barman, who was busy polishing a glass with a tea towel, shook his head at her sadly.

'Now you've come to your senses, I *suppose* I can forgive you for totally not appreciating how awesome I was when I was alive,' Andy said. 'As long as you give me permission to haunt the crap out of Oliver.'

'Not just yet – I don't want him to know what we know until we have some more evidence,' Emily said. 'I'm certain Oliver shot this film, but we don't have any way of proving that from this clip. The original video must be somewhere, and it might tell us more about what happened. Like, this clip's sound is covered with music, but maybe you can hear Oliver on the original. We just need to find it.'

'Or maybe there's more footage, where he says, "Oh no! I can't believe I killed that handsome man!"'

'Also very likely,' Emily said.

They sat in silence, thinking for a moment. 'I don't suppose ghosts can access the iCloud, can they?' Emily asked. 'Because that would be really helpful.'

'Nope. I couldn't even do that when I was alive,' Andy said. 'I was always rubbish at technology.'

'Then we have to check Oliver's phone and see if it's still in there,' Emily said. She glanced at her watch. 'If only we had some way of getting into it without him noticing. Like a ghost who's learned how to touch stuff . . .'

'Hey, how are you feeling?' Jada said, when Emily arrived in the office. 'Also, what are you doing here just before home time when you're supposed to be off sick, and what have you done with Emily?' she added, looking theatrically under the desk.

'I'm afraid New Emily is dead,' Emily said, slumping in her chair. 'She suffocated on a hydrating face mask with Omega-3 infusion and super-plumping peptide nodules.'

'Wow. You look amazing,' Simon said, poking his head over his laptop and staring at Emily. Her usual uniform of figure-enhancing dress and sky-high heels had been replaced with high-waisted jeans tightly cinched at her waist, over a strappy top and baggy cardigan. She was wearing a minimal amount of make-up, and her hair was loose around her shoulders. Emily had found it a real treat – and a huge relief – only spending fifteen minutes getting ready that morning.

'Are you *blushing*?' Jada said, throwing a highlighter pen at Simon's face, who was too busy looking shell-shocked to duck. 'What's all this in aid of then?' she added to Emily.

Emily glanced over her shoulder at where Oliver was leaning over Chrissie's desk, probably teaching her how to do something she was pretending to have forgotten.

'I can't explain right now, but in a nutshell, I've realised that Oliver is a prick, obviously, and that holding your stomach in for six years straight is really boring. Which is also pretty obvious, now I think about it. Plus I'm sick of trying to kill off Old Emily, because she's refusing to die quietly.'

'Does this mean we can go on a field trip to The Pink Lagoon?' Simon said, hopefully. 'Prima Doner's kebabs sound amazing, even if you often have to eat them quite near a pile of sick.'

'New Emily isn't *completely* dead. I'm not going to start sparking up twenty Marlboros a day and regaling everyone with tales of my torrid past. The Witches' Coven would enjoy that far too much. But I'm certainly not going to bend over backwards to impress the likes of Oliver, either.'

'I can't believe what he did to you,' Jada said, shaking her head. 'It's bad enough when men somehow manage to take credit for ideas you had in a meeting where LOADS OF PEOPLE heard you say it first. But deciding you can't handle the Cat's Miaow presentation because of a couple of days off sick ... He might as well just tell you not to worry your pretty little head about it and be done with it.'

'That's not even the half of it. It turns out he's much *much* worse than even Zoe thought. And she didn't like him from day one.'

'What's he done?' Jada said, her eyes widening.

'I'm not one hundred per cent sure yet, but that's why I'm here,' Emily said, looking back at Oliver. He'd returned to his desk, and Andy was standing behind him, watching over his shoulder as he punched the security code into his mobile phone. He gave Emily a thumbs-up, and she grinned back. 'Hopefully, I'll be able to tell you soon enough.'

As if he'd felt his eyes on her, Oliver glanced over, then stood up and swooped towards Emily's desk.

'Ah, you're back,' he said, raising his eyebrows at Emily's outfit. She crossed her legs and held his gaze, daring him to say something about it. 'Feeling better, I hope? Could we have a word?'

'Of course, Oliver, I'd love to,' Emily said sweetly, grimacing at Jada and Simon behind his back as she followed him towards The Upside Down, a meeting room that Al had insisted be designed with all its furniture stuck to the ceiling.

'Sorry, this is the only room currently available,' Oliver said, gesturing to the bean bags strewn across the floor.

'Oh, no, please. After you,' Emily said, smirking as he tried to sit down with a modicum of grace, and failed miserably.

'Do sit,' he said, gesturing at the neighbouring bean bag.

'I'm fine, thanks,' Emily said, folding her arms and leaning against the wall. 'Bad back,' she added, in case he insisted.

Oliver cleared his throat. 'I just wanted to check that you were happy with our decision about the Cat's Miaow pitch. You understand how important it is – and, of course, how important you are to the team. You're incredibly talented, but it's understandable that the pressure of such a big leap forward might be a bit much at this juncture.'

'Yes, at this juncture. Of course,' Emily said, nodding, and Oliver frowned.

'So you're OK with me taking on the presentation?'

'Absolutely,' Emily said, smiling genially. 'It makes sense that someone of your calibre should head up the pitch. And it doesn't matter who presents the ideas, as long as we land it. There's no "I" in "team", is there?'

'Right,' Oliver said, looking slightly confused. 'So we're all fine, then?'

'Of course, why wouldn't we be?' Emily said, then tried not to smirk as Oliver attempted to remove himself from the beanbag, eventually resorting to rocking back and forth to build up enough momentum to spring out of it. She watched as he stalked out of the door, then yelped as she saw Andy standing behind it.

'Quick, grab this,' he said, checking no one was looking before shuffle-boarding Oliver's phone along the carpet towards Emily's feet.

Emily bent down and grabbed it, before shutting the door behind her.

'What on earth are you doing?' Emily said, as Andy launched himself onto a bean bag. 'You were supposed to just find the video.'

'I tried to get into his phone, but it didn't work,' Andy said, waggling his fingers. 'I don't think I'm electricky enough.'

'So you can turn off my oven by just glancing at it, but you can't use a touch-screen phone? Incredible.'

'I told you I needed a handbook. I still have no idea how this stuff works. I got his password, though.'

'Is it six-six-six, by any chance?'

'No, but it is one-two-three-four-five-six. If I'd known he was that stupid, I wouldn't have bothered spying on him. But anyway, I knew I had to steal the phone for you without anyone getting freaked out by it floating around in mid-air, so I knocked it under his desk then slid it across the floor when no one was watching. The perfect crime.'

'OK, so let's do this before he comes in here looking for it,' Emily said, turning her back to the door, unlocking the phone and opening Oliver's photos folder. 'You keep watch.'

'Roger that,' Andy said, jumping out of his bean bag and peering through the window in the door. 'He's patting his pockets . . . now he's looking through the piles of paper on his desk. I think he's realised it's gone, so hurry up.'

Quickly, Emily brought up the picture search bar, and tapped in the date of Andy's death.

'Bingo,' she whispered. There was only one video shot on that date, and the opening frame was an image of Andy grinning over his shoulder at the camera as he clambered onto the bright-red air vent on the roof of Barter, Bugle and Hegilly.

'He's coming,' Andy warned, as Emily quickly emailed the video to herself, shutting everything down a moment before Oliver pushed open the meeting-room door.

'Are you looking for this?' she said, waggling the phone at him. 'I thought you didn't approve of people bringing phones into meetings, so I was surprised to see you'd left this in here. I found it under this bean bag.'

'It must have slid out of my pocket. I thought I'd left it on my desk,' Oliver said, plucking it from her fingers. Then he looked around the room. 'Why is it so cold in here?'

'No idea,' Emily said, grinning at Andy as she followed Oliver out of the door.

Chapter 41

'OK, are you sure you're ready for this?' Emily asked, as she opened up her laptop on the coffee table. 'Because I don't know what we're going to find in this video, and it might be hard to watch.'

Agreeing to look at the video together so they could both offer Andy moral support, Zoe had headed to Emily's flat straight after she'd left work, Andy following from Emily's office via ghostly teleportation, to avoid the Tube.

'I guess so,' Andy said. 'I need to find out what happened to me, even if it's hard to watch. So let's do this thing.'

The three sat perched on the edge of Emily's sofa, Andy in the middle, and Churchill curled on top of Emily's feet. Since she'd realised Churchill was just trying to be himself, rather than a hellcat from Hades, and started treating him as such, he'd become completely attached to her, following her around the flat like a puppy.

As Emily hovered her mouse over the Play button on Oliver's video, Zoe gave Andy a supportive thumbs-up – then they watched as, on screen, Andy scrambled onto the air vent.

The voice behind the camera said something too quiet to make out.

'Hang on, rewind that,' Zoe said. Emily turned the volume up and skipped backwards.

'That was great,' the voice said. 'Now we've warmed up a bit, do you think you can do a backflip?'

'Oh my god. That's definitely Oliver, right?' Emily said, and the others nodded. They stared as, from the top of the air vent, Andy turned his back to the camera and did an ungainly back flip, before giving Oliver a thumbs-up.

'Perfect,' Oliver said. 'Shall we try something a bit more dramatic?'

'What do you want me to do?' Andy said. 'I could try jumping over these bollards.' He pointed at some metal struts embedded in the roof.

'I think we need something more. Something big, that will really blow their minds,' Oliver said. 'Do you think you could make a jump to the next roof? It's not that far.'

The camera wobbled as it followed Andy to the edge of the roof.

'I'm not sure. It looks dangerous,' Andy said dubiously, looking down. The camera wobbled as it focused on the next roof along. Emily swallowed as she saw how far away it was, and glanced at Andy.

'Come on, it can't be more than twenty feet. You've already jumped further than that up here, and that roof is lower than this one, so it'll be easy,' Oliver said from behind the camera. 'If I can capture you making this jump, we'll definitely land the AirLab campaign.'

'You mean you'll be a *shoo*-in?' Andy said, grinning at his own joke.

'Yes,' Oliver said, slightly impatiently. 'And I promise you, if you do this, they'll have to use this clip, because it'll look superb. You'll go viral, and everyone will know who you are. Then this girl you've been telling me about . . . Emma, is it?'

'It's Emily.'

'She won't be able to say no when you ask her to be your girlfriend, will she?'

Emily paused the video and turned to Andy. 'You did this for me?' she said, her eyes already filling with tears. 'To try and impress me?'

Andy looked crestfallen. 'I still don't remember all this,' he said, gesturing at the screen. 'But I remember wondering why sometimes you seemed really into me, then at other times you seemed to cool off, when I hadn't done anything wrong. I guess I thought doing something like this might seal the deal. I mean, it does look pretty cool, right?' Andy gave Emily a small smile, and she realised she'd give anything to be able to hug him properly.

'Carry on,' Zoe said gently, squeezing Emily's hand. 'We need to see what happened.'

Reluctantly, Emily pressed Play. On the screen, Andy turned to the camera.

'I'll go viral?' Andy said, thinking it over. 'I tell you what, if you use one of Remington 11's tracks in the pitch, I'll do it. Then maybe Emily will say yes, *and* we'll be famous.'

'Absolutely,' Oliver said.

'He didn't even do that, the bastard,' Emily said. 'But then I guess he couldn't, could he? It was risky enough using footage of Andy at all. I guess he knew it would be good for the pitch, but that it was unlikely anyone outside the industry would ever see it, so it was a risk worth taking.'

On screen, Andy looked over the edge of the building again, then at the camera.

'I guess I'd better take a run-up,' he said. He sounded like he was scared, but trying not to show it, and Emily's heart clenched. 'Here goes nothing.'

Emily's heart thudded as she watched the camera focusing on Andy from the edge of the roof as he did a run-up. It followed him as he leaped through the air and towards the next roof. He was close to making it, but started falling too soon, plummeting sickeningly downwards, his arms scrabbling for purchase in thin air. Emily swallowed as a muffled thud could be heard off-camera.

'Shit! ... shit!' Oliver breathed, the camera wobbling as he ran to see what had happened, his phone still clutched in his hand. Its lens hanging over the edge of the roof, the camera moved in and out of focus, until it finally settled on a horrifying image: that of Andy's body lying crumpled on the ground below.

As the video ended, Oliver swearing under his breath as he switched off the camera, everyone held their breath, before Andy broke the silence.

'I guess we know what happened to me now,' he said, in a wobbly voice.

'Jesus,' Zoe said, softly. She placed her hand through Andy's. On his other side, Emily did the same, ignoring the cold, treacly feeling.

'I don't know what to say,' Emily said, swallowing hard. 'I can't believe what happened to you was partly my fault.'

'Of course it wasn't,' Zoe said, firmly.

'It's not your fault Oliver has all the scruples of an alley cat,' Andy said, angrily. 'Sorry Churchill, no offence. And who knows, maybe it would have worked if I'd made the jump. You'd have realised how amazingly sexy I am, agreed to be my girlfriend, and we'd have lived happily ever after.'

'How are you feeling now?' Emily asked.

'Weird,' Andy said, ruffling the back of his hair. 'I don't expect many people get to see a video of their own death. But at least now we can make sure Oliver gets what he deserves.'

'I can't believe he still used that footage to land the AirLab campaign, despite what happened,' Zoe said, shaking her head. 'There's ruthless, and there's . . . well, that.'

'I can't believe he was stupid enough to *keep* the footage,' Emily added.

'And to protect it using the password one-two-three-four-five-six,' Andy said. 'What a dickhead.'

'So what do we do now?' Zoe asked.

'Easy,' Emily said. 'We get revenge. And I think I've figured out the perfect way to do it.'

Chapter 42

'The sandwiches haven't arrived yet. Fuck my life,' Jada said, picking up the phone and stabbing in the number for the local deli.

'Why are you on Sandwich Duty anyway?' Emily said, looking nervously over at Andy. He was at Oliver's desk, waiting for him to leave his laptop alone for two seconds so he could find the file they needed to execute their plan. He shrugged at Emily helplessly, and she looked at her watch. Just forty-five minutes to go.

'Ellie's off sick, so Charles has given me the inestimable honour of ordering a load of manky, curly-edged sandwiches filled with dead animals for a load of white, middle-class men to stuff their faces with,' Jada muttered, covering the mouthpiece. 'Weird how he didn't ask Simon to do it, isn't it?'

'Men can't do things like make coffee and order sandwiches,' Simon said, seriously. 'We've simply got way too much penis.'

Jada poked her tongue out at him, before taking her hand off the mouthpiece and shouting at whoever at the deli had had the misfortune of answering the phone.

'Who's that over by Oliver's desk?' Simon asked, squinting across the room.

'Who?' Emily said, turning around.

'The guy in the stripy T-shirt. He's just . . . standing there, staring at him. It's a bit weird. And didn't I see you talking to him in The Upside-Down yesterday? Who is he?'

'Shit,' Emily muttered.

So far Operation Ditto, as Andy had insisted on calling their big idea, wasn't going according to plan. As well as Oliver being inconveniently glued to his laptop, scuppering Phase One, Charles had been out of the office all morning. Emily needed to convince him to let her sit in on the Cat's Miaow presentation before the account executives arrived, but she hadn't been given the chance to talk to him yet, thwarting Phase Two.

And now, she realised, she'd completely forgotten that Simon and Jada had been at her flat the night Andy had come back from the dead, which meant they could see him too. It added yet another hurdle to Operation Ditto that Emily really could have done without.

'He's, um, shadowing Oliver. He's the new intern, poor bastard,' Emily babbled, her stomach flipping as the lift pinged open, and a group of glossily dressed executives poured out of it.

'Look at him, the smarmy git,' Simon said, shaking his head as Oliver leaped from his seat and jogged enthusiastically to the lift, grinning widely. 'I bet his handshake is really firm, because he read somewhere that it makes him look more alpha. I can't believe he's going to get all the credit for your hard work. What a twat.'

Oliver ushered the team towards the boardroom, which was

officially titled The Board Room, and featured a table made from vintage game boards as a 'hilarious' nod to its name.

Emily glanced anxiously over to where Andy was now sitting in Oliver's chair, looking helplessly at his laptop. He looked at her and shook his head.

'Hopefully, what goes around comes around,' Emily said, jumping out of her chair as Andy headed towards her.

'Loo break,' she announced loudly, widening her eyes at him. Taking the hint at the last minute, he swerved away from her desk and towards the bathrooms.

'Keep away from Simon and Jada,' Emily whispered when she'd locked herself in a cubicle with Andy. 'I totally forgot they'd be able to see you.'

Andy grimaced. 'Even worse, I can't get into the laptop,' he said, breathlessly. 'My stupid fingers won't work the trackpad, and he doesn't use a mouse.'

'Andy, no one uses a mouse any more. So I guess we're going to have to enact Plan B.' Emily pulled a USB stick from her pocket and waggled it. It had a heart drawn on its metal case in Tipp-Ex.

'Hey, I hope you didn't delete my super-romantic amazing song for this,' Andy said.

'It's for a good cause, and I've got it saved on my laptop anyway. Wouldn't it be cool if this very USB led to Oliver's downfall?'

'Good point,' Andy said. 'Plan B is a go.'

'As long as I can grab Charles before he gets to the board-room, and he lets me sit in on the meeting, we should be OK. And he totally owes me one after booting me out of my presenting role.'

'Good luck,' Andy grinned. He'd always loved an

adventure, and Emily was glad that even this one, which was so closely linked to his demise, seemed to be entertaining him too. Once Andy had made his way to the meeting room through the bathroom walls, to avoid being spotted by Jada or Simon, Emily left the bathroom and almost crashed headlong into Charles.

'Just the man I wanted to see,' Emily said, brightly.

'Can it wait, Emily? I'm about to embark on my pre-meeting ablutions,' Charles said, looking slightly pained. 'My bladder, alas, isn't what it once was, but we can't keep the cream of advertising's creative minds waiting, can we?'

'It'll take two seconds, I promise, then your bladder can have all the wees its heart desires.' Emily winced, and Charles raised an eyebrow.

'You paint quite the picture,' he said. 'Go on then, you may have fifteen of my finest seconds.'

'I just wondered if I might sit in on the Cat's Miaow presentation?' Emily said, trying to sound like it was of little consequence whether he said yes or no. 'As Oliver said, I'm probably not quite ready for the responsibility of presenting, and I totally appreciate your decision. But if I sit in, even if I don't say anything, I'll see how everything works, and I'll know what to do when you feel I'm ready.'

Charles sighed, which Emily hoped against hope was a good sign, rather the bad one it almost definitely was. 'Emily. You're a bright young woman with a fantastic future ahead of you, but I think it's best that you leave the pitch to Oliver and his team this time,' he said gently, placing his hand on her shoulder. 'Oliver told me about your ... episodes, and this is simply too important to all of us at HoRizons for anything to go wrong. You do understand, don't you?'

'Episodes?' She frowned.

'Yes. Rest assured that it was strictly between him and I, and that it will go no further. He was simply worried about you. And of course, it absolutely won't affect your future chances of promotion.' Charles patted her shoulder reassuringly. 'Now I really must go. The water closet calls.'

Emily bit back angry tears. Whatever these 'episodes' Oliver had invented for her involved, she didn't imagine they cast her in a particularly flattering or professional light. And now she had to work out how to get into the pitch meeting without actually being invited.

Back at her desk, her legs jiggled as she watched the boardroom door while various executives nipped out for the loo or to take a call before the meeting started. She knew Charles and Oliver would be schmoozing them with chit-chat before the presentation proper began. But she couldn't work out how to get inside.

'You seem more nervous than I am about those bloody sandwiches getting here on time,' Jada said.

'Jada, you're a genius!' Emily said, grinning. At the same moment the giant, numberless clock above the New HoRizons coffee bar clicked into place to mark the hour, the doors to the board room were ceremoniously swung shut, and the lifts pinged open.

A flustered-looking teenager carrying a stack of platters so high he could barely see over the top of them wobbled into the office.

'Thank fuck,' Jada said, leaping up to take them from his arms.

'Do you mind if I deliver these?' Emily said, as Jada dumped the stack on her desk.

'You don't have to do that for me,' Jada said, squeezing her arm. 'For starters, you have to lay them all out on the table then bring in the drinks, which is a fucking pain in the arse, as well as SEXIST.' She shouted the last word towards the closed boardroom doors. 'And for seconds, do you really want to have to watch Oliver presenting your work in there?'

'It might sound weird, but that's *exactly* what I want to do,' Emily said.

Jada shrugged. 'Fill your boots, then.'

Emily gave her a loud smack on the cheek before piling the trays onto a waiting trolley.

Outside the meeting-room door, she paused, her heart thudding.

'You'll all know Oliver, of course,' she could hear Charles saying through the frosted glass. 'We obviously wanted our brightest and best working on this project, which is why we got Mr Beauchamp here, who headed up the notorious AirLab campaign, to apply his brains to Cat's Miaow.'

As the execs broke into applause, Emily pushed the trolley through the meeting-room door with a loud clang, mouthing, '*Sorry*,' as everyone turned to look at her. Charles frowned, and Oliver looked furious. Andy, who was standing in the corner of the room next to the presentation screen, gave her a gleeful thumbs-up.

Good, I've rattled him, Emily thought, as she began spreading the platters of food out on the tables set up at the back of the room as slowly as humanly possible. Although Oliver would be shooting daggers at her back, she knew he wouldn't want to show himself up in front of the execs by telling her to hurry up. He was the kind of man who would claim to his peers that he treated everyone alike, from paupers to princes, while secretly treating service staff like crap. 'Thank you for the kind welcome, Charles,' Oliver said from the head of the table. 'I must say, I was hugely excited to be given the Cat's Miaow account on my very first day here at HoRizons, and I'm confident you're going to love where we've taken your incredible product. So let's begin with the strapline I developed for the campaign.'

Clicking the remote control held in his hand, a giant slogan appeared on the screen behind him.

Every cat is unique.
But all cats love Cat's Miaow.

Emily turned around to look, and gasped. She'd known Oliver would be presenting the campaign on her behalf, but she'd assumed he'd have improved upon her initial ideas – something he'd boasted about enough times – or at least acknowledged that there was a team behind them, rather than pretending they were the fruit of his genius alone.

'The internet is full of memes about cats being evil geniuses and only caring about their owners when they want food,' Oliver continued. 'These stereotypes can be annoying for cat-lovers like me, because when you've got a pet you know it's special.

'So *my* idea is to turn that whole evil-genius cat trope on its head, and show customers that we're on their side. That we understand them, and the way their pet is unique, better than any of our competitors ever could.'

Forgetting the sandwiches she was supposed to be laying out existed, Emily gaped at Oliver. He was using the presentation she'd written, word for word. And he was doing it with an exceedingly annoying look on his face.

Charles looked over, and gave Emily a single, warning shake of his head. He looked troubled, and Emily realised that he'd been as in the dark as she was about what the finished pitch looked like. He'd trusted Oliver to improve on her ideas, not to present them verbatim – but she knew there was no way Charles could correct Oliver mid-meeting without putting the pitch in jeopardy.

And she knew that Oliver, who was smiling at her genially from across the room, knew that too. He'd once told her that his personal motto was, 'Ask for forgiveness, not permission,' which she should probably have seen as a huge red flag. But if Oliver landed the Cat's Miaow account using entirely her ideas, Charles would have no choice but to forgive him. She had to hand it to him: he might be a big fat fraud, but he was certainly smart with it.

Still, it was about time she put a stop to the presentation – and to wipe the disgustingly smug smile off his face. Nodding at Andy, he gave her a thumbs-up before plunging both hands through the presentation screen. It flickered a couple of times, then died.

'I did it!' Andy said.

'Oh . . . umm, we seem to be having some technical issues,' Oliver said, stabbing at the buttons on the remote he held in his hand. 'One moment, please.'

Emily nodded her head slightly at Oliver's laptop. Andy walked across to it, closed his eyes in concentration, and slammed the lid shut. The woman beside Oliver's empty chair jumped.

'Your laptop just shut itself,' she said nervously.

'Sorry about all this,' Oliver muttered, moving around to his seat and pulling open the lid. Andy pushed his hand through the keyboard, his eyes closed in concentration, as Oliver punched at the keys. 'It doesn't seem to be working,' he said. Emily could see sweat gathering on his forehead, and grinned.

'Isn't it delightful the way technology buggers up the second you really need it not to? Perhaps our presentation screen aspires to be a printer,' Charles said, sending a nervous laugh around the room. 'Would you like to use my laptop, Beauchamp?'

'I'd love to, Charles, but the presentation was saved on my desktop. I appreciate it isn't company policy, but it contained delicate material.' Oliver shot Emily a look, and she knew straight away that he hadn't trusted her not to mess about with the presentation once she was banned from the meeting. Quite rightly, as it happened. That was why she hadn't been able to find it on HoRizons' shared server, where it belonged.

Feeling like Cinderella presenting her missing glass slipper to Prince Charming, Emily plucked the USB out of her pocket. 'Sorry to interrupt, Charles, but I have a copy of the presentation here, if it's of any use to you. I did a little bit of work on the campaign,' she explained to the executives, who had turned around in their seats to look at her. 'Of course, Oliver was the mastermind behind it all, but I made a copy because I was so proud of working with someone as famous and successful as he is.'

'That's very kind,' Charles said, as Oliver glared at her with suspicion. 'But it's not much use if the presentation screen is broken, I'm afraid. Would you mind calling IT for us?' At that, Andy leaped over to the TV and shoved his hand through it again. With a startled buzz, it flickered back into life.

'Wonderful,' Charles said, clapping his hands together. 'It seems you've saved the day.'

'Yes, thank you so much,' Oliver said, through gritted teeth. 'Emma, isn't it?' he said, pointedly.

'Emily, actually,' she said, smiling sweetly as she passed the USB to Charles, whose face, as he looked from Oliver to Emily, was a picture of confusion. Inserting the USB into his own laptop, he connected it to the screen.

The slogan Emily had written flickered into life, and a small smattering of relieved applause went around the room.

'As I was saying,' Oliver said, dabbing his forehead with the handkerchief he kept in the top pocket of his suit. Emily noticed that it was monogrammed with his initials. *What a tosspot*, she thought, as Oliver continued.

'Instead of playing up the similarities between cats,' he said, 'I thought we could show cats behaving totally out of character. More like dogs, in fact.' Emily shook her head as Oliver churned out her presentation, apparently without a hint of embarrassment. Luckily, she knew that embarrassment was going to be the least of his worries in just a few seconds.

'We'll ask cat owners to send in content showing their cats' individuality,' he said, smoothly, getting back into his stride. 'Photos of cats sitting on their owners' heads. Films of cats fetching sticks, etcetera. To show that they're not all the same.'

'Three, two, one . . .' Emily muttered, as Oliver pressed the button to bring up the next slide.

In her original presentation, the fourth slide contained her compilation of cat videos. But in the new one, a hand-held video appeared of a man standing on an air vent wearing a stripy T-shirt and a pair of AirLab trainers, about to do an imperfect backflip.

Chapter 43

'Sorry about that. Wrong slide,' Oliver stuttered, turning pale. His hands shaking, he clicked over to the next slide. Reaching over Charles's shoulder, Andy waggled his eyebrows at Emily as he pressed the arrow key on the laptop keyboard to restore it.

'Perfect,' Oliver said onscreen, as Andy completed his backflip. 'Shall we try something a bit more dramatic?'

'Shit,' Oliver muttered, sweat shining on his forehead as he pressed the remote again to change the image on the screen.

'Nope,' Andy said, clicking it back to the video. 'This is going to get really boring, really quickly, don't you think?' he asked Emily, who nodded.

Wandering over to Oliver, he slapped the remote control out of his hand.

'What the fuck?' he muttered, as his onscreen counterpart said, 'I think we need something more. Something big, that will really blow their minds. Do you think you could make it to the next roof? It's not that far.'

The camera wobbled as it followed Andy to the edge of the roof. Charles frowned, and the people around the table started to mutter.

'Sorry about this,' Oliver said, reaching down to grab the remote. Andy kicked it out of his way, and Oliver leaped backwards. No one but Emily had noticed, as everyone's eyes were firmly fixed on the screen.

'I'm not sure. It looks dangerous,' Andy was saying dubiously, looking down.

'Come on, it can't be more than twenty feet. You've already jumped further than that up here, and that roof is lower than this one, so it'll be easy. If I can capture you making this jump, we'll definitely land the AirLab campaign.'

The room gasped and looked at Oliver.

'Stop watching. Stop it!' Oliver said, lurching towards Charles's laptop. By leaping through the table, Andy got there first and closed the lid with a bang onto his fingers.

'Jesus,' Oliver said, clutching his hand. He was trembling all over. 'What's happening here? Who's doing this?' He looked wildly around the room.

'You'll go viral, and everyone will know who you are,' Oliver was saying on screen. 'Then this girl you've been telling me about . . . Emma, is it?'

'It's Emily.'

Everyone in the room turned and gaped at Emily.

'She won't be able to say no when you ask her to be your girlfriend, will she?'

'Is this your doing?' Oliver snarled at her.

'Sit down, Oliver. Now,' Charles said, icily.

Oliver slumped into his chair. Even he couldn't tear his eyes away from the screen as Andy took his run-up. The room fell silent, and everyone seemed to be holding their breath as the camera followed Andy leaping through the air and towards the next roof, before he plummeted to the ground, and the video ended on the image of Andy's body lying crumpled on the pavement below.

Oliver dropped his head in his hands, and everyone turned to stare at Emily.

'You covered it up, didn't you, Oliver?' she said. 'You didn't want anyone to know that you'd had a hand in Andy's death.'

'I don't have to listen to this,' Oliver said, standing up and striding out of the room. But Emily and Andy followed him.

'You deleted his texts from his friend's phone, bribed his mum not to ask questions, and quietly left Barter, Bugle and Hegilly, still covered in glory,' she said. 'You didn't care about the people who loved him who were left behind, wondering what had happened to him, did you? All you cared about was your career.'

Oliver swung around, and grabbed Emily's arm. 'Do you blame me?' he hissed. 'Look how fucking famous I became, thanks to that AirLab campaign. Not to mention the fat bonus I got for putting the agency on the map.'

'So why did you come to HoRizons?' Emily said, her eyes filling with tears. 'Did you know I was Andy's ex? Did you ask me on a date on purpose, to make sure I kept quiet too?'

'You think I'd come to a two-bit agency like this just to shut someone like *you* up?' Oliver laughed. 'No. I was asked to leave when they found out I'd lost a pair of their precious trainers. And that the AirLab campaign wasn't mine. Some jumped-up junior copywriter came up with it.'

'Let her go!' Andy shouted, trying to pry Oliver's fingers off Emily's arm.

'But like you, despite her best efforts, she was as common as muck and had no class whatsoever,' Oliver continued, digging his fingers in even harder. 'She didn't have the panache to pull it off. So I stole it. And as for you ... well, everyone likes a bit of rough, don't they?'

'You ... *absolute wanker*,' Emily yelled. Already, a few people were watching them, but now the rest of the office turned and stared.

'You heard the man. Let her the fuck go,' a voice said behind them. Simon was staring at Oliver, panting, his hand clenched into a fist.

'My pleasure,' Oliver said, dropping Emily's arm. She rubbed it, knowing he'd have left a bruise.

The moment he let go of Emily, Andy took a deep breath and yelled, 'Hai-ya!', pushing his fists towards Oliver's chest. He sailed through the air and onto the floor.

'Hey, it worked.' Andy looked at his fists. 'Squish like grape!'

'Yep. Squish like grape,' Emily said fondly.

'Nice work, intern dude,' Simon said, looking impressed.

'Who did that? Tell them to stop!' Oliver moaned from the floor, covering his head with his arms. He looked terrified, his face as white as a sheet and covered in sweat.

'I think you'd better leave,' Emily said. 'It looks like you're having some kind of ... *episode*? Perhaps the stress of the campaign has become a bit much for you?'

On his hands and knees, Oliver shuffled as fast as he could towards the office lift, Andy giving his bum a shove with his foot as he went, causing him to scream in terror. As he reached the doors, they pinged open to reveal Zoe standing inside with two police officers. Her job in Operation Ditto had been to show them a copy of the video, and make sure they arrived in time to intercept Oliver after the meeting. And they'd arrived right on cue.

Along with the rest of the office, Zoe looked at Oliver squirming and whimpering on the floor and raised her eyebrows.

'It worked then?' she said, cheerfully.

Emily gave her a quick thumbs-up, then turned to Simon. 'Thanks for that,' she said, smiling gratefully and giving his arm a squeeze, before heading back into the boardroom.

'I'm so sorry about all this,' Charles was saying apologetically to the room, which had descended into chaos, everyone talking at once. 'I can assure you I had no idea about Mr Beauchamp's past as a fairly dubious film-maker. He will, of course, no longer be working with HoRizons.' He beckoned Emily to join him at the front of the room, which gradually hushed.

'I sincerely hope that after the drama of this afternoon, you are still interested in what we have to say, ladies and gentlemen? Because as well as – apparently – being a bit of a super-sleuth, Emily here is a very talented young copywriter. One whose ideas, I'm sorry to say, seem to have been appropriated by Mr Beauchamp.

'With your permission, I'd like to reschedule this meeting for a week's time, in order to give Miss Blott the opportunity to present her ideas to you. Ideas I'm confident you'll be keen to use for the Cat's Miaow campaign, which will doubtlessly be thrown firmly into the spotlight when Mr Beauchamp is brought to justice for his wrongdoings. All those in favour say, Aye.'

The assembled executives looked at each other, before nodding a collective, 'Aye.'

'Thank heavens,' Charles breathed. 'Now, shall we tuck into these sandwiches before they're as unrescuable as Mr Beauchamp's career?'

Chapter 44

Sneaking back out of the meeting room, Emily caught up with Zoe, who was waving a handcuffed, scowling Oliver into the lift, and Andy, who was miming high-fives at her.

'We did it!' Zoe yelled when she spotted Emily, grabbing her in a giant hug. Emily winced as she pressed the spot on her arm where Oliver had grabbed her. 'Andy told me how you pulled it off. I wish I'd been there. It sounds amazing.'

'It was all Andy, really,' Emily said, grinning at him. 'All that practise you did with him came in handy after all. I might even forgive you for destroying my vase.'

'That was even more fun than playing with the band,' Andy said. 'Although I was worried at one point that Oliver might have a heart attack, and I'd have to buddy up with his ghost for eternity. Brrrr.'

'What the hell was that all about?' Jada demanded, scurrying over and joining Simon at Zoe's side. 'One minute you're hijacking my sandwiches, and the next Oliver is storming out of the boardroom and manhandling you. I thought Simon was going to pop. Then this guy starts kicking him,

Zoe appears with two policemen, and Oliver's carted off in handcuffs. Is this kind of thing going to happen on the regular now Old Emily's in town? Because if so, I'm here for it all day long.'

'What was he arrested for in the end?' Emily asked Zoe.

'Gross negligence manslaughter, whatever the hell *that* is.'

'De-buildinging someone with intent,' Andy said.

'And you can add assault to that, I reckon,' Simon said. 'Your poor arm. We're being rude,' he added, sticking out his hand towards Andy. 'I'm Simon, and this is Jada.'

'Hi, I'm Andy. And I'd better not touch that.'

Simon withdrew his hand and looked at it, frowning. 'That's funny. That's the same name as ...'

'Please don't finish that sentence,' Emily warned. 'Because that is a thread that should definitely *not* be pulled.'

'So what happens now?' Zoe said. 'Oliver goes to jail, presumably. I'm going back to Essex, and Emily? What will you do?'

'Make things up with Mum, I guess.' She shrugged. 'Buy some more pairs of jeans and onesies to help me embrace the old me. And maybe look for another boyfriend. Preferably one who lets me be myself, rather the kind of wanker who thinks nothing of covering up someone's death to advance his poxy career.'

'And what about you, Andy?' Zoe said, turning to him. 'What happens to you? I kind of thought you might disappear when Oliver was arrested. Closure gained, end of story, and all that.'

'I'm not sure,' Andy said. 'Although ... hold on. I think I can see a light.' He squinted at the wall next to the lift. 'It's getting bigger ...'

'Let me guess,' Emily said, folding her arms. 'You can see a taco truck driven by Kurt Cobain waiting for you in heaven?'

'No, really,' Andy said, turning to Emily, his eyes shining. 'I can see it. My way out. It's really happening.'

'What, really? Now?' Emily said, panicking, pressing her palm against the bare wall. 'But I'm not ready for you to go.'

'Um ... What is he on about?' Jada said, looking nervously at Andy.

'I'm not ready either,' Zoe said, tearfully. 'Can't you hang on for a bit? We never had that game of Punch the Potato you promised me. And I was going to show you around Greenleaf.'

'I'm sorry, guys,' Andy said, rubbing the back of his hair. 'I'd like to stay a while too, but I guess there's nothing left here for me to do. I stopped Emily ending up with Oliver, said goodbye to my mum, and solved the mystery of my tragic demise. I can't really ask for more than that. Not bad for a dead guy, eh?' He squinted at the wall. 'Bloody hell, that really is bright. When I get there, I'm going to recommend they change the wattage.'

Jada and Simon frowned at each other.

'Please don't make jokes. Not right now,' Emily said, tears falling down her cheeks. 'What will I do without you? I'm not sure I can be Old Emily without your help. You always really liked her, much more than I ever did. It's too hard.'

'I loved her,' Andy said softly, turning to face Emily. 'But you don't need me around to be yourself. Just look at what you've done. You've worked out what's really important, and faced up to the mistakes you made along the way. You helped me find out what happened to me, even though I know you didn't really want to. And you stood up to Oliver, and told the world who he really is. Although I'm pretty sure *Bijou* would completely disapprove of you getting your date arrested. That's *soooo* non-U.'

Emily managed a laugh and swiped the tears from her cheeks.

'And look at who else you've got in your life. People who *all* love the real you. It doesn't matter where she lives, Zoe will always be there for you.' Emily held out her little finger towards Zoe, who hooked her own around it. 'You've got a little sister on the way, who I just know will totally adore her big sister. You've got Jada, who's never less than honest with you, without ever being mean. And Simon, who you should probably ask on a date, what with him being completely in love with you and stuff.'

'What?' Simon said, looking startled as everyone turned to look at him. 'I never said I was in love with Emily. Who says that?'

'We all do, because you blatantly are,' Jada said.

Simon opened his mouth to argue, then closed it again, settling for a defeated, 'Oh.'

'See? My Spidey Senses reckon he'd be your perfect wonky puzzle piece,' Andy said. 'In the absence of the original and best, of course.'

Emily turned to Simon and looked at him, as if for the first time – then grinned through her tears.

'I'll miss you, Andy Atkins. You really were one of a kind,' she said.

'Then remember me by always being yourself in future, and trying not to care what anyone thinks of you. Anyone who's worth your time, anyway. Why would you try to be someone other than yourself, when you're so awesome? Aaaand now I'm crying too.' He touched his face, marvelling at the moisture on his fingertips. 'Who knew that was a thing ghosts could do? I'm totally writing that handbook myself when I get up there. So . . . I guess I'd better go now. I'll miss you all.'

'I'll miss you too,' Zoe said, laughing through her tears.

Taking a deep breath, Andy stood in front of the wall. Looking back to the group, he gave everyone a small wave. Then he stepped forward, his palms raised against a light only he could see. And with a small popping sound, like a lightbulb pinging out, Andy walked through the wall, and was finally gone.

Epilogue

'Are you absolutely certain you want that to be her middle name?' Emily's mum muttered into her ear. 'Because if you change your mind in the next ten seconds, we can rescue her from a future of people constantly taking the piss out of her.'

'Mum, her first name is Chanel,' Emily whispered back. 'Her middle name is the least of her worries. And besides, you promised I could choose it.'

The vicar shot a pointed look at Emily. 'Are we ready to proceed?' he said, and she straightened up and nodded. 'Then I baptise you, Chanel Andi Biggins, in the name of the Father, the Son, and the Holy Spirit,' he said, dribbling water onto the baby's head.

'Isn't she gorgeous?' Auntie Suze said at Emily's elbow, blowing her nose loudly. 'She's going to grow into a stunner, just like you.'

'Hooray!' Zoe shouted from the front pew, throwing a handful of confetti in the air, then blushing as she realised no one else was joining in.

'So you decided to name your sister after your dear departed ex-boyfriend, did you?' Simon said, catching up with Emily and squeezing her hand as everyone filed out of the church. 'I'm not sure how I feel about that.'

'I'm pretty sure you'll learn to live with it, seeing as the chances of us being together if it wasn't for him are practically nil.'

'Hey! My genius tactic of slowly winning every quiz show on British TV to showcase my giant intellect would have won you over eventually.'

'Aww, it's sweet how well you know what women want,' Emily said, pinching his cheek.

'Whaddup, clowns?' Zoe said, stumbling into Simon and Emily's backs as she careered out of the church. 'And what happened to your face?'

'Churchill happened,' Simon said, ruefully, fingering the scratch on his cheek.

'Simon is, of course, delighted that Mary let us keep Churchie. It's just taking them a bit of time to adjust to each other,' Emily said. 'Besides, there's not much I can do when Mary's exact words when I tried to return him were, "If you were stupid enough to take him in the first place, you'll have to learn to live with the miserable sod." He'll come round to the idea of someone who isn't Andy hanging around eventually.'

'Speaking of rounds... It's yours first, isn't it, Simon?' Zoe said.

'Why is it always my round first?'

'Because if you're not from Greenleaf, you have to earn your place in the Dog & Duck hierarchy. And that takes time.'

'It's been nine months,' Simon muttered.

'Then you've only got another year or so to go then, haven't you?' Zoe said, grinning at Emily.

*

'Alright, Einstein, what'll it be?' Bob called over to Simon, as the Christening party clattered through the doors of the Dog & Duck, everyone talking at once.

Emily's mum was pushing an empty but ridiculously ornate pram, while Baz was holding Chanel in his arms, looking at her with a dopey, adoring look that hadn't left his face since she'd been born three months earlier.

'Champagne all round, please, Bob,' Simon said, as they wove their way towards the bar at the back of the room.

Bob cackled. 'You'll be lucky,' he said, scratching his stubble. 'I've got a couple of bottles of Cava, and I can do you some white-wine spritzers.'

'Sounds perfect,' Simon said, looking slightly relieved. Emily squeezed his arm, then made her way over to the tables where her mum's guests were busy cramming themselves into chairs of various heights.

'Here, Baz, can you give Simon a hand with the spritzers? I'll take Chanel,' Emily said, holding out her arms.

'Of course, love. Careful of her head,' he said, handing the baby over like she was made of glass, and kissing Emily on the cheek before making his way to the bar.

'See? I told you so,' Emily's mum said, pointing her phone at Emily and Chanel and taking a photo. 'Baz is a lovely dad.'

'When are you going to stop saying I told you so?' Emily said, sticking out her little finger for Chanel to curl her tiny fist around.

'When I'm ninety, *if* I've gone doolally,' her mum said. 'But I've been so right about so many things, it'll be very hard to stop.'

'I can't wait to give her her first haircut,' Zoe said, reaching over and gently stroking Chanel's head, which was covered in a light dusting of soft blonde hair.

'Which reminds me, you've got to do mine,' Auntie Suze said. 'Will you pop over next week?'

'No problem,' Zoe said, squeezing into a seat beside her parents. 'I'm doing Mum's on Wednesday after the salon closes, so I'll do yours at the same time.'

Since moving back to Essex, Zoe had moved home, and set up a small hairdressing business of her own, close to Greenleaf. When Chanel had arrived, she'd decided it was about time she moved to a house-share nearby. Which just happened to be convenient timing, what with Auntie Suze needing to move out of Emily's mum's place so her room could be transformed into Chanel's new nursery. Zoe's parents had welcomed Suze into Zoe's old room with open arms.

'The more the merrier.' Zoe's mum smiled. 'I miss the days when you'd cover our kitchen in hair.'

'I don't,' Zoe's dad grumbled, and she reached over and squeezed his arm.

'What did I miss?' Paul said, causing a bright shaft of sunlight to flood into the dingy room as he pushed open the door and ambled towards the table.

'Paul, taking off the top of your overalls doesn't count as smart casual.' Zoe sighed, tugging at the oily blue sleeves he'd tied around his waist as he leaned down to kiss her on the cheek.

Zoe had started dating Baz's new apprentice at the garage and, in true Greenleaf style, they'd been joined at the hip ever since they'd made things official a few months earlier. Emily wasn't surprised Zoe had fallen for him; with his scruffy blond hair, broad shoulders and easy grin, he reminded her of Andy.

'I didn't want to miss anything,' Paul said, looking down at himself sadly.

'Don't worry, mate,' Baz said, returning to the table carrying a tray filled with wobbling bottles and glasses. 'I don't think the Dog & Duck has a dress code, unlike Mary Mags.'

'Here we go. Spritzers, Cava, and a bottle of whisky for . . . well, whoever wants whisky,' Simon said, causing the table to let out a cheer.

Hands reached across the table to crack open bottles, pass around glasses, and slosh ice into tumblers. When everyone had their drinks in hand, Emily stood up, picked up her glass, and rattled the ice inside it to get their attention.

'I'd like to make a toast, if that's OK?' she said, turning pink as everyone looked up at her expectantly.

'To baby Chanel Andi Biggins, obviously, who is the belle of today's ball, and plenty of balls to come, no doubt.'

'Hear, hear!' Baz grinned.

'To Baz, who I know is going to be an absolutely amazing dad, Auntie Suze, who is clearly going to spoil Chanel absolutely rotten, and Mum, who I'm sure will do a bit better this time, now she's had her practice run.'

'Oi!' her mum yelled, good-naturedly, as Auntie Suze honked her nose into a tissue, even more loudly than before.

'To all the friends and family here today, from Greenleaf and beyond. I'm glad you're in my life, and I'm even gladder that, after a teeny, *tiny* blip, I'm back in your lives too. I know you're going to give Chanel the best possible start, and have her back every step of the way, so I can't think of anywhere better she could have been born.'

Heads around the table nodded in agreement.

'But I especially want to toast those who can't be here with us. The people we've become better people for knowing, even if we didn't appreciate them enough when they were here. They're the ones who are looking out for Chanel, and for us, from who-knows-where, and who we miss so much, every day.

'And I know, with all my heart, that one day we'll see them again. So here's to Dad, and to Andy, and to all those we've loved and lost,' Emily said.

'To all those we've loved and lost,' everyone repeated solemnly, clinking their glasses together.

Above the table, the lightbulbs in the dusty candelabra flickered once, then twice. Emily looked up at the ceiling and smiled.

Acknowledgements

The first people I want to thank are the BookTokers, reviewers and readers who took the time to read *The Time of My Life*. Scrolling through some of your lovely comments when I was grappling with *Ghosted* gave me the impetus I needed to get through it. Anyone who gives up their time to read this book is equally appreciated – thank you.

Thanks to Mum and Dad for being so unfailingly positive about my writing, and for Dookie for putting up with another year or so of moaning – especially for those times I made him pause his game of Destiny for a bit so I could work through a gnarly plot point out loud.

Thanks to my lovely agent, Jo Unwin, and all at JULA, for their hard work and faith in me.

Thanks to everyone at Little, Brown who helped make this book what it is, especially Darcy Nicholson, Rebecca Roy and Jon Appleton for their rigorous but kind editing, and for keeping the book on track. And thanks to @agnesbic for her fab cover illustrations – you've captured the book brilliantly again.

Thanks to L.M. Chilton for being a primo beta reader, as well as an extremely patient friend. I'm looking forward to being publication buddies this summer.

Thanks to Thread for joining me on the journey, to Katie Espiner for the wise words and booze, and to Adam Kay for the plotting advice. And thank you to Emily Niâ O'Malley for giving me her name to use in this book.

About the Author

Rosie Mullender has been a journalist for over twenty years, and is the author of the novels *The Time of My Life* and *Ghosted*. She lives in Worthing with her fiancé and an impressive collection of tat.